"What shall I call you, little crell? Hael says you will live. Do you want to live?"

"I am Estri of Astria, Hadrath diet Estrazi," I said. I thought the second question rhetorical. I watched his face closely, but my name meant nothing to him.

"No," he said to me, "you are not. You are an unnamed crell, bound for the appreiada of the Nemarsi. Your chald," he ran his hand under the eighteen-strand belt at my waist, "means nothing here. You have but one choice open to you; you may live, crell to me, Chayin rendi Inekte, cahndor of the Nemarsi. Or you may, at this moment, choose to die. Choose now, for the choice will never again be given you."

Bantam Books by Janet E. Morris

THE HIGH COUCH OF SILISTRA
THE GOLDEN SWORD

THE GOLDEN SWORD

Janet E. Morris

BANTAM BOOKS · TORONTO · NEW YORK · LONDON

THE GOLDEN SWORD
Bantam edition / December 1977

ISBN 0-553-11276-7

Published simultaneously in the United States and Canada

Bantam Books are published by Bantam Books, Inc. Its trade-
mark, consisting of the words "Bantam Books" and the por-
trayal of a bantam, is registered in the United States Patent
Office and in other countries. Marca Registrada. Bantam
Books, Inc., 666 Fifth Avenue, New York, New York 10019.

PRINTED IN THE UNITED STATES OF AMERICA

to
Sydny Weinberg

Contents

The Golden
Sword

Replication

⸻⸻⸻⸻⸻⸻⸻⸻⸻⸻⸻⸻

The dayglass, alone, posited upon the black square of controlling Will on the board of catalysts.

As events are conceived by all-pervading Will and brought into time by the Weathers, so are they given spatial reality by Replication.

Replication gives instruction and molds the world in its image.

Replication has no foes, nor can a thousand armies stand against it. There is no obstructing the time of Replication, when the crux wind blows across the earth and all things assume their true nature.

The wind of the First Weather blows across the sea and the tides are remade in their rhythm. It blows upon the land and great forests are tumbled to the ground. In this way is the old made new and that which has served its purpose cleared away. In such times it services one to delve into one's own fitness and make ready.

Adjuration: The dayglass is upended and the salts begin the journey that divines time within space. Each grain must wait its turn and pass through the narrowed middle in a predetermined sequence. No grain may refuse to pass from top to bottom, nor is the order of passage subject to alteration or review. Should a stubborn grain thwart its destiny it will be ground to bits by its fellows and the resultant powder will in the end assume its place.

With the woman as agent:

Around the waist there is nothing. That task to be accomplished is of such gravity that a chald of eighteen chains becomes meaningless by comparison.

The inward ear hears success and is not discouraged by the message. Replication suspends natural law. That which is folly by reason is demanded in times of Replication.

She receives the light of the north star Clous into her right hand and is not blinded by its beauty. In times of Replication, when only that which is preordained may be done, a material sign is always given at the outset.

Adjuration: She who receives the light knows herself not exalted, but drafted into exacting service.

—excerpted from *Ors Yris-tera* (Book of the Weathers of Life), by the dharen Khys, hide-year sixty-three

I. Ors Ȳris-tera

In the bloody sun's rising, the desert was a sea of gore, the crack-riddled, barren earth between it and the ravening crags east and west a vitrified corpse. The fuming sun straddled the mountains, triumphant. Vanquished was the beneficent night. All creatures great and small scuttled for cover, lest the vampire in the sky suck them dry of life.

A dry wind sprang up out of the desert. From the southwest it came, driving the sand before it in great clouds. Red-dark up from the south met the dawn and devoured it. Deracou, the wind that devours, is such a storm called in Parset. Deracou stalked the cloaked figure. The sighing, groaning sand it drove scoured the dead sea bottom, until every crack was filled, making it again sea; roaring sea, sea of sand. Deracou claimed the waste, covered it, drowned it, and the high tide wave of it made once again shore of the rocky place where the still form lay. I lay quiet as the desert, back turned to its courting. As it had claimed the cracked wasted dead sea, so would Deracou claim me.

Out of caprice, it reached out its arm to me, when I thought I had escaped. The temptation was strong

3

within me to sleep. To let my body be covered forever by the sand, to take the peace nature offered. I had, after all, fulfilled the chaldra of the mother. To fulfill the chaldra of the soil, to give back what I had borrowed, to die here upon Silistra—indeed, the temptation was strong within me.

The Shaper's seal sign of my father, its great spiral, myriad points of light worked into my cloak's back, glittered and twinkled before my sand-sealed eyes. My father, it said, did not deliver me home to Silistra, to the Parset Desert, to die. My father, it reminded me, had need of me. My father, Estrazi, it cajoled, would expect more from his daughter.

I lay, arms crossed over my head, with the cloak pulled close about me. When the south wind died away, all that could be seen of me was the scintillating spiral sparkling in the sand.

The receding wind bore the darkness with it, and the light of sun's rising was again upon the land. It rainbowed the Shaper's seal that was upon the cloak that my father had given his daughter.

Sensation consumed me. My eyes and nose and mouth were filled with grit. My swollen tongue was unable to give comfort to my cracked and blistered lips. My savaged feet throbbed and pulsed.

Surely, I told myself, my father had good reason for depositing me here. Doubtless, I comforted myself as I lay in the dark under my cloak, that reason would be made clear. My lungs burned and ached. They had been hard put to adjust to the thinner Silistran air, although it was Silistran air I had breathed for three hundred years, until my need to discharge the chaldra of the mother had led me to the Falls of Santha, to the cavern beneath them, and to Mi'ysten.

I thought of Mi'ysten, that world out of time, of Estrazi and Raet, child of the Shapers, while my body lay resting. I could not ask more from my tortured flesh, not now, with the heat of the day upon the land.

Estrazi, my father, for whom I had forsaken my

position as Well-Keepress of Astria, for whom I had searched so long; it was he who had put me here. By his design was I created, in his hands was I pawn. On Mi'ysten had I given back to him his ring that I had worn threaded through my chald across the plain to Arlet, amid the mountains of the Sabembe range, below the Falls of Santha. Even in the solitary confinement of the crystal cube of Mi'ysten had I worn it, even while at the mercy of Raet had I retained it. To give it back to him. To discharge my chaldra, my responsibility and my duty, to my dead mother, Hadrath, had I withstood Raet and met with Estrazi upon his world, Mi'ysten.

And when it was done, when the ring was removed by my hand from my chald belt of interwoven chains and placed in the bronze-glowing hand of my father, Estrazi, I had found myself, naked but for cloak and chald, upon my back in the Parset desert, looking upon the constellations of the night sky of Silistra. So many questions unanswered, he had delivered me home. I had lain a long while looking up at the sky. That the sand under me was Parset sand I had determined from the placement of the stars above me. Groistu, the stones-wielder, was only half-risen in the north. Wiurer, the winged hulion, held court directly above Groistu's head. The tip of his tufted left ear, where the north star Clous twinkled, was barely discernible upon the horizon. From no other place upon Silistra would the night sky so display herself.

I had wept for joy, to feel Silistra again supporting my flesh, to breathe the thinner, righter air of the planet of my birth. I had not thought, then, of what the desert day would bring. I had been so long away from the cycle of day and night, and from weather, and from nature herself, I had forgotten. But the morning sun taught me, after I had wasted the night cool in introspection. I quickly relearned my vulnerability. My Mi'ysten schooling did me little good. I had shaped water, creating a bare trickle with my limited power, and the desert sucked it away. As it tried

to suck away my life, in the three days that followed.
By the north star Clous, and the crouching crags of
the southermost tip of the Sabembe range, did I set
my course, northeast to Arlet.

I had, I reminded myself in the dark of my tented
cloak, come far in three days. I blew breath hard out
of my mouth, trying to spit the grit from my gullet.

In a little while, I would set out again. I was safe,
in the heat of the day, from dorkat, the stalking carnivore, from slitsa, the slithering fork-tongued, from friysou, the leather-winged scavenger, and from all that
scuttled and crawled upon the desert sands. In the
heat of the day, the desert slept. Doubtless I could
sleep, unmolested. Truly, I had no choice. My limbs
would no longer obey me, and my dreaming mind
would no longer hold a train of thought. I sank into
the cool dark, where pain could not find me, nor heat,
nor hunger, nor thirst.

I dreamed of Raet, son of the Shapers, and that
he worked his will once again in the worlds of time
and space. I dreamed that he came and bound my
hands behind me, and caused my chald-belt to rust and
fall from my body. I knelt where it had fallen, but it
was only powder on the sand. I protested to him, and
he replied to me that I could not be allowed to interfere. And my father was beside him, nodding, the
bronze glow from his skin growing brighter and
brighter, until I buried my head in the sand to shield
my eyes from the glare. And I was lifted up from the
ground; Raet's arms were so hot they seared my skin.
But that was wrong. Mi'ysten flesh is always cool. I
struggled, crying out.

"It is more than a jeweled cloak Deracou has
blown you, Cahndor." The voice belonged to the face
that swam blurred before me. It was a Parset face,
dusky brown, severe; the whites of the eyes staring
into mine were softened by the Parset nictitating
membrane. The language was Parset, and my sluggish
mind took long to make sense of it. The sun's set shad-

owed the forms before me. Dreamecho chased their words into my ears.

I would have raised my hands to wipe the sand and sleep from my eyes. I could not move them. But I knew I no longer dreamed, for my body's complaints were loud within me, the pain a rippling film between me and the shadowed forms bending down in the fading light.

I opened my mouth to speak, to explain, but no sound could I coax from my parched throat.

And then I smelled it. My nostrils drank first, of the particles the air carried to me. I will never forget the strength of that odor, the coolness, the life my nose and throat received from the very air. Water. It was on my lips and in my mouth and spreading through my dust-covered innards. The feel of it as it dribbled upon my chin will stay with me as long as I live. My throat knew no longer how to swallow, my tongue had forgotten its task.

The faces in front of me sharpened, took focus. I tried with my eyes to thank them. I managed a wordless sound. I felt again the bladder's rim against my lips, the ecstasy of the liquid in my mouth. There was an arm under my head, hands at my throat. The cloak fell away.

"Quiet, little crell, do not waste your strength." The voice came from above and behind me. I was held, high in the air. Strong arms supported me, as if I weighed nothing. My abraded flesh felt tight-curled hairs, moist and warm, where he held me to him. I remembered. Cahndor, one had called another. "Will of the sand" does that word mean. And crell, one had called me. I tried to protest. I was Estri Hadrath diet Estrazi, former Well-Keepress of Astria, surely no crell. Crell is a Parset word, for nowhere else upon Silistra does such a status exist. A crell is other than chaldless, other than human; that beast of burden which walks upon two legs rather than four. But my protest came out a moan, and I sank back exhausted, my head against the dark chest of the man that held me, my gaze lost in the forest of curling black hair upon it. Tiny beads of sweat meandered among the hairs, split in two by the root shafts, and in two again.

"Will she live, Hael? What think you?" came the voice from above and behind.

A face loomed close to mine; breath tickled my cheek. It was a bearded face, and that beard was curled and dressed and beaded and gray with dust.

"Would you raise apprei here, and rest the night and day with her? If so, I could be sure of it. Without shelter and attention, I cannot say."

"I would not lose the time," the deeper voice of he who held me came again.

"Then, Cahndor, I think her chances slim." The bearded face receded from my sight. A hand touched my face, my brow, raised the lids of my eyes. There was a roaring in my ears, a great pulsing beat in my head. It seemed unimportant what they said, what they did. Only sleep mattered to me, sleep and escape from my body.

There was silence then, and I felt the stride of he who held me, he whom the other had called Cahndor. I tried to open my eyes to see, but my lids were weighty beyond my strength.

I smelled the threx before I saw it; the warm-damp musty smell that belongs to the great four-legged omnivore who is the preferred riding beast of Silistra.

I coaxed my lids open once more, as I was shifted from one pair of arms to another. Before me I saw, in the fading light, the carved and tooled Parset saddle, with rolls of bright-colored web-cloth strapped around it. The short-coupled back upon which the saddle rested was sand and shadow, dark at the withers, dappling light toward the barrel. The threx's broad chest, parallel to my face where I was held well off the ground, gave me the impression of immense size. Then my sight of it was obscured by a muscular, dusk-dark back, upon which my father's cloak, with the Mi'ysten Shaper's seal, had been carelessly draped. He who wore the cloak swung up in the saddle, and held out his arms from the back of the dancing threx toward me. I was placed in those arms and lifted up onto the threx's back, laid across the saddle before the great beast's rider, so that the grip dug into my right hip, and my hair, flowing loose, almost dragged the ground by the threx's tripart hooves.

The blood rushed to my head, and the red-grained pulsing swallowed my sight.

I felt a callused hand upon the small of my back, large, rough. Then the threx leaped into motion under me, the air was driven from my lungs, and I was glad of the steadying hand. Sand and grit thrown up by its hooves filled my nose and mouth and eyes, pelted my skin. The ground beneath my head rushed by under me, blurred into a dark band. No longer could I see the cracked earth, the jumbled rock, the coarse jeweled sand.

Endlessly did the threx plunge across the barren dead sea floor, endlessly did I suffer the shower of clodded earth its hooves kicked up. When dark was full upon us, when I thought I could not fight for one more breath, the Parset slid the choppy-gaited beast to a halt so abruptly that in its rearing one of those rock-hard hooves grazed my temple.

He who wore the Shaper's cloak vaulted from the threx's back. His grip upon me removed, I felt myself sliding. In mid-fall he caught me and laid me upon the crusty, abrasive earth. I heard the blowing of the winded threx, the creak and jingle of harness, the rustle of bodies about their business in the dark. Then the bladder was again at my lips. A horny hand brushed clod-caked hair from my face. Water washed new strength into me. I choked and sputtered. The bladder was withdrawn. A damp cloth caressed my mouth, my eyes, my temples. I winced when it touched the cut I had sustained by the threx's hoof. Then it too was withdrawn, and I was once again alone. The night breeze had the chill of the abyss about it, and I did not welcome that coolness. I

looked up into the starry night, using the north star
Clous as focus. When it ceased to dance and circle
above me, when my eyes once again obeyed my
mind's commands, I turned my attention to my body.

With all my strength I tried to move my arms,
that I might sit up. I could not do so. As my awareness sharpened, my flesh gave forth its message. My
wrists felt their bonds, my waist its encircling loop.
My hands were confined by a rope, and that rope
passed once around my belly. I did not remember it
being done. Perhaps I had been so bound to keep me
from falling from the threx's back as it plunged its
way through the barrens. I thought not. But it certainly had not been done to prevent me from escaping
or doing harm to my captors. With the realization that
this was so, that I was captive, rather than rescued,
my mind was suddenly clear, my thoughts coherent.
As I lay there upon the rocky ground, I considered all
that I knew about the Parsets, while around me the
moon rose full and red-ringed and the wind sorted the
sand, sighing, and the men's gruff, rapid exchanges
rang unintelligibly in my ears.

I recalled that which had been taught to me in
the Day-Keepers' school. I had learned there, among
many others, the Parset language. And I recollected
also what I had heard from the wellwomen, the Slayers, and the Day-Keepers themselves about the flam-
boyant, tattooed desert dwellers.

I had heard it said that the men of the Parset barrens were the most insular, prideful, arrogant men
upon Silistra, and their women the most indolent and
imperious. Long ago, when the remnants of Silistran
civilization emerged from the hides to rebuild a deci-
mated planet, the Parsets took another path. Their
Day-Keepers and forereaders split from their brothers
and sisters. History has it that the *aniet* hide Day-
Keepers had engaged in genetic manipulation; that
the Day-Keepers of the rest of Silistra had found them
out. Whatever the reason, there was from hide days
little communication, and only a strained tolerance

between the Silistran Day-Keepers, guardians of the past, manipulators of the present, charters of the future, and their Parset brethren. The forereaders, as long ago as my great-grandmother's time, predicted that someday great harm would come to us all from out of the Parset desert.

So the Parsets had chosen. They speak a dissimilar language, wear a different chald. The chains of chaldra which have bound them from hide days are not the same as those which bind the rest of Silistra. I recalled that the Parsets had instigated no Wells, where a woman might go to get herself with child. I knew also that their jiasks, warrior men, and tiasks, warrior women, were not bound by the Law of Seven, as were the Slayers of the north, east and west. And that they alone, of all the peoples of Silistra, still made war.

I heard the flap and snap of wings about my head, saw a shadow cross the full moon. It was bright as day upon the barrens, but a day sucked dry of color and tone. I recollected stories I had heard about the Parset Lands; that many had entered them and few had returned; that one was better off to give up one's body to the chaldra of the soil than to walk the Parset barrens uninvited. Because their chaldric chains differ so markedly from those worn upon the rest of Silistra, all not Parset are, to them, chaldless.

Occasionally I had seen Parsets at games or festivals. Once I had been, before I reached my majority and took up the Keepress' robes in Astria, at Day-Keepers' Rollcall, that greatest of gatherings held four times a year on the plains of Yardum-Or. With my teacher Rin diet Tron, first of the Slayers' Seven of Astria, had I been there. I had seen a number of Parset jiasks, swaggering bold among the crowd, with their feather-plumed helmets, their tiasks beside them. At such gatherings they do their trading. They come to barter their woven rugs, their precious metals, their rare drugs. I was standing with Rin beneath the Slayers' awning when a pelter from Galesh accidentally jostled a tiask woman in the crowd. Her mate turned, aired steel, and struck in one motion, and the pelter's headless body took several steps before it fell and pumped out its lifeblood upon the grass. I remembered the fury in Rin's face, how his hand grew white upon his sword hilt, and how he turned away. By the Day-Keepers' edict, the Parsets have immunity. To the jiask, the pelter was nothing. He struck within his chaldra, as a Slayer might an outlaw in the forest, whom he had hunted for sport, or as a woman the wirragaet sucking blood from her arm. It was well past eighth bell, after evening meal, before Rin diet Tron, of the Slayers' Seven of Astria, had again spoken, had regained his good humor.

Occasionally I have seen a Parset man within the walls of Well Astria, there to partake in the normal fashion of the fruits of Silistran womanhood. But never has Astria been petitioned to admit a Parset woman, never have I heard of a Parset man so much as allowing one to compete in the Well testings. How they keep their birthrate at an acceptable level was a question much bandied about. I had seen a number of women, such as Celendra, Well-Keepress of Arlet, who had been sired upon wellwomen by Parsets. It is said among the wellwomen that the Parsets are the most potent of Silistran men, and that a woman couched by one is almost certain to conceive. Some maintain that this is because of the strong infusion of Gristasha blood in the Parset hide days. When the hide aniet was put into use at the time of crisis, when the Day-Keepers and the forereaders went underground to avoid annihilation, the hide aniet was only half-filled. Then did the Day-Keepers of aniet invite into the hide as many as could be accommodated of the fierce and primitive Gristashas, those anachronistic tribesmen who had kept their line pure from the very beginnings of Silistran prehistory. The Parsets bear strong and clear the Gristasha stamp, even do they still tattoo themselves, as did their ancestors before them.

Again the wind from the abyss blew chill about

me as I lay beneath the full moon, though the evening
was so warm that the air wavered and rippled in its
heat. I did not welcome that cold, which upraised every hair upon me and caused my skin to pebble and
crawl. No, I did not welcome the wind from the
abyss, which had blown me from the keeps of Astria,
whipped around me where I lay with Dellin in the
Slayers' camp, whistled through the halls of Arlet. The
cold of it seeped deep inside me, chilling me as it had
when it drove me forth into the Sabembe range. It
keened in my ears as it had at the death of Tyith bast
Sereth. It roared as it had roared beneath the Falls of
Santha. Upon Mi'ysten I had been free from it. Until
this day had I been free from it, and the evil portents
of its fetid breath. Now again it blew around me, and
my belly cramped into a knot so tight I drew my
thighs up against my chest as the Parset came toward
me, silver-gilded in the full-moon light, my father's
cloak thrown carelessly over his shoulders.

Where I lay, upon my side, he squatted down by
my head and reached out a hand toward me. Upon his
chest I saw what I had not seen before, swinging from
a heavy golden chain. As he raised me to a sitting
position, it swung inches from my face, that palm-
sized medallion upon which was worked the likeness
of the uritheria, that mythical beast of the desert who
is winged and scaled, clawed and horned, and from
whose mouth came the fire that ignited the sun in the
sky. Its jeweled eyes glittered in the moonlight, cruel,
sentient. One of the other men had called this one
Cahndor. Such is a title of respect among the Parsets.
But this man was Cahndor in the word's formal meaning—war chief of a Parset tribe, will of the sand, who
held sworn death oaths from every man, woman, and
child under his protection.

I swayed, dizzy, my weight against the arm that
held me upright. His grip upon my shoulder tightened. His hand, horny against my skin, seemed ex-
ceedingly large. Black eyes, all pupil under bushy
straight brows, examined me minutely, appraising,

thoughtful. His other hand was at my belly, at my back, and my bonds fell away.

I rubbed my wrists, crossed my legs under me, felt him withdraw his support. My eyes were caught by his; I felt the insect in the webber's snare, waiting, paralyzed. I looked away, at my wrists in my lap, at the rope print upon them.

"How is it with you, little crell?" he asked in Parset, slowly, distinctly. I could not place the dialect. He shifted back on his heels. The silvered light played on his heavy-muscled thighs, upon his thick neck and corded arms. He was a large-boned thick-maned man, in his prime, massive but not clumsy. Tight-curled hair poked through the chain links about his neck, forested his chest, thinning as it approached his navel, where it fanned out on his flat belly, to disappear beneath a metal-studded breech. Over this was buckled his sword belt, which held the undulating Parset short sword, a small sheathed knife, and the coiled length of braided leather.

I did not answer, but only looked up at him.

"Hael, attend me!" he called, and that one came to join him, sitting cross-legged beside his master. Hael was of almost identical stamp, save that his skin seemed a trifle more black, his lips a bit fuller, his nose flatter above his full beard.

The one called Hael brought from his belt a tiny bladder, as small as my palm, and removed the stopper from it.

"This will strengthen you. Open your mouth," he said. I was sorry that I had done so when the bitter, burning liquid hit my tongue. It was fire inside me, and that fire slowly spread through my whole body, calling every artery, every vein, every capillary to my attention.

"What was that?" I choked. My vision dimmed and sharpened, my ears rang. The drug was strong. I heard the air rustle; the two men breathing sounded loud as the roaring of Santha. My heart was a kapura drum keeping double time.

"So you speak. Good. Here. Only drink three swallows," the bearded one said, and handed me a larger bladder.

This I smelled before I tasted, and it was water, cold and good. I was reluctant to stop after the third drink, but their eyes were upon me, and I handed it back. Hael took it from my grasp and corked it. He leaned over me and put his thumbs to my eyelids, each in turn, and then to my temples and wrists. He turned to his cahndor and nodded. That one grinned, white teeth flashing.

"Chayin," said the one called Hael, putting his hand upon his cahndor's shoulder, "we should either ride or raise apprei." He got to his feet. "She is strong and resilient. When she is healed and clean, she might even be pleasing. If you would find out, you should leave her be, let her rest." And he turned and was gone without waiting for answer or dismissal.

I thought it strange that a jiask would talk to his cahndor so. To raise apprei, the portable cloth house of the Parset, or ride on was surely a decision the cahndor was capable of making on his own. A Slayer would not have spoken so to one of the Seven.

The cahndor gazed after the one called Hael. He spat upon the ground, and turned back to me. He raised my chin with his hand, gently, so that his eyes met mine once more. I saw the nictitating membrane for a moment; then it was gone.

"What shall I call you, little crell? Hael says you will live. Do you want to live?"

"I am Estri of Astria, Hadrath diet Estrazi," I said. I thought the second question rhetorical. I watched his face closely, but my name meant nothing to him.

"No," he said to me, "you are not. You are an unnamed crell, bound for the appreiada of the Nemarsi. Your chald"—he ran his hand under the eighteen-strand belt at my waist—"means nothing here. You have but one choice open to you; you may live, crell to me, Chayin rendi Inekte, cahndor of the Nemarsi.

Or you may, at this moment, choose to die. Choose now, for the choice will never again be given you."

The look upon his face convinced me he did not speak in jest. The wind from the abyss buffeted me. To renounce my chald, my heritage, my Well, my freedom, to renounce all of those for my life—what choice was that? And yet, death renounces life.

"What if I do not wish to choose?" I asked him. My voice trembled in my own ears.

"Then I will choose for you. But if that be the case, then you are bound by my will."

"We are all bound, Chayin rendi Inekte." It was my voice that spoke, insolent and defiant, but I had not willed it to do so.

I saw the anger in his eyes. I swallowed, my fear-dry mouth sour and sticky. If he chose death for me, so be it. If he chose to make me crell, then it was not by my will, and I was not bound by his choice. I was not unhappy that the power within me had so spoken.

Chayin rendi Inekte, cahndor of the Nemarsi, took up the rope in his hands. He slid its length between his palms, coiled it around his fists. A long-legged, narrow-beaked pandivver landed, snapping its wings, near my knee. It regarded me, unblinking, head cocked. I could see the pulse beat in its throat. Finally, satisfied, it furled its pinions and began to hunt, stabbing its sharp beak into the ground, throwing its head into the air to swallow, then repeating the process. Its long legs carried it away, bobbling, its feathered rear raised to the moon.

"You know nothing, crell, of our customs. Uncommitted, your lot will be hard. Perhaps too hard. As a favor, I will bind you here and leave you for the desert," he said as he rebound my hands behind my back, and passed the loop of rope about my belly, tying it in front. "I have not the time for you."

He got to his feet. I looked up at him from where I knelt on the sand. The horror of my situation had me frozen. I had thought he would take me, or kill me quickly, mercifully. But he would leave me bound and helpless in the barrens, food for whatever first happened upon me. He turned his back to me, and the moonglow fired the Shaper's seal on the cloak he wore. My father had done this to me, placed me here in the path of pain and dying, that I might not interfere in his plans. Of all I had suffered at the hands of men, his stroke had been the cruelest. Pawn had I lived, pawn would I die. Defiance rose in me. I would not be so easily dealt with!

"Cahndor," I called softly to his retreating back, though the word came hard and bitter to my tongue. I would beg for my life, bide my time. This was no Mi'ysten I faced, but a desert primitive. I had not spent so long in Well Astria for nothing. I would play the conquered, but eventually, it was I who would conquer. As he had bound me with rope, so would I bind him, with desire. I would spread the knowledge I had gained upon Mi'ysten and free us from the Shaper's Mi'ysten manipulation. To do so, I must live. To live, I would do what was needed.

"Cahndor," I called again.

Chayin rendi Inekte, cahndor of the Nemarsi, turned and came to stand before me.

I put my cheek to his booted foot and kissed it. Kneeling, my hair in the dirt, my lips against the rough leather, I waited.

"Speak, little crell, speak the words." His voice held amusement, triumph.

"I choose to live, I beg to live. Do with me as you will."

"Say, then, that you choose to live as crell to me, and speak my name."

I did so, though the dust blurred the words and my voice was weak and shaky. For a moment I thought he would not accept me, but would leave me, even though I had prostrated myself before him.

"I think," he said, after a silence in which my heart thundered, deafening, "you shall be Miheja. It is a good Parset name. Live up to it." And he lifted me to my feet. I was much shamed; my sense of purpose, my plan did not ease me. The smile that tugged at the corner of his lips, danced in his eyes, burned my skin. My legs were unsteady under me; I weaved upon my feet.

"A crell does not gaze into the eyes of her cahndor, unless so commanded," he informed me. I dropped my eyes.

"Nor into the eyes of any man or woman of the Nemarsi," he cautioned. His voice seemed far away, the words unclear. The ground beneath me reached up, calling. A haze of red consumed it; then the red was dark, and I felt his arms about me, and the dizziness faded. The drug was wearing off, the stimulant effect receding. I was again conscious of my throbbing feet, my thirst, my hunger, my weakness. He picked me up in his arms and carried me. His skin was hot and slick against mine.

Among the others he set me down. I counted ten of them, squatting on the rocky ground. Bladders of drink and wraps of meat littered the sand. Beside the bearded Hael he placed me, and sat himself. Hael's eyes were for his cahndor. My eyes were for the wrap of leather upon which rested a half-eaten joint of meat. The smell of it had me salivating. My stomach voiced its need. Chayin rendi Inekte picked up the meat and gnawed at it.

"What name have you given her?" Hael asked.

"Miheja," Chayin answered around a mouthful.

I lay between them, hands bound under me. My cahndor had not seen fit to free me. Hael looked at me; his eyes searched mine. I looked away, remembering.

Hael uncorked a bladder and lifted my head that I might drink. In the bladder was not water, but some warming brew with which I was not familiar. He then cut some meat and fed me pieces, slowly, with his fingers. After three bites, my shrunken stomach could hold no more. I turned my head away. His hand on my forehead turned it back to him, so that I could not avoid his bearded face. He smiled down at me, and his smile was gentle.

"Perhaps you will win, in the end, little Miheja," he said in a voice so low the others could not hear. He leaned over me, his hand once again on my forehead. I felt strength pour into me through his palm, the heat of it burning. He had the healer's touch, and I wondered what other touches he had, what he meant by his obscure comment as his hands did his work.

"Put her up before you. I would not overly tire Saer. If we leave now, we will make Wiyuta jer by sun's rising. There we will raise apprei," Chayin said. He got to his feet and strode to the dozing threx, huddled together, heads drooping. The men were up and moving, hurriedly reclaiming their bladders and meat. None spoke as they worked. I thought it strange that so many men were so quiet. It is not that way among the Slayers.

Hael picked me up and carried me to the threx, where he sat me astride a large black and swung up behind me. I would not ride, this time, upon my stomach, with my face in the dirt. He reached around me and drew up the reins. Chayin's threx was already started, a cloud of dust marking his trail. Hael kicked the black into a run. Its gait was easier than the cahndor's mount, but with my hands bound behind me I had no way to keep my balance, and was glad of Hael's arms around me on the reins. The threx's bristled neck snaked low as he hit his stride, and I could see the pointed ears flicking back and forth as he picked his way at breakneck speed across the treacherous ground. Foam sprayed up, rising on the wind from his frothing mouth. Hael gave him more rein.

When the black threx was so close to Chayin's dapple that each bristle of its tail was distinct from the others, Hael reined him up, content to follow. The Shaper's seal sparked in the moonlight like some festival firestick before us in the night.

"How did you come by that cloak?" Hael asked in

my ear. His beard itched my neck, his matted chest hair my back as I leaned against him.

"It was a gift from my father, when I entered the desert." I turned my mouth to his ear, that the wind would not snatch my words away.

"And what did you seek here?"

"A way home, to Astria. And a man of Arlet. And a Day-Keeper."

"What father," said he, "would allow his daughter to seek where she cannot find? The home you will see will not be Astria. Except among the crells, there are none of Arlet with us. There are few enough in Arlet. But a Day-Keeper, now, that is another thing. If you sought one, then you have found one." His arms tightened about my waist as the threx swerved to avoid some obstacle, then veered back behind the cahndor's mount.

I had thought as much. The way he had spoken to Chayin, the concern he had shown for me, his healing skills, all marked him. And he had the cryptic tongue of his kind.

"It is a certain Day-Keeper I seek, one for whom I have a message."

"Although there is little exchange between us and our past-brothers, the times have pushed us closer. I could deliver such a message."

"For a crell?" I asked bitterly.

"That cloak marks you. Chayin is ignorant by choice of what does not please him. He will learn. One does not instruct the cahndor. There is little enough I can do for you. You should accept my offer."

"To Vedrev of Arlet, then, take this message. I am Estri, returned from discharging the chaldra of the mother. I had success in that, and it should be so written. Say also that Sereth crill Tyris' actions on my behalf were above reproach."

I felt his arm tighten, heard the intake of his breath, felt the imperceptible shake of his head.

"How long have you been upon this chaldra? And where have you been that you do not know what has occurred?" At his words, I felt the ice wind again upon me. "Even in the Parset barrens, we have heard that news."

"What is the date?" I asked. "I have been long sequestered." I could not tell him more, not yet. "What news is it that I have not heard?"

"The date is Finara second first, 25,695."

It had been more than two years, Silistran time, since I had been with Sereth beneath the Falls of Santha.

"And what is it," I asked again, "that I have not heard?"

"That Vedrev has taken up the chaldra of the soil, and at the hands of Sereth crill Tyris." Ahead of us, Chayin slowed his mount. Hael did likewise. I was aware, but vaguely, of the silhouetted tyla palms, the smell of fresh water in the air. Amid the barrens was an expanse of life, and growth.

"We approach Wiyuta jer, little crell. Name me another Day-Keeper to whom you would like this message given."

I hardly heard him. Vedrev dead, and at Sereth's hand? What had happened? How could such a thing be true? And what of Sereth? It is unthinkable, a heinous crime, for a Slayer to kill a Day-Keeper.

"Ristran, perhaps," I answered, when he repeated the question. "Ristran of Astria."

I had to know. I asked what was in my mind, what constricted my heart and made my tongue huge and unwieldy in my mouth.

"Does Sereth live?"

Hael laughed. I did not like the sound of that laugh; there was no humor in it.

"Indeed he does. But enough talk of these things. For you, all that exists is the Nemarsi, and its cahndor. You had best forget Sereth of Arlet. I will do what I said, and deliver your message, but you might be better off if I did not. Things are much changed in Arlet; indeed, upon the face of all Silistra. Sereth crill Tyris is much changed. You are better off crell to Chayin than you would be if the past-Seven of Arlet knew you yet live. I would not, if I were you, speak your given name again, as long as you yet breathe. Forget who you were. Let Estri, Well-Keepress of Astria, remain unfound. I thought it might be you when I saw that sign upon the cloak." He reined up the black threx, lest he pace abreast of Chayin's dapple in his haste to reach the grassy jer.

"Tell me," I pleaded, "why you say these things." He shook his head, and did not speak again to me, but let the threx he rode have its head. The black came up beside the cahndor's threx and was then content to match him. The dapple's ears went back, he snorted and snapped, and the cahndor slapped him sharply with the flat of his hand. The animal jumped and lunged, and Chayin pulled so upon the double bits that the foam dribbling from the threx's mouth turned red.

The black was much unnerved by this, and danced and quivered beneath us. Once again Hael reined him back. He leaned forward to sluice the new sweat off the sleek shoulder.

"Would he have left me, truly, upon the desert?" I asked.

Hael's head snapped around, his eyes narrowed. "What transpired? Did you choose for him?"

I nodded, and told him what Chayin had said, and how I had responded.

"He is canny," Hael said when I was done. "There is no way to change it now. You are his. I might have objected, claimed you myself. We came upon you at the same time. I might have been tempted. You could have value beyond that which seems apparent. But he saw that. Privately, but valid nonetheless, you have spoken the words. Nothing can change that."

"He does not know who I am. My name meant nothing to him," I protested. I would have much preferred to belong to this Day-Keeper, if I had to belong to any of them.

"Do not be a fool. There are none upon Silistra

who do not know that name. The halls of Arlet ran with blood upon your account. He knew, before you told him. He made no sign, because he was not surprised. The haste with which he took your commitment proves it." His voice was wry. The threx's footfalls were muddled upon lush grass. Chayin was already dismounted, stripping the carved and tooled Parset saddle from the steaming dapple's back. He slipped the headstall, with its bloody double bits, from the threx's mouth, hobbled its front feet, and turned away to seat himself beneath a tyla palm. I thought it a wonder the animal was sound, if such negligence was the cahndor's practice. The threx was badly overheated, steaming.

Hael lowered me to the ground, to the luxuriant grass that grew in the jer. Chayin, from where he sat under the tyla, watched me. The dark was fast receding, the sky greening in the east, the stars fading away. The night noises were gone, the moon absent from above our heads. I heard the jingle, snort, and blow that was the rest of the Nemarsi jiasks straggling into the jer. Hael rubbed his threx down and turned him loose. He dragged his carved saddle with its webcloth rolls and voluminous saddlepacks to Chayin. Color and tone came almost perceptibly to the jer, silhouette became substance, as the sun's first rays burst over the Sabembes.

When there were nine more threx loose in the jer, the jiasks went about raising apprei. From their saddles they took the web-cloth rolls, from their bags arm-length tubes of green stra metal. These tubes they fit together into long stanchions and set them deep into the earth. Over the pyramid frameworks they fastened the web-cloth panels. By the time the sun showed its full disk, three appreis, each resplendent with those psychotropic designs favored by the Parsets, stood beneath the tyla palms.

Into the largest of the three went Chayin, his saddle thrown over his shoulder, the tooled leather packs almost dragging to the ground. I still stood where

Hael had left me, my hands bound behind me, my feet upon the moist, cushiony grass.

I heard a rustle, a crackling, and Hael slid down a tyla's trunk, a cluster of fruit stuck in his sword belt. Two of the jiasks were busy with a fire, another two with a haunch of meat. Gear was strewn everywhere. The jer rumbled with their mutterings as they unstoppered bladders and passed them back and forth.

The Day-Keeper motioned me, and I followed him meekly into the largest apprei.

The apprei was a clutter. A Parset keeps his treasures around him, wherever he may be. Chayin squatted in a corner, pulling still more from the bottomless saddlepacks. I saw a full set of threx shoes, and all that was needed to set them. I saw a small brazier, piles of clothing, boxes, and rolled mats. I saw wraps of meat, plump full bladders. Over the grass the cahndor had spread thick-piled mats; from the stanchion in the apprei's middle he had hung his harness and sword belt, coils of braided leather, and a lit oil lamp.

"Sit, little crell," Hael said to me, and knelt down himself, to unpack his own gear.

I sat upon my heels, conscious of my bonds, of the rope upon my belly. It was cool in the apprei. The mat under me was all red and gold, rich, warm. I let my eyes follow the dancing patterns. I sank within them, searching.

In Chayin I saw a beast in a blood rage, a dorkat wounded. I deep-read him, and what was there made me shiver. He was law unto himself, but he knew no law. Stealthy desert stalker, he craved the kill. Within him was a terrible anger. He cared only for his satisfaction. He was what a Slayer might have been, were there no Day-Keepers' laws to restrain him.

And Hael, the Day-Keeper, I read also. I liked what I saw no better. The picture I had for him was that of the kepher, that tree dweller from the swamps of Galesh, with its warted skin and suckered, webbed feet, that waits invisible upon the bark for unsuspecting wirragaets. I saw its long, sticky tongue shoot out, waving. I could only wonder at the vision's meaning.

The two knelt together, fitting pieces of wood like demented children with a puzzle. As I watched, the three-level board took shape under the light from the middle stanchion. It was the yris-tera, part game and part oracle, that is played by forereaders and Day-Keepers for its auguries, by Slayers and advisers for its strategies, by children for the fun of the contest.

When they had it built, they settled around it with the leather shaker, in which were the sixty game pieces of carved bone, and began to play. I was forgotten, ignored, as the first throw was cast.

Upon the first level of the board fell the spear and shield, and the dayglass. Through the slots in the first level tumbled two threx and the woman and man symbols, to land upon the second, and the fire and spear, and the Well, to land upon the third.

Chayin spat, disgusted. He still wore the Shaper's cloak, thrown back over his shoulders. Upon his arms I could see his tattoos, rippling as if with their own life as he shook the leather cylinder, to throw again. Upon his right arm was the slitsa, curled around the undulating Parset blade. On his left the uritheria, symbol of his rank covered his entire bicep, winding around it, its tail trailing down his forearm. Its fanged mouth was open, its forked tongue seemed to dart and writhe in the uncertain light, its leathery wings about to snap into flight.

A jiask entered, bearing two full bladders, one larger than the other. He passed me without notice, and stood before the cahndor and the Day-Keeper, bent over the board. Chayin nodded absently to him. The jiask laid the two bladders by Chayin's side. He looked at the board, and his brows knit together.

"Is it for Frullo jer?" asked the jiask.

"For what else could it be?" The cahndor's tone was sour. The jiask squatted down to watch. Hael leaned forward as Chayin threw again. The oil lamp picked out the Day-Keepers' signs in blues and reds upon his shoulders; the compass, the dayglass which contains the world, the eight-pointed star in circle. Within that star I saw glyphs I did not recognize. All except for one. That one I had seen upon Estrazi's ring, and upon the platform beneath the Falls of Santha. The glyph means "messenger" in Mi'ysten. I wondered if it were by chance that he wore it.

I was not pleased by my reading. Doubtless, I thought, it was the drug they had given me, blocking my talent. I, who wore the deep-readers' chain, had gotten little help from my strongest skill.

The second throw gave Chayin another woman upon the top level; an ebvrasea, winged fury, opposite one threx, and a sword upon the other, on the middle; and two men and one woman upon the bottom. The placement of these was most unusual, one woman and man beside the Well, and the other obstructing them with the fire and spear. These, certainly, were no random falls. Sometimes one can get much from the boards, sometimes little. It was my guess that this game might show the cahndor and the Day-Keeper more than they wanted to see. It was a board of crisis and polarization, of struggle and death. It had fallen so upon only the second throw.

Hael pointed to the top level.

"On the board of catalysts, the spear and shield, upon the red, are what is needed. The dayglass, upon the black, represents the will that controls. Thus we have what is preordained by the demands of time. Into this is drawn the woman, upon the gold, the place of the prime mover, through which the dayglass works. What think you, Chayin?"

"Besha," cahndor said. The jiask shifted his position. His brow was furrowed.

"Perhaps," said Hael. "But I think not. Upon the mid-board, of movement and manifestation, we have a threx on the gray of death, and one upon triumph's purple and loss's yellow. We see a woman, near the dying threx, within the swirl square of change. And the man, almost atop the threx that abides in both triumph and loss. Coming to challenge these we have the ebvrasea, opposite the man, and upon the square of overriding purpose. Thus, the ebvrasea will use the threx and man to its ends. And lastly, the sword, upon the threx in the death square, its blade pointing to the woman within the square of change. Remember, as you consider this board, whose symbol the ebvrasea has become, and what rumors about its flight we have just recently heard. I think, as it falls, that Besha lies here." He pointed to the woman in the swirl.

Chayin nodded, leaning forward, his eyes narrowed, his chin resting upon his fist.

"And last, the board of outcome," Hael continued. "The Well in the white of what may be gained, with the fire upon its home, what is needed, and the spear upon the square of the heart. Into this come two men and one woman. One man takes up the spear with the power of the fire at his command, and opposes the man and woman who stand before the Well. The woman stands in hate, and the man in love. I think we have thrown for Frullo jer, and gotten a glimpse of something else, of which the races at Frullo jer are only a small part. Only in the mid-board are the pieces concerned with our question." He looked up from the board, at Chayin.

"If the ebvrasea seeks your aid, will you give it?"

I wondered who the ebvrasea represented to them. I knew of no Well or city, town or tribe, who used that great soaring mountain carnivore as a symbol.

Chayin met Hael's eyes.

"Would you, brother, were our positions reversed?"

The jiask, silent, watching, had his hand upon his sword hilt.

"I think I would. The board demands it. The time demands it. And yet, much blood would flow, if such a thing were done, for reasons that are none of our affairs. Or were not, until this day. If one made this move"—he reached to the top board and plucked the woman from it, and placed it atop the ebvrasea upon the second—"one could perhaps avoid the entire sequence. With the prime mover surrendered to the square of overriding purpose, one might avoid what follows. It would have to be done before this occurs." He pointed to the threx within the square of death.

Chayin regarded the changed board. He reached out and removed all the pieces with the exception of the ebvrasea and the woman Hael had placed beside it in the green square. He tossed the bone pieces in his closed fist.

"Could you not be wrong, could that woman not be Besha also, and the ebvrasea the speed of the threx, the purpose of the race itself?"

Hael smiled and shook his head.

"When did you last throw the Well, brother? There is but one Well," he reminded Chayin gently, "among all the pieces."

"I threw it six passes ago, sets before we went to Rollcall at Yardum-Or." He grinned ruefully.

"And did you not, while in Yardum-Or, ride close to two hundred neras to see Well Oppiri?"

"It was an impulse, drunken and ill-conceived."

"But you did, against your own judgment and intentions, enter into a Well soon after you threw one. Had you ever thrown the piece before?"

"You know I did not ever before throw one. And you know what you would make of this board," Chayin said sharply. "I say it is Besha that is our problem, at the moment. If the Menetphers attend, and Aknet aniet Boshast rides the Son of Tycel, who has taken the Golden Sword three years in a row, then Besha's Guanden is our only hope. Saer has not the stamina for the two-nera run, and your Quiris has not the speed to take a Tycel son."

It was clear to me at that moment that the Nemarsi had been upon the desert to toughen the threx. I had wondered why they carried no helmets, no spears, no shields. Nor had I seen the deadly Parset lash, the huija, upon any of the men. Readying the threx for racing, they traveled light.

"I, also, would hate to see the sword go again to the Menetphers," Hael agreed. "But I think you still miss the point of the board."

"The point, as I see it, is that Besha is insufferable. She is more lofty than her station. I would be as loath to see her triumph as I would the Menetphers."

Chayin gestured to the jiask, who unstoppered one of the bladders he had brought and handed it to his cahndor. He drank deeply and handed the drink to Hael.

"Still," Hael said, wiping his mouth with the back of his hand, "Guanden should run. Besha will be only more difficult if you leave her behind. Perhaps something will occur at Frullo that will remind her of her place. But neither you nor I, such as it would pleasure us, can be the one to do so. Doubtless her insolent manner will attract some other jiask, someone not of the Nemarsi. Let us cast again." Hael pointed to the board, to the pieces Chayin still held in his hand.

"Marshon!" snapped the cahndor. The jiask jumped to his feet. His blue eyes were startling in his sun-weathered face. I saw he was younger than I had thought. He wore only breech and sword belt, and his ribs showed clear under his binnirin-colored skin.

"Marshon, take this crell and get her cleaned and fed and return her to me. And have a meal brought to us." Chayin dropped his gaze to the game and threw the bone pieces.

Marshon the jiask was leaning over me, obscuring the board, and I did not see how the throw fell out.

"There is nowhere for you to run," said the jiask, looking me up and down, "and no use in you causing yourself trouble. I will unbind you, and we will walk to the pool. I would not have to wash you like an infant."

I nodded, and he removed the rope that bound my hands in back of me. Then he led me through the tylas to the deep, wide pool, cool in their shadows.

The young jiask reached among the vegetation and broke from its stalk the fruit of a large succulent.

"This will take the dirt from you," he said. "Watch." And I watched while he thrust the plant beneath the water, swirled it around, then snapped it in half lengthwise and rubbed the exposed whitish pulp against his skin. I tried the strange whitish plant upon my arm. It slid across my skin, and where it had been, I was shades lighter. Convinced, I lathered and rubbed and dunked and lathered again, until the water was murky with silt and suds. Moving deeper, I worked the strange, fruity gel from the plant into my hair. When that was done, I lay upon my back and floated still upon the pool's surface. My abraded feet throbbed my heart's rhythm.

I turned the game's fall in my mind. I wished I had been there to see the play. Chayin's next throw would have designated the pieces to be used, as well as showing the result of surrendering the woman from the prime mover's square to the ebvrasea of overriding purpose. Then the pieces would have been assigned, placed on the board, and the dice cast. And cast, and cast. And through the dice and the pieces and the two players' abilities would have come the probabilities inherent in the approaching time. One, eventually, would win, capturing the other's pieces. How this win was accomplished, and upon what squares the drama unfolded, would greatly influence how the cahndor and the Day-Keeper pursued their goal. The power of yris-tera is very great. Sometimes I have wondered whether it is not too great, whether the game does not condition the time, rather then predict it.

I sighed to myself. The first two throws had seemed to speak directly to me. Hael had hinted that he, too, saw me upon the board. I could make no sense of the mid-level, nor why the Day-Keeper had chosen to move the woman there.

"Enough, crell! There will be nothing to eat but bones."

I opened my eyes and regarded the jiask. I climbed dripping upon the bank, my copper skin gleaming in the bright sun. The slightly abrasive plant fibers had buffed me silken smooth. I ran my hands over my flat belly, sluicing the drops from me. I split my sopping mass of thigh-length hair and brought the halves forward upon my breasts. Running my fingers through the snarls, I remembered that upon Mi'ysten I had learned a better way. I raised my hands to the crown of my head and did as the Shaper woman had taught me, bringing my hands slowly down, fingers spread. My scalp tingled, the strands crackled, and my hair lay without knot or tangle upon my breasts. So I had brought at least one Mi'ysten skill back with me. Not all of what had been learned beyond time and space could be used within it. But if one skill could be brought to bear, so might some others. Shaping—creating from the molecules free in the air what one desires—had eluded me in the desert. I thought I might try again, when I had the chance.

The jiask's eyes were upon me. He was staring.

"It is amazing," he said, "what a little puiia and water will do."

I smiled at him, boldly meeting his eyes.

"Your cahndor awaits you, crell," he growled, his eyes on my chald.

"And his brother, does he too await me?" I queried, as he took my arm and led me back through the tyla palms, toward the appreis. "Are they truly brothers?"

"Dharener Hael? He is also the son of Inekte, by the same rendi woman, Tasphersi, who was a Nemarchan until Inekte died." He stepped over the dead tyla trunk that lay fallen across the path. I followed suit, and gasped as I trod a sharp stone.

"Who is Nemarchan now?" I asked, limping as we crossed the clearing to the fire, burning low, untended. The other jiasks had already retired to the shade of the appreis. They had left a joint of meat and a half-full pot of binnirin, boiled until the grains had dissolved into a brown starchy mass. Beside the joint, cooled so that the fat and blood had congealed upon its charred surface, lay a quarter-filled bladder.

"Can you not wait to find out? Liuma Sataeje aniet Erastur reigns over the tiasks, over the time and the life, at the side of Chayin rendi Inekte, chosen son of Tar-Kesa." He intoned the ritual with more than a little fervor. Tar-Kesa, ancient god of the gristasha, still held power in the desert. If Liuma reigned over the time and life, then she was forereader. Chayin had a formidable court, with his blood brother the dharener, first among the Day-Keepers of the Nemarsi, and his couch-mate Nemarchan and forereader. With the three elements in accord, the Nemarsi might be wielded like a single razor-sharp sword in the hand of the cahndor. I knew the ritual of Tar-Kesa, and if Chayin had become his chosen son, he had undergone its testing: arduous, but worth the pain and risk to a man who would become a flesh-god, a living legend, above reproach and question. Dorkat, indeed, was Chayin, who loved power so much that he had laid his life down as wager upon the altar of Tar-Kesa.

I picked at the charred meat, at the mass of binnirin in the pot. The jiask gulped his food so fast he must have swallowed each bite whole. He drank long from the bladder. The sun beat down hot upon my back. When he surrendered the drink to me, I found it to be brin, headless and flat, but welcome. The intoxicant eased my mind, lightened my heart. I drank more. I was not hungry, I decided, but only thirsty. I was conscious of the apprei, looming behind my back. Its cool shade did not entice me. I had almost managed to forget why the cahndor had allowed me to wash and feed.

Marshon the jiask got to his feet and wiped his greasy hands upon his thighs. He tugged at my hair. Reluctantly I rose. He unlaced the flap and held it open for me. I saw that my plight amused him. All within the apprei looked green and indistinct. I stood for a moment, the urge to turn and run strong upon me, but there was nowhere to run. I stepped inside, and the flap fell back in place.

"As is often the case," Chayin said from somewhere before me, "Hael was right. When that chald is cut from you, you will be very lovely. Lace the flap." I turned and did so, the laces and holes slowly detaching themselves from the grainy dark as my vision cleared and sharpened. When that chald is cut from you, he had said.

"Do not take my chald from me." I faced him, my back against the laced flap, my hands clenched behind me.

"Crells do not wear chalds. It lessens their beauty, their usefulness, their humility. It slows their adjustment. What use is a chald without meaning? Come here."

I went to him, where he lounged with his back against the middle stanchion. I remembered, as I knelt before him, not to meet his gaze.

"Crells do not wear chalds," he repeated, his hands taking up the hair over my breast and gently brushing it back, that he might see me better.

"Then I will remove it if you wish." I would not have my chald defaced.

"Do so," he commanded.

I put my hands to my chald, running the strands through my fingers. I found the juncture, took the tiny key from its housing, and fitted the key in the lock. The ends parted. I took my eighteen-strand chald in my palms and looked at it. I saw the silver chain with white interwoven, that of Well Astria. I saw the red, due for changing, of the chaldra of the mother. I saw the bronze of birthing, unfulfilled. I saw my chains of patronage; to the Day-Keepers and the Slayers and the gol-masters, I closed my fists in, upon my platinum deep-reader's chain, and that of Astria's dependent city, Port Astrin. My eyes swam with tears. I could not see my clenched fists, but still I saw the strands of my chald. I saw the six brass mixed, of my schooling, and that of the singers of titrium and iron, and that of the musicians, of copper and bronze, and the green stra metal of the threx breeders, and the Well-Keepress' chain, of white gold set with white-fire gems. That one had been mine when I was born. The others, I had spent three hundred and two years acquiring. What is a Silistran without chaldra? I brought it to my lips and kissed it, and handed it to the cahndor of the Nemarsi. I had never before felt so exposed. I shook my head to bring my hair forward, that it might cover my nudity. It settled in a cloud around me, soft and sweet-smelling. I crossed my arms over my breasts.

His hand, which held my chald, was still outstretched to me.

"And the key, little crell." This, also, I handed over to Chayin.

He fitted the key in the housing, laid the chald aside. He looked me over, long and slow, where I huddled shamed before him. I could feel the heat of my blood, racing to my skin.

"Such a position suits you," he commented. "You might have been born crell." I did not meet his gaze, nor answer him. I was crell. A crell does not raise her eyes to her cahndor.

II. Chosen Son of Tar-Kesa

～～～～～～～～～～～～～～

The apprei was red-lit with the sun's setting when I awakened. Chayin slept soundly. He had not removed the Shaper's cloak, but wrapped it around his chest, though the day was fireside-hot. His alien chald glittered in the dim light. I could make nothing of it, but I must honor it. He was chalded; I was not. There were fourteen strands, of various metals, some with teeth and charms, tufts of hair and gems depending from them. It was loosely woven, more so even than the chalds of Arlet.

He had not used me as a wellwoman, but as an animal. If such was a crell's couching, I wanted no more of it. He had forced upon me more of the stimulant drug Hael had given me in the desert, and my heart pounded against my ribs. He had made no attempt to sate my needs, and my heat burned within me. I lay upon my side, my loins pressing against his thigh of their own accord. I hated him. He slept. I could not. He had taken my chald from me, made me crell. In my mind, he was every man who had ever misused me. He became for me Raet, and Estrazi, and Dellin. Even Dellin, whom I once loved, at that moment I would have killed upon the spot. My breathing deepened, and my senses became sharp and clear. Through this man, I would teach them all a thing about women. I studied Chayin's cloaked chest, rising and falling before my eyes. I would kill him. He, abuser of the helpless, cahndor of the chaldless, did not deserve to live. His breech and sword belt lay where he had thrown them, upon the mat, within easy reach. With his own sword I would skewer him, not only for myself, but for all the other helpless crells. I would plunge that undulating Parset blade into his heart. He would make no outcry, and then I would slip past the sleeping jiasks and steal a threx. The black one, Hael's, the one called Quiris, would I take and ride northeast, into the Sabembes, to Arlet. There I would see for myself what had occurred, whose blood had been spilled in my name. I would find Sereth and do what was needed. And Dellin, whom I once loved. Then I would go to Astria, and take up the Keepress-ship once more. I would need, I reminded myself, my chald, which lay in Chayin's saddlepack under his head. I would be once more chalded and free.

I lay a long while considering my stroke. While I pondered, Chayin groaned in his sleep and turned, to lie on his stomach. The Shaper's cloak, still fastened about his neck, was drawn tight around him. The spiral glittered upon it. Where the stones were thin, upon the western arm, would I strike. Between his ribs, into his heart would I thrust the recurved steel.

Stealthily, holding my breath, I rolled from his side and crawled to the sword belt he had so casually thrown upon the mat. Did he think that because I was crell and chaldless, I was bereft of will? Soundless, the blade slid from its sheath. The hilt was welcome in my hand. The blade was heavy, but of good balance. It was intricately chased, the hilt inlaid with titrium and gold. It was a cahndor's weapon. By it would a cahndor die.

On my knees I crawled back to him, the blade held between my breasts. I crouched above him, not daring to breathe. My arms trembled. I had never killed a man before. This man, I reminded myself, badly needed killing. Both hands upon the hilt, I raised the blade above my head, and brought it down, my whole body behind my thrust. Between two jewels of the spiral, I aimed the point, and followed it down with all my weight and all my force.

When the blade struck the Shaper's cloak, drawn tight around Chayin in his sleep, it shattered like ice. He was upon me; his hands imprisoned my wrists. He forced the jagged-bladed hilt from my grasp. Breathing hard, one knee at either side of my head, the shattered hilt now in his one hand, both my wrists crushed together in his other, he leaned close to me. His pupils were tiny points in his dark eyes, his lips mucus-sticky, his face beaded with sweat. His breath had the smell of fear about it.

"Crells do not raise arms to their cahndor," he rasped. "This act of yours begs discipline. Shall I cut you here?" He brought the jagged hilt to my face, ran the edge across my cheek. His knees, upon my hair at either side of my head, gripped tightly. I could not turn my face. I struggled to free my wrists, but in one hand he held them, easily. His grip upon them tightened until I thought surely the bones would snap. I met his eyes, defiant. Chance had defeated me, ill luck attended my bid for freedom. It was not by his skill that he had triumphed.

"Kill me now, Chayin," I suggested, "before I have another chance. It was the Shaper's cloak that saved you. My next attempt will surely prove successful."

He laughed, and ran the broken blade down my throat, across my breasts. Burning moistness followed its passage. I wished he would strike and be done with me.

"Chayin . . ." The voice was low and calm. It came from the direction of the apprei's entrance.

The cahndor turned his head, grunted, threw the hilt aside. He dragged me to my feet, twisting my arms cruelly. Leaning against the apprei wall was a figure. Next to it the unlaced flap blew in the first evening breeze. It was Raet. There was no mistaking that bronze glowing skin, that shimmer that surrounds a Mi'ysten. I shuddered. Chayin forced me down on my knees, facing the intruder. His free hand jerked my head back. I saw once more the figure by the door, and it was Hael who stood there, his arms folded across his chest, a smile flickering upon his beard-fringed lips.

"How long have you been there?" Chayin demanded.

"Long enough," Hael answered.

"This crell tried to kill me in my sleep." Chayin gave my head a savage shake.

"I saw." The Day-Keeper moved to stand before us.

"You saw? And you did nothing? Brother, would you see me die?"

"I saw what the boards told me I would see. I saw the sword raised against you crumble, as did the bone sword when it struck the wood. As the pieces fell, so did it happen." His voice was water upon the fire of Chayin's fury. "What did you expect?" he continued. "That she would calmly submit to you? A Well-Keepress, designated prime mover, dosed with enough uris to keep a jiask at the kill for a week? Did you expect her to sing you to sleep?"

The cahndor grunted. He dragged me through the litter to the middle stanchion and forced me to my knees before it. The uritheria upon his arm glared balefully at me as he bound my wrists before me to the pole. When his arm brushed my face, I sank my teeth into his bicep, into the uritheria's fanged head. Chayin cursed and struck me away. My temple crashed against the stra metal stanchion. The lash upon my back was far away, as if it was another whose flesh was parted. I bit deep into my arm, that I would not give him more satisfaction by crying out. And somewhere within me a thing gave way, and the pain mixed with passion and became something else. And that too was gone, and I was but a woman beaten by her master, and the pain was only pain, and I was content to lie passive and receive it. There was little blood.

Chayin came and squatted before me, the thick braided-leather strap in his hands.

"Are you satisfied, crell?" He jerked my head up. "What your mind expected, your body demanded, I have given you."

I shook my head, wordless, but my flesh knew what my heart denied. My eyes misted and cleared. I felt a hand on my shoulder, and knew it to be Hael.

Chayin looked past me, at his brother the dharener.

"She is yours, Hael. I give her to you. In that way, perhaps things will set themselves aright. We will throw again and see."

He turned his gaze back to me. His voice was low, his grip upon my head gentle. He laid down the braided lash. I could see my flesh upon it. He traced the side of my face with his fingers.

"It would have been amusing," he said to me, "but I have not the time for you. You tempt me, with your flesh and spirit, your wellwoman's skills. I cannot afford you." His voice was a whisper. "I am not Sereth of Arlet! Into your circle I must not step, lest I lose all I have gained."

His eyes searched mine, his tone a strange mixture of sadness, longing, and determination. Around his mouth were lines of strain.

My back counted my pulse for me. "You fear yourself, cahndor, for you certainly cannot fear a crell." I thought he would strike me when he heard my words. I did not care. He did not strike, but smiled.

"You understand too well. I will let you pass. Let Hael try you. With his Day-Keeper skills, he is more your match." He leaned forward and pulled my face against his, kissed me. It was not the kiss of a cahndor to a crell. And I returned it. When he took his lips from mine reluctantly, I did not meet his gaze. Confusion had my mind like the slitsa the furry yit; and it attempted to swallow me whole.

Uris. Uris. I had not realized. It is a drug to take with utmost care. It looses that part of us which must tear and rend and kill. It frees of inhibition, retards moral judgment, masks fatigue and pain with its own strength. I had never submitted myself to it in the past. The word pulsed great red letters before my eyes, and I could see little else. I could not see Chayin, kneeling again with the shaker in hand, nor Hael. I could not feel my bonds, the strain of my weight upon my arms, still lashed to the stanchion.

After a time another thought came to me, and the red mist faded, to be replaced by a blackness through which I wandered without form. I heard Chayin's words again, echo chain: What your mind expected, your body demanded, I have given you. And I answered it "no" until from sheer exhaustion I stopped, cold, alone, mid-place between nowhere and nothing, and knew what I had done. And the dark became lighter. I had form once more. I walked the halls of Mi'ysten once again. My feet trod the saw-toothed Mi'ysten grass. This time I needed no guidance, no collar of stabilization around my neck.

I found Estrazi behind the first door I chose to open of that endless hallway of same-seeming doors. I felt no surprise that he should be so easily found, he who is seldom enfleshed. He sat upon the ground, and I joined him, sitting close beside, content to watch the flameglow dance upon his skin for a longer time than I have yet lived.

And he spoke to me; a smooth strong breeze in my mind, for my ears did not hear him. Finally he folded his arms over his chest, and those eyes that touch what they see burned within me. He said to me that I must do as he bid.

I replied that I could not do so, that I would do what mortal flesh could do, but no more.

My father pointed out to me that if I did not use my skills, others would use me through them. That I myself would be my greatest enemy.

And I replied that it was he who had made it thus, and he must unmake it, for I would not and could not be what he would have me be.

And Estrazi laughed that gentle laugh that is like the first spring water bubbling, while at his right hand, Raet, Shaper son of Kystrai, appeared out of sparkling air.

I would have risen, but I could not. Raet sat, completing our triangle.

He hested a blue-white ball of jagged-edge crystal through the air toward me. I raised my hands before me, but it was what I found behind my eyes that stopped it, whirling, midway between us.

"Take it," Raet said, pushing it hard toward me, while his fingers played upon the knee of his crossed legs. The ball was suddenly closer, a small distance. I evened it.

"I will not." And my words were for Estrazi, as I tried to send the fiery ball toward the greatest among the Shapers.

"You will, in the fullness of time," said Estrazi kindly. The blazing blue-white form regained the middle between us. "Look what you do, with so much ease before us. Remember. When you are ready, it is yours."

I shook my head. I would not.

"So that I can be a better plaything for Raet, a more efficient instrument of your designs?" I took my eyes from the ball for just a moment, to look in my father's eyes.

"Surely," he said, and the jagged crystal ball, unimpeded, hit me in the head and exploded within my brain. It illuminated within me every crevice and dark place of hiding. I shrank from the blinding light, but not even my spirit cast a shadow in that cruel glow. I writhed and rolled to be free of it, and heard my own voice, screaming.

And I opened my eyes, to see Hael peering down, the mid-pole of the apprei rotating with his head as its center. The distance between us became less and less, and the rotation of the world slowed and ceased.

Hael only knelt above me, his face but scant inches from mine. I could see grains of sand entrapped in his wiry black beard, cracks where the desert wind had scoured his full lips dark and deep.

"I had thought you entrusted with the chaldra of the soil," he said softly, wiping my forehead with a cool cloth. So close I could see the pink tongue dart in his mouth, he peered into my eyes.

"I was with my father," I said, unthinking. My mouth would not form a clear word. The lamplight flickered over the apprei walls, which sighed and groaned in the dim.

"You were, in truth, elsewhere. We will be within the appreida by sun's rise. Three days you have been unconscious, with precious little breath moving in you. And yet I found this, here by your side, when none have been within but I. I have not left this apprei between the time I last examined you, when there was no such thing here, and just now, when you with your screaming roused me to look again." Hael held in his hand a blue-white pulsing, jagged-edged. It nestled innocent in his palm, glowing. I could not see the black filaments within it from this distance, but I knew they were there, floating, waiting. I shuddered. I would have run, had I had the strength to move.

"You do not know it! Do not hold it so, against your naked flesh. Wrap it in something, tas-, parr-, apth-hide. Put it away! Wrap it and put it in the deepest pocket of the roomiest saddlepack among the Nemarsi, and make sure that it lies not near the flesh of man or beast!" My words came out of me a hissing croak.

Hael dropped the crystal. It bounced upon the Parset rugging and rolled toward me. I stopped it, unmoving.

"Get the skin!" I demanded, not taking my eyes from the blue-white helsar. Already it brightened, close to me That it was mine, I had no doubt, nor did it. That I had somehow brought it with me, against my will, was impossible. It was here because somewhere inside me I wanted it.

The dharener of the Nemarsi, rushing to do my bidding, dropped a thick apth wrap over the glowing helsar and made it fast. He then picked the thing gingerly up by the thongs and packed it carefully in his own saddlepack with great attention to its position. Only when it had been finally seated among the bladders and braziers, pincers and pillows, rolls and wraps of his store, and the lace lashed tightly shut, did he turn to me.

Sitting cross-legged by my head, he offered me water, lifting my head that I might drink.

"Why? What is it?" he finally asked me. We were both suddenly aware that it was not as a dharener he had done my will, nor as a crell had I ordered him.

"Call it a toy, if you will," I answered him. "A toy of a race such as is your Tar-Kesa, and nothing to be held in the human grasp. Give it to him, upon his altar, if you will. I am sure the receipt of it would bring him pleasure." And I was sure. I met Hael's eyes steadily, demanding his recognition.

"You do not believe in Tar-Kesa?" he said to me, in question form.

"On the contrary." I steadied my voice, that it might somehow match my gaze, rather than my quaking heart. "I know he exists. I respect and revere him. I do my best to keep his laws, and out of his way." I tested my arms' strength, gauged it sufficient, and sat up, drawing my knees around me. The creamy Parset web-cloth slid down to bunch across my thighs. I was not cold.

"What harm could it do, this god's toy?" the dharener pressed me.

"It could engage you in its teaching, forever and ever. It could drive you mad. It could suck all the life from you without your notice, pleasantly, so that you went more and more to its use and your death. Is that sufficient?" All truth and no lies had I told him. But the helsar was so much more; a primal catalyst, the seed of a universe yet unborn. I rubbed my hands on my arms, loving the feel of flesh against itself. I have a horror of being without this tactile sense of being, and I had been three days removed from my body and its needs.

Hael shook his head from side to side, hand wandering in his beard.

"How do you know all this? Do you know the thing's use and purpose, and what is to be gained from it?" His black eyes were keen, the nictitating membranes flickering back and forth in his excitement.

"Ask Tar-Kesa," I suggested. "What I know of it, I have told you. It could do you great harm." I did not tell him that another's attempt to use the helsar could put me in very real danger. Doubtless the link was already made between us. I could feel it, warm, waiting at the edge of my perceptions. I had no choice now; I must use what I could of my Mi'ysten skills. Perhaps I had been fooling myself, since my return, that I could do without them. If one is the first of a group of children to learn to walk upright, one does not return to crawling for the sake of the group. One walks upright, and is sooner apprised of danger and better able to meet it.

The dharener stood abruptly. I could hear the whispered voices of the jiasks as they began dismantling the apprei around us. We faced each other in awkward silence. I could feel his mind gently probing. I snapped up my best Mi'ysten shield, smooth and shining. There it had been child-weak, useless. Here it was more than sufficient. Hael pursed his lips. I reached out through the shield and met his, in my own turn testing. Day-Keeper he was, and adequate. I saw there a great agitation and intricately wrought defenses, about what seemed to be, in part, concerned with me. To read what is consciously hidden, one must get the thought to the surface.

"If you try the helsar, dharener, see that your sorting is strong and free from fear," I advised him softly. And there it was. What I had sought, he considered in his excitement. Monitoring my mind while I lay unconscious, Hael had seen more than he would have chosen.

"The key, then, is in the sort?"

"You must have the sort to get there," I conceded. "Sort" is a forereader's term for the stochastic process, for isolating the probabilities available from a specific moment in time.

The jiasks had one of the apprei walls rolled and were starting upon another. The night showed clear and star-flecked, the moon nearly full and low over the Sabembes. Hael snatched up his saddle and hefted it upon his shoulder. The fully distended packs almost dragged the ground.

"Walk before me," he ordered. I did this, through the jiasks kneeling about the stra framework of the apprei, toward the large darker shadows that must be the hobbled threx. There was hard, stony ground under my bare feet, and mountains towered both to my right and my left. I judged us to be well north of the dead sea, where the tail of the great Yaica range parallels the Sabembes.

There was a great thudding and snorting and clinking. Chayin, phantom upon his dark-dappled Saer, circled the plunging beast around us. Moonlight sparked off my father's cloak in the darkness. Foam from the animal's tossing head sprayed my arms and face; small stones from his hooves pelted my naked legs as he danced in place.

"Bestir yourself, brother, or we shall miss our only opportunity for bloodletting this night!" And he laughed down at us while Saer walked a dozen steps upon his hind legs, wheeled him toward the north star Clous, and was gone.

"What mean you, Chayin?" Hael called to the

empty air. "Fool," he groaned softly, his free hand on my back, guiding me among the threx. As he threw the saddle over Quiris' back and cinched it, I asked what was in my mind.

"Did the sword really break upon the square?"

Hael grunted and thrust his knee against Quiris' black belly as he tightened the straps around the threx's distended middle. The animal let out its breath in a whoof, and Hael got the girth a hand's length tighter.

"It did," he said, his back to me. "It shattered into splinters. But for that, the throw was the same. Small chance, that such could be the case. Even another woman was forthcoming to replace the one we moved to the ebvrasea's square. The time is deathly tight." He moved around the threx to fasten the breastband to the cinch rings.

"And were you so sure it would break, to take such a chance?"

"Am I so sure of you, that I do not bind you?" he retorted. It was true. He had not restrained me. My hands were free.

The dharener's head appeared above Quiris' back, and he regarded me sharply.

"I had to judge the truth of the board. How else but to test it?"

"And if you were wrong, if the yris-tera was wrong, what then? Do you love the truth so much, or your brother so little?"

"It might have been better, had I been wrong," Hael replied in a strange tone, and came around to Quiris' head with the double-bitted head gear in hand. "You have seen how he is, how the jiasks are around him. And he is in one of his better times. A man should not live with such pain. His agony touches us all. Our destiny lies in his hands, and those hands support him forever dangling from the edge of the abyss. One day soon his grip will weaken, and he will fall. It is my charge to see he does not take the whole of the Nemarsi with him!"

"I do not understand," I said as he finished checking straps, boosted me up forward of the saddle, and swung up behind me.

"Chayin is a forereader," he continued, turning Quiris on his haunches and setting him at a run after Chayin's dust trail, just visible far ahead like low-riding fog. "He suffers from the forereader's disease. When he underwent Tar-Kesa's testing and took the cahndor's sword, he had not yet had a woman." Foreseeing ability first becomes obvious at puberty, never before, and often not until some little while after. "Once he was invested, nothing could be done, for the chosen of Tar-Kesa is all-knowing." He sighed and shook his head. "There was no peer from whom he could receive instruction. Therefore, he did not receive it."

I considered this. I had never heard of a male forereader. I had been taught that male drives and the passive surveillance of the forereaders were mutually exclusive. I knew well enough what agony an untutored forereader's life could be, for I had been called a latent, and schooled sufficiently to protect myself, should the talent come tardy upon me. Even with years more training that I had received, working forereaders face always the grim specter of forereader's disease. One in seventy, it is said, succumbs to it and goes irretrievably mad. Now I knew why I had gotten such a chaotic reading from the cahndor; such confusion, such fear and hate. He saw only violence around him.

The neras passed under Quiris' pounding tripart hooves, and soon we were close enough to Chayin to shout across the distance. Hael charged him to halt and wait for the jiasks to catch up. This the cahndor was willing to do. In the high moonlight, Saer was white with foam and dust.

"Know you," said Hael in my ear, "the book of Khys?" as he slowed Quiris to a walk. The threx's muzzle seemed to graze the ground in front of me. He blew dust clouds with his heaving breath. It had been a mad pace Hael set to catch his brother, who had so great a start, upon a threx carrying a lesser burden.

I shook my head. I had not delved deeply into the *Ors Yris-tera,* which holds the true wisdom of the board game.

"The dayglass was upon the board of catalysts, and within aspect of a human piece, the woman. Thus it works, through her, the will of the First Weather. In the citing of this arrangement of pieces, Khys said that in such times a material sign is always given at the outset. And it likens that sign unto starlight. It seems to me that what we have apth-wrapped within my saddlepack is such a material sign."

I could see Chayin's face, limned by the moonlight, as he leaned his forearms upon the grip of his saddle, watching us. I felt a stab of compassion for him. He and I faced similar struggles, both with powers we did not want and information we could not use, and for neither of us was there any alternative. A male forereader was surely as alone as a Shaper's daughter on Silistra. And for our questions it seemed to me then the Day-Keepers had no answers. Somehow, seeing him and knowing, I felt less lonely. He struggled to resolve the law within and the stimulus from without, as did I. I sat straighter, up before Hael upon Quiris' back. I sent a gentle probe of strength and comfort, deeper than the cahndor would consciously feel.

The threx greeted one another. I have often wondered that such high-pitched sounds can come from out of those great beasts.

"I asked you if you saw yourself upon the board of catalysts," Hael reminded me softly. Saer slobbered upon Quiris. Quiris stamped, tossed his head.

"Perhaps. But one cannot know it," I said.

"Perhaps one cannot know it, but one can surely do no better than one expects, either," he answered, sidling Quiris against Saer until my knee brushed Chayin's and we were but handbreadths apart. The cahndor's face, previously abstracted as he toyed with

his reins, changed when his eyes met mine. I dropped
my gaze, wondering what part I played in the endless
traps and tortures his mind made for him, what hor-
rific futures incessantly threatened.

His hand under my chin raised my face to his,
but he spoke to Hael, and his eyes searched the dark
terrain over which we had just passed.

"Here they come. Good. We will need everyone.
If you have a weapon within your pack you might
choose in battle, get it out now. We will catch us some
threx with sun's rising, I think."

Hael said nothing.

The cahndor reached back and unlaced one of his
own packs and pulled forth two short gol-knives. He
put one in his belt and handed the other toward me,
almost absently. Hael reached around me to take it.
Chayin snatched it back.

"Not for you. For her. She will not use it upon
me. She must use it, though! So I have seen it!" And
he pointed it at me.

"No, Chayin," said Hael gently. "You cannot arm
a crell. And what against?"

The first of the jiasks sighted us and slowed his
beast to a walk. I could make out the forms of three
others.

The blade was still in the cahndor's outstretched
hand. The moon played tricks upon his face, and he
had but dark holes for eyes. He leaned back in his
shadow, tossing his head like an apth with sand in its
ears. Then, once more he offered the blade, and his
voice was strong and sure and clear.

"It is no matter what you think, Hael. I am apprised of what is to come, and in time you will be
also. You shall not gainsay me. It is your life I would
protect."

I took the gol-knife. Hael did nothing, but I could
feel the muscles cord in his arms. The jiasks were almost upon us, with their uncanny silence. It would be
better to show an armed crell to them than open dis-
cord. Hael would rather take the chance that I would

turn upon him than expose Chayin's indisposition to the cahndor's death-sworn men.

"Arm yourselves, and make all haste. Look well about you, for our enemies steal triumphant through the night. Upon your lives I charge you. Regain what is rightfully ours!" And he jerked Saer cruelly around and sped off toward the north. Quiris, anticipating his master, leaped to follow. Hael did not stay the threx's headlong flight, but turned to peer behind him into the dark. My gaze followed his, and I saw the knotted jiasks milling in a circle; then the circle became a line of twos, and that line followed in our dust. Hael reined Quiris into an easy lope, fast enough to keep Chayin in sight, yet slow enough that the leading pair of jiasks soon came abreast of us. Quiris tossed his head and fought restraint, his ears flicking.

"Is the veil again upon him?" the jiask upon Hael's right shouted.

"I know not," Hael called back. Quiris leaped a shadowed depression before us that did not suit him. I was thrown violently forward at his jarring impact upon the far side. I hugged the threx's neck, and Hael's hand upon my shoulder gave me aid as I righted myself. If I had fallen, then, with the jiasks mounts racing to pace us, I would have been pummeled lifeless by those metal-shod thundering hooves.

"Keep as close as you can, but not upon us! Be ready!" ordered the dharener, and his flat hand came down hard upon Quiris' croup, and the black sprang away from the other threx as though they stood grazing upon sweet jer grass.

I had not imagined Quiris capable of such speed. The night roared around us as he strained to catch Saer. But it was not so easy to draw abreast of the cahndor. Slowly we gained upon him. I could see Chayin's arm rise and fall upon his mount's bunched quarters. Almost imperceptibly we closed the distance, Quiris' superior stamina telling as the ground blurred by. A northern threx would have died of burst lungs long before Saer's rider slid him to a halt atop a rock-strewn rise in the cold moonglow.

"Another nera, and I would have caught you!" called Hael as he brought Quiris alongside.

"I know it," Chayin allowed, his eyes searching the flatlands ahead. Nothing bigger than a pandivver could cross that open ground unseen in the bright clear night. "Back down the slope, that they will not see our outline!"

Hael did this, and set our sweat-slicked threx walking in a long ellipse that he might not injure its legs standing still while so badly overheated. Chayin paced us.

"Only some few enths remain until sun's rising, and the appreida is but thirty neras from here at the most. Where is your enemy, Chayin?"

"Even now they sneak stealthily through the web-weavers' appreis with their loot. This is the place where we will meet them, upon the plain, when the sky is greened before sun's rising. It is as I have seen it. We are only early enough to rest the threx. We wait here."

I heard Hael sigh softly. His body seemed to slump slightly in the saddle. We walked the threx and waited.

When the jiasks were all among us, Chayin set them to likewise walking their beasts in circles. He would not suffer them to dismount and charged them to maintain their readiness. Then he himself dismounted and crawled to the top of the stony rise and lay there, his head nestled upon his arms, watching.

After a time, we went to join him, leading Saer and Quiris as close as we dared to the ridgetop and tethering them to the scraggly harinder bushes that grew there in relative profusion. No harinder bush or even puny boulder was upon the plain below us. Nothing moved. I lay between Chayin and Hael, looking over the rise. I knew stinging embarrassment for the cahndor. He would be much shamed before us all if no foe appeared upon the plain. An enth passed, and still nothing stirred upon the silent expanse before us. No yit squeaked nor friysou cried. The sky was lightening, a presaging green haloed the peaks. The jiasks whispered and grunted behind us. There was much restlessness among them. Another enth passed. I wondered why Hael did not speak, put a stop to this ugly farce.

"There!" Chayin whispered. I sighted along his outstretched arm and could barely see a dust cloud rising. At first I thought it just a trick of anxious eyes, a quiver in the predawn light. Hael pulled himself forward an arm's length, as if that short gain would bring the distance into clearer focus. A thousand breaths did I take, and still the dust cloud grew upon the horizon. Hael wriggled back the short distance he had gone from us. His face as he looked past me to meet Chayin's eyes was painful to look upon in his joyous relief. He reached his left hand across me and grasped Chayin's shoulder, his fingers making valleys in the Shaper's cloak the cahndor wore.

"Let us go down and do battle, brother!" the dharener said, and suiting action to words, hastened down the slope in a crouch.

Chayin put his hand upon my arm. "Go with him. May your gol-knife quench its thirst this rising." And he pushed me gently before him toward the others.

As I mounted Quiris, and Hael swung up behind me, I entertained thoughts of death. Perhaps I could slay the dharener, make away upon the threx in the confusion of battle. The helsar was in Quiris' pack. But I knew, somehow, that I would not.

Silent were the jiasks as single file they made their way over the rise and down the slope, together waiting in the dark pool of shadows at its base. Soundless, recurved swords of stra and steel were drawn and held low, that the glint of them might not warn our approaching victims. And still the dust cloud enlarged and the greening moved higher and higher in the sky, until the dust had dark shapes within it, and those shapes resolved themselves into mounted threx, a dozen or more. And whispered orders formed the five pairs of jiasks into a spear point, with the cahndor and dharener at its tip. So close they were that I could see they carried neither spear nor shield, and still the cahndor did not stir his waiting men, though his arm was raised pointing to the sky. As I raised my eyes to his hand, that I might see the signal given, another thing, and strange, did I see. A M'ksakkan egg-shape glowed silent, like some speeding creamy comet across the sky: a Liaison's ship surely, for no other may fly the gravitic-drive hovers through the skies of Silistra. And yet there was no port in the Parset Lands for such a craft, and none due north, from whence it came. It danced for a moment motionless over the plain, then veered northeast and was gone. Chayin's hand came down. As one, the jiasks of the Nemarsi swept down upon their prey.

Barely had I time to steady my seat after Quiris' first leap and ready the gol-knife in my hand, before we were among them. Crouched low on Quiris' neck, that I not impede the dharener's longer blade, I found my knife of use first upon the gaping mouth of a threx who sought to clamp his jaws around my arm. Its pupils glowed gold and huge in white-walled eyes rolling in that deathly head. I split its nostrils, and it reared away in agony, giving the cahndor clear strike at his opponent's armorless chest, which he made with the ease of a man slicing cheese. The first rays of the sun color-glowed the plain and fired the sparking swords, and the whole world was blood-soaked. I saw for a moment the fallen jiask before I followed him, tumbling upon the corpse as Hael's mount kicked out with both hind feet at a new tormentor and whirled to meet an attacker coming up from behind. I disengaged from the corpse, up and running, lest I be trampled by the beasts as they tried to savage one another. I saw a riderless threx, unable to escape, so close-quartered was the fighting. His lifeless rider was wedged, head dangling down, between two live combatants' threx. He had no top to his skull, and the gray pulp dripped upon the feet of the fighting men. Somehow I made my way to its far side, and, unthinking, squeezed behind Saer's rear. I had just grabbed the mounting strap when I heard a great singing above my head. Chayin's sword snicked the head from a man whose own blade was in mid-strike at my back. I dodged the free-falling weapon and caught it in my right hand by the blade near the hilt. I looked up and grasped Chayin's arm as it was extended to me, and he all but threw me upon the riderless threx's back. Our eyes met for a moment. He laughed his joy and turned away, still smiling, to seek a new foe. I grasped the threx's back with but the strength of my knees and thighs, the stirrups being so far too long I could not even use the strap loops. I grabbed the reins caught around the saddle grip just as the great dun beast reared and brought his steel-shod hooves down upon the neck of another threx, who thought to get him by the throat. And I saw Hael, badly pressed by two foes, Quiris bleeding. I slammed the flat of the short sword against the threx's rear, and he fairly jumped upon the back of the nearest attacker's threx. The man's head turned, and I saw his startled expression as I plunged the gol-knife in my left hand into his throat, while his sword arm was raised to parry Hael's blow. The quarters were too close for the short sword to have helped me, though I still held it in my bleeding right, along with the threx's reins. The gol-knife was gone now, somewhere below in the dust, in a dead man's neck.

Hael, free to engage properly his opponent, skewered him with dispatch. He brought Quiris head to tail with my dun threx. I looked around me. I saw only Nemarsi still mounted. I searched for Chayin, seeing Saer was among the riderless, and felt a great relief when I spied him standing upon the ground over a lifeless form. He was speaking, it seemed, to a threx. I could hear his coaxing tone but not his words. The dust slowly settled. Everywhere the jiasks were catching up the riderless animals. I did not see Marshon,

the jiask who had taken me to wash in the jer, among
them. Hael's eyes were fastened upon the threx I rode.

"A Menetpher!" Chayin called out, holding high a
blooded blade.

A sardonic smile appeared upon Hael's full lips. His
cloak and beard were white with dust. I looked away
from him, at the corpses. I counted fifteen. There was
much blood upon the moving jiasks, but no telling
whether it be theirs or their victims'. One limped slowly
among the dead. Another, holding a useless arm, stood
staring at the body of the jiask Marshon. The sun's rising
was ruby mist upon the land. Hael still stared around
him, smiling. Chayin snatched up the dragging reins
of the steel-blue threx he was stalking and led her toward us. The men's voices were growl and hiss in
their throats, and many shook their heads to and fro as
they collected threx, weapons, and chalds from among
the fallen. If a Parset dies in battle with an enemy of
his peer group, his chald is returned to the Day-
Keepers by the enemy, that his death may be entered
upon the Day-Keeper's Roll. Those possessions upon
him at the time of his demise are retained by his
killer. There would be a formal rebuke and presentation of these Menetpher chalds to the Menetpher Day-
Keepers, for the traditional truce surrounding threx
meets had been broken. The Nemarsi who had died
victorious in battle fared better. Their effects would
be shared between those in the tribe with whom they
had sipped blood. If, however, the Menetphers had
triumphed and left no clue as to the identity of the
assassins, all the worldly goods of the fallen would
have been thrown out upon the sand. In mysterious
death among the Parset tribes, there is no beneficiary.
Thus do they keep murder from their backs. Only if a
man is willing to take up the chaldra, the responsibilities and family of another, does he raise arms against
him other than in war. If the death is unseemly, such
as death at the hand of a chaldless, or while pursuing
some immoral end, then also are all worldy possessions of one so slain cast away, serving no one, that all

trace of his ignoble memory be lost forever and ever, and even his name be scoured away by the desert. Such are the Day-Keepers' laws upon the Parset Lands.

Hael still smiled, like a proud father at his son's first chalding.

"Does death so amuse you, dharener?" I asked him. He grunted.

Chayin, mounted once again upon Saer and leading the steel-blue threx, joined us.

My arms were shaking uncontrollably. I pressed them against me.

"She sits upon Guanden, proudest possession of the tiask Besha, and fastest among Nemarsi threx, and she wonders why I find the situation amusing. I would have been far from amused had we returned home and found thirteen of our best stolen from under our very noses." Hael chuckled aloud.

For a moment, I was with the helsar. The battle had excited it, even wrapped away within Hael's pack. It had made use of some of the life energy lost in battle. It was warmer, closer. Then it was gone. But I marked it stronger.

"And Besha this way comes," said Chayin in a distant tone. I searched his face. Now the veil was surely upon him. His eyes stared, enraptured at what only he could see, while he wiped great toothmarks of bloody open flesh upon his mount's neck with a cloth sticky with dark salve. He must have used it first upon his own arm and shoulder, and upon a place high over his eye. Through the gel upon his skin one could almost see the blood clot and dry.

"There is no solution for what is between us," he said solemnly to me, profering the cloth. I took it and wiped my slashed right hand, where I had caught the sword in mid-fall. I wondered again what the cahndor envisioned "between us."

I rubbed the cool salve upon a long slash running diagonally down my right side from collarbone to breast. I did not recollect how I had come by it.

"This cloak of yours twice saved me," Chayin muttered, as if only now remembering.

I did not answer, but handed the healing cloth to Hael, who had greater need of it than I. A wound of some depth upon his chest bled copiously, though he had pressed a strip of cloth to it. I moved to dress his cut, and the Day-Keeper urged Quiris forward and let me attend him.

"How did you determine them to be Menet-phers?" Hael winced as I peeled away the cloth adhering to his wound.

"By this." He handed Hael a blade he had taken upon the field. "And also did I remember a face among them, from the battle of Macara last. They wore little that would mark them in their perfidy." I could hear the pride in Chayin's voice, that the time had upheld him.

Hael grinned at his brother, sharing the cahndor's triumph. His flesh quivered with pain under my hand. He examined the blade peremptorily and secured it in his saddle sheath. I slid my own blade into a similar scabbard upon Guanden's saddle. The threx tossed its head, and its long bristles rattled. Most threxmen keep neck bristles close-trimmed; one might otherwise lose an eye should the beast throw his head high. But Guanden's brown bristles were as long as my forearm, and each was beaded, so that they rattled and flopped as he moved. He bared his teeth and snapped irritably at Saer. He was an ill-tempered beast, always shifting on his feet, never easy on the bits.

There was much jabbering among the jiasks, all mounted now, all leading recaptured threx. Upon one was draped the body of Marshon. Another, the beast whose nose I had so savagely slashed, bore a similar burden. Two Nemarsi dead. Among the victors there was not one unscathed, but only three seemed seriously wounded. They clustered their mounts around us.

"They are all ours!" exclaimed the one whose arm hung useless, blood still streaming down his shoulder despite a salve-soaked bandage. His face was very pale. "Upon what did they ride from Menetph? Think you that like some star-trader they left us their useless splay-footed mounts in exchange for the best of ours?"

There was general dissent at this, and unease in their anger.

"They chose well," put in another, whose flesh seemed near unmarked. "Surely there is nothing left in the appreida worth putting one's pack upon!"

I did not mention what I had seen floating high over the plain, and then speeding northeast.

"Let us get them home safely, that there be once again threx worth riding among the Nemarsi," Hael suggested. "Where there are some Menetphers, there may be more!"

And Chayin slowly raised his head. He regarded the men gathered close around him as if they were strangers. Then he nodded and urged Saer through their midst, the threxmen making way for him. He still led the steel-blue female by her reins. Hael's eyes caught mine, and we threaded our way through the confusion engendered by so many riderless mounts on leads. The jiasks would have no easy time forming up with so many skittish beasts to control.

Guanden effortlessly gained Saer's left. I had him so tightly held that his jaw rested against his chest. My arms ached from his constant pulling. Hael, upon Chayin's right, sent me some hand signal I did not understand, but seemed to be satisfied when I kept Guanden even with the others.

I might have then made for the northeast, upon the fastest of the Nemarsi threx. If I could outdistance them, I might go free. Chaldless, but free. And Hael would have the helsar. I sighed and tried to find a comfortable position. My knees and thighs were rubbed raw from the constant friction against the leathers. I spent a time adjusting the straps so I might get some purchase from their loops, which afforded me a better seat but gave my raw skin another surface to chafe against. It had somehow become full morning. I looked around me, at how the summer sat upon the northern Parset Lands. It was not as forbidding a sight as the dead sea bottom in the desert, but was precious little green. Even the sky had to it a yellow tinge. In back of us the jiasks gave up upon forming, and led their charges single file toward home. Mount Opir was mist-enshrouded to the west.

There was only the snort and thud, creak and jingle of loping threx under saddle. Nothing else. Neither Chayin nor Hael spoke. The cahndor was again abstracted, sunk somewhere within, loose and easy upon his mount. He and Saer were long familiar, and it almost seemed that as he gave more and more of his attention to his thoughts, just that much more care did Saer use in seeking out the smoothest and safest route. The reins flapped untouched from the saddlegrip, and Saer judged the way, nose in the dust.

I was shaking. My mouth was dry and my heart struggled to free itself of my confining chest. During the battle, I had been only cold, and in a very slow time. It had been as if I watched myself, and the sound was so far away. Not now. I could yet see the bodies back there upon the sand. Nemarsi take no prisoners. They have no word for "prison." Their only word for captive is "crell." They were careless of life, these people, more careless than I found seemly. And I thought of Chayin, and his affliction, and Hael's astounding statement that his "charge" (a strong word he used for it, with meaning near to "commitment") was to keep the Nemarsi safe from their cahndor. And I had killed a man, for the first time in my life, with my own hand. A part of me raged, a portion wept, and somewhere else deep in me was a strong thing that had grown stronger.

Sparse grass was under the threx's hooves. Mountains rose high and impassable to the west and east. We rode in silence.

My mind, drifting free, found Sereth crill Tyris. I sorted for a way that would lead me to him. The probabilities fanned out before me; scenes from time not yet realized, only a handful I could use. I chose among them and set my will in motion, that my choice and no other's manifest in real time. Thus does one hest the time-coming-to-be and make it one's own. I sensed the helsar again. It was interested in my choosing. There was death upon that altered path thus opened before me, but in such a harmonic position that I felt it not discordant. There had been death upon all the usable futures. It was only a matter of proximity. At that time, I thought it all so simple.

Simple to take that which might be and alter its balance? Estrazi once said to me of hesting that the weakness is always in the conception, never in the power. But one cannot hear without ears.

Feeling confident that events would turn to my advantage, I began to consider the intricate relationship between Tar-Kesa and the yris-tera. I raised my head and spied, above Guanden's bobbing bristled head, the Nemarsi appreida, its banners breeze-rippled on the horizon. And from that direction was a dust cloud fast approaching.

I leaned over and touched Chayin on the arm. He jumped. I pointed, and he nodded, grinning. Hael had also seen.

When their individual forms were discernible to us, Chayin reined up and waited.

Hael queried him as to this.

"I would not meet Besha too close to the web-weavers' appreis," he said solemnly, rubbing the back of his neck with a dust-powdered hand. It was the first time I really looked at him in daylight. His skin was the color of strong-brewed rana, his form was lithe though not truly spare. There was no hint of the veil about him. He leaned to me. It was the first time I had seen him grin but in battle. I gathered this meeting had some of that same flavor to him.

"In the middle. Upon the red threx in the front. See her? The owner of your mount seems anxious to find him. I expect she will be effluent with gratitude to have him back." He straightened up and spat over

Saer's shoulder. His hands were crossed upon his saddle-grip.

Besha, from a distance, was an imposing feather-draped figure. As the threx bore her closer, it seemed to stagger under her bulk. Fully as wide of shoulder and thigh as any man, she sat the beast with a stiff, imperious manner that caused her beaded feather trappings to flop rattling about. As the band of ten tiasks bore closer and dropped to a walk, consternation could be seen among them. Besha, blade in hand, rode straight up to Chayin, only stopping her red threx when the beast was nose-to-nose with Saer. This close, Besha's imposing figure seemed more due to a general rotundness of figure upon ponderous bones than the feathered helmet and cape she wore. The purples and greens were startling in the tan-to-brown landscape. Behind her, I could make out the dark shapes that must be the web-weavers' appreis. Such are always upon the outskirts of a community. Untutored minds are a discomfort to webbers and weavers alike.

"*Gaes d'ar, tiask.*" Chayin demeaned Besha with the formal greeting. "You stand before me" demands obeisance in reply. Though the tiask speaks first to the jiask, the cahndor speaks first to all.

Only the lower part of Besha's dark face was visible beneath the feathered helmet. Her weathered lips twitched. The sword she still held pointed at me wavered.

"*Irat s'es d'or harekte,*" Besha replied. "I but kneel before magnificence." The words came hard and clipped between her teeth. A friysou cried overhead, winging south to the feast we had provided. Behind Besha, her tiasks were a line of statues.

"What do the tiasks seek so ardently in the desert, and in such formal garb this early in the day?" Chayin queried in his deep, rumbling voice. Besha's sword drooped even lower as she realized his intent. She held it barely above the heaving red threx's ears.

"You know what we sought, Cahndor," the tiask hissed.

"And how is it that this sorry state of affairs has come about?" Chayin's voice cracked sharp like a striking huija. "Can I not leave the appreida for a set's time without fear for the safety of what I would leave behind me? Must I fight my way home through my enemies, and they turning my own war beasts upon me?"

Besha said nothing. Chayin was not satisfied.

"And where are your brothers?" he continued. "Surely you could have roused a jiask or two, judging from your lengthy preparations. We met the Menetphers at sun's rising upon Qadar ridge, and you only now leave the appreida's outskirts. May I assume that you raised the alarm before you left, in case more Menetphers are about?"

Besha shook her head, mute.

"Did you count upon us, returning, to intercept the thieves? Surely you did not think to catch them, upon inferior mounts, when they had such a lead?"

What could be seen of Besha's face was as purple as her feathers.

"Speak, tiask," Chayin urged. "Your cahndor awaits an explanation. What circumstances are there that could possibly excuse such negligence?"

Besha shifted her considerable weight about in the saddle. When she finally spoke, her voice quivered with temper ill-restrained.

"We awoke," she said, "to find them gone, shortly before sun's rising. So stealthily was it done that the sentries raised no alarm. Restless through the night, it was I myself who discovered the theft and roused these others to give chase."

"Who were the sentries?" Cold as the peaks of Mount Opir was Chayin's voice, and as forbidding.

There was a movement among the feather-trapped tiasks, and five urged their mounts forward.

"You," snapped Chayin at the foremost of the five. "Is that how you dressed to stand your watch?"

"No, Cahndor." The tiask's head was so sunk upon her chest that her voice was only a distressed whisper.

He waved at the remaining four who had stood the posting.

"And the rest of you! Were you perhaps so bedecked at your posts?"

The four hesitantly admitted that they had not been so accoutered.

"How long did it take you, tiask, making ready to give chase after our enemies?" he demanded of the tiask he had first questioned.

The answer was unintelligible.

"Speak louder, that your brothers and sisters may hear you," the cahndor commanded.

"Perhaps an enth," the tiask repeated, toneless.

"You shall, all five, go about your duties naked as the crells than whom you are little better. A set's time will you bear this chastisement." He waved them back to the others with evident disgust.

Hael, upon my left, rubbed his jaw with his hand, that his mirth might not peal unrestrained over the silent congregation.

Chayin turned his attention back to Besha.

I still have not heard why there are no jiasks among you. Could it be that there is such a rivalry between tiask and jiask that it obtrudes even upon the performance of tasks of this magnitude?" he said, dorkat toying with yit.

"I sought my own in the confusion of the moment," Besha said clearly. Her tone admitted no error. I could feel her gaze upon me. Guanden stamped and snapped the air as the shifting breeze brought him the scent of his mistress.

"Can you assure me the speedy return of these beasts to their stalls, tiask? I would minimize this ignominy before the people of Nemar."

"But give to me that which is mine, and I will gladly return home, my cahndor. That you set a crell upon Guanden is all that prohibits my departure." Besha raised up her blade, once again pointing it at my chest. Nude and chaldless and filthy, my station was obvious to the tiask. Upon impulse I slid the recurved short blade from my saddle sheath and hefted it in my hand. Hael shot me a warning look. Besha's head bobbled.

"This is no simple crell." The dharener spoke for the first time. "She is a skilled northern forereader whom I hold for questioning and eventual disposition back into the lands whence she came. She is my charge, and none are to touch her but by my order." What scheme had Hael in his head, that he would speak for me?

"Spawn of apths!" spit Besha, her temper beyond her control. I watched her calm herself. "Perhaps the northern forereader, who has misplaced her chald, who is armed as a tiask and naked as a crell, might be petitioned to get herself from the back of my threx!"

Chayin inclined his head and indicated, stern-faced, that I might ride the steel-blue female he led.

Throwing my leg over Guanden's back, I slid to the ground, sword still in hand. I handed Guanden's reins calmly to Besha, conscious of the stillness and the tiasks' eyes upon me. It was harder to turn my unprotected back to her and walk unconcerned those few steps to the steel's side. Chayin extended the reins to me, and I grasped them and mounted. It was a relief to be free of Guanden's constant testing. The steel stood calmly under me, eyes half-closed.

"Attend me at mid-meal, tiask," said Chayin with a motion of dismissal.

Besha regarded us for a moment. Then she wheeled the red threx, and leading Guanden beside her, raced away toward the appreida upon the horizon.

All was confusion as the tiasks and jiasks apportioned the recovered threx between them. Chayin dismissed the men also, and there were left only the dharener, the cahndor, and I upon the sparse-grassed rolling plain.

Chayin raised his hands behind his head and kneaded the muscles where his neck met his shoulders. He sighed deeply. The uritheria upon his bicep writhed lifelike in umbers and ochers. The Shaper's cloak, thrown back from his arms, rustled softly in the stiffening breeze.

Tears of laughter squeezed from Hael's eyes, and great roars of mirth shook his large frame. The dharener leaned forward upon his saddlegrip for support, convulsed with amusement. Chayin only stared after the fast-receding line of threx. There was no humor in him at this turn of events. His eyes were narrowed, and he still rubbed his right shoulder.

"If they tear like that through the web-weavers' appreis, I will be graced by the company of the First Weaver," he remarked dryly.

"I would have given much to see her face," Hael chortled.

"We will see it at mid-meal. For me, that will be more than soon enough. What prompted you," he asked the dharener, "to so twist the truth as it pertains to this crell whom I have given you?" And he started Saer at a swinging walk toward the appreida.

Hael sighed, wiped the tears from his eyes, and kicked Quiris into motion. My mount followed of her own accord, quiet, head down, easy-gaited.

"I but opened an alternative path for us concerning her, should we choose to travel it. She did," reminded Hael, "strike down the Menetpher who might have laid me lifeless upon the field of battle. I could not see her helpless before Besha's anger. Perhaps my expressed interest will stay the tiask's hand, although yours would surely have had that effect." His tone was wry. "Have you ever," he continued, "seen another upon Guanden's back?"

"No," Chayin allowed, "I have never seen it, before this day. I had hoped that I might continue to see it, but she was remarkably restrained."

"That probability," Hael confided, "occurred to me also. However, that which is meant to be will come in the fullness of time. Those things destined to meet cannot be held apart indefinitely."

"Like a certain sword and specific flesh." And Chayin finally smiled, his white teeth bared just an instant.

It was a slow and easy pace we kept across the stony-soiled barrens of Nemar. As we neared the appreis of the web-weavers, there appeared before us an old, old man, in the middle of the cobbled way between the weavers' tents. He was shaking his fist and jumping up and down in agitation. Upon his shoulder danced his webber, itself so old that some of its sensory hairs were white.

Chayin winced when he first spotted them, but made no move to avoid this new confrontation. He headed us straight for the slight, wizened figure, and halted so close that I could see the filmy membranes that seemed to be permanently across the old man's eyes. The grizzled webber on his shoulder stared at me with emerald eyes and clicked its sable mandibles together. It was as wide across as my body at the waist, and two of its eight legs were wrapped about the weaver's throat.

"I cannot allow it!" the old man screeched, a raspy whisper of a scream. "I cannot allow it! Chayin! Is that you?" He came close and peered up into Chayin's face. "Can you not control your people? Would you like to come in and see? See what they have done with their curses and their clatter and their awful thumping of the ground? Would you?"

Chayin reached down and put his hand upon the old man's arm. "Calm yourself, Tenager. You will put a snarl into the weave yourself. T'nis is sorely disturbed." And it was true. Colorless fluid dripped from the webber's underside, and its leg hairs were stiffly extended.

"My boy, you must do something about controlling your army! There is a place for peace and quiet upon this land, and it is here! Let them race elsewhere. Who will stand the reparations? Who, I ask you? Twice in one day is too much to bear!" And the webber upon his shoulder clicked to uphold him.

The old man's noise had drawn several other web-weavers to the doors of their appreis. They stood there, blinking in the daylight, with that elsewhere look upon them so common to their trade. Each had been wrenched from that inner world of beauty that is the domain of webber and weaver. Silent, they only watched us. It is said that among themselves they might not speak a single word for years unending.

Chayin was still soothing, leaning down to whisper in the old man's ear. What he suggested calmed the old weaver visibly, and he scuttled off to the shade of the nearest doorway, pushing a young weaver girl within.

The cahndor straightened up. We rode forward. When I looked back, I could still see one of them staring after us.

Once past the web-weavers' appreis, of which there must have been a hundred, the collection of ambiguous shapes upon the horizon separated themselves and became perhaps a thousand appreis of varying sizes. I was shocked to see so many. Here and there, towering stone edifices pointed spires to the sky, and between the appreis many cobbled ways extended in geometric perfection. The threx's metalshod feet rang against the stones. To my far right stood an imposing structure hewn from the solid ornithalum face of a cerulean cliff that loomed sheer and forbidding a nera high into the skies of Nemar. The appreida covered the whole valley floor between those cliffs in the east and the craggy feet of Mount Opir and the Yaicas in the west. Upon those feet I could see great patches of cultivated fields, bright green, yellow, and a brownish purple, and the irrigation ditches of stone that fed them. In the center of the valley was a large and obviously manmade reservoir. I had never seen it upon any map.

I recalled that once there had been no valley here to connect to the Skirr in the north. This depression had been blasted from the mountains in that terrible explosion that boiled away the Parset sea and made desert out of much of the surrounding land. A long time gone since then, more than twenty-five thousand years, but the cliffs recollect the event, as does the still, dry sea to the south.

"The summer quarters of the Nemarsi, Miheja." Chayin used the crell name he had given me upon the desert. He veered Saer sharply to the right, taking an easterly thoroughfare, the surface of which was riotous with stylized stone mosaics.

"You ride upon the Way of Wings," Chayin said, his pride unconcealed. "Only the Way of Tar-Kesa eclipses its beauty!" And as I looked around me at the great winged beasts upon the avenue, I realized that the apprei panels, grown larger and more ostentatious, repeated this theme of flying beasts. Not only of this world were those creatures who danced beneath the threx's hooves. Uritheria was there also; and Cathe, winged slitsa; and the ei-jos, the five-named human spirit, was limned in fire tones against the blues and creams of the way. I raised my head to speak of its beauty to Chayin, and tapestried pyramids leading in greater and greater magnificence to the thrice-towered keep hewn into the ornithalum cliff left me wordless.

"Is it as beautiful as the keeps of Astria?" Chayin asked.

I had to admit that it was.

"How can you bear to leave it to roam the desert, Cahndor?"

"We summer here, take the autumn in the east, the winter in the south, and the spring upon our lands in the west. To own a thing, one must make use of it. We are never all in one place, but most of us make the yearly pilgrimage. If I knew not the welfare of the south with my own eyes, how could I presume to see to it?"

Looking at the imposing appreis of priceless web-weave, I tried to imagine tiered foundations empty, stra stanchions, some as big around as my waist, collapsed, and the valley deserted but for a handful of stone buildings, watercourses, and the half-wheel of pictorial ways spreading from the eastern cliffs across the valley floor.

"Do all the Parsets do likewise?"

"Menetph, Itophe, Coseve, and even decadent Dordassa still retain that much grace of spirit," he informed me.

There were the noises of gregarious life, and children upon the ways. Masked and concealingly dressed women stared at us. Men in gossamer jewel-toned cloaks leaned together against stanchions and whispered as we passed. Some stopped what they were doing entirely to watch. For the first time since I had sorted for my future, I felt again captive.

I was afraid—afraid that I had not truly seen, and thus that the events upon which I waited would not come to be. It is a forereader's fear. I deep-read Chayin. Perhaps it was his doubt I felt, for his affliction made him ever doubtful. Perhaps it was his fear, and not my own. Forereader's illness brings one terrors of one's own creation, masquerading as owkahen, the time-coming-to-be, through which the forereader ever sorts the safer, more fertile path.

And as I reached into the cahndor's mind, he was himself busy sensing. His mind had sought the dharener's while Hael attempted to penetrate the helsar.

We stood in one another's subjective present, invader and invaded all at once. I broke the link.

Hael reached over and gently slid the blade from my saddle scabbard. His face was guarded.

"You will not need this, among the crells," he said. The wind from the abyss carried his words to me. I shivered under the bright hot sun.

The threx crossed a wide bridge of dressed ornithalum as we made our way into the cerulean court before the cliff.

III. Crell

Before the first of a hundred broad steps up which one might mount to the palace of Nemar North, Chayin halted the threx. Atop a grisly scene of a wounded dorkat rended by friysou, armed men with short storm-blue capes crowded around to attend their cahndor. Among them was a tiny woman, covered all over but for her bejeweled bulging child-belly. Just left of the steps was a sheer high wall that had set in it two barred rectangular openings, each twice a man's height and wide enough for three threxmen riding abreast.

Hael came to the steel's side and helped me dismount. I was chaldless among them, and the indignity of my state stiffened my movements and flushed my flesh.

Hael gave orders. Two jiasks hustled me to the farther of the barred doors, and it was slid aside from within. I looked back and saw Saer's rump just disappearing into the other passage. The dharener was speaking earnestly to the tiny pregnant woman, upon whom his arm rested. Chayin stared after me. I would have stopped. The men pushed me roughly ahead, around a bend to the left.

Specific instructions had Hael given them concerning me. My meal schedule was to be "four," my work status "seven," and my designation "ten." I was to be quartered in section one. My eyes adjusted to the torch-lit dim, and I saw numerous turnings, some with barred gates. Where there were gates there was always one or more short-caped jiask. It was cool in the passage. The stone under my feet was smooth and all of a piece. The jiasks' footfalls and the clink of the metal they wore echoed around us.

When I lost count of turnings, they stopped before a barred gate identical to the others I had seen. The attendant roused himself from his cross-legged doze upon the cool stone and accepted me from them, sliding the barred door aside to admit us.

He picked up my wrists and examined them critically, then bade the two with me await him. Grumbling, he retired to a small chamber cut in the tunnel wall and returned with a selection of metal wristlets joined by some few links of heavy chain.

"She is a 'ten' you say? Pity," he said to the jiasks. "Hold out your hands. Go on! You have come this far. Now is no time to be difficult!"

And I did, and he fitted my bonds to his satisfaction. His short, stubby fingers were gentle and efficient, his dark eyes not unkind as he met my gaze. He then led me, with the others following as Hael had instructed them, into what I would come to think of as the crellpits. The large chamber was empty, the crells being at their daily labor. It was low-ceilinged and almost featureless. At certain places upon the floor were grates that opened onto some lower level. At other places, large rings that accommodated a number of chains were set into the stone.

I wondered what it meant, to be a "ten," as the crellkeep chose a spot seemingly like any other upon one chain and fastened me to it by means of heavy metal anklets that were spaced along its length.

"I put you next to Aje. You will sleep through the nights," he informed me, as if I should be grateful for some thoughtful service. Seeing me safely bound, the two jiasks turned and left the chamber.

"What is your name?" the crellkeep asked.

I almost told him, and caught myself. It took me a moment to remember the crell name Chayin had given me.

"Miheja," I said finally.

"Mi-he-ya," the crellkeep corrected me gently. "The East-most Star's Daughter. Suits you. So you have the dharener entranced, do you? A ten, indeed. Crell life is no burden to one so highly numbered." He stood up, rubbing his back, "I go to get Aje. You will like him. They all do," he said, and patted my naked shoulder. Moments later I was alone in the deserted, ever dusk of the crellpits. A single torch burned in the chamber's entry, throwing life into the featureless rock walls.

I crawled the length of my tether, and by lying stretched out could just get my fingers upon the central ring. I tested its strength, as had countless crells before me. There was no weakness in it. I had expected none. I then examined each link of my chains with my fingers, to see if perhaps somewhere there was one unsoldered among them. There was no error among the 387 links that bound me firmly to the central ring. Its twin was sunk where the cold stone floor met the wall behind me. Perhaps there was a weakness in that area, but I had not enough tether to explore it. I lay down upon my left side and curled my knees against my chest. I could not think. I merely lay there.

After a time I heard shuffling feet, and I was glad there was life in the world. The crellkeep entered, and I sat up, to see beside him a naked blond man who wore upon his wrists crell chains. He was taller than the crellkeep, and his body had the angular bulk and stoop of long, arduous labor.

Grunting as he bent down, the crellkeep snapped

the metal anklet nearest mine around the blond man's left ankle.

"This is Aje. Meheja. Aje is a neighbor on your chain. You will breed. Then I will feed you." He turned to walk away.

"No," I said.

The crellkeep turned in mid-stride. The man beside me raised an eyebrow.

"You must be bred," explained the crellkeep, standing over me. "We cannot have you later claiming pregnancy by the dharener."

"Hael never touched me."

"Oh. Someone must have. You are crell. You must be bred after any contact with your masters." He was getting an edge upon his patient tone. "You will breed, and then I will feed you." And he went to stand in the corridor, that we might have privacy. As if that made any difference.

The man called Aje put his hand on my arm. His pale eyes were friendly; his pale hair fell over them, shadowing.

"Come, now, let us get this behind us," he said in a low voice. "Things get no better for a crell. It need not be unpleasant. I have some little skill." But even in that dim light I could see that his body had no great interest in mine.

I drew my legs up around me, clasping my arms over my knees, shaking off his touch. I said nothing.

"I am Lalen gaesh Satemit, musician of Stra," he offered. I did not answer. The crellkeep coughed in the passageway. Aje sighed and drew his own knees to his chest, regarding me over crossed arms. His chains rattled. I thought I would start screaming and never stop.

"That is all we have to give each other," he said finally, in an intimate voice. "Our real selves, which the Nemarsi deny us. Who are you, Miheja the crell?"

If I had told him, he would have understood. His eyes searched my face, and for a moment I thought he knew me. The moment passed. He sighed and reached out toward me again.

"Before he comes in here and stands over us, lie down!" he said urgently. He pushed me backward, and I let myself fall, and lay there until I had been officially bred. I heard the crellkeep grunt to himself with satisfaction and lumber away.

When he returned with two hot bowls of binnirin gruel, Aje still held me. He stroked my hair and pressed my head against his chest, and little by little the tension drained out of me. It was a great kindness.

The crellkeep put the bowls upon the floor and departed. It was another little while before the light-haired crell bestirred himself, kissing me upon the crown of my head and raising me up with him.

He made the polite compliments that might be between two free people at such a time. It was strange to hear them. I put my hands around my bowl. I wondered if the place were truly cold, or if it was an inner chill I felt. I pressed closer against him, for warmth.

"The crellkeep will be bringing the others in soon. How is it that you are the dharener's ten and have not lain with him?"

"I do not know what a ten is. I was with Chayin, before he gave me to Hael. It is very complicated."

"Good. We will have lots of time. Besha will not want me tonight. She has problems with the cahndor. I am also a ten. Tens spend most nights with their owners. I do little stonework anymore."

I wondered that he knew so quickly of Besha's encounter with Chayin.

"I will tell you about my capture only if you will tell me those things which I desire to know." I could hardly have cared less at the time.

"Anything, if I know it."

"First, about the tens, and second about what occurred in Arlet two years, three passes back. More specifically, what transpired there between a Day-Keeper and a Slayer. I have been told this is common knowledge, but it is knowledge I do not have." And at that moment there was a stabbing brightness behind my eyes. For a second I could not see, only afterglow. It was Hael, with the helsar.

"Are you unwell?" His voice was solicitous.

I told him I would survive. I hoped I would.

"I know only hearsay, but Khemi, who is upon my left on the chain, was, I think, in Arlet at that time. I was crell even that long ago." His soft voice was wistful.

"And about the tens?"

"The tens eat better. Their work, whatever it is in nature, is reduced in hours. It is a number of favor. The jiasks and the tiasks and the crellkeeps will treat a ten better. Prize your status. You can go no higher. You have a work number. What is it?"

"Seven," I answered.

"With the threx," he informed me. "It could be much worse." He rubbed his hands together. Those hands when upon me had little of a musician's touch to them. They were scarred and twisted and rough. The room again exploded. I saw a thousand lights.

"Do you think the dharener will call you this night?" he asked. I almost laughed. I pulled away from Aje, running my hands through my tangled hair. My upper lip was beaded with sweat, though I had been so recently cold. I could see an overlay of another room, faint but real as I looked around me. Hael had unwrapped the helsar and sat before it.

"I said, do you think the dharener will call you?" repeated Aje.

"No," I said. "I do not think he will."

"Tell me about what occurred on the desert," Aje suggested.

I did so, and while I was in the telling, the crellkeep brought groups of crells in and fastened each in place, until there were fifty-three of us in all. Then food brought by two crells on a rolling board was passed around. Our old bowls were collected, and Aje and I were fed again, on the heels of a meal.

I moved to send my bowl back.

"Keep it," Aje hissed. "There are some who do not get enough."

I kept the bowl, continuing my story. I did not tell him how I came to the desert.

On my one side was Aje, upon my other only empty chain. Beyond him sat dark-eyed, dark-haired Khemi, and behind and beside us the rest of the fifty-three. They talked and joked among themselves. They shared their food, and some even laughed aloud. I could not see that they had anything to laugh about. The cool stone under me was becoming clammy; the press of flesh warmed the air. Aje took my untouched bowl from me and sent it down the line.

With the helsar, Hael got nowhere. I sensed his agitation, and a cessation and darkness as he covered the thing once again.

I breathed an inward sigh of relief.

"That is all, save we came straight here and the dharener assigned two men to deliver me." I was finished with my account. I had paid little attention to the telling.

"Did you see a woman upon the court?" Khemi asked.

I said that I did, and described her.

"And was the Nemarchan affectionate to the cahndor, father of her child?" There was petulance in her tone.

"More likely to the dharener," Aje put in.

"I only saw her speak at all to Hael," I clarified. There was much interest in the affairs of their owners here among the crells.

"Aje, will you fulfill your part of the bargain now?" I asked him, lest the moment be lost. He turned to Khemi, who lounged upon her side, her braceleted leg crooked.

"Tell Miheja what you know of Arlet, when Sereth became past-Seven and Vedrev gave himself up to the chaldra of the soil," he bade her.

And Khemi looked at me curiously, but started the tale.

"I know not all of this story, but I shall tell you what I saw and what was told to me," said Khemi in a musical voice. "On Macara first fifth of that year, when I had been wellwoman precisely one year in Arlet, it came to pass that I put down my duties to go into the hide bast beneath the Well, and study there the forereaders' way. If I seem bitter in this telling, it is that I too lost something in the common hall upon the first sixth of Jicar, when the floor ran slick with Arletian blood." Khemi sighed.

"Hence I was below ground the whole time that Estri, Well-Keepress of Astria, was in Arlet. I never saw her, but rumors of her doings reached us even so far beneath the Well. It was said to me by my sponsor, who was close to Vedrev bast Iradea, that some great crux wind blew around her affairs, great enough to involve the learned northern dharener himself.

"At that time there was in Arlet a new Liaison, Khaf-Re Dellin by name. In fact, he and the Astrian Keepress arrived together, and it was said that Dellin had more interest in his traveling companion than in Celendra, who was Keepress in Arlet then. Dellin was a strange Liaison, with stranger ways than the old. It was said he was close to Sereth, Seven of Arlet, and closer with Ganrom, who might sponsor him for the Slayer's chain.

"This is only rumor," she continued, "but it is said that the Keepress of Astria bested Celendra at gol-knife upon their first meeting. It is also rumored that some little interest sprang up between Estri and Sereth crill Tyris, former couch-mate of Celendra and father of her only son, Tyith. And it has been postulated that this, coupled with the indignity Celendra suffered at Estri's hand in the circle, and Dellin's relative indifference, greatly angered Celendra bast Aknet." Most of the crells had grown quiet, listening.

"Whatever the truth of it, it came about that Sereth crill Tyris was tithed by the Liaisons and commanded by Vedrev to get this Astrian Keepress to the Falls of Santha, that she might look upon an artifact there and discharge some chaldra.

"Now, Sereth, Seven of Arlet, was a man who heard his own voice only, and one not easily ordered about. He and Vedrev had in the past found numerous occasions for altercation between them. And the Liaison Dellin, by trying so desperately to please everyone at once, soon found himself in the middle between them, and between Estri and Celendra also." Khemi shook her head, remembering.

"In mid-Macara there was Feast of Conception for Genisha and Jerin of the Slayers. A man of Baniev, wearing the clothes of a Morrltan, died a mysterious death during the night. Its cause was never determined. The tension was thus heightened all around, for we waited to see if such awful death would come again upon the land.

"Perhaps because of that, the Seven decided to take his one son, Tyith, apprenticed for the Slayer's chain, with him upon the trail to Santha.

"When Celendra heard this, she locked herself in her keep and commenced a fasting and a keening that lasted a full set's time. When she once again opened her door, she went straight to Vedrev and demanded an inquiry into what had occurred upon the trail. Vedrev answered her that it was doubtful they even reached the falls by that day. Celendra then informed Vedrev that her son was dead, that she had seen Sereth, in a vision, bind the boy up in a brist pelt and throw him into a great crevice. And that he had failed to protect Estri of Astria, who was lost now forever to the spirits beyond, and that Sereth had killed four chalded men and left them, their chalds upon them, for the hulions and the harths. I know this, because it was to my lecture hall she came, and demanded Vedrev at once attend her will.

"This the Day-Keeper did, leaving us thirty would-be forereaders in the learning hall, waiting. Celendra's unquiet voice rang through the hide corridors, and in our ears, as she charged Sereth with all the un-Sevenly acts I have mentioned, and more besides.

"Vedrev tried to calm her, but the seeds of doubt were planted in his mind, and he went himself upon the trail to the Falls of Santha, taking with him Ganrom, Celendra, and at Celendra's bidding, the Liaison, for it had passed between Dellin and Celendra that they would take the one-year couch-bond traditional between Keepress and Liaison.

"One who should have known once said to me that but for this pledge to Celendra, Dellin would have stood for Sereth in his need, and had that been true, things might have taken a different turn. But he did not.

"Let me point out that at the time Celendra first approached Vedrev, it was with forereader's knowledge. It was her forereading Vedrev trusted, and as it proved true in some things, it seemed true in all. It was her forereading that destroyed Sereth." Her voice was wistful, and I knew she saw him before her eyes, even as I did.

"Just upon the plateau of Santha," Khemi continued, "Vedrev's party found some badly savaged bodies.

"Embedded in the chest of one of them was a knife with the Seven's device engraved upon the hilt. There was the Slayer convicted before trial, for he had not collected the chalds of his dead.

"The body of Tyith was not among them. Celendra demanded that they press on, and the dharener's party continued, until they found their way was blocked by a great crevice in the earth. Deeming it impossible to pass over the chasm's width or around its length, they turned themselves around and headed back to Arlet. The fact that the crevice was as Celendra had described it was enough for Vedrev.

"By this time I had finished my seminars and was released to my wellwork for a pass, to put what I had learned in the hide into practice upon the customers.

"It was market day in the Inner Well, first first of

Jicar. Vedrev and his party were still in the Sabembes. Sereth crill Tyris came riding through the gates with a coin girl at his side, and she upon one of his finest threx. Tyith was not with him, nor was the Keepress of Astria.

"I was standing with a chalder near the outer gate. I had long coveted the Seven's attentions, and always greeted him when the opportunity arose. He had in the past often stopped to speak with me. This day he did not stop, and his face was awful to look upon. He rode straight to the hostel and disappeared within, taking the coin girl with him. He did not even see to his threx himself, but handed them without ceremony to the slayer at watch. What more eloquent statement of something sore amiss than Sereth crill Tyris not caring for his prized racing stock?

"There was a great buzzing in the Inner Well that day. Sereth had brought a coin girl into Arlet. None dared to question him, but behind his back the people wondered aloud at his brashness."

"And where was Tyith? And the Well-Keepress of Astria?"

"It is said that Sereth called then upon Vedrev, and finding him gone from Arlet, and Dellin and Celendra and Ganrom also, was apprised of what had occurred by some Slayers whose loyalty he still retained." Khemi coughed, shifting in place.

"By Vedrev's order, the Seven was confined within the halls of Arlet until the Day-Keeper's return. There were few among the slayers who would have moved to restrain him, should he have chosen to flee to the south or west. But Sereth was a proud and arrogant man, and he told his fantastic story before his men, and a great many of them believed him. He did not flee, but settled himself and his coin girl into the Slayer's hostel to await Vedrev's return.

"On Jicar first second did Vedrev, Dellin, Celendra, and Ganrom return out of the Sabembes, to find Sereth, Seven of Arlet, there awaiting them.

"An open hearing was set for the first sixth, four

days hence, within the common room of Well Arlet, that all concerned might attend. The hall was so crowded with the Slayers of Arlet that I could only find standing room in the back.

"I saw Ganrom and two other Slayers of rank lead the Seven in. They passed so close to me, I saw the tears in Ganrom's eyes. Nor was he the only one among the Slayers so moved. Sereth walked between the two, Ganrom just ahead, making way through the crowd to the makeshift dais. He wore his formal leathers and the Seven's sword, and his chald lay shining around his waist, that it might be easier for Vedrev to strip him of them.

"Open hearing or not, the outcome of it was long decided, and all knew it.

"The Slayers of Arlet were by this time polarized into two groups: those who believed their Seven and those who were for some reason or another glad to see one so mighty brought low. There were weapons aplenty in the common room of Well Arlet that day.

"The Seven were brought to stand before Vedrev, upon whose right was Celendra, and upon her right, the Liaison Second. It became very quiet. I squeezed through the crowd until I was parallel to them, between a number of restless Slayers. Vedrev read the charges. He presented the chalds he had found in the Sabembes. He asked if Sereth denied that he had killed those men and left them chalded." Water was passed, and Khemi stopped and drank, her dark hair falling over her shoulder.

"Sereth admitted to that. Vedrev then presented Celendra's allegations and asked the Slayer to produce, if he could, Tyith and Estri, or explain their absence.

"Sereth crill Tyris told his story in that chill voice of one who has done so many times and has no hope of being believed. He spoke of the crack that opened before them in the earth, of the malignant spirit that assailed them, of Tyith's death and Estri's disappearance beneath the Falls of Santha.

"At his mention of Tyith, Celendra threw herself upon him, scratching and shrieking, and Dellin needed the help of two Slayers to get her from the common room. He did not return.

"Vedrev, resplendent in his Stothric priest's robes, stood on the dais. He said that he had seen the crevice and no man could have crossed it, and therefore all after that point was mere fabrication. He asked again of Tyith and the Well-Keepress. Sereth stood with his head bowed. Vedrev repeated his charge of negligence, unseemly murder and misuse of power and sentenced the Seven to be stripped of all rank and cast chaldless from the gates of Arlet, never to return. Then Vedrev pulled out his curved Stoth blade to cut away the Seven's sword and chald. When Sereth saw this, he raised his head, and his own sword flashed in his hand, and he cut the belt from Vedrev's waist with an easy flick.

"I did not hear the words of his challenge to Vedrev. The common hall erupted in a roar around me. Some Slayers drew their blades to disarm the Seven, and others to restrain them, that Sereth and Vedrev might have what each other had long desired of the other. In moments, death whirred over my head and all around me. There was swordplay everywhere in the great hall as Slayer turned against Slayer. Those who supported the Seven hacked their way toward him, drawing me with them. A Slayer held me against him by the neck as he fought, a human shield. And a good one. None struck at me. I could see anguish upon faces of men suddenly enemies, of men who had slain friends with whom they had this day ridden. I saw two, recognizing each other, put up their swords. One was struck down from behind. The other knelt in the frenzy. The stone slabs were slippery with blood; men skidded and fell. I saw one fall onto a blade and die there. I saw Vedrev dead, and Sereth leaping bodies toward the door. The Slayer still dragged me before him. Out into the Inner Well we went, and from somewhere threx were produced, and, like a number of other wellwomen, I was captive of the renegade Slayers until they had ridden the night long into the south. There I was dumped with no ceremony by the side of the trail. I did not see Sereth at any time once out of Arlet, but I have heard he lives. I would not tell any more, for I do not like to remember what followed, and I have a long day ahead tomorrow." And Khemi smiled a shy smile and turned upon her side with her back to us, not knowing what effect her words had upon me.

I was glad for the darkness. I lay down upon my back and stared blindly at the ceiling.

Aje's hand touched my hair. His chain rattled as he shifted his body closer to me. His arm went around my shoulders.

Khemi's story, though distorted in gossip and retelling, doubtless had truth to it. It was strange to hear about myself in the third person, and about these affairs from such a different perspective. I rolled against Aje in the darkness.

How could Dellin have behaved in so unprincipled a manner? I thought bitterly of the M'ksakkan, for putting Celendra's goodwill and the trade balance in Arlet before his own honor. Perhaps he had none. I could understand Vedrev, for he and Sereth had long been at odds. And Celendra was either a disastrously incompetent forereader or a vicious liar, though I had never seen her as either.

And Sereth—who could help him now? He had slain a Day-Keeper, a dharener even worse. There would be no straightening out of this tangle by a simple explanation. Estrazi had told me both of us were needed to set the balance aright. But to what authority could we take a plea? And upon what grounds?

How different things would have been if my father had allowed me to send my word to stand for the Seven. What purpose could be served by Sereth's ignominy? I worried these thoughts into nightmares that had no sense and no ending.

I was awakened by the crellkeep with the others,

and went to my first day of crell life upon an empty
stomach. Khemi, also on the seven schedule, worked
beside me straining the sand in the threx stables of
wetness and muck. Once a set, the sand must be taken
out of each stall, and clean sand put in its place; then
the soiled sand must be strained and wheeled in carts
out the back door of the stable, where other crells
wait to tend to its disposal as fertilizer upon certain
crops. This was that day. The work was strenuous,
and we were soon filthy smelly and coated with the
foul sand, which clung to our sweating bodies. Once,
when water was brought, I looked up, to see Chayin
watching me from the harness area, thirty stalls down
the row. He was waiting while Saer was made ready.
I turned and leaned against the stone partition, the
water dipper in my hands. I drank slowly, staring
back, but he did not look away.

Khemi got up off her knees and came to stand
beside me.

"Lower your eyes," she warned me in a soft voice,
taking the dipper from my hands and filling it again.
The crell with the water cart fidgeted. "You will bring
down his wrath upon us both."

"I think not," I said to her, but dropped again to
my hands and knees and took up my two-handed
scoop. When Chayin rode out, he chose the long way,
which by happenstance brought him past the very
stall where I was working. He stopped Saer directly
behind me. I could see the threx's legs by looking between my own. I continued to work on my knees,
bending over that I might scoop the sand up from the
lower floor of the stall's doorway. Khemi, inside the
stall and facing me, blushed and smiled at the cahndor, but I did not look up. After a time, he rode away.

Khemi and I did our ten stalls each; we were
given some grain gruel for lunch, and a quarter each
of a green tuber where we worked. Then the threx
were brought in, all filthy from rolling outside, and
we cleaned and polished their hides and picked their
tripart hooves and set about their feeding. It seemed

as if no two of them got the same meal, and each special diet had to be mixed by us from great bags of grains with the device of Yardum-Or upon them.

Among the threx we fed were Besha's Guanden and the red threx whose name I never learned. It is possible that I somehow mismixed his feeding. I think more likely it was some previous negligence.

We were checking stall locks before being taken to our own stalls for the night, when I noticed the red was down upon the sand. Low groaning noises came from deep within him; his nostrils were flared wide and running with mucus. There were bloody chunks upon his bloated belly where he had bitten himself. I was in the stall in a moment, calling Khemi. In vain did we struggle to get the beast up on his feet. We pulled him by the head, but though we could drag him up, we could not keep him standing. He sank back three times, and with a gasping groan upon our fourth attempt he laid his head back on the clean sand and died.

Khemi looked at me in horror. I was crying. I always cry over animals.

"Besha will be furious!" she whispered, her eyes wide.

"Sheltering wing of uritheria!" cursed the jiask summoned by Khemi's wails. He in turn got the crellkeep. Khemi and I were not taken back to our chain for the night, but kept there in the threx's stall to await his owner, Besha, my owner, Hael, and Khemi's owner, the cahndor.

The crellkeep and the threxmaster were engaged in spirited debate with three jiasks as to the cause of the threx's death. They fell suddenly silent.

The dharener stood in the stall doorway, surveying us. I was crouched by the dead beast's head, Khemi stretched out on the sand on her back. She sat up.

Hael put his hand to his forehead and closed his eyes. When he opened them, he said, "Threx upon the square of death," and sat himself down in the doorway, his bearded chin resting upon his fists, his elbows upon his knees. He stared at us.

"I am exploring the material sign," he said to me casually.

"I know it. You have already caused me some discomfort," I answered.

"Nothing beyond your capacity to endure, I trust?" he asked solicitously.

Khemi's head swung between us as she listened without understanding.

"Nothing I cannot survive. Keep in mind that what the helsar sees is shown to me also," I suggested to him.

"When are you going to do me the great service yris-tera promised?" Hael inquired. Just then Besha's bulk loomed dark and menacing behind him. She stepped over Hael and in three strides was at her beast's head.

"I have seen your face too often," she said to me, pushing me away from the corpse. I rolled to the wall near the dharener.

Having examined the beast, she rose from him and came toward us. Her huge hand came down upon Khemi's fragile shoulder, and Besha hurled the crell across the stall, so hard that the girl hit the far wall and crumpled senseless at its base. Hael bent over the fallen Khemi. Besha came toward me, hands raised. I could retreat no farther. I put my chained wrists before my face, to defend myself. The tiask struck my wrists away and slapped my face so hard my temple cracked against the stone wall. I saw another universe, and suddenly I could not breathe. I curled into a ball. My back exploded in white pain. Kicks rained upon me where I lay.

Far away, I heard voices. Eventually I could see the sand beneath me, and I was conscious that they moved me. I remember being carried into the dim crell chamber and locked into place upon the chain. I remember Aje's voice, but I did not answer. I found no sleep, but worked as best I knew how within my body to ease it. A part of me raged and paced. After a time, I was conscious that the crellkeep came for Aje. Besha wanted her plaything. Aje paid a heavy price that he might be a ten.

When I felt no pain in me, I lay gaining strength. I had almost calmed the raging within, when Aje was carried into the chamber by two jiasks. The crellkeep scurried along beside them, carrying a torch, and in the torchlight upon Aje's body I saw for the first time what a Parset huija can do to human flesh. The steel-burred lash had torn muscle and sinew from the crell's chest. I wondered, as they chained his ankle, if he would live.

The jiasks who had brought him departed. The crellkeep remained, standing over Aje, holding the torch high. His face was sorrowful. I too felt some sorrow.

As he moved to lower his torch, I lured the crellkeep toward me with artful moaning. He knelt beside me, setting down his torch upon the stone.

As he bent closer to examine my face, I opened my eyes, smiling while I slid his knife from its sheath. My chains rattled as I plunged the knife between his ribs. The crellkeep fell upon me in his death agony. I took the keys from his slitsa belt, removed my wrist bonds, and unlocked the manacle from around my ankle.

Many of the crells had seen. Some were sitting up staring, but none said a word. I tossed the key ring down the line. I wished Khemi had been there, so I could have freed her. She had not been returned with me this night. I leaned over Aje. He needed skilled attention. I had not much in healer's skills, but I took precious moments to do what I could.

The crell who caught the key ring did not free himself, but laid it down, regarding me levelly.

I looked down at myself, and in the flickering torchlight saw what he saw—that I was covered in the crellkeep's blood.

"Free yourself," I urged him.

"Why?"

I looked around me. My chain-mates appeared uneasy and frightened. They were not happy with this choice I offered them. I looked at Aje, once Lalen, musician of Stra. I did not understand the crells' indifference.

"I need someone to get me to the court. I do not know the way. Is there not one among you more oppressed by this life than afraid to flee it?" I spoke that the moment might match my vision.

There was one. I got the keys from beside the crell who would not use them and threw them down the chain to the dark, curly-haired man standing. He unlocked his bracelets, freed his ankle, and came to stand beside me, the keys in his hand, rubbing his wrists.

"We will need these for the gates." He hefted the key ring in his hand, grinning around him. "None else for a clean and easy death?" he asked them. The wind blew in his husky voice. His white teeth flashed like a carnivore's.

In an easy motion he had the torch and the dead crellkeep's weapons in his hand. He dragged the crell-keep to his vacant place on the chain, then, motioning me to follow, slipped into the corridor.

I followed, wondering if I could move in such silence, down the corridor and into the crellkeep's cubicle before the barred steel gate. There he sconced the torch and rummaged in a deep wooden chest.

"If you are in for the small wager, would you stay in for the great?" I whispered to his back.

His curly head came up from out of the chest, followed by his arms, in which he held assorted weapons and belts. Among them was a huija.

"What mean you?" he said, tossing all but the huija and a short blade at my feet.

I knelt down and chose a sword belt with a light blade and a gol-knife that suited me.

"I would exchange a friendly greeting or two

with the tiask Besha before I leave this fair land," I explained, rising.

"Hold the torch for me," he said, and I did, as he fitted the key in the lock and slid aside the barred gate, which he then locked behind him. He took the torch from me and discarded it.

We sidled down the corridor, pressing our backs against the smooth stone.

"So you would see my mistress," he grunted, jumping from out one shadow into another. Around the corner, he awaited me, his head flat against the corridor wall.

"Did you hear something?" His voice was harsh. I strained my ears.

"I hear nothing," I said.

He laughed. "We will both be hearing things soon. We will be here sneaking about at sun's rising, at this rate. And you would seek audience with a tiask! If I sought out every Nemarsi who has laid hands upon me, we would be still here next Detarsa." He turned his head, and our faces were very close. "Where would you expect to find her, this time of night, after such a busy evening?"

"She is your mistress," I reminded him. He chuckled and sprinted off down the corridor. I followed him down that one, and then to the left and past three, and then to the right. There we halted. I gasped for breath. He whose name I did not know pressed me back against the wall.

"Up those stairs," he whispered, "are the kitchens, and among them one room where food and drink are always provided. They often go there to while away the time. She goes there, when her irascibility invades her sleep. But remember that the Nemarsi use all twenty-eight enths of the day, and others may be there also. Men right out of the desert often have trouble sleeping through the night." And he did not ask after my fears, but took the stairs in a dozen leaps. These corridors were larger, muffled with tapestries, almost well-lit. He silenced me when I tried to speak, and shook free the huija in his hand.

Then he simply stepped from the stairwell into the middle of the corridor, the huija slithering like a living thing beside him. I tightened my clammy grip upon the gol-knife and followed.

After a time of aching silent progress, we stopped, just short of a wide-open doorway on our right. From within, light, sound, and the smell of baking bread poured forth into the corridor.

"What better could we ask?" he whispered as we peered within.

The room was intimately lit, and L-shaped, and through three high windows I could see the spent evening sky, the stars fading away. There were a number of plank tables, all deserted save for one, at which sat Besha and a jiask unknown to me. Across the remains of a meal they leaned toward each other, engrossed in earnest conversation. It had been their low, angry voices we had heard out in the corridor. The kitchen help clattered about, somewhere around the far corner.

My companion touched me upon the arm and walked boldly through the doors. The sound of my body's movements was deafening. My skin prickled, my mouth was dry, yet the soles of my feet seemed slick with sweat. My eyes upon Besha's broad back, I sheathed the knife and drew the short blade at my waist, for I was reminded of her girth and reach, and knew I must keep my distance to keep my life.

They did not look up until, standing a man's length from them in the aisle between the tables, my companion spoke.

"There is a certain fitness, Diyjar, in meeting death upon a full stomach," and the huija flicked out even while the jiask Diyjar was drawing his sword and still rising, wrapping itself around the blade. My companion snapped his wrist back, and the jiask's blade skittered across the stone floor. Then again did the huija strike, and the jiask wore no longer gol-knife or scabbard at his waist.

Besha stared, her recurved stra blade wavering, her eyes going from my companion to myself and back again. She took two steps backward, then held her ground.

My companion had the jiask backed against the wall.

"Speak my name and petition me for your life," the curly-haired man suggested to his terrified victim.

"I know it not," stammered the perspiring jiask, "but leave me my life, and whatever is mine shall be yours."

"You no longer have what I want. You had it once, and it was named Mera. Remember me now, jiask?" And the horrified realization was still on the jiask's face as the deadly huija curled hissing about his throat and snapped tight. He slid lifeless down the wall, to crumple upon the floor, his neck at an unlikely angle.

The dark man knelt over him and pulled the burred lash away from the flesh in which it was embedded. He turned and regarded us, coiling it carefully in his hands.

"Carth . . ." Besha's voice was uncertain. She searched for a commanding tone. "Give me that, and naught shall come of this." She held her free hand out to him.

He shook his head, grinning.

"I will not hurt you, mistress," he said. "I stand here only to see that you two are not disturbed." And he hunkered there over the corpse, the huija in his hands.

Besha turned to me, and her eyes were blazing with fury. Her dark lips curled back from her teeth, she made a great number of allusions as to my probable parentage and the condition of my female parts.

She advanced toward me, thrashing the air with her blade. Now that the moment was here, I could think of nothing to say. I had not the knack for talking and killing at once.

I think I somehow expected my companion to dispatch Besha for me, knowing that I desired it. But he had taken me at my word, and only watched as I retreated before the bulky tiask, trying somehow to get a sense of her. She bellowed with every new leap, and her cuts descended right to left and ascended always the same way. She sought by sheer force to batter me to the ground, but her bulk made her slow. I danced and jittered to keep out of her reach on those furious downward swings. Each time my blade met hers, my arm was rocked in its socket. I sought to score her while the inertia of her cut left her open, but she caught herself and ripped her own blade up my side. I ducked a clumsy attempt to cleave off my head, and blooded her sword arm. My ribs burned.

I fled around the table from her. She huffed and wheezed. No longer did a steady stream of filth run from her mouth. I caught sight of my companion, grinning, as I whirled out of the way of Besha's longer reach. Her thrusts became predictable, but my arm was leaden from her concussive parries, and sweat ran into my eyes and blurred my sight. As I retreated before her, I suddenly grasped the double-eight pattern of her tiring sword arm. I could not last much longer. I could barely keep her spark-throwing cuts from my breasts.

I feigned a stumble, and landed rolling. She flung herself through the air toward me, thinking to crush me under her enormous weight. I closed my eyes in that final thrust, that I might not see my ending. Besha impaled herself with such force upon my blade that it was torn from my hand. Her ponderous hulk thudded to the stone beside my head, so close that her great thigh landed upon my face. Only a handbreadth of misjudgment, and I would have been dead beneath her. I lay there and trembled, too weak for a moment even to lift the flaccid weight of her thigh from me.

I heard the snap and hiss of the huija, and scrambled to my knees. My companion stood between me and the doorway, and in that doorway were a number of jiasks, and the dharener of Nemar.

Without thinking, I rolled Besha's corpse and retrieved from it the weapon that had so fully served me. The tensed muscles knotted and twitched in my companion's dark back as he made the huija dance and writhe on the azure floor around him.

I knelt there over Besha a moment, despair and triumph chasing each other around within me. I wiped the blade on my naked thigh and went to stand beside the curly-haired man. I could hear at our backs the buzzing of the kitchen help, who peeped around the corner. I wondered where I had gone wrong in my sorting, and then, not even that mattered to me. I stared at Hael, who leaned nonchalantly against the doorframe in breech and belt only. His arms were crossed over his chest, and he seemed pleased with himself. I wondered what they would do to us—two crells who had slain Nemarsi and been caught while still about it.

"We stand upon the swirl of change, past the dying threx, and the sword has found its destined scabbard," he remarked.

I failed to see what bearing yris-tera had upon this moment.

"Shall we go now and see the cahndor?" he asked, bestirring himself from the wall to approach us. The huija hissed and cracked. Hael stopped. His face was calm. The jiasks, six of them, stood waiting in the doorway. There was no escape for us.

"You will have to take this from me, dharener," I warned him.

"Retain it," Hael said. "And you also." He spoke to my companion. "Retain your weapon. But coil it up and come with me to the cahndor." Such an odd smile the dharener had upon his face.

I chanced a sidelong glance at him who held the huija. In his eyes was a dawning understanding. He pulled up the lash, coiling it carefully, metal burrs meshed inward. I touched him.

"What means this?" I whispered.

"That we may yet go free," he said in a low voice. "It is a chance only, if the Day-Keeper means what he implies. But we have no other." And he put his left arm around my shoulder. I sheathed my blade and let my companion propel me toward the door.

My gaze met the dharener's, but he gave no answer to my questions, only walked beside me on my left. The jiasks melted from our path and fell in behind us.

Down numerous corridors and up three flights of stairs we went, and upon each level the corridors became more opulent, the hangings more beautiful. Torches here were frequent, and cushions appeared in windowed alcoves curtained with vibrant web-weave draperies rippling in the predawn breeze.

We came to a pair of carved thala doors, and the dharener disappeared within, leaving us with the six jiasks, who watched us warily, silent.

After a time, Hael returned and ushered us into the cahndor's presence.

The cerulean room had carved pillars, and layer upon layer of blood-tone rugs, and eight paneless windows that kept a hundred gossamer web-cloth panels constantly in motion. There were many cushions, and some low tables upon which were heaped uncountable items of valued Parset clutter. Amid pillows, two women slept, naked, and their skin shone with oils. Scents I had not smelled since Arlet were soft on the air, and I was minded of Celendra's keep, so long ago.

Chayin wore a sunset robe loose about him. He had lit an oil lamp and set it upon a low stand amid the cushions.

"Join me, tiask," he said softly, indicating a place by his right. My companion had to push me forward. I was speechless. I collapsed before Chayin, thinking of my filthy state. The wound upon my side still bled fitfully. I felt rather than saw the dharener and my companion seat themselves.

"You have done us a great service, though no greater perhaps than that done you by this crell whom you so recently aquired." The cahndor turned his un-blinking stare upon my companion. "I am sure that I speak for your mistress when I offer you whatever you desire that is within our power." Chayin looked at the nameless one inquiringly.

My companion regarded his hands for a time. Then he raised his head and spoke.

"That message which I came here bearing so long ago has been by other means delivered." He looked at Chayin, and his manner was not that of a crell's.

"That which has been lost," he continued, "cannot in this world be regained." He turned to Hael, and his voice held censure long restrained. "I wore when I came here the arrar, chald of the messenger. Any-where else upon Silistra one who bears upon his very skin the glyph of service would have protected and succored me. You cannot serve two masters, dharener. What has gone before will be noted by him who sent me here." And he turned back to Chayin, giving Hael no chance to answer.

"I want only my chald and a mount, and suffi-cient weapons and provisions. I return to the north-west."

"It is done," Chayin agreed. "I will even send two jiasks with you to the borders of the Skirr."

"It is not necessary," the curly-haired man de-murred. I had lost all thread of understanding.

"Hael, see to these things," Chayin ordered. The dharener and my companion stood.

The curly-haired man put his hand gently upon my head. "Blessings, small one, and success in all you do." He bent and kissed my forehead. "When you come to the Lake of Horns, seek me there," he said softly.

"And after whom shall I inquire?" I asked.

"I am Carth, only, in service to the dharen." This

last was a whisper. "Not even tiask Besha dared give me name other than that." And he straightened up and was gone out the doors with Hael.

Chayin stretched and rubbed his neck. A smile played about his lips. He extended his hand to me. In the corner, one of the women moaned in her sleep.

"Explain to me," I pleaded softly, my hand in his.

"Surely." He chuckled. "Besha is dead. She has been killed either by a northern forereader whom she was willing to engage in single combat, or by a crell in ignominious and unseemly death. If it were admitted that a jiask and tiask had been bested by two mere crells, we would invite trouble." He ticked his points off on his fingers. "Also consider that in unseemly or mysterious death, all possessions are given up to the desert. That would include the threx Guanden, and our hopes for the race at Frullo jer. So either you accept Besha's chald and be tiask in her place and ride the race at Frullo jer, or we will kill you, quietly and with all formality, so that in single combat the threx Guanden will pass into some jiask's or tiask's hands."

"So I do not win my freedom, as Carth did," I said bitterly. I understood only that. "The tiasks will never accept me."

"Besha was high among them. You outrank all but nine others if you take up her chald. She was a woman with many enemies, but by your works they will accept you. Frullo jer looms ever closer."

I thought that over. A strong sweet breeze ruffled the hundred hangings.

"You could never be sure of me," I said.

"Nor you of me. But nothing is sure in Nemar. And there are times when even the self cannot be trusted. I give you life and a kind of freedom." He leaned closer to me.

"Win for me the golden sword at Frullo jer!" His black eyes gleamed. "Make true my vision, and I will serve you in kind. We both twist the time around us.

Let us combine our strengths, upon one common objective after another!"

"I do not twist the time, forereader. I but move within it."

Chayin laughed.

The woman moaned again, and I heard the rustle of her body turning in its sleep. I thought of Khemi, once a wellwoman, and Aje, who lay bleeding from Besha's abuse. If I took up Besha's chald, all that was hers was mine, Aje included.

"Hael says it will go this way. I see it. Why not accept this life for a time? And more that I could offer you!"

"If I do this, will you help me find Sereth crill Tyris?" I bargained.

"I would rather do any other thing." He leaned back in the cushions, stroking his chin with his hand.

Hael came through the double doors and closed them behind him.

I looked at Chayin questioningly, awaiting his word.

"Win for me the golden sword, and I will put you before him within a pass," Chayin promised in a strange voice. "I would have, at any rate," he added.

"Do you two still delay the inevitable?" Hael interrupted.

"No." In that moment I decided. I stood in accord with my sorting. This was the way. "Send someone to my crell Aje. I want him whole and well, and no crell labors upon him. I will be your tiask and uphold whatever chaldra is involved," I committed myself.

"After you are officially chald-bound as tiask," the dharener temporized.

"This moment," I insisted.

Clearing the Way

⚛︎⚛︎⚛︎⚛︎⚛︎⚛︎⚛︎⚛︎⚛︎⚛︎⚛︎⚛︎

The spear and shield together upon the red, what is needed, on the board of catalysts.*

The armed man, by his own design, serves the will of the Third Weather.

He sees around him decay, and hastens to make reparation.

The shield keeps his council, and the spear is indefatigable in his service.

At such times it is unseemly for a man to do other than what he chooses.

He need not question the fitness of his actions, for his left arm bears the shield of righteousness and his right the spear that clears the way.

His actions are precipitous without folly.

---

* When multiple pieces inhabit one square upon the board of catalysts, the diviner is enjoined to read also the oracle for each alone upon the square in question, and to take note of any pieces inhabiting congruent squares upon the boards of manifestation and outcome.

All that he touches turns to his purpose, for he is in harmony with the time.

Under the influence of Clearing the Way, a man not only serves himself, but his brothers also.

There is no adjuration.

The spear and the shield together are the manifestation of the Third Weather in the material world. The man bearing them turns his strength to the cause of a maligned leader to whom his heart holds allegiance. There is no error in this, not even in laying his weapons at the leader's feet.

The time of Clearing the Way obviates all previous assignations. When the spear and shield are offered willingly into the service of one who is capable of bringing order out of chaos, they will certainly triumph.

Even should he offer up his own volition into the bargain, the commitment would not be too great.

—Khys, the Second Appendix,
hide-year sixty-three

IV. Tiaskchan

I lay in the warm scented bath, and neither the healing water nor the skillful ministrations of the two crells Chayin had roused from their sleep to attend me could ease my mind. I stared upward at the muraled ceiling, into the tropical fantasy foliage that had never grown in Nemar. The morning's breeze blew through gold-green web-cloth panels, and one of the sleek-skinned girls added another steaming kettle of the herbal brew to my sea-green archite tub.

I rose dripping and went to lie upon my stomach on a padded bench, that the crells might knead my aching muscles, dress my wounds, and anoint my skin with the precious oils of the south. I would take up the chald of Besha when the sun stood high. So it had been decided by the dharener, before he went upon my bidding to see to Aje.

When I had, in Chayin's presence, demanded return of the helsar, the dharener refused me. He would go this very day to the hide aniet, directly after my enchalding, and he would take the helsar there with him. I objected. His retort was that I might ask him again after Frullo jer. Then he turned to Chayin and informed the cahndor that he would take the Nemar-chan, Liuma, with him. Chayin opposed this for the safety of his child-to-be that Liuma carried. Hael replied that because they took the undertunnels, there was no danger. I thought it less odd at that moment that the dharener would command the cahndor as to the disposition of the cahndor's couch-mate, than that Hael would speak of the undertunnels, secret ways through which the carriages of the Day-Keepers move at dizzying speeds from one hide to the other.

But Chayin, for his own reasons, was then agreeable to what Hael proposed. When the dharener was gone from us, he bid me make ready for the ceremony, after which, he promised me, we would take a meal and he would answer what questions he could of mine. We would have time for this, since by custom a new tiask spends her first night with her cahndor, that her loyalty might be adjudged by him and a firm basis for cooperation established between them.

The girls' hands were efficient and gentle, but the muscles in my shoulders and back were beyond their power to soothe. I sighed and sat up.

They dressed me in makeshift fashion, for I am smaller in frame than Nemarsi women, though as tall as many. They combed and bound my thigh-length hair, and put over my head one of the feathered masks of which tiasks are so fond. Around my shoulders I wore a cloak of slitsa strips worked also with plumes and beads, and under it a simple wrap of white silk, for there had not been time to have proper tiask's garments made for me. So I stood when Chayin came to collect me; my copper skin and hair gleaming, all masked and robed in whites and desert colors, but with the dark fires of unease shining out of me.

Through the day-bright corridors we hastened, Chayin keeping the silence with which I had greeted him. He was resplendent in his robes of state, but I thought he must be as warm as I beneath them. His cloak was thrown back over his shoulders, and the ur-itheria upon his arm glared balefully at me, intruder into its domain, usurper and unbeliever among the faithful.

Around and around we went in the maze of the palace of Nemar North, until we stood finally in the dharener's offices in the southernmost tower, where the hierarchy of the Nemarsi awaited us. The Nemarchan was there, impossibly delicate amid these robust people, her ripe belly wound about with strings of fire gems. Behind her stood her forereaders, ten of them, and ten from Hael's Day-Keepers, each accoutered differently after the leanings of his heart. And ten jiasks stood to their right, and nine tiasks to complete the circle around Hael, upon whom every feather glowed black as deepest night. Before the dharener burned the chalder's fire in a great bronze caldron, over which the chalder had arranged the tools of his craft. Above Hael's head hung a great tapestry in night shades, upon which uritheria was depicted with his tail wrapped around the world, which spun upon the palm of Tar-Kesa, whose eyes were two huge red gol-drops set into the weave. And that form of Tar-Kesa had a familiar glow to it, and a certain familiar countenance that set my heart to scrabbling about my ribs in search of escape, for I knew then that I stood in the presence of my enemy Raet, with his servants ranged about him.

And I hardly heard Hael rendi Inekte's voice as he intoned the ceremonial words and named off to me that chaldra to which I was henceforth bound, though I could not yet read the Nemarsi chald.

"And do you take up also the web-weavers' chald as patron, and swear your sword to their perpetuity and your efforts to their betterment?" Hael continued.

"I do so swear," I answered for the sixth time the same, and the chalder then picked up a strand of blued iron bound around with web-thread and wound it among the others in the chald he was building for me.

"And do you take up also the threx breeders', and swear your sword so their perpetuity and your effort to their betterment?" And again I answered him the same. When fourteen facets of Nemarsi life had my word behind them, and when the cahndor's hand was kissed and my life's blood sworn to his service, I stood again on my feet while the chald was bound upon me and the last links made fast.

Then all present but the cahndor and the dharener knelt down, and the blessing of Tar-Kesa was invoked upon us. My skin crawled as I received it. I would have sooner received an apth upon my couch than that one's word into my heart, as his priest adjured us.

At the end of the ceremony one of those miniature bladders was passed around, and when it came my turn, I found it to be uris, that drug of which I had had so much in the desert. I blocked the bladder's mouth with my tongue, but even the small amount of bitter liquid produced immediate results. Colors brightened, and I stood suddenly on a high precipice overlooking myself amid the Nemarsi.

From that vantage point I picked from among the tiasks two who looked likely, by the standards with which women judge each other. These I deep-read with shameless skill, and what I learned, I put to use upon them.

To the first, whose name was Nineth, I gave that which had been Besha's clothing, telling her that I could not use them, which was true, and that I thought her to be almost as tall, though much slimmer, which was not true, for she was easily as wide as Besha.

To the second, Pijaes, I spoke in low tones of threx, and praised her skill, of which I had heard nothing, but seen in her mind and her carriage, and asked her advice about the number of contracts to take for Guanden at Frullo jer. Once given an opening, Pijaes extolled to me the virtues of particular threx bloodlines, until Chayin pulled me gently away to meet his couch-mate, the Nemarchan.

I stood before Liuma reluctantly, for I had seen her, and it took no deep-reader to mark that though she carried Chayin's announced child, her body and heart were Hael's. Such situations always bring me discomfort. I wondered whether Chayin did not know, or knew and did not care. And, after the ways of a woman, I wondered whose child truly kicked and turned within that taut, dusky, fire-gem-encrusted belly.

She held out her tiny hand to me, and I looked into eyes deeper than sleep and calm beyond mortal composure.

"*Presti, m'it tennit,*" she said to me in the language of the north, perfect and without accent.

"And you also," I said, but in Parset, "feel free to approach me, at your leisure. What have you within?" I asked the polite question, the answer to which I already knew.

"A son for the cahndor." Her voice was velvet soft, but assertive.

"What takes you into the hide?" I made conversation as Chayin left us together, alone in the crowd, and sought the dharener. Watching him, I again saw the night-dark hanging, with those blazing eyes that seemed to follow me.

She turned her head also, to watch her couch-mate. "He is well today," she commented. "It is not always so easy for him. Think you," she demanded suddenly, "that you can succeed where we have failed?" Her black eyes had midnight ice in them. So deftly did she turn aside my question, I did not even notice.

"I . . . I do not know," I stumbled. "He feels me kin to him through our struggles. He might be right. Can the bondrex, up to her knees in sucksand, help her brother, sunk in to the hips?"

"Often, even among the bondrex, one is sent ahead to scout out the safer way, that the balance of the herd not be risked upon untried ground. I had thought perhaps you were such. We call them first-come, and I have myself predicted such a one's arrival among us. Could it be that you, who match my vision, do not know yourself, nor the use to which we will put you? Did not He-whose-name-we-will-not-mention prepare His representative?"

I tried, cautiously, to think of some answer that would not reveal me as less than the Nemarchan chose to make me, and yet pierce the veil within which she swaddled her words. Liuma made dextrous use of the forereader's cloak, obscurity, and in the dark so engendered. It is easy to fall and hurt oneself.

I was still trying, my eyes upon her serene smiling face, when the dharener came up behind her, and at his touch upon her shoulder, Liuma melted to him. Again I felt sorrow for Chayin, that such could occur even in his presence.

"Chayin will begin your indoctrination. Stay close to him until I return. There is little time before Frullo jer, and you must be able to comport yourself in a tiask's manner by then. When I am back from aniet, I myself will attend your schooling." Liuma looked adoringly into Hael's bearded face. I reminded myself of whose power he invoked to protect his people. How could he go from here, down into hide aniet, where the philosophy of the Weathers held sway, and feel no ambivalence?

The cahndor at that moment appeared and steered me over to meet his jiasks.

"You must greet them first," Chayin explained, his lips close to my ear. I turned my head to answer him in kind, and saw Hael and Liuma just stepping out the door.

"What shall I say?" I whispered.

"It does not matter, but a tiask is accorded the privilege of first address among jiasks with whom she ranks equal or higher."

"You mean they cannot come up and talk to me at their inclination?" I asked incredulously.

"You must go up and talk to them at *your* inclination," Chayin explained gently.

"I will find that very difficult. I would rather be

sought. How does one avoid importuning upon their privacy?"

He laughed. "I do not know. I am cahndor. I speak first to all, and it does not cause me embarrassment. You will get used to it."

We stood now before the ten highest among Nemarsi jiasks. They were dark, large men. The gristasha stamp of their ancestors and the Parset nictitating membranes were all that marked them apart from any Slayers of the north. Most wore only breech and weapons belts; some had lashes coiled diagonally around their chests.

And I was introduced to them as Estri of Nemar only, as we had earlier agreed.

They looked at me, expectant. None said a word.

"Jiasks, Chayin has told me of the customs between jiask and tiask, and I have much to learn and much to live up to. I thank you all for confirming me." I took from my face the tiask's mask, though I knew this to be a sign of sexual availability among them.

"There is one custom, however, that is so against my nature that I find myself constrained to alter it between us. As it is said in the towers among which I was raised, I will say it to you, and with like meaning. At any time, approach me," and the men looked startled, but their smiles were truly warm and welcoming as they crowded around me. As we walked, the jiasks, Chayin, and I, to that room where I had earned my tiask's chald, I could sense his approval, his relief that the jiasks, and to some extent the tiasks also, had accepted me. The Day-Keepers and forereaders had been cold and distant, but for Liuma. They were hesitant to accept other than aniet-born among them, although, as the dharener himself had explained to me, there was a precedent—the mother of both Hael and Chayin, the rendi woman the cahndor Inekte had brought into Nemar.

"Chayin," I said as we seated ourselves at one of the plank tables, "you once said to me that there appeared no solution for the problem between us. Things seem to have worked themselves out." His face grew grim, then regained its former humor.

"There is not, on the larger scale. We live in a pleasant interval, where fantasy, for a time, can give us succor before events strip our pretensions away. Let us enjoy it while we can," he advised.

The jiasks and tiasks settled themselves noisily about us, pushing together tables and benches, until Chayin and I sat at the middle of one great board. Upon my left sat the cahndor, and upon his left the tiasks, each of whom was commander, or tiaskchan, of three hundred. Upon my right was a jiaskcahn I recognized from our triumph over the Menetphers, and beside him another, who bore a fresh scar the length of his arm from that battle. The "chan" Silistran root word has been adopted almost unchanged into the Parset language; only in its division into male and female does it differ in usage from the north. "Will of" is a popular Parset concept.

None sat opposite me or any other upon that long table, for friends in Nemar sit beside one another, never opposite.

As the kitchen help brought great heaping trays of food to us, I looked in vain for signs of my confrontation with Besha, but not one drop of blood remained upon the seamless ornithalum floor.

"How is Khemi, Chayin?" I broke the silence between us. Upon my right, the jiaskcahn heaped his plate.

"Who?" Chayin asked, as he served himself, and put upon my plate some greenish meat with a jellied skin and pungent odor. Upon few of the serving trays did I see food familiar to me.

"What mean you, 'Who?' " I was angered that he did not recall her, for she was his. "That crell of yours that Besha pummeled senseless over the death of the red threx!"

Chayin motioned a server to him, and that one

ladled onto our plates black lumps in some viscous sauce.

"There are thrice a thousand crells in Nemar North alone, not counting those who serve in the fire-gem mines or the uris fields or in maintenance in the west, south, and east. Should I concern myself with all of them, I would have time for nothing else." He leaned forward and called down the table to his left: "Yisri, how many crells did Besha own?"

The tiaskchan Yisri put down her two-pronged fork. "Around sixty, cahndor. I am not sure of the exact number," she answered.

"And how many of those are in Nemar North?" Chayin pursued the matter.

"A score. Of that I am sure," Yisri replied, puzzled.

Chayin turned back to me. The tiask, after a moment, returned to her meal.

"Have you seen to your own crells? Name them for me, and give me a report on their health and well-being."

"That is unfair!" I protested. But he had made his point. I had been too busy even to ask after Aje, whom I knew was badly injured. I resolved then to do what I could for those crells who were mine. And there was the matter of Carth.

"And Carth, who wore the arrar! Is ignorance your excuse for mistreating an agent of the dharen?"

Chayin sighed and put down his fork. The muscles in his jaw twitched.

"These things are not table conversation," he reprimanded me, his eyes narrowed, voice low. "I knew it not. But Hael knew, and did as he saw fit. The dharener receives all crell chalds. We will speak of this later. Attend your brothers and sisters, and make friends among them. That is why I have called them together." He rapped my stra plate with his fork. "Eat your food," he commanded.

"Thou art my will," I mocked him, and turned my attention to my plate, as an approving cheer from the jiaskcahns greeted the arrival of servers with pitchers, and a purple, frothing beverage was poured into our bowls.

I pointed to the green meat upon my plate, nestled between the black lumps and some yellow vegetable in red sauce. "What is that?" I asked. "And this, and this?"

"Tail of apth, a great delicacy. And the black are the unborn eggs of kelt. And the yellow the fruit of the succulent which produces uris."

"I am really not hungry." I pushed my plate away.

Chayin grinned and repositioned the plate before me. "Eat!" he repeated.

I tasted the yellow chunks. They were spicy, not unlike sour narne. Gaining courage, I nibbled the green apth meat, which I found quite tasty, once one got over the source. The eggs of kelt, a smaller relative of the golachit, I could not bring myself to try. But the cahndor was satisfied. The purple beverage was invigorating, and possessed of a tingly tartness. I drank it down, and a clean-scrubbed, deferential crell scurried to refill my bowl.

The jiaskcahns had long been at this refilling of their bowls, and their mood was much lightened. The man upon my right was telling in a loud voice an exaggerated account of my prowess as it had been shown to him in our skirmish upon the desert, and in a very proprietary manner. He put his arm around me and pounded me upon the back, and another who had been there took up his tale. I did not mind, but thanked whatever unconscious grace I possess that predisposes men toward my favor.

I judged it to be late day when Chayin pushed back from his place and rose and stretched mightily. Long ago had cloaks been discarded, and formal headgear and weapons joined them upon the floor. Some wagering had been made as to which threx among the active sires was most well-endowed, and a number of those present prepared to adjourn to the stables to find out.

Chayin demurred when enjoined to accompany them, and he and I took up our raiment from the floor and walked a different way through the halls until we entered through a well-concealed door in a shadowed alcove into Chayin's chamber.

He slid the bolt and rearranged the ruby-toned tapestry that secreted this entrance from view. "If you ever need to come to me unobserved, you now know the way," he remarked, stripping off all his trappings but breech, and leaving them upon the floor. I threw upon the pile my elaborate weapons belt and the feathered cloak. There was a soft rustling, and I turned to see the two silken crells hovering silent behind us, gleaming in the torchlight. The room was dim, though it was still day, for heavy web-cloth draperies had been drawn across the eight windows.

Chayin commanded them to withdraw, and one of them raised pleading eyes to him. I did not understand the dismay I saw in their faces as they searched among the cushions for their flimsy robes. Chayin touched my shoulder and went to them, where they hesitated by the double carved doors. He spoke in low tones and kissed them each atop their harth-black heads, the highest of which only came up to his shoulder.

I recognized then with a pang of empathy that piteous dependence upon a man's will that brought them one moment to the abyss of misery and the next to the precipice of joy. Those two crells were deep in love with their cahndor. Chayin slid three bolts upon the door behind them. When he turned to me, his face was distracted. He had hardly seen them. I had been in their place, one time, with a certain man, when a touch brought me to grateful tears. I shrugged the memory away. Not again would that happen to me. Chayin smiled. I was not amused. I flopped down upon a heap of sunset cushions and stretched full out on my side, my clean fragrant hair falling loose about me. The silk I wore against my flesh was memory of countless times I had worn silk and given pleasure before. Yet this was different. I found a struggle within: I was not so sure of myself as I had been, or my place or purpose. I did not want to play any game at all with Chayin rendi Inekte, no lovers' games, no women's game of submission and manipulation.

He came and lay close, his hand upon the silk at my turned hip, but his eyes were turned inward. He, too, felt the tension between us, that impropriety of the time that made my body cold to his touch, though he was a fine and handsome man and I had even then a great respect for him.

"Chayin," I said softly, "if you were to tell me that which you feel I do not know, that which so concerns us both, it might help. It will be a long and painful time until I guess the right questions. I am no forereader."

His eyes had anguish in them, and his voice was shaky. I could see the sweat beading upon his forehead. He sighed and rolled to his back, staring at the ceiling.

"If one sees a thing, one may think several ways about it: that it is true, that it is the product of one's fears, that it is the dream of one's heart. That is what I have been taught. You bring another way. I see you changing what would have been otherwise with your will, and I see that you cannot always control it, and are perhaps at some times unaware. The sort was for you to fight Besha beyond the web-weavers' apprei, but you did not choose to do so. When I first took you, I did other than what was natural for me, and I have a sense now that you drafted me into your service. I have from this determined that I myself have upon occasion brought my own fears into the time, as I have long suspected."

I said nothing, waiting.

"If one may bring a thing into time by will, then surely it is imprudent to speak of what might be, even when it is what one sees as truth. I do not desire that which I see. Therefore, it would be wise upon my part to try to conceive another ending to this affair, rather than give support to what I fear."

"Some of what you say may be true, but one must first determine all the available probabilities, then choose between them. You cannot bring your choice into being if it is not among the time tracks. There is never only one way a thing may occur, but we both know there is crux, and within crux, what occurs is fixed. One cannot take responsibility for more than one's personal behavior. We must trust that we sort and act in the best possible fashion when we work from the law within." I crawled to him and put my head upon his shoulder and stared into the forest of curling hairs upon his chest. He still wore the uritheria medallion on its thick-linked gold chain. "Tell me what bothers you, and I will turn my small skill toward it."

"Many things bother me, little one. Nemar is no simple land, and that which ails my mind is nothing that can be helped."

"I am not so sure," I said.

"Sereth will surely kill you," he said simply. "And you hasten with loving eyes toward your death. I cannot sit and pretend I do not know it, because it serves me to have you, unaware, do my will until I hand you to him, as Hael would have me do. Sereth is no longer the man you knew. He is an outlaw with a fierce band around him, and the people of Yardum-Or call him the Ebvrasea and fear him. It is said his men will have no women among them, and that to no living thing do they give quarter."

"Sereth would never hurt me. All you have is gossip. Have no fear for me at his hands." I almost laughed when I said it.

"I know it from his own mouth, for I met him when I was on the plains of Yardum-Or, and under circumstances which left me owing him a blood debt. For that I gave him asylum from those who hounded him, and the whole of Mount Opir as his own. Do not

tell me of his feelings—I know them." He turned his
face into my hair. "I must present you to him, else
violate the spirit of the bond between us. And yet I
have feelings for you that I thought never to have for
a woman." His voice was barely a whisper. "Yet I see
losing you wherever I look. I cannot have you near me
without memory of the pain I will come to feel at
your loss. This once I wish my foresight would fail
me." And he pulled me close and held me tight. "All
that time, since I saw you and saw what would be
between us, I have tried to shut it out, that I not feel
this pain. It grew as I foresaw it, this caring, though I
have denied myself your use. I would no longer go
without it."

"Then let us do as you said, and enjoy this pleasant interval."

His touch upon me proved the truth of his words,
and I was caught in the tide of his intense emotion,
for I opened my mind to his. When at last we were
both exhausted, I got up from beside him and opened
the draperies, that the night sky might shine in upon
him. My mouth and, it seemed, even my stomach tingled long after from the taste of him, so potent was
his gift to me.

"It is said here," he murmured to me when I
again lay in his arms, "that a Nemarsi takes his duty
with a tiask, his lust with a crell, and his love with his
brother. We seem to be the exception that proves the
rule. Would you be Nemarchan beside me?" His tone
had no hint of the veil about it. The couching seemed
to have stabilized him.

"But you have a Nemarchan. Can there be more
than one?" I asked, playful.

"There could be one who was in truth what
Liuma is in name," he said.

"But she bears your child," I pointed out.

"Perhaps, and perhaps Hael's or Tar-Kesa's, for
all I know. She is little more than Hael's eyes and ears,
though she fancies herself a strong influence upon

me." I could feel his body stiffen with this truth, and its strain upon him.

"One cannot couch a forereader without couching also the Day-Keepers she represents." Bitter was Chayin about the restraints Hael held upon him. "I think she would be relieved, should I put her burden upon another. And there is no way they could stop me. My father did the same, displaced another for my mother. And surely you are, whatever your protestations, as much of a forereader as any of them."

I thought about this, silent, about all the reasons I could not do this thing.

"Chayin," I said softly, "let us take some time together, a short-term couch-bond, if you will, and see what the Weathers bring us. You know nothing about me. I can truly say that I have never cared more for a mortal man. There would have to be great change in Nemar for me to reconcile this life with the law that resides within me. And I have certain things that I must do. If I live through the latter, we can come to terms with the former." I sighed, knowing this to be the time.

"Your god Tar-Kesa and I are not upon the best of terms. I serve another, whose power is even greater and whose demands are heavy upon me. I think you and I must consider what we are allowed to do, rather than what we choose to do. Make no mistake: if such a thing could be, I would be most blessed of women." And I kissed his throat, running my tongue in the dark hollow there.

"The chosen of Tar-Kesa is himself a god," he reminded me, his voice dark as his skin.

"Then my tasks should be greatly lightened by your aid; and by your will, success must surely come to me. Only until the new moon let us keep this couch-bond, and if at that time you still want me, provided we both live, I will be your Nemarchan, if you will meet certain conditions which the time between now and then will doubtless make clear to you."

And seeing that I would not be dissuaded from

this, Chayin agreed to let Liuma continue as his Nemarchan until that time, and more that I asked of him.
He would return to me my Astrian chald that Hael
now held, and the helsar also. When I explained that
Hael's use of the helsar caused me pain, he became
agitated, demanding to know why I had not told him
before, and it came to light in that conversation that
Hael was meeting with the other four dhareners of the
Parset Lands to try to get some unified policy for
dealing with the Bipedal Federate M'ksakkans, who
had approached each tribe separately with certain
proposals. An uneasy feeling in the pit of my stomach,
I guessed aloud what those proposals were: bases in
the south and direct access to the drugs grown here,
those drugs catalytic to the serums that are our only
restraint upon the M'ksakkans, for they have not suc-
ceeded in synthesizing them.

As Chayin so aptly pointed out, if the Menetphers
had hovers and star weapons, it would behoove the
Nemarsi to treat for them also.

I expressed my disapproval of the scheme, and
aired some considered opinions I had gathered from
close and continued contact with the B. F. representatives, the Liaisons, in the north. I put it to Chayin
that only disorder could result from treating with
these materially fixated beings, and he promised me,
in return for certain information, that I might sit in on
the final negotiations, to be held at Frullo jer, where
all the Parset lords would be gathered. Furthermore,
he promised me that he would under no circumstances treat with M'ksakka, and that he would convince Aknet of Menetph to refrain also. If the two
most powerful of the Parset nations did this, he was
sure that the others would follow their lead.

"At some time," I had said, "I must return to Astria, and take up again my duties there. I would like to
send a message to my uncle, adviser Rathad, that I am
well and safe, and that I will be home when this business with Sereth has finished."

"I thought you knew, surely, for you did not ask me

to return you," he had said incredulously, propping himself upon his elbow to stare down into my face.

"Knew what?" I asked him, my lips suddenly stiff and cold. And in a way I had known, for among the probabilities of my sorting had been none concerned with my beloved Astria; no way home.

"Knew," he said, hesitant, "that Rathad lives no longer, that Jana, who was Well-Keepress there, has long since disappeared, none knowing whither, and that Celendra bast Aknet rules in Astria."

And I have never been gladder for a man's arms than at that moment, when so many things became clear to me, and the pieces all fell together, and I saw with the clarity of true seeing what awaited me upon the plain of Astria.

And glad I was too that he would make me his, for of a sudden I was homeless, without family but for Estrazi. Had Chayin again asked me, while I wept and he held me, to become Nemarchan of the Nemarsi, I would have accepted. But he is a righteous man, and he did nothing but what was needed. He held me throughout the long Nemarsi night.

In the morning, upon awaking, I remembered and and took refuge; I couched him upon my own initiative, and drove away once again that feeling of aloneness within me.

I thought that day, as we rode the threx around the perimeters of Nemar North, of Rathad. Chayin knew only that he was dead, not how. My mother's brother had been all family to me.

We rode also to see the child of Besha's, who was now my responsibility, for as the Weathers would have it, I now wore around my waist the strand of birthing fulfilled. The boy was near adult, and a web-weaver, as had been Besha's father, Tenager the First Weaver. The youth was not noticeably disturbed; it seemed he hardly even noticed us. The whole time we were there his webber was busy upon the frame and his eyes were elsewhere focused. Tenager, on the other hand, was visibly grief-stricken, and Chayin sat talking to him well over an enth.

As we left the weavers' appreis I mentioned to Chayin a dream I had had, in which I stood in the middle of a seven-cornered room. He interrupted me there and described to me exactly what I had been about to describe to him—the seven occupants of the room and the aspect that each presented. He was as excited as I that another had seen what had been to each dreamer so real, and we set about speculating upon the identity of the seven men and the meaning of the dream, but we came to no supportable conclusions.

That night we spent in his keep, and the next day I viewed all that had been Besha's—each crell, each threx, the appreis, and the palace quarters. Her most amazing possession was a great apprei upon the Way of Tar-Kesa, for which Tenager himself had created the web panels. There was more wealth than I found seemly, and more material things about which to be concerned than I liked. I gave all to Chayin but one apprei, the threx, and crells, and bade him distribute it. I kept the threx upon impulse, and the crells because I felt responsible for their welfare. When we returned to Chayin's keep that night, a Day-Keeper awaited him with the news that Hael would be late in hide aniet. He bade us await him, that we delay our departure to Frullo jer until his return to Nemar.

Chayin dismissed the man without a word and slammed about the keep, kicking unwary cushions out of his way. He stripped off his sword belt and threw the exquisitely crafted weapon against the far wall. Finally he sat, hands clasped behind his neck, staring at the floor.

"What means this?" he whispered, when I went behind him to knead the knots from his shoulders. I had for him no answer.

"Curse them! Curse them all, the forereaders and the Day-Keepers and Tar-Kesa and the Weathers! I am so tired of suiting my actions to their will! Someday I will throw every manipulative one of them into a pit of hungry apths! This secretiveness is more than I can bear. The two of them, loose among their kind; who knows what harm they will hatch up!" He trembled with rage.

"I have often thought, these last few days, we might be better off without them," I commiserated. There was one particular Arletian forereader whom I would have liked to add to Chayin's candidates for the apth pit.

"Do you really have one?" I asked him at last.

"One what?"

"An apth pit."

"Surely, although they are old and lazy," he answered. "It takes them days to fully devour their victims. Would you like to see them?"

"No." I shuddered.

He turned and faced me, reaching up to pull me to my knees by the hair.

"We leave for Frullo jer before morning. I want you to wear this. It will keep the jiasks from you, even if you are maskless. And you will be safe even from other tiasks." He grinned, and took the golden uritheria medallion from about his neck and placed it about mine. It lay cold and heavy between my breasts. A superstitious chill ran through me.

"I would not take this, it is too great an honor." I could not say I would not have Tar-Kesa's sign upon me.

"You must." His smile was proud and gentle. "I command it." And for his sake I agreed. Then he went and rummaged behind his hangings, and a great pile of Parset gear began to grow beside him. He threw toward me the Shaper's cloak.

"You might as well wear it, and these also." And to the cloak he added a gol-knife in red-gold sheath and a stra straight blade, such as is used in the north, with a hulion's head carved into its archite hilt.

He strode to the double doors and passed through them, and I heard a great chiming. Chayin returned to his pile and dressed himself from it until there was nothing left of the pile and he stood armed and ready for the desert in brown web-cloth cloak and breech and untrapped leathers. I had seen him strap all manner of weapons about him, from tiniest sticker to razor-moons and gol-knives, but this armament was so cleverly hidden that one saw only a gol-knife at hip and short sword beside it.

He grinned through narrowed eyes at me, silently staring. I picked up the Shaper's cloak and put it over my arm, and threaded the gol-knife through the sword belt before I belted the familiar northern straight blade about me, just below my Nemarsi chald.

There was a clatter in the hall, and another, and two jiasks burst through the double doors and skidded to a halt before their cahndor. Before Chayin could even turn to face them, two more followed. These two were noticeably winded, and both familiar to me from my confirmation.

"I leave for Frullo jer within the enth," Chayin told them. "Wiraal, it is on you to get the remaining threxmen there safely." Wiraal nodded.

"Yimon, Nemar North is in your hands," he said to the second, and that one bowed his head.

"Asi, prepare Saer and Guanden, with a light hand. Send all I would have carried with Wiraal. Just see it is not forgotten, for I will need it, first first of Amarsa. And send to fetch desert gear for Estri. Those things I ordered are surely ready." And the jiask Asi backed hurriedly from the room, without protestation as to the lateness of the hour.

Chayin turned to the fourth, a heavyset, grizzled veteran whose age I found it impossible to judge. He wore his scowl of disapproval as might another his weapon.

"Isre, I—"

The older jiask did not let his chandor finish, but broke right in. "You are not going again into the desert without me, Chayin! That last was my only folly.

If anything had happened to you, your father's spirit would surely—"

"It is time, Isre," Chayin interrupted in kind, his hand raised palm up to the jiask. "That the father's son be left on his own. I have my own spirit to temper in the caldron of time. You cannot do it for me. I must leave more than one man whose love is unquestioned in Nemar North."

"I will not stay here," said the jiask, crossing gnarled arms thick as thala saplings across his breasts.

"You will, for I shall not return with the others from Frullo jer, but continue on to Mount Opir. Would you leave Yimon to stand for Nemar against Hael upon his own? Surely your responsibility to the jiasks outweighs all else that might be balanced against it."

The jiaskcahn Isre had that look of a man who only sees the trap when it has closed upon his ankle.

Chayin made a sign, and the three bowed down, and the cahndor, in his capacity as living god, blessed them and their endeavors in his name. He then bade them rise and leave us, which they did, as a fitter-woman with sleep still in her eyes stumbled through the double doors with the weaponmaster. Both of them carried armfuls of their craft before them, the little fitterwoman such a load it was a wonder she could see around it.

At my feet they dropped enough to garb a yra of tiasks, rather than one.

From this assortment I soon found myself dressed a double to the cahndor, concealed weapons included, even down to the razor-moons in my thigh-high boots. My cloak, it was decided, was weapon enough without the wires and stickers Chayin's contained, but still they insisted upon slipping the Shaper's cloak within a brown double thickness of web-weave and sewing shut all the edges, so that the cloak was totally encased, except for the starburst clasps, which they dulled with some paste so that they no longer shone.

What occurred fit so exactly with my sorting that

I was afraid to break the spell, and we rode long silent neras out of Nemar North to the southwest, through the decline of evening and sun's rising and at midmorn we stopped in the middle of a dried-up streambed to rest the threx. The veil was heavy upon Chayin then, and in a sense it was on me also, for I made no move to alter what was to be, nor any judgment upon my part in it. We waited, silent, until the threx were rested, and we shared water, but neither ate, and then once again we set their noses toward Frullo jer. Halfway through that harrowing, silent trek, Guanden ceased his pulling and fighting. He had had, finally, enough run to suit him. And when the threx would have slowed, I urged him on, half in revenge for his ill manners.

The full moon was high when we made the ridge country, and higher when we reined them up to gaze upon Frullo jer—a long day-bright hollow between two parallel ridges, ringed with a thousand torches beneath which a sea of appreis shone like jewels. In the center were huge pavilions, with the device of Nemar, a slitsa wound around the recurved blade upon a field of crimson, emblazoned upon them. Frullo jer lies in Nemar, and the midsummer festival of Amarsa is always hosted by the Nemarsi. Three years in a row had Aknet of Menetph beaten the Nemarsi, upon their home ground, and taken back with him to Menetph the Golden Sword. This year Nemar would regain it. Men's hoarse shouting came to us on the breeze, and the smells of food and threx and life. Appreis and pavilions were still being raised, work still being done. To our left, some gaen, Parset draft beasts, pulled a huge rake along a nera-around circular track, in the center of which were more web-structures. It was toward these we headed, down the slope, among the busy throng that seemed not to know or care about the night's waning. I was to learn that Frullo jer, like many Parset institutions, is a day-and-night, nonstop affair. A tired Parset tastes his uris and keeps going, that he not be interrupted. This we did, also, as

Chayin guided Saer across the beautifully graded track among the pavilions to one with the Nemarsi device upon it. Behind us was another, easily as imposing, that bore the amber star upon the black field of Menetph.

We were challenged by a querulous Nemarsi. Chayin casually dismounted, and I did likewise. The man, seeing his cahndor, reached out his hand for Saer's reins. I handed him mine also, and we followed the threx's rears to see where along the ropes they would be placed. Never have I see more fine threx under one cover. A great part of the purpose of these festivals is to mix bloodlines, threx and Parset both, the rest being the meeting of tribal leaders and Day-Keepers and the checking of weights and measures to reaffirm them lawful. At such threx meets also it is not infrequent to see greedy grain merchants from Yardum-Or, for there is a truce of sorts about these affairs, and even safe passage for a few chosen outsiders. There are many northern threx breeders that would give a man's weight in silver for a chance to stand where I stood; more even to contract for service of their best threx by such proven producers of race stock as Aknet's Tycel. The Parsets do not cross-breed their stock outside their own tribes, and even among them, security about the threx was tight. All of thirty jiasks stalked the aisles between the ropes, constantly vigilant.

We passed along aisles where owners worked upon their beasts' coats with razors, patterning their rumps, and with dyes upon their tripart hooves, and with all manner of beads and ribbons and brushes and combs beautified them. Many men were stripped down in the heat of the night, and their dark skins shone slick in the torchlight as they worked.

We regained the track and crossed it, and were among the awnings, where all manner of threx gear was available. I saw stone-studded headstalls and gold-worked rounded reins and great ruffed saddle-pads of vibrant coloration. Parsets browsed and haggled about the stalls in all variety of dress, some eating or drinking as they wandered about. Chayin's hand at my waist guided my steps; his voice was proud in my ear.

"Nowhere in all of the Parset Lands is there another meet to equal that of the Golden Sword. My people have been months preparing. Two hundred have been at this spot for three sets, that the track be perfect and the grounds free of slitsas and apths."

"It is indeed overwhelming," I said, as a prelude to a plea for food, but at the last of the threx-fitters' stalls I saw what I wanted, and put my arm about Chayin's waist and stood on my toes to speak in his ear.

"Buy me that," I said, pointing to a bitless headstall with a nosepiece of metal wound with parr-hide, as is used in the north. This one had silver buckles, and the leathers were gilded, but it was the only one I had seen.

"Anything," he said, and paid twice what it was worth to the merchant, without comment.

"Thank you," I said as he handed it to me. "Since Guanden has no mouth, we will see if he has nerves in his nose." And he knew what I meant: the threx had so much scar tissue in his mouth, he hardly felt the bits.

"Food?" he suggested, guiding me toward a number of fires that glowed up into the night.

"Your forereading is astounding," I answered.

"And then some rest, perhaps?" His hand slipped from my waist to my hips.

"Indeed, for we must be up again by midday to take them around the track," I reminded him.

"We have today and another before first first of Amarsa," he objected. "They have both run this track." We were among the food vendors, each of whom had spread deep-piled rugs upon the ground before their fires, that their customers might sit and eat.

Chayin sat me in a vacant corner and went to the fireside. Some jiasks, farther down the mat, regarded me curiously, talking in low tones to each other. I was maskless, I reminded myself, and of what that meant to them. Chayin met someone he knew, and they stood talking, bowls in hand. The jiask was Chayin's height, but broader and darker, dressed similarly to the cahndor, but in black. They turned and headed toward me. The black-garbed one had a bladder over his shoulder.

I was getting to my feet when the spinning took me, and I sank back to my knees, and then I could no longer feel my body, or hear through its ears, or see through its eyes. I was in a different place, of pink phosphorescent seas and fuchsia cliffs where hump-eyed herbivores rose from the waves, their mouths dripping with brown vegetation. And then, not there, but another place, with a blaring angry call in my mind, that I had no business in that place. Hael's mind, and others behind it I felt, pushing with the wrong tools upon the helsar, desperate, for now en-twined in it, they had not the skill to free themselves. I thought the helsar would surely shatter from their force, the wrong way, at the wrong time. Sorters all, they had not thought to hest the filaments into order, but tried to push through them. And I had no choice but to aid the helsar, for its fate and my own were even then too closely linked.

From the inside, beyond the first gate, I set the filaments spinning in reverse; contrapuntal, it spewed them out. But I had by that step committed myself. A portion of me lay trapped behind the golden gate, and would remain there until I could run the helsar in se-quence and reacquire it. I slid out. The helsar was not unhappy at what had occurred, and what it had traded to me in return went with me, to see a world which for it is only a dream.

Then I knew that Chayin shook me, holding me by the shoulders, and I could feel the rug pile under my knees. Then sight, and his face, eyes narrowed in concern, membranes full across his eyes in his concen-tration. My mind met his before I found the skill of speech, and his sniffed mine all around, like a worried mother threx her newborn.

"Hael," I said when I could, "knocked upon the gate, and he contrived to get his foot stuck there, he and his friends."

"What did you leave there?" he demanded.

"Only a little time," I reassured him.

"For him? I would have let him languish!"

"For myself; it is within my keep he would wreak his disorder and shriek his pain. How could I do otherwise?" I sat back on my heels and shook his hands off. The black-garbed jiask stood a little behind the cahndor, who knelt beside me. He stared. I tossed back my hair and wiped the beads of sweat from my upper lip. I could feel it running in rivulets from under my breasts down my ribs.

"It is done, and with little harm, Chayin." I touched his face. "Let us eat our meal."

He growled like a dorkat, but managed for me a wry grin, and handed me a bowl in which were a number of fried harth parts.

"Will you never introduce me, Chayin?" demanded the jiask, pulling on his beard with his hand.

"Jaheil, cahndor of Dordassa, Estri of Nemar," Chayin complied.

"Cahndor," I acknowledged.

"You are too much of a woman to be the deadly tiask that Chayin paints you," he said, leaning forward to take the hand I offered in Astrian greeting. This man had been in the north. He negotiated the three-turn grip with easy familiarity.

I smiled at his compliment but said nothing.

"I have been trying to convince Jaheil to take a yra of jiasks and accompany us to Mount Opir and beyond." Chayin's tone deepened suggestively. "Of all the cahndors, Jaheil is the only one to whom I would trust my back. I am going to have to turn it sometime in the near future."

"It would suit me, such a romp. I have been too

long a cahndor. I have not blooded my sword for a score of passes."

"Even a cahndor, in Nemar, gets more exercise than that. Have you heard of Aknet's attempted foul play?"

"I have heard." The black-eyed jiask nodded.

"Estri, tell Jaheil what you saw that day in the sky."

"A M'ksakkan craft, big enough to have held that many Menetphers. It came from Nemar and then veered northeast," I said.

"Think you what I suspect?" Jaheil demanded of Chayin, tugging so at his beard that his jaw wobbled.

"That the M'ksakkans aid the Menetphers? Doubtless. And they will aid us all against each other until there are none left to say what they may do in the desert!"

"What would you do about it?" Jaheil queried Chayin.

"Refuse them any ground. Unite all the cahndors against the M'ksakkans. If you will see to Itophe and Coseve, I will convince Aknet that it is not to Menetph's benefit to treat with the star men."

"And how will you do that? You and Aknet under the same web-cloth is reason enough to have one's sword well whetted. Since I have known the two of you, the only agreement between you has been when to enter into battle. Have things so changed between Menetph and Nemar?"

"Know you only that I will do what I say! I can be very convincing." And Chayin showed that smile he wears only upon the kill.

"Are you also a living god?" I broke in, for I saw many around whose ears were fairly pricked in our direction.

Ostentatiously Jaheil rolled back his wide sleeves to exhibit his marks of godhead. "Certainly We are all gods, eh, Chayin?" And he uncorked his bladder.

"Can the gods tell who will win the Golden

Sword?" I asked him, taking a drink of some tart kifra and handing it back.

"Surely you know that already?" he evaded.

"Ah, within, within," I quipped, "it is all within, but so much rests upon us learning to fetch it out where we can see it. Omniscience must be exhausting." The banter served its purpose. The jiasks down the mat took up their own talk, and the small group behind me wandered into the night.

"To get what is within without"—Jaheil's eyes twinkled and sparked in his dark face—"one must set the lure and wait. A high mind receives that which by nature belongs upon that level," he pronounced.

"Enough! I hear such drivel too often! The higher the mind, the farther the horizons for which it pines!" Chayin snapped.

"Will you, Jaheil," I said smoothly, "accompany us to Mount Opir?"

"My lady, I doubt if I have a full yra of jiasks to whom I could trust my own back! If I find that I do, I may later join you. Hard is the lot of a cahndor!"

"Hard is the lot of a man who has upon his couch Aniacaer? Come now, Jaheil!"

"All love grows dim with time, Chayin. The fuel burns, the fire low between us. And you, the same with Liuma?"

"The same," said Chayin in a clipped tone. "Whom did you bring with you, then? Doubtless the cahndor of Dordassa will not sleep alone at Frullo jer?"

"What I brought, I would not be seen with in public. I am not so lucky as you, to have such as Estri among my tiasks. I brought two crells, of whom, if you wish, you may partake, and I had thought to take a maskless tiask who does not outweigh me. As a matter of fact, what drew me to you was this maskless lady, for I did not recognize you in the dim light."

"I have heard it is a common saying in Dordassa that all we of Nemar look alike," Chayin teased him.

"If that were true, how could I sit before one as

ugly as the cahndor and as beautiful as the tiask of Nemar at the same moment? It is a blessing of stronger gods than we, that produces such beauty." Jaheil, sucking prodigiously at the kifra bladder, leaned toward me.

I shifted against Chayin, and he rose, sensing my unease, and held his hand out to me. I took it, and the uritheria of Nemar jiggled between my breasts.

"A productive search to you, Jaheil. You have reminded me of my duty, and I must hasten to it." Chayin bade him farewell, and we threaded our way through the crowd to a cluster of large appreis that bore the device of Nemar, and between them into a central one that awaited us.

Chayin unlaced the flap and held it open for me. Mats were unrolled, and two oil lamps lit, and both our saddlepacks had been brought there.

I unlatched my cloak and let it fall with a sigh of relief, and my boots and belts and breech and band I stripped off also, before I saw the figure that lounged in the shadows. Chayin had his back to me, bent over his saddlepack, searching something from its depths. I knelt casually and picked up my boot, sliding my hand around the grip of a razor-moon. Then I let the boot fall back.

"Chayin," I said softly, "we have a visitor." And the cahndor was at my side, blade glinting in the lamplight.

A laugh came from out of the figure in the shadows, and at that sound the razor-moon dropped from my nerveless fingers to stick upright in the thick pile rug. Chayin bared his teeth and sheathed his blade.

"I sent word to you," Hael said, stepping out of the shadows.

"I received it," Chayin acknowledged, "and if I had heeded it, I would sit still in Nemar, awaiting you."

Hael spread his hands. There was a stiffness to his movements, and his face seemed somehow rearranged. I bent and retrieved the razor-moon, forcing my limbs to do my will. It was Hael's debility, and his sending of it, that had numbed me. I sent it back to him, and saw his face blanch as I returned to him his gift.

"By what means," Chayin demanded, pretenses abandoned, "have you contrived to be in two places at once? What Day-Keeper's tricks can you find to excuse your presence here?" He glowered at Hael, who stood slightly weaving upon his feet. I wondered if what he had gained in the helsar was worth this price to him, and whether it would cost me so much, when my turn came.

"I have communed with Tar-Kesa," said the dharener at last. "I have conferred with my brothers in aniet. I but do the will of the time. The M'ksakkans arrive momentarily. I had thought to save you from what promises to be an unpleasant confrontation." His voice was not so sure as his words.

"And the Golden Sword? Do you prize it so little?" Chayin snapped, accusing. "I have seen the results upon Estri of what you did in aniet. I have seen she who must stand for us all upon her knees, helpless by your machinations. Would you lose us our only chance to win?"

Hael's face regained some animation. "Even that!" the dharener exclaimed. "Even that is a puny price to pay, for what might be gained." And he looked at me defiantly, his uncertain hand quivering as he pointed at me. "Nemar lies upon the line, because of her. She is accursed by Tar-Kesa! You dally with your doom, Chayin! And all of us must be drawn in your wake. Blood is upon her path, and it is Nemarsi blood!" His words rode upon some chill and ghostly wind. "Any who aid her shall be by his will destroyed. I have seen it." Hael glared at me, then at Chayin.

"I too have spoken with Tar-Kesa," said Chayin, folding his arms across his chest. "What he has shown every dharener, he has shown his chosen son also. Have no fear, brother, for those messages so clear to you have not been withheld from me. About the M'ksakkans, He has instructed me. And about this woman also. His will be done!" And he held out his hand, palm upward, to Hael.

"The mind-tool"—and his voice was silk-sheathed steel—"give it to me." And, as Hael hesitated: "Surely you do not doubt His will as it is manifest through His son?" And Hael handed the tas-wrapped helsar to Chayin, who hefted it in his palm.

"Now, go, and see you to the Nemarchan and your dharener's duties. But I warn you, stay your hand from my affairs, and your mouth also." And Chayin turned his back to his brother and knelt once more at his saddlepack, helsar in hand.

Hael stared, unbelieving, for a moment at Chayin. Then he wheeled and strode through the flaps and out into the night. But the promise his eyes had made mine in those last moments was unmistakable.

I went and laced the flaps, that they not rattle and snap in the rising wind. When I turned from this, I saw Chayin stripping off his gear. When that was done, he went and extinguished one of the oil lamps and sat himself upon the cushions in the semidark.

I went to him and laid my head in his lap. He stroked my hair, and we spent a time in silence.

"It is true, you know," I confessed, "what he said about me. The race that fathered Tar-Kesa spawned me also, and this world's future lies in contest between us." And admitting it, my voice sounded hopeless even to my own ears.

"I do not believe in curses. I have lived every torture conceivable; every curse ever spoken has been laid upon me. I was by chaos sired, and out of fear's belly did I come. The accursed knows his siblings, and you are not one. Long before I met you, Terror consumed me and made the leavings Her agent." He tossed the helsar into my lap, like some worthless bauble. "How could I fear you?" His voice softened. "When I am with you, my own curse comes less often upon me; should I fear that which alleviates my pain?"

"That is no conscious skill of mine, but a hereditary gift that eases you. You are soothed by the calm within the crux that surrounds me. But it is my primal self that hests the time and has all my life done so. You have even said this to me. I try now to control it; make the hesting a conscious skill, before the power turns back upon me. I must do so. I hold in my mind that which I wish; hesting. But I have not the dexterity to sort and correct and hest all at once. So I am in effect blind until my will comes to be. I may not win, Chayin, nor can I see past my choosing, or determine what will come if I fail."

"And can this mind-tool help you?"

"Perhaps. And if not, the ending will be quicker. It is premature, but Hael has left me no choice. I will need your help."

"Anything."

"I need safety for my body while I am away from it. Three days, at least. While I am gone, will you watch over what remains?"

"Can it wait until we are upon Mount Opir?"

"If you can keep the thing from Hael, and safe, it could wait that long. But it is a tool from the school of another race, the helsar, and you should not handle it, nor should I until I can give it my full attention." I could feel it calling.

"I will secrete it where it will be safe until we ride for Mount Opir, and then return it to you."

"Do so," I said, and gave it to him, and he rose in the dim light and went to the middle stanchion and fussed awhile about its base. When he returned and lay beside me, he was empty-handed. And we began what by rights should have taken more than an enth, but was ended before being barely begun by a braying of Chayin's name outside the laced flaps.

He groaned and cursed and wrapped his breech around him before ripping out the laces to admit Jaheil, cahndor of Dordassa.

I made no move from among the cushions, thinking that Jaheil would speak his piece and depart, and we could return to what concerned us, but at Jaheil's first words I knew such would not be the case.

"The M'ksakkan ship has arrived," he announced, walking past Chayin and across the apprei, to throw himself down beside me upon the cushions.

"I importune!" He leered at me. "Forgive me, tiask."

"I do not find your choice of moments at all amusing," I said to him, "but I will excuse you this once, if you will promise not to repeat your error." And I rose to my knees and began searching about for my clothing.

"Have you done your part with Itophe and Coseve?" Chayin inquired as he pulled his sword belt and the breech I was missing from under a mat. He threw me the breech, which Jaheil intercepted and handed to me with a flourish.

"It is just done, but I would wager you have not had time for Menetph."

Chayin smiled and latched his cloak at his throat.

"You are truly godlike in your omniscience, Jaheil. I have not seen Aknet. I go now to do so. Delay them for me, with some clever stratagem, until I join you."

Chayin stood awaiting me. I grabbed up the Shaper's cloak.

"They would not start without the two of you," Jaheil remarked.

"They will start without one of us for certain," said Chayin, holding the flap that I might pass out before him.

He hurried me through the waning dark along the aisles of appreis, until we stood before an imposing circle of them, each bearing the device of Menetph. Through these to the one encircled we passed, and before the flaps Chayin called Aknet out to meet him.

After an interval the flaps were unlaced, and a

large man stood backlit before us, cloaked and fully armed. Aknet aniet Beshost was black as a northern harth, in middle years, powerful, and girthy, with a layer of fat laid deceptively over his strength.

"What has the son of Inekte to say to me?" he demanded in a growl.

"I would discuss with you some things in private," said Chayin. "Such things as are not spoken of between appreis."

"Such things as need a witness?" The older cahndor demanded.

"Such things as might." And Chayin's voice was icy.

With a curt motion the Menetpher waved us within. He followed. The apprei was night tones—darks of red and purple and blue, all ashadow.

A man raised his head from among the cushions.

"I, too, have a witness," Aknet said. The man stood and busied himself dressing.

I felt the tension between them, and though I knew of their rivalry, I did not understand.

"I had not thought you this courageous, to come to me after what has occurred. But I would have sought you out after I had had the satisfaction of once again laying claim to the Golden Sword."

"I, too, had thought to wait," Chayin replied. Neither made any move to seat himself, and both men communed with their sword hilts. "But the M'ksakkan ship is here. Gainsay their aid, and we shall both walk out of this."

"You know I am already committed. If I were not, I would even so take up this offering of the lands of Nemar. I have long wished to retreat before the summer's heat."

Then I understood.

"And I before the winter's chill. Upon my life I wager you." And Chayin's voice was eager and joyous.

"The chald of Menetph against the chald of Nemar, all descendants and claimants waived, the one survivor possessing all. Witnessess have heard it." Aknet laughed, drawing his blade.

With Aknet's first lunge, I saw Celendra in him. He attacked fiercely, trying to drive Chayin back before him, but Chayin would not be driven back. He gave no ground, and his riposte of Aknet's stroke sent sparks flying. I found myself hunched down near the other witness, Chayin's back to me. He feinted, and Aknet followed through and left his right side open, but Chayin could not connect. They were perhaps too equal a match, and their blades snicked through the air, blurred with speed. Around the middle stanchion. Aknet pushed Chayin, but he could not pierce the younger man's defense. Aknet battered the harder; I could hear his stentorian breathing. Chayin is no lightweight man, but next to Aknet he seemed of lesser stature, and my mouth was dry and foul as I watched them. Aknet's blade took hairs from Chayin's head, and in his follow-through Chayin finally slashed him. Doubly surprised at his sword's failure to connect and Chayin's quick attack, the cahndor stumbled. I caught a close glimpse of Aknet's face, contorted in blood lust, for he staggered close to me, and he wore no sneer any longer, for he knew then, and that knowledge further stayed him as Chayin's blade arced and rose, and killed him before he could even parry the blow. While Aknet was still upon his knees did Chayin strike the head cleanly from his body, and it rolled, to stop against my knee. I saw those eyes, and I was sick upon the cushions, and even upon the head of Aknet aniet Beshost, former cahndor of Menetph.

There was a score of jiasks crowding into the apprei, though I had not seen them gather.

Chayin reached down to the headless corpse and cut the chald from it with his blade. He wrapped the reigning chald of Menetph around his fist and turned to the jiasks, frozen in horror and uncertainty at the grisly scene.

"Greet your new cahndor, men of Menetph! And

go from here and spread the word. Aknet wagered me Menetph, and I will collect my debt."

"It is true," stated the male witness, and I added my own affirmation.

"Clear the way," Chayin demanded, and the men opened a path through their midst. Chayin held out his hand to me, and I ran to take it. It was the hand around which he had wound the chald of Aknet. I expected any moment to feel a blade between my shoulders as we walked among the Menetphers, but such did not occur.

"This is one chald," he whispered in my ear as we passed the last staring men of Menetph, "that I have long been willing to bear." And he nibbled my ear as we passed out of that area and toward the food vendors' awnings.

"You could not possibly want to eat!" I objected.

"Just a drink to celebrate." He was happier than I had ever seen him. By the time we stood among the vendors, I had spotted the M'ksakkan ship, not a small hover but a great golden friysou's wing of a craft, glinting in the first rays of the rising sun. It sat upon the track, near the threx pavilions.

Chayin purchased some kifra, and I was glad for it to wipe the taste of my sickness from my mouth. When I was done, he tilted the bladder back and drank prodigiously, emptying the bladder and tossing it to the ground. He slapped me on the rump.

"Let us be off to greet the M'ksakkans," he suggested, pulling me by the hand at a half-run. He seemed much younger, then, flushed with victory, and sure of himself.

"That is no small show of power, that ship," I remarked to him as we threaded through the thickening crowd that browsed among the threx fitters' stands. "I have beheld such in Port Astrin. See you that golden network? I have seen pictures of such craft in deep space, with sails unfurled, and that network abillow with the winds between worlds. They seldom land them, though such a ship may drift like a hover upon gravitic lines of force."

"Shall we take it and sail the seas of space?" Chayin suggested.

I shuddered. "Leave me the ground under my feet, cahndor."

"It was just a thought." We reached the track's edge. Chayin stopped and took from his belt a uris pouch and partook of it. I did likewise. Upon the track were three knots of men, at varying distances from the M'ksakkan ship.

"Put upon you the tiask's mask, and show the medallion you wear," Chayin ordered.

I did as he bid me, lifting the golden uritheria from between my breasts so that it rested on the leather breastband, and securing the tiask's mask about my head. The uris blew a coldness about my eyes, and my jaws ached already from the excitement it heaped upon my frayed central nervous system.

"How do I look?" I asked him, feeling stiff and restrained by the mask.

"Like a respectable tiask, albeit a small and unusually soft one," he said.

As we approached the first knot of men, they spread into a line before us. The M'ksakkan crew members were uniformed in black and brown, and were pale and slight. They stood spread-legged and uneasy as we approached them. As sentries, they were less than formidable, but the small oblongs of star steel each carried more than made up for their physical deficiencies. They did not make way for us.

"Show cause, that you may pass," said a golden-haired man no taller than I, in clumsy Parset from tight lips, his hand upon his weapon.

Chayin threw back his cloak and extended his arms, that all might see the marks of his godhood upon him. The blond M'ksakkan waved his men back, and we passed through without comment, toward the groups gathered before the ship in the new day's light. As I watched, one figure detached itself and hurried toward us, and two walked at a more leisurely pace behind the first, their forms red-limned in the dawn.

"You slitsa!" howled Jaheil, pounding Chayin upon the back so that he staggered. "Convincing, indeed, is the cahndor of Nemar! What will you do with Menetph? Will you take up the sea, now that you have a port city? Coseve and Itophe are understandably unnerved, positioned so precariously in the middle." He lowered his voice for this last. "I have reassured them, but you yourself must speak of your plans." And it was obvious that Jaheil himself was unsettled, and felt the need also of some reassurance, for Dordassa lies conjunct the southern boundaries of Nemar, and would be first struck if Chayin's intent was one of continued expansion.

"Have you fear of me, Jaheil? I thought us better acquainted. I will set a regent in Menetph, later. Now we must divest ourselves of these intruders." He waved his hand toward the alien ship, his eyes narrowed in concentration as he awaited the two remaining cahndors of the Parset Lands.

When the green-clad cahndor of Coseve and his companion in the gray of Itophe were before us, Chayin repeated what he had said to Jaheil. The tension in the yellow eyes of Omas of Coseve was not noticeably eased, nor was the stiff carriage of the light-skinned Locaer of Itophe relaxed by Chayin's reassurance.

"Speak, then, for all of us, Chayin," said the flame-haired cahndor of Itophe. "For we bow to your will in this affair."

"No, Locaer. Each must speak for his own. I can only adjure you to reject the alien's offer. Neither Menetph nor Dordassa nor Nemar will treat with the star men, for reasons Jaheil has made clear to you. It is your choice, each of you."

"And if we should choose to avail ourselves of the M'ksakkan weaponry and aid them in return? What

will you do?" demanded Omas of Coseve, biting his
dark full lips with his teeth.

"If you take up the star weapons," reasoned
Chayin, "you might be able to withstand the attack
that would fall upon you from the north and south."

"The dhareners are greatly agitated. They may
not let you keep Menetph. They are saying it is too
much power for one man, and they like not the seeds
of empire you sow," added Locaer, his hands at his
sword belt, nervous, ever-moving.

"Let them try to divest me of it," Chayin growled,
baring his teeth. And at that moment the keening of
the Menetpher death wail came to us upon the wind,
which blew ever stronger, and from somewhere in the
Menetphers' appreis a gong tolled the years of Aknet's
life. Sand stung my naked arms, and dust whorls
danced upon the track's raked surface.

The cahndors regarded each other for a time in
silence. Chayin was the first to break it, with a word
to me, and we walked ahead of the three cahndors,
straight to the five dhareners and past them with only
a curt nod to Hael and his companions, resplendent in
their diverse Day-Keepers' formal wear, to stop before
three in the black-and-gold knit coveralls of M'ksakkan Liaisons. I could feel Hael's eyes upon my back.

The faces of the M'ksakkans bore the same
shadow that had been upon the faces of the cahndors,
and upon those Day-Keepers who stood to our right.
News had doubtless reached them.

I heard Jaheil, Omas, and Locaer come up behind
us. The Liaisons waited, as custom dictated, for
Chayin to speak. He did not, immediately, but scrutinized them so thoroughly that one turned a reddish
color and the other two could find no comfortable
place to rest either eyes or hands. Jaheil, behind me,
cleared his throat. The dhareners soundlessly closed
around us. When I thought my eardrums would burst
from the quiet, Chayin gave them imperious greeting.

"You stand before me," he allowed.

"It is our honor to do so," said the tallest of the

three, whose hair and skin were the same shade of tan. Not only did he speak flawless Parset, but he neatly avoided direct obeisance without giving offense. I felt Chayin stiffen. He rested his right hand upon his hip and spat deliberately close to the M'ksakkan's shiny black boot. The M'ksakkan took no notice.

"I am M'kai, Liaison Fourth to Yardum-Or," he introduced himself. "This is the Liaison of Liaisons, who has traveled the seas between the stars to meet with you. Har-sai M'Erris, the cahndor of Nemar, Chayin rendi Inekte." The blond man indicated put out a freckled hand, which Chayin did not meet with his.

"And of Menetph, am I also cahndor," said Chayin. M'Erris let his hand fall to his side.

"And may I introduce your couch-mate?" asked the Liaison Fourth, to smooth things over. Chayin had the chald of Menetph in his hands, and he played with it deliberately.

"You might if she were here. This is Estri, Tiask-chan of Nemar, and temporary regent of Menetph." The insult was not lost upon the Liaison Fourth. The M'ksakkan's face grew pale, and he raked his hand through his hair.

"Cahndor, tiask, this is Fer-En M'Ras, who would be Liaison between my people and yours." The man nodded cautiously to Chayin, not willing to risk his hand. He had a harth beak of a nose, and his eyes were mere slits upon either side of it.

"I doubt that such a position will be established. Perhaps you were premature to fill it," Chayin said.

The Liaison Fourth looked like a man forced to choose between two equally torturous deaths.

"Perhaps I could speak with you and your regent alone?"

"Perhaps," Chayin said.

Rapidly M'Kai introduced the two off-worlders to the remaining cahndors, then invited us to follow him up the steel ramp into the M'ksakkan ship. We entered the small cubical chamber, and the Liaison

Fourth waved a tan hand over a red glowing light. The steel door slid soundlessly shut, cutting us off from the outside. My stomach rose and fell as the M'ksakkan punched out his destination and the lift shot upward. Lights chased each other across the control panel, steadied, and the door slid aside. We emerged into a round room the walls of which were viewers filled with Frullo jer. I saw the three small springs that watered the jer, the appreis spread like tiny yris-tera pieces upon the ground far below.

Chayin paid no attention, though he was surely less familiar with M'ksakkan technology than I. He sat himself down upon the floor, ignoring the Aquastan contour lounges, and motioned to the Liaison Fourth to seat himself opposite. The tanned man did so, with obvious unease. Friends never sit opposite in the Parset Lands. I did not sit, but leaned against the wall at Chayin's side, trying to control my feelings in this M'ksakkan place.

"Would you refresh yourself, Cahndor?" queried M'Kai.

"No. Speak that which you would to me." Chayin gave the M'ksakkan no title.

"We have but moments before the others arrive. I beg you to consider our proposals. Your people could reap a great benefit."

"Are you born of woman or test tube?" Chayin asked, and the M'ksakkan flinched.

"Of woman," he answered. "Your point is well taken. Most of the benefits have been in the past for the Federate group, but we would change this and give you that which would make life easier for you: great ships to sail the skies, wonders of distant worlds, and the capacity to visit them." These things he offered Chayin were specifically forbidden by the agreement made between the Day-Keepers and the M'ksakkans at first contact. No weapons were to be brought upon Silistra for Silistran sale, and no vehicles of any kind were to be upon the planet except for the Liaisons' use. Not even off-world tourists could ride hovers through our air.

"What need have I for these things?" Chayin demanded. "I have no hurry. How long did your mother live?"

The M'ksakkan sighed. "She is still living. She is seven hundred and forty M'ksakkan years old. My grandmother, test-tube born, lives still also. And my great-grandmother died of natural causes at age ninety-seven, before Silistra was brought into Federate Group. We acknowledge our debt to you. But there are a great many more worlds that have not yet had the serums, where men still die after a handful of years. We would spread your fame and your generosity upon these worlds, give the gift of life to those who have not yet received it."

"For one with such altruistic motives, you have proceeded in a very unseemly fashion. Do you deny that you aided Menetph against Nemar?"

"No, I do not deny it. It was not my decision, nor would I have approved it if I had known. The Liaison of Liaisons was precipitous in his actions. He knows little of—" And the steel doors opened to admit the two M'ksakkans and the three remaining cahndors, who looked about them with unconcealed amazement. Jaheil, staring out the view wall, backed into a pedestaled Torth sculpture and cursed loudly as it fell and shattered upon the star-steel floor. The Fourth was up to soothe him, and soon had them seated upon the lounges all in a circle. Then he came back to us and in a whisper begged Chayin to join them.

This the cahndor was willing to do, and I followed his lead, perching myself on the edge of one of the recurved chairs, which gave it much consternation as it tried to form to me. The harder I tried to maintain my edge seat, the more the lounge lurched and rolled in an effort to enfold my backside. I battled it for a few moments and then stood up again. Chayin reached out to me and set me on his lap, wordless. The Liaison of Liaisons was speaking.

Har-sai M'Erris spoke eloquently and at length to the cahndors of responsibility to galactic society and the recompense the M'ksakkans would offer for access to an additional three shiploads of serums per Silistran year. He intimated to us that if we would but allow them to do the cultivation and refinement themselves upon Silistra (and in the process teach them how), that even greater rewards would be ours. He spoke of galactic commerce, planetary gains; how anxious the Federate Group was to welcome Silistra as full-privileged among them. I watched him dig himself deeper and deeper into a pit of his own prejudices. The Liaison Fourth's expression became more hopeless the longer the M'ksakkan leader spoke.

The M'ksakkan seated himself. Omas, most interested of the cahndors, looked truly troubled. The Fourth asked us to voice our questions, hesitantly and with obvious trepidation.

I could not resist. They did not know me.

"What could you give me, that I do not already possess, M'Erris? I have weapons enough and time upon my side. In my hundredth year I had sufficient wealth gathered around me to feel secure. I need not one more bauble or pelt, and I want no machines about me. Can you give me peace of mind? Can you give me the enlightenment I seek? Can you free me from my body's bondage, from my mind's quandary? It seems to me we seek different ends. If you must, bury yourselves in your profits and losses. The desert is not in need of an additional million grains of sand." I could feel Chayin chuckling.

"We could turn the Parset Lands into a garden, fertile and green. We could fill the dead sea and make rivers run again where only dry beds now stand," said M'Erris of M'ksakka. Omas and Locaer murmured to each other. Jaheil looked openly toward Chayin, who shook his head and motioned me up off his lap. When I had done this, he stood and went to the view wall that overlooked the northwest. He stared out at Opir and the shining that was the Opirian Sea, and I knew he weighed that temptation against what he knew was right. Nemar, green and fertile. Is that what they had offered Aknet? To sail ships again in the Parset sea, as our ancestors had done centuries ago. It was a danne dream, nothing Chayin had ever conceived as possible. Faced with it, he took his time, and I could feel the veil coming over him, as he sought the sort. Eventually he turned and leaned against the view screen. It seemed that he rested there upon thin air, with his fingers wound in the chald of Menetph. Abruptly he threw it to me.

"If this were done," he said in a slow and troubled voice, "there would be no more Silistran serums, for only in this climate upon the sands do the plants grow, and the insects fly, and the animals which complete the chain flourish." His eyes saw other than the room around him. "Think you, brothers, of dorkat and apth, of friysou and wirragaet, and all who thrive upon the sands. And another thing." He faced M'Erris. "It is no harm to us if the serums be lost, nor to those of you who have had them, for as you know, once the adjustment is made, it becomes hereditary. But why would the M'ksakkans destroy what they say they want? There is less than truth here, or some twisting of it I fail to comprehend."

The Liaison Fourth rose and walked to where I leaned against a counter with an inset computer terminal. He punched up a drink, and a panel slid aside that he might obtain it. He looked at me above the rim of the glass. I realized my own thirst and joined him there. The board was similar to that in my former couch-mate M'Lennin's keep, and I punched up two jeris. The Fourth raised an eyebrow but said nothing. I took the two glasses and returned to Chayin's side, handing him one. He sipped it cautiously.

"These changes would take time, Cahndor," explained M'Erris, accepting a green M'ksakkan drink from the Fourth, "enough time so that the animal and plant life might adjust, and your people also, to a new and better life."

"You dare to speak to me of time?" said Chayin incredulously. "What is the time now?"

M'Erris consulted his wrist chronometer, and gave Chayin answer in M'ksakkan reckoning.

"Time is more than numbers upon a chronometer's face, off-worlder! And what you propose has the smell of the abyss about it. A wise man precipitates no action born of another's conception, and what you propose is beyond mine. My answer is no!" And he seated himself once again upon the lounge. "I do not trust you. I believe you could do this thing, and I do not think it should be done." He sipped the jeri.

"I beg you reconsider," said the Liaison Fourth. "Perhaps at a later date we could meet again?" He spread his hands wide.

"In a hundred years, then," said Chayin, unsmiling, "approach me. If between now and then I have changed my mind, we will supply you with the three shiploads, retroactive to this date."

"Could you produce so much?" wondered M'Erris, greed tempering his disappointment.

"Dordassa alone could produce that amount," boasted Jaheil, "were there ever the need."

Chayin leaned toward me and whispered in my ear. "Can you work the lift controls?" I allowed that I could. Chayin stood.

"Consider this, brothers," he interrupted Omas' query as to the life span of a M'ksakkan hover. "If such a craft were desirable, we could simply go down into aniet and make our own!" His voice was harsh. "And such cowards' weapons also are extant there. Take up star weapons, and I might be tempted to make such a journey."

M'Erris' head whipped around sharply. His gaze followed us to the lift entry, eyes widening as I keyed the door open.

"And lastly," said Chayin, his anger no longer hidden, "I bring to your attention the purpose of our gathering here upon the lands of Nemar! I, for one, am most interested in the Golden Sword. I have threx to work, and a race to win. I want this craft off my track within the enth. Keep you in mind, off-worlders, that if men walk the land of Nemar uninvited, they find themselves crells in our service. That hospitality I will extend to you also. Within the enth, begone from here!" And he backed into the lift. I followed, and the door slid shut behind me. I punched up the ground hatch, and the lift obeyed me, disgorging us onto the ramp and into the wind-yellowed morning, where the dhareners still huddled in the shelter of the ship's bulk.

Chayin ignored them and strode so fast across the track that I jogged to keep up. The wind whipped around us, and I wished I had a Parset membrane to protect my eyes from the grit and dust.

I heard pounding feet behind us as we reached the line of M'ksakkan guards, and Hael and another dharener joined us, puffing in their undignified haste.

"Chayin, what happened?" Hael demanded.

"I told them to approach me at a later date," he said, not slowing his pace. The second dharener's face was striped laterally with blue and green lightning bolts, and he wore his tight-curled hair in two great swirls about either ear.

"You must meet with us, about the Menetph situation," Hael demanded.

"I meet with my rugs and mats. I am in need of sleep. Set me a dozen guards, that I may rest undisturbed. If the wind dies before dark, wake me. The temporary regent of Menetph will rest with me. I will come to you when I seek conversation."

"There is much consternation among us," said the Menetph dharener. "Surely your sleep could be postponed for a little while." His eyes were red, and I thought it not from the dust. Aknet had been much loved among his people. We were among the threx fitters' stalls, all curtained now against the gale.

Chayin sighed and rubbed his neck as he strode through the almost deserted aisle "I bow to your need," he said. "Give me until mid-meal. Have with you at that time suitable viands for four. Then will your regent and I speak with you. Now, leave us!"

"But—"

And Chayin stopped still in his tracks and glared at Hael and the objecting Menetpher.

"Do my will, Menetpher, exactly and without question! I am not Aknet. If you would live to keep another day, you had best get your self from my sight!"

Hael put his arm upon the Menetpher's shoulder and turned him away, wordless. Chayin stood watching until they disappeared among the appreis. He spat upon the ground and squinted into the yellow-green sky.

"If this wind does not let up, it bodes ill for the race," he muttered. I put my hand on his arm.

"It will. We have another day before first first," I reassured him as he pulled me into the shelter of his arm and we made our way through the food vendors' stalls to the Nemarsi appreis.

V. The Golden Sword

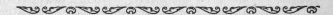

The wind had not let up by mid-meal, when Hael and Dyis, the Menetpher, awoke us from too little sleep with a host of clumsy crells and a meal that would have fed thrice our number. The apprei growled like distant thunder with the whipping wind upon it, and the sand riding those hot gusts out of the south hissed its way into the apprei with their entrance, and my ears rang with the gale's constant keening.

"Even the air weeps for Aknet." Dyis voiced my own thoughts as he sat himself upon my right and shrugged off his cloak. The last of the crells departed, and Hael laced the flaps against the yellow dusk at midday. Truly, the very sky seemed to mourn Aknet's passing.

"Has the M'ksakkan ship departed?" Chayin demanded. He did not sit up, but still leaned naked upon his side, his body curled around mine, so that my buttocks were against his belly. Hael lit a second oil lamp and sat beside Dyis.

"As you instructed them, they left within the

enth. Even now the obstacles are being built upon the track. All will be in readiness. If the wind lets up, we can work the threx tonight. Moonlight is better than this yellow dark."

Hael reached out and filled a bowl for Chayin, and one for himself. The Menetpher did the same for me. And we ate in cold silence, though the day was more than warm.

Chayin licked his fingers and refilled his bowl. None seemed willing to speak first.

"You want to tell me, I suspect, that I cannot have a female regent in Menetph." Hael started to speak, but Chayin raised his hand. "Let us save what time we may. My appointment of Estri as regent was qualified by the word 'temporary.'" We had discussed this before we slept, and I knew what Chayin wanted of me.

"I have no interest in Menetph," I agreed.

"I am pleased to hear it," said Hael, "for we would not allow such an unprecedented regency."

"You had better close your mouth before a stray wirragaet lands in it, brother, and hear what I have to say, else you may once again regret the looseness of your tongue."

Dyis shifted uncomfortably.

"It is my intent," Chayin continued, "to put Liuma as regent-in-trust to Menetph, her holding it for the son she bears in her womb. And it would not be unfitting, under the circumstances, if her favorite dharener accompanied her there. I am willing to abide a Menetpher Day-Keeper in Nemar, that we may more quickly unify the two lands."

And indeed Hael's mouth fell open, and the dharener of Menetph examined the nails of his right hand. Ready to threaten and argue, they were unprepared for Chayin's proposal.

"What say you to this? Perhaps it is not a woman in Menetph which displeases you, but only the identity of her who sits in that place of power." And he leaned back, amusement tugging at the corners of his mouth. He had, in effect, given Menetph to' his brother, to do with as he might choose.

"I . . . I am overwhelmed," said Hael, with more honesty than I had thought in him. "We would not have asked so much of you. For Liuma, and for myself, I accept, if Dyis agrees." He looked at the Menetpher, who spread his fingers wide and steepled them before his face. The tattoos upon his cheeks seemed to glow in the lamplight.

"We must get the other dharener's approval, of course. This is one contingency for which we were not prepared," he admitted. "I would be agreeable to such a move, in the name of peace."

"In the name of peace, then, get you from my sight and arrange what you will. If this is not acceptable to you, perhaps I will have new dhareners to whom I might later make the same proposal, after I have united all the Parset Lands under the device of Nemar," Chayin said softly.

"You leave us little choice, brother."

"Such was my intention. Go and persuade whom you must. I will hear no more on this subject until after the race. Hael, send Liuma to me, and someone clean up this clutter!"

And without another word, Hael and Dyis departed, leaving me with the feeling that the thing had been too easily done.

"Think you that you are truly rid of him so easily?" I asked him. "Is that confrontation you sorted now obviated?"

"It is too early to tell, for the probability I seek to make real was not a strong one, while that which I intend to avoid would have surely occurred. Is Menetph enough for them? I cannot tell. But for the meanwhile, Hael is diverted. We will see what we shall see, when you and I go to Opir. If his lust is not sufficiently sated, we will know it then." He laced the last flap and came to sit beside me.

"It is the hand of Tar-Kesa in this I fear," I said,

laying my head in his lap. "Hael may be distracted, but such a one as his master is not so easily fooled."

"Sometimes I think you have a touch of forereader's disease, Estri. Can you not hest your will? Bring into being some other way, if what I chose does not please you."

"If one bends natural laws excessively, the pressure of the mass of distortion can make it impossible to even move within the sort. I would not create more disturbance until I have taken the helsar's teaching. Should I bring an alternate future into time now, I open myself to those stronger at such skills than I. You be my eyes and ears this little while longer, and I will repay you later in kind."

"When all this is over, and your blindness leaves you, you must teach me this hesting," he said, while his hand wound in the chain around my neck. "At this moment you may begin making reparations for the further inconvenience you will undoubtedly cause me. Divested as you are of all rank and privilege"—and he tightened his grip upon the golden chain, drawing me up against his chest—"you are helpless before me." He growled, his teeth and tongue upon my neck.

"Helpless," I agreed, "and without hope of rescue."

"Utterly without hope," he affirmed, pushing me down upon the mat, where I attempted to begin discharging my obligations. I found it suitable at that time to recollect certain of my Well-Keepress' skills, and was still at my remembrances upon Chayin's prostrate form when a cacophony of angry voices reached us from without the apprei.

"This is absurd," I whispered, and rested my head upon his muscle-taut belly, looking into his face.

"Let us ignore this disturbance," he commanded, his hand twisting in my hair. I could feel the pulse of him against my cheek.

"It is your couch-mate, certainly," I gasped when he let go his grasp for a moment.

"She will wait this short time longer." And his

tone brooked no argument, nor did his eagerness need more than the touch of my tongue to bear fruit, nor was my own body hesitant to take what pleasure the moment afforded.

"I promise you," he said, hunting up his breech among the mats, "that before we leave Frullo jer we will get you properly couched," and he pulled my hair and went and once again unlaced the flaps. I did not bother to do more than roll upon my belly to watch, the uritheria medallion cool and hard between my breasts.

In she swept, all swathed in the sheerest emerald web-cloth edged with tiny gold beads that jingled against one another as she moved. Black eyes painted with sun tones were all that was visible of her face, but her belly was exposed and wound around with golden links, and in her navel rested a shiny gold nugget the size of a well token. She threw herself into Chayin's astonished arms in full view of the crells and guards who clustered around the apprei. I got up and laced the flaps.

The Nemarchan wept copiously, her face pressed to Chayin's chest. He stroked her multiplaited black hair, from which the emerald cloth had fallen. His eyes met mine, and he rolled his upward. I was not amused. I sat back among the mats in the apprei's darkest corner before Liuma regained her self-control and raised her perfect face, somehow unmarked by tears, from his shoulder. I had to admit she was beautiful, with her delicate, almost miniature features and those huge evening eyes set aslant in her head.

She sank down before Chayin and put her head to his feet.

"Please, Chay, please do not send me away," came her muffled voice, soft but distinct from beneath the hundred plaits of her hair. "Whatever you feel for me, you would not slay your son." By this time Chayin was on his knees beside her, his arms about her shoulders, trying to raise her up. This the Nemarchan allowed, and now her face shone wet with tears.

"He is your son! No matter what you think! If you were not so ill"—she smiled bravely, reached out her hand to touch his mouth with a trembling finger—"you would know it. The child is yours. I am yours. Do not send us away." And she again collapsed against him where he knelt beside her.

"I thought it what you wanted, Liuma," he said, stroking her head helplessly. "It matters not to me whose the child is. It is enough that Nemar has an official heir. And Menetph, too." His voice was all confusion. "This is no banishment, but a chance for you to rule your own life and do that which you choose." He grasped her by the shoulders and held her at arm's length, and I turned my head to the apprei wall and wished desperately that I were elsewhere.

"It has been long since there was more than politeness between us, Liuma. I am overwhelmed by this sudden show of devotion." His words were strong, but his voice betrayed him. He coughed. "I cannot change this arrangement. I have given my word. Surely Hael did not send you here to refuse it."

"No. He cannot see what lies before his face. I know what you are doing!" Furiously she wrenched her shoulders from his grasp. "I saw. You and the northern woman! I will not die the death you have in mind for me! I will not!" And she got to her feet, and her midnight eyes flashed. "The uritheria and the hulion, upon the plain before a place of rainbow towers! And the opening sky, and you and Hael! I saw it all! Even the vengeance He will wreak upon us all for your defiance! By all you hold sacred, Chayin, keep me and our child at your side. It is our only hope!"

Chayin rubbed his shoulder with his hand and got slowly to his feet. He stared down at her, and finally he shook his head slowly from side to side.

"You did see, Liuma. I had not thought you possessed that much skill." And the confusion was gone from out of him. "But you only saw the beginning, or you would not ask me to do that which cannot be done. You must be in Menetph. I must be where I must be. The child will survive."

"And Hael? And I? Even yourself, do you know that? Oh, please, forgive me!"

"Only that the child will live. That is the only assurance I have to give." He spread his hands and dropped them at his side. "You were as much a part of the forming of this future as I. There is only that which will come to pass. There is no forgiveness or blame, no amnesty or safety, except what one's own self can provide. Go now! This quaking before owkahen does not become you!"

And I saw the stunned disbelief in her face as he escorted her to the apprei's entrance and beyond into the small knot of crells and guards that still waited there in the abrasive whining wind. It snapped the open flaps with a sound like the strike of a huija, and sand devils danced upon the mats and dust darkened the air. I paid it no mind, but lay watching as Chayin stood with Liuma leaning against him in the haze, and the crells who had been awaiting this moment entered the apprei to clean away the remains of our meal. In the process, one of them, a female, tripped in the flickering dust-hazed lamplight and sprawled among the cushions, showering me with crumbs and bones and dregs of kifra. I cursed her and leaped to my feet and kicked out at her as she knelt among the garbage, sending her sprawling, prostrate in the mess she had made.

By the time I had collected my temper, the crell had still not moved, but cowered, head pressed to the mat, buttocks in the air before me. Shame coursed hot through me, and I bade her clean up and get herself from my sight. I turned away and went to stand in the apprei's doorway. Chayin still attended the Nemarchan, oblivious to the wind. The crells sidled by me with whispered excuses on their lips, eyes downcast. Chayin turned from Liuma, and two of the guards escorted her into the yellow ambience. The last crell, the clumsy one, had just finished her reparations when Chayin crossed the apprei's threshold. She went down upon her knees to him. He waved her up impatiently.

"Get you up and out of here, crell," he dismissed her, holding the flap, which writhed and snapped with a life of its own. "It is thick as sucksand out there," he said to me. But I had seen Khemi's face as she rose and hurried out, and Chayin struggled with the flaps against the insistent wind.

I watched with folded arms as he jerked tight the knot and stalked around the apprei. He was as light as a M'ksakkan, all covered with the yellow dust. He threw himself down upon the mats and stared at the apprei's undulating walls. Liuma had done her work well, and the veil was heavy upon him. After a time, I went to him, but he did not see me. I raised his head and slid my legs under. I ventured into his pain that I might lead him out of it, and there I met that probability of which Liuma had spoken, and it was nothing spawned of mortal conception. Uritheria blazed and writhed its anger against some great midnight beast for which a hulion might have been microscopic model, and that thing answered with breath of ice, and their roaring ripped apart the firmament, exposing the grids of nonspace apulse. There I found Chayin, he frozen with horror at what he would do, and it was all I could do to bring him back with me, against the current, as time-space poured through that hole the beasts had made in their death struggle, and plain and towers crumbled around us as we fled.

He reached up and put his hand on my neck, and I bent and kissed him. His face shone with sweat.

"How does one know," he asked me softly, "which among them all is the right way? Who should die, and who should live? So many ways, and no criteria with which to choose between them." He turned his head against my belly.

"I do not know," I replied. "But I too seek that answer. If there ever was some future in which all received benefit and none became sacrifice, it is no longer. With power comes powerful burden."

"And yet, one cannot refuse to choose, else we be but pawn in some other's choosing."

"Which might be worse than our own. I know too well." I laughed bitterly. "It is a road upon which there is no turning back, for it forms before us as it dissolves behind. Layer upon layer of relevance, floating on a sea of chance, which recognizes only change. My father once told me that there is no value but the value one chooses, that which we manifest through our conception."

"It was my conception that Liuma would take joy in that which I did." He raised himself up upon one elbow, looking into my face. "Have I unknowing consigned her to her death?"

"Did you see it so?"

"Not hers. Hael's or my own, but not hers. Was I blinded by what I would not accept?"

"Chayin, she plays with you. She saw what you saw and made a guess at what guilts could be pulled therefrom. Even if a woman no longer loves a man, she wants no other to have him. She thought to turn your illness against you, and with wily skill, for she is an accomplished forereader. If there is one thing I know, it is such manipulation. She would not stay her hand from Menetph. She merely wants you as well as Hael under her spell, that she might rule through you both."

"How could it be my child in her?"

"You will have to ask her that," I said.

"I did so. She says it is my son she bears, and even Tar-Kesa will confirm her. But I have hardly touched her this last year."

"God or man, it is still sperm and egg. What did you expect her to say? That it is the dharener's child she carries, and thus lose herself all she will gain by being mother to the heir of Menetph and Nemar? In the north we have ways of determining these things. Send her north and find out, if you will."

"She would not do that," he said positively.

"Exactly. She would not loose her hold upon you. Nor would she endanger her life by holding strong to thoughts of death. She has no forereader's disease."

He reached up and pulled me down beside him. "Jealous she-apth!" he accused.

"Doubtless," I admitted. "But remember: for what is between us, there is no solution." And I twisted in his grasp so that my back was to him.

"One can do no better than one expects. When I said that, the veil was heavy upon me." His body was of a sudden like stone against mine.

And I was sorry that I had said it, and tried to turn back to face him, but his arms held me like a vise and I could not.

"Lie still," he ordered, "or sleep by yourself." And I did as he bade me, and sleep took us our separate ways.

He woke me a time later for a savage and word-less couching, and when I sank back into dreams, they were so troubled I could not bear them. I lay long enths staring wide-eyed at the apprei walls. Long I thought upon the dreams' meanings, and of what I had seen in Chayin's mind, and since such things could not come to pass, I called them allegory and mind mischief to ease myself. I could not believe it, even then.

When we awoke, the wind had stopped, but only when he shook my shoulder did I realize it, for the hel-sar, growing ever stronger, had lured me from my stance between sleep and waking with its whispered songs. I sat up cold and trembling, and he mistook my confusion for displeasure, apologizing for what had passed between us. I leaned against him and said nothing.

One of the oil lamps had gone out while we rested. He filled and lit it, and opened the flaps. Two guards stood revealed at their watch against a still and starry night. Dust lay like golden snow upon the appreis and the aisles between them under the full but waning moon. We had slept the day away.

The two guards were quick to attend him. He motioned one in, and the man stood nervous between the flaps, his eyes flitting everywhere that they might not rest upon me. I stretched luxuriously and busied myself with my sleep-tangled hair.

"Speak, man. What holds your tongue?" demanded Chayin.

The guard sighed and shuffled his dusty feet.

"Cahndor, Wiraal has arrived from Nemar North and begs audience."

"How long ago?"

"At first dark, when the wind had just stopped." The guard wet his lips. "The dharener has been here and left word that he has seen to the threx, and the cahndor should not trouble himself. Jaheil of Dordassa has been here thrice and left invitation for you both to join him in his apprei at your convenience." He cleared his throat. "And the dharener and high chalder of Menetph have come twice here. And"—he seemed to search for a word—"your couch-mate also left her greeting."

"No doubt. Is that all?"

"No, Cahndor," he said hesitantly. "All nine of the tiaskchans came here together, and they would see you with certain complaints they aired to me but which it would not be my place to repeat. And the threx masters sent a message that at sun's rising all who ride must be weighed and weighted, and the threx master of Menetph begs consultation before that time."

"And is there any more?"

"No, Cahndor."

"Send a man to fetch us food, and rana if any can be found." The guard nodded and turned to go.

"I am not yet finished." Chayin's voice snapped him around. "I will see Wiraal as soon as you can get him here. Have the chalder and dharener of Menetph, and Hael also, meet me at the threx masters' pavilion

an enth before sun's rising. The Menetpher threx master wants to know who shall ride in Aknet's place. Tell
him the choice be his. And repeat this to him exactly.
I want no call of unfair play. If he can beat Nemar, let
him do so. It is not men but threx we race here on the
morrow. And one more message, to the tiaskchans,
that their complaints have been noted, and only I am
qualified to adjudge the solution."

"But you do not—"

"Know what their complaints are? Your cahndor
is a god, man! The tiaskchan Estri's conduct at my
service is no business of theirs."

"You want me to tell them that, Cahndor?" The
man was horrified.

"Send someone against whom you have a grudge
to do it," Chayin advised. "Now, begone before my
hunger makes me irritable."

The guard backed out of the apprei, and then began much shouting and pounding of feet as he delegated the tasks that Chayin had set him.

"What about Jaheil?" I asked as we dressed.

"I think we will accept his invitation." He peered
through the open flaps at the stars, he dug out his
uris pouch and handed it to me. I wondered, as the
taste of it sent a thrill through my body, how I ever
did without it. Thus emboldened, I hested my hair
clean and tangleless, not caring that Chayin saw me or
that the helsar shifted where it lay.

Chayin raised an eyebrow. I grinned at him. "I
have no comb here," I explained.

"I will buy you one, lest you usurp my godhead
from me with such tricks."

"That is all it is," I assured him, "simply a trick of
polarity."

"You had best save some for Sereth the Ebvrasea.
I had a dream of dire portents." And he finished pulling on his boot and leaned close, taking me in his
arms.

"I have no fear with you to protect me," I told
him.

"I have told you that I am bound by his will in this matter, and before his wrath I cannot stand for you. Before Hael I can protect you, or Liuma, or even all the tiaskchans of Nemar, but not to Sereth will I raise my hand. It is not that I would not, but that I cannot." He grasped me by the shoulders and held me at arm's length, as I had seen him hold Liuma.

"I understand," I said, though I did not, and a great commotion presaged the entrance in quick succession of Wiraal and our meal, and as we ate, the jiaskcahn gave his report. Nothing had been overlooked. He had even brought the crell Aje, as I had instructed him to do if his wounds were healed. They filled three places fallen empty in the cahndor's personal yra of twenty-one jiasks that would follow Chayin to Mount Opir, and the three of us searched for a way to circumvent with a likely story the tiaskchans' displeasure at being excluded.

"I do not think it will work," commented Wiraal.

"It had better. I cannot take tiasks among northern men, lest they kill each other instead of the enemy."

"Then tell them that," Wiraal proposed, rubbing his jaw with his gnarled hand.

"You tell them. I have not the time or the inclination to bother with them."

"They are not pleased at our conduct; they sent some representatives here with complaints," I interjected.

Wiraal looked at me out of icy eyes. "None of us are easy about you, tiask." I rose and got the bitless headstall Chayin had given me, and walked out into the night.

"Wait," said Chayin, and joined me outside.

"I am going to try this upon Guanden," I said, shaking his restraining hand from my arm. "I will see you when you are finished with the dharener and the chalder and the threx masters and your ill-mannered subordinates."

"I must send two men with you, then," he in-

sisted, and snapped his fingers at two of the score that
waited about the apprei to do his will.

With the jiasks to protect me, I had no trouble
among the aisles, or even upon the track, for they sad-
dled their own mounts and accompanied me as I
walked Guanden around the course, that he might
sniff the obstacles newly built there. The bitless headstall proved successful; he even carried his head
lower, and it took just the slightest pressure of the single braided rein upon his nose to make him obey. I
worked him longer than needful, even chancing a full
nera's run, and found busywork upon my gear until
sun's rising, when I turned him to the threx masters'
yellow pavilion, the restless and tight-mouthed jiasks
following dispiritedly behind. They had had other
plans for this time.

"And I did not blame them. The polyrhythmic
thrum of dhrouma and kapura players mixed with
voices raised in song, and the jer fairly seethed with
life. Hundreds had arrived during the night, and festival was upon them with the dawn of Amarsa first
first.

It was slow going through the pedestrians, many
drunk and reeling, to the threx masters' pavilion. I dismounted and led Guanden, whose ears were flat to
his head above rolling eyes. Within the pavilion were
scales upon which we were both weighed. Guanden
was taken from me by a threxman to be tested for
health and pronounced free of drugs or devices.

I drew third slot from the inside, out of fifteen
positions, between a tiask of Dordassa, who had second, and a spare rangy Menetpher, who had fourth.
Then we were each called up and received a flat racing pad with pockets for deadweight in them. Mine
was heavily loaded, for I was lightest weight among
the riders. Chayin lounged against the huge pavilion's
far wall, Jaheil beside him.

When Guanden was returned to me, I set the racing saddle, which weighed almost as much as I with
stra rods in its pockets, upon his back and went to

receive waiver from the high threx master that I might use the bitless headstall. When that was done, I relinquished him into the care of the threxmen and found my way across the threx-crowded pavilion to Chayin and Jaheil, my two guards close behind me. I could not even get near my mount again until second section was called and I and the fourteen other riders went to see which five would race the final section.

"What number did you get?" Chayin demanded, as I sidled through the jiasks to join him. My guards stood uncertain with their mounts in hand, watching.

"Dismiss them," I begged him. Chayin did so. "Three in the second section," I answered.

"And I am seventh in the first," the cahndor told me. "And Jaheil, with Dordassar luck, has first in the first. You should have no trouble with the elimination; all your competition runs first section."

"Except Menetph, which has three mounts in my group," I reminded him. "And I have almost my own weight in stra to carry."

"I told you to eat a bigger meal." Chayin grinned. A gong sounded loud in my ears.

"First call," Jaheil chortled. "Give me a kiss for luck," he demanded, and I did so, and Chayin also did I wish well, and then ran through the crowd into the new day to find a place near the ta-nera pole, that I might see the winner pass it. I squeezed my way between two men in plain leathers, who had upon their breast armor no device, but each wore around his waist a scarlet sash, and I knew them to be some who attended as guests of Nemar.

My stomach was an aching knot, and my throat was dry, but I knew my nerves. My indisposition would pass when I sat upon Guanden's back.

Another gong's stroke ushered the threx out of the pavilion, and they formed up into a ragged line of snorting frothing excitement. Facing left upon the track, they waited the huija crack that would start them. I was so close to Jaheil's red mount that I could see the sweat break out upon his flanks. Chayin, down the line, sat Saer with the calmness of a man ready to jog around his holdings, and the dappled threx stood with ears flicking and head held low, as if he were in his stall in Nemar North.

For one moment, each of the beasts faced front, and all was in readiness; the threx master gave the signal, lest the opportunity be lost. So close upon the huija's crack did the beasts spring forward that the sound was lost in the thunder of their start.

By the time the dust settled so that I could see, they had passed over the tyla-palm break at the first turn and were close upon the ditch at the sa-nera pole. I jumped up and down to peek over the heads of those before me, and the plain-leathered man upon my right picked me up bodily and sat me upon his broad shoulders. I yelped and pounded upon his helmet when I saw Saer's dappled form fly over the ditch with Jaheil's red mount close behind. A pure white beast with the Meneteph black-and-amber hooding his head did not fare so well, but misjudged his leap and floundered, to be pummeled by a dun whose saddle pad proclaimed him of Coseve.

Then they were at the half, and a black began to move among the bunched threx.

A deafening roar rose around me as the black began to move upon the leaders. The white threx who had gone down at the ditch had not risen. Gaen were hurried onto the track to drag him from it before the second lap. The dun threx who had crashed into him was limping slowly toward the inner field, his rider beside him. Two out.

The black threx, whose pad was of Nemar, had closed upon the leaders as they entered the stone chutes set diagonally across the track. Two grays of Coseve followed them into it, and when the leaders reemerged, the grays were close upon them. With enviable skill the Coseve riders had paced their beasts at the perfect speed for the chutes, exploding from them with a burst of speed that brought their muzzles to the tails of the leaders, still collected up from the chutes' narrow confines.

I saw Chayin throw his mount sideways as the grays flanked him. Then they were packed tight at the ca-nera pole and straining toward us, Chayin's Saer on the inside, one gray pocketed behind him by his mate on the outside, and Jaheil's red behind. The black threx, who I now saw was Quiris, came up to match Saer, blocking the Cosevers' path again. And while Chayin and Hael held the grays in check, they slowed their own mounts. Jaheil, as if expecting this, had dropped back and out, loosing his red in a great burst of speed upon a clear track. Past me Jaheil sped, and again over the tyla-break and into the second lap, while the grays were still held entrapped between Quiris and Saer and the tight field closing behind them.

Then, as if of one mind, Hael and Chayin loosed both Saer and Quiris after Jaheil, while the unobstructed grays of Coseve matched them stride for stride, not a nostril's difference between them as they took the tyla-break four abreast.

Jaheil had the half, and started slowing then for the chutes. He could have walked him through them, such a lead did the Dordassar have upon the rest.

I saw Saer snap out at the gray, who seemed to bump him, and Chayin's hand raised from his mount's neck, and the two of them fell back, while Hael and the second gray matched each other, less than a threx-width between them over the ditch. The moment they landed upon the far side, Jaheil passed before me in a red blur, and the volume of the shouting doubled as Parsets screamed themselves voiceless.

The man whose shoulders I rode reached to lift me down, and when I was on the ground, Hael passed before me, a quarter-length behind the first Coseve gray, and at that one's tail was Chayin, and the other Coseve gray a half-length to the rear.

I was still struggling through milling, close-packed Parsets when the gong rang for second section.

In my haste I jostled a man queued up to collect his bet, and coins went flying. He cursed me as I ran. I laughed.

Into the yellow pavilion I stumbled, just as a roar behind me signaled the brief presentation of golden knives finished. I would not have time to congratulate the first-section winners.

Down the rows of restless threx I hurried, until I reached the line of second-section threx in order before track entry.

I smiled at the man who held him. Guanden snapped at me nervously. He was already damp and trembling. He had done this before, and the crowds were nothing new to him. He was ready and anxious for what he knew awaited us. I checked my saddle girth, every strap and buckle, and his feet one at a time, though I knew it had already been done. I made a mental note to shave his bristles, which flopped bead-heavy around him. I took off my cloak and handed it to my threxman, and donned the tiask's mask of plain leather, that I might have some protection for my face against flying dirt and stones.

The gong chimed, and I took the leg up the threxman offered me. Then it was just Guanden and I, and what we would do this day. I took up the braided circle of rein and stood once in the saddle, then settled myself, my knees tight against his ribs, prominent through the padded web of the racing pad. The rana-brown rear of the second-place threx, ridden by the Dordassar tiask, moved before me, and I took Guanden out onto the track.

When his feet touched it, he stopped, his nose raised up to the sky, turning his head to and fro, questing. He shivered, and in answer to the pressure of my knees danced to his place between the brown and the golden mount of the Menetpher who was fourth.

Not one moment could I keep his four feet upon the ground. He walked upon his hind legs, he screamed his high-pitched challenge to the others, kicking and snapping. The golden Menetpher threx answered him, and for a moment the two of them stood together upon the air, teeth flashing. I wrapped length after length of rein round my fists, until his head was pressed to his chest. I saw the Menetpher strike his beast viciously between the ears, and the golden threx came down heavily upon his four feet, head between his knees. The Menetpher grinned at me, where I still struggled with Guanden. I might have struck such a blow myself, if I had had a free hand. At last I got him, for one instant, upon four legs and facing straight ahead, and the attentive threx master's huija cracked out loud in the stillness.

Guanden's first leap near to pulled my arms from my sockets. I loosed two loops of rein and let him go. I could do little else. He was oblivious of me. I crouched down, my head upon his neck. The ground sped by my tearing eyes. The golden Menetpher threx was the only one I could see before me. His rider headed him into the tyla-break at an alarming speed. I fought with Guanden for control, that I might aid him at the leap, but he would have none of me. He soared over the five-palm break with such a mighty thrust of his hindquarters that we landed a length beyond it, and almost upon the Menetpher's tail. Guanden screamed his challenge, and the gold threx's answer came to us on the wind. I saw the Menetpher's hand rise and fall on the beast's flanks, and he leaped away from us once more. I risked a look around and saw the Dordassar tiask and three others close behind. The ditch past the half was beneath us, and still I did my best to hold Guanden, and the harder I tried, the more he screamed and twisted, that I might release him, and he catch the beast who dared run before him. But I did not. Not until we twisted right, left, and right again in bone-jarring leaps and came out of those fiendish stone chutes did I free him. The threx knew what he was about. Not once had he broken stride in the chutes. I gave him more rein and closed my eyes, my cheek pressed to his hot, slippery neck. I barely opened them in time to see the ta-nera pole flash by. The golden threx loomed ever closer. Over the tyla-break we gained a stride, and at the ditch another. It was a two-threx race. I could no longer see the others through our dust. I gave Guanden the final two loops I held as we came again into the chutes, and threw my weight to the right as the threx changed strike-foot. Then left, and right, and as we hit open track, I smacked him with the flat of my hand upon his rump.

In vain did the golden threx's rider ask him for speed, in vain did he urge his mount to keep his lead. Guanden's shrill high voice rang once again upon the track, to be swallowed up in the stamping crowd's roar as we came abreast of the Menetpher. Nostril-to-nostril for three leaps, and in that time the Menetpher's hand flashed out, and a leather whip struck Guanden in the chest. Guanden bellowed, leaping ahead. As we passed the ta-nera pole, he was a threx length in front of the Menetpher.

It took me almost a quarter-nera to turn him. I would not call foul upon the Menetpher. He had won us the race with his unseemly gesture. I could feel Guanden's rage, as we came abreast of the Menetpher and his golden threx awaiting their reward before the threx master's yellow apprei. The brown Dordassar threx had placed third, a tan with black legs from Itophe was fourth, and another golden Menetpher beast had the fifth position.

I rode Guanden to the place of honor before the threx master, putting his tail in the face of the Menetpher threx who had been second. I stroked his neck. He was not too tired to trumpet his disdain for his rival in ear-shattering tones, nor to attempt to take a chunk of the threx master's arm as the man handed me the gold-hilted knife we had won. I accepted his congratulations, feeling cold and undeserving and alone among them. I had only done what the time demanded. I felt no triumph or joy until I saw Chayin, his face alight, with Jaheil behind him, making their way toward me through the crowd.

The threxman assigned to Guanden was at his head, stroking it, and amazingly enough, the ill-tempered beast stretched out his crested neck and closed his eyes, that the threxman might scratch the wet hide under his jowls. I dismounted, that the threxman might cool him and care for him until the final race at mid-meal, and the man handed over to me the Shaper's cloak encased in brown web-cloth that I had entrusted to him. He touched my arm and showed me the place upon Guanden's chest where blood dripped from a flesh wound. I leaned closer to examine it, and our heads met.

"I would not mention to the cahndor how this cut came to be here," he said.

"I had not intended to," I whispered back.

"Good." And his glance was conspiratorial. "Rest assured, we will take care of this matter, when the time is right." He straightened up and led Guanden into the yellow pavilion. I latched the cloak at my throat and threaded the golden knife upon my weapons belt. When I looked up, Chayin stood less than a threx length away, engaged in discreet conversation with Hael and the Menetpher dharener, while Jaheil made exaggerated faces and impolite signs behind the Day-Keepers' backs.

I threaded my way toward them through the crowd, only understanding Jaheil's gestures when a hand clapped me heavily upon the back. It was Pijaes, the tiaskchan with whom I had conversed at my enchalding, and beside her Nineth, she to whom I had given Besha's clothing. They were both maskless.

I accepted their effusive and slightly drunken congratulations, and begged my leave of them. Over Nineth's massive shoulder I saw Chayin and the dhareners fall silent, staring apprehensively in my direction.

"You are going with Chayin to Mount Opir?" Pijaes demanded, her hand upon my arm.

I admitted that I was.

"Surely with your great influence upon him, you could persuade our cahndor that a yra of tiasks would not be out of place upon this journey. It would do you much good among your sisters." And Nineth leaned her bulk toward me suggestively.

"Could you fill me a yra of volunteers who would go maskless and take up the customs of the north? What is normal practice among northern men might be cause for a death match in Nemar. It would take tiasks of great restraint and understanding to spend time among such as the Ebvrasea's renegade Slayers."

"I could do that easier than preserve peace in Nemar if such an honor is denied us," Nineth sniffed.

"I will volunteer, and even more, guarantee ten others," said Pijaes.

"And I will find the other ten, though I cannot go myself," said Nineth. Chayin beckoned me urgently from behind their backs. "Many will be anxious to follow her who was victorious at Frullo jer."

"I have not won it yet," I reminded her. "But if Pijaes will truly go, and be responsible for the tiasks' conduct, and promise me that no blood will be shed other than at the cahndor's order, I will arrange it." And at this they were satisfied, and let me by them to Chayin, who took me into his arms and swung me off the ground.

"What passed with them?" he whispered urgently as he held me close.

"We will have a yra of tiasks with us upon Mount Opir, with Pijaes at their head," I answered him as he put me on my feet once more. "I could do no different."

He stepped back from me. "I think you have overstepped your authority." His face was stern and his tone far from loving.

"They are your tiasks." I would have said more, but Jaheil stepped between us and crushed me against him. When I thought I would die of his congratulations, he released me. I felt gingerly of my ribs, lest some might be broken from his ferocity. Hael and Dyis stood by Chayin, and each wore the other's chald.

"Why the drawn face?" Hael asked me. "If you are so conditioned to struggle that you cannot experience victory when it manifests, in time it will cease to visit you."

"Are you now dharener of Menetph?"

"Your eyes do not deceive you," he said, fingering the strange chald of Menetph at his waist.

"Then save your counsel for Menetphers," I advised him. I turned to Dyis.

"What is the time, dharener?" I asked him.

He raised his hands, palm upward toward me. "Put me not in the middle between you, tiask."

"I asked you what you see."

"I have studied the yris-tera throw for this time," he admitted. "I am not objective."

"Talking to one is talking to any. They are interchangeable," Chayin growled.

The Menetpher-now-Nemarsi dharener grinned, and the green-and-blue lightning bolts tattooed upon his cheeks wriggled.

"What has you in such a foul mood, Chayin?" I asked him.

He stared at me coldly, then took my arm and led me away from the others to the corner of the threx masters' yellow pavilion. There he let go of me, and his hands toyed in the doubled chald he wore. I heard the gong for the third section chime.

"I must spend some time with Liuma," he said to me. "There is much to do before this evening. We leave for Mount Opir at sun's rising. The jiasks . . . and tiasks"—and he shook his head—"will stay an extra day here. The Ebvrasea's emissaries are among us. You and I will go ahead with them. Wiraal knows the way and will be in overall charge." He leaned back against a stanchion and rubbed that place where his neck met his shoulder. "Make sure your tiasks understand this.

"You would be advised," he continued, "to keep your mask upon you until you stand before Sereth, and to conduct yourself as much like a tiask as you can manage until that time."

"What would you have me do while you are busy with Liuma?" I asked softly.

"Whatever you choose." A great roar signaled the end of the third-section race.

"I choose to do your will." I wondered who had won.

"Why did you have that crell brought here?"

"Aje? I had thought to take him north with us and free him."

"Free him now, then. A tiask couching the cahndor of Nemar and Menetph should have no need of a male crell." The membrane flicking across his eyes belied his calm. "I have arranged for you to spend the night in Jaheil's apprei. I want you safe under his protection."

"And who will protect me from Jaheil?"

He shrugged. "Do as I bid you. And another thing. Speak to no one you do not know!"

"I will have to speak a number of times to those I do not know in order to get Aje suitably prepared to take up his freedom. I would not turn him out threxless, weaponless, or without proper provisions."

"Jaheil will accompany you." And he started back toward the others.

"Have you no special strategy for the race?" I asked him, hurrying to keep up.

"None that involves you." And he knew that I knew what he and Hael had done. "I would not discuss such matters, were I you," he warned me as we came upon Jaheil and Dyis, Nemar's new dharener.

So it came to be that Jaheil was with me when I went and bought, upon the credit that the uritheria medallion gave me, a good young red threx for Aje, and an assemblage of plain but well-crafted weapons, such functional trail clothing as one can get for an other without knowing size, and enough provisions for the trail to Stra.

We went then, loaded threx in hand, to the pit where all the Parset crells were kept together.

The crellkeep was a long time finding him, and Jaheil gloated nonstop about his triumph and pulled intermittently upon a kifra bladder he had with him. He was giving me the history in great detail of the Tycel son, Tycet, the golden threx who had been second to Guanden, when the crellkeep returned with Aje.

"Take those chains from him! I left instructions that he not be bound." Aje's confusion was mirrored in the crellkeep's face as he freed the crell's wrists.

"It is your business what you do with him in your apprei, tiask," the crellkeep muttered, "but I cannot have unbound crells in the pits."

"I will not be bringing him back," I said. The crellkeep looked at me askance.

"Come here, Lalen of Stra," I said gently, and he came and stood beside me, eyes upon his feet in good crell fashion. I touched his shoulder, where the huija had left great toothmarks upon him. Even the brown salve of the south had not been sufficient to repair, scarless, Besha's work.

"Look at me," I suggested. He did so, pale eyes devoid of understanding. "You are free. This threx is for you, and what is upon her also, and this." I held out in my hand a pouch. He did not move to take it. I shook it so the coins jangled. I took his hand and put the pouch in it. He looked from his open palm to me.

"You will have to buy your own boots." I grinned at him.

And slowly his face lit up, and he too smiled uncertainly, as if remembering some skill long forgotten. I went to him then and put my arms around him, for I knew he would not dare such a thing. Jaheil snorted and muttered, and I saw the lingering crellkeep's scandalized face.

Then I stepped back from him. "I could not get your chald."

"It does not matter," he said. His eyes were upon the red threx.

"Do you like her?" I asked, and I pulled from my belt the red sash I had purchased. I was sure that Chayin would not mind if I stretched his permission into protection.

"Lalen of Stra"—I laughed—"do you like her?"

"I love her," he said wonderingly, running his hands down the threx's legs.

"Wear this," I suggested, handing him the sash. "It is good as a chald here, though why I should worry about the son of Satemit is beyond me."

"You knew, then?" he asked, incredulous.

"I have been much among Slayers. The exploits of the Third of Stra, your father, are not unfamiliar to me, nor did those hands ever play instrument other than steel and gol."

"I would not want him to know what ignominy I have brought upon his name," said Lalen gaesh Satemit.

"I know," I said. And I did know. "What will you do?" I asked him.

"I have no idea." Jaheil glowered at us, arms crossed over his mighty chest, from where he stood a threx length away from the crellkeep.

"You will not return to Stra?"

"I cannot, chaldless." He sorted through the weapons in the saddlepack.

"There are two here, who wear the red sash, with whom you might wish to strike up an acquaintance. They are from the camp of the Ebvrasea. I have heard that one of the primary requirements for entry into that camp is a chaldless waist, and the other is a skill level the like of which is possessed by only one in a hundred Slayers," I said thoughtfully to him while he dressed and armed himself from the things Jaheil and I had bought. When he stood up at last, dressed Parset except for his bare legs, his stance was very straight and his eyes met mine unwavering.

"Perhaps I shall search them out," he allowed, and mounted the red threx, who danced beneath him.

"Tasa," he said to me, stroking her neck.

"Tasa," I replied, and turned away to Jaheil lest he see the unaccountable tears that filled my eyes.

Jaheil left the crellkeep, and his face was twisted as if he had eaten something sour as he looked at me.

"Let us get some food before it is too late." He squinted into the yellow-tinged sky and pushed me ungently toward the food vendors.

"If you were my tiask, I would beat you until you were blue from head to foot for such behavior. And before a crellkeep yet." His voice was gruff. "Have you no shame? Or even if you do not, how can you so demean Chayin's attentions?" he demanded.

And instead of answering him, I pressed myself against him there in the middle of the aisle, and with my masked face against his great chest, let the tears I could not stay flow until I could cry no more. And Jaheil stood there helpless and stroked my back in the way of men before a woman's despair, muttering senseless words of comfort about the safety of Lalen of Stra, though it was Chayin who had brought the tears upon me.

When I was relieved of tension, and the pain was no more than a dull ache within me, I stood back from him, glad for the mask that hid my face from view, and we walked slowly through the aisles to the food vendors, where Jaheil saw to it that I ate and drank. Though he queried me about my pain, I had no answer for him, nor for Chayin and what lay between us. And though I closed my mind as best I could to it, the helsar twisted and turned within Chayin's apprei as Liuma worked her wiles upon him.

When I could, I bade Jaheil go and rescue him from her, lest the veil fall so heavy upon him he could not ride. He went, though I could see in his face he believed me not.

While he was gone, Nineth and Pijaes came and sat with me. I told them what Chayin had said, and cautioned them again as to their deportment. The sun neared its zenith, and Jaheil and Chayin did not appear. Pijaes and Nineth still went maskless. After some delicate inquiries into the success they had had finding couch-mates, during which time I saw Lalen of Stra pass by with the two helmeted, red-sashed northeners, it became clear to me that Nineth had long nursed a desire to spend a night in the arms of the cahndor of Dordassa.

I allowed as how I could introduce them, and since I was to spend the night in Jaheil's apprei, that Nineth might consider visiting me there. She was at first scandalized, then intrigued by what she called my northern strategies. I wondered aloud that she did not simply approach him. She answered me that she could not speak first to a cahndor. To this I replied that in my experience I had found the couching urge oblivious of such niceties as rank and protocol. She smiled and lowered her eyes demurely, an expression almost ludicrous upon one so powerfully framed as she. The gong for the final section rang out, and I begged my leave and hurried to find Guanden.

Under the yellow pavilion I found not only my mount, but Chayin and Jaheil as well, standing over Hael, who knelt, holding Quiris' left front hoof in his hands.

"I will not chance it," Hael said decisively, rising. I peered at the hoof and saw what disturbed the dharener—a hairline crack running vertically a finger's length up Quiris' mid-hoof. The threx bit at his leg fretfully, holding it off the ground. Hael jerked his head up, lest he injure himself further, and led him away.

Chayin looked at me, his eyes distant and brooding. "After the race, attend me," he ordered. As the threx master came around with a deep bowl and we each drew our numbers, I wondered what I had done to further displease him. I drew fifth, Chayin third,

Jaheil eighth. The threx master blared the lineup at top voice, and the threxmen shuffled their charges into order. The golden Menetpher threx, Tycet, had first position.

I was glad to get upon Guanden's back and away from the strained silence. I tried to call it the pre-race tension, but I knew better. Thus we rode out onto the track without any well-wishing between us, and Guanden caught my mood and turned it into a blessing. He did not trumpet, neither did he leap about, but only snorted softly, facing front with ears atwitch, waiting in the blazing midday heat.

The crowd was deathly still, watching. The fourteenth threx, a Coseve gray, finally stood upon four feet. I took two loops of Guanden's rein. Tycet of Menetph, in first position, screamed his challenge. Guanden shivered and made reply to him. The huija cracked out, the crowd roared like an enraged hulion, and Guanden's first leap brought him upon the rump of the fourth-position black, who had broken diagonally from the start. The black went to his knees, and Guanden leaped over him. I saw the Itophe rider's anguished face pass under my stirruped foot. Before us the packed field was only a cloud of yellow dust. I gave Guanden all the rein I had, and two smart slaps upon his rump. We caught the field just beyond the tyla-break, spread even across the track. There was no way through them, no hole big enough for Guanden between those straining haunches, and we trailed them close into the half and over the ditch.

Guanden saw the opening before I did, and he was through it, so close that my knee brushed that of a Coseve rider. Guanden snapped out at the gray and got his teeth in the other's bristled crest. The gray squealed and lunged, and his rider's angry cries faded behind us. Into the chutes we thundered, only five before us, and the pace the leaders set took its toll there. A Dordassar beast lay lifeless in the chutes just before the sharp right turning, his head twisted at an unlikely angle, his unconscious rider pinned beneath.

I barely saw this new obstruction before we were upon it, and Guanden twisted in midair like a slitsa, that he might avoid the chute wall and the corpse and make the turn.

But make it he did, and the last right twisting also, and we had four in front and a straight track before us. Guanden's froth and sweat spattered my face, his neck snaking even lower, while the wind whipped streaming tears from my eyes. We closed steadily upon the leaders. The moment stretched out distorted, each bound taking enths to complete, as if time itself thickened to obstruct us.

A gray Coseve threx came up upon my right, slowly, so slowly, though the track beneath us was blurred by our speed. Guanden shivered and snorted his anger. He leaped away from the straining beast in a snap of effort that shattered the dream sense of the time and brought the crowd's roaring loud to my ears as we gained the ta-nera pole. At the tyla-break we caught Saer and passed him in four strides, and there remained only three before us. Over the ditch we encountered Jaheil and his frothing red beast; then they were gone in Guanden's dusty wake.

I tried to rein him up for the chutes; the dead threx still lay there, and I adjudged the leaders too far ahead for us to catch, but as I did so, Tycet's victory squeal came back to us on the wind. Guanden bellowed his rage and twisted through the gut-wrenching turns so hard I hugged his neck for my life's sake. On that last short straightaway he flattened himself to the ground, and his hooves barely touched it. In my sight was only yellow dust and his straining strike-foot. Then I saw another hoof, upon a golden leg. Guanden came up on Tycet of Meneteph. And as he passed his rival, he took time to close his teeth upon that golden neck. I slapped his head away, while a scant two lengths from the ta-nera pole the Menetpher's enraged beast broke stride and pawed the air.

We were gone past the finish, and this time Guanden was easy to stop and turn, his intent being to kill the golden threx who had twice affronted him. The Menetpher beast was not averse to such an encounter, nor could his rider do more to dissuade his mount than I could mine. The field of racing threx scattered to avoid us as Guanden and Tycet engaged each other. I battered helplessly at Guanden's head, dodging Tycet's snapping teeth and metal-shod hooves as the two kill-trained threx stalked each other upon their hind feet. Men broke from the crowd and raced across the track toward us. I saw Chayin, regardless of Saer's safety, leave him riderless and jump for Guanden's head. He hung there, his hands twisted in the headstall. Guanden shook him like a rag. Then another man, and another, and finally the sheer weight of them brought the two threx squealing and snorting to the ground.

Hands reached up to help me down. I could not move; my grip was frozen upon the reins. I heard my name, and it was Chayin's voice. I let myself down into his arms and endured his examinations of my limbs. I saw the threxman whose charge Guanden was, shoving and pushing his way through the crowd around us, and the Menetpher rider, he being helped, limping, from the track by two of his brothers. Their snarling demands for clearance rang in my ears. I twisted in Chayin's grasp to go to Guanden, but he would not allow it, and the ground wriggled in and out of focus as he led me off the track and into the threx masters' body-packed pavilion.

We stood in the small cleared area with the threxmen and the Menetpher rider, who still leaned upon another for support. His thigh bore teethmarks where Guanden had torn his high boot away. There also was the green-trapped Coseve rider, who received from the threx master the fifth prize. Then Chayin left me to receive the fourth. As Jaheil stepped up for his third, the Menetpher leaned toward me, a strained grin upon his dark face. I asked after his wound, whereupon, free then to speak, he proposed that we meet later. I agreed, and he went to receive the lesser sword that was second prize. As he did so, a great howl rose up from those gathered around us, only rivaled by the deafening shouts that greeted me when I in my turn went to accept the Golden Sword from the five Parset dhareners who had the care of it.

As I took it from Hael's hands, I felt, finally, a great elation, and a warmth within me, and I took a moment to give thanks that the time had so matched my hest and need.

Then did I kiss the sword's golden-chased hilt and do what was expected of me there; I went down upon my knees before the cahndor of Nemar, who took in his own hands the sword. After putting his lips to it, he handed it over to Nemar's new dharener, in whose safekeeping it would lie until next Amarsa first first, when again the five tribes would contest for its custodianship.

From beyond the tent came a great pounding of dhrouma and kapura, and a chiming of gongs together, announcing the beginning of two days' feasting, of which the winner of the sword is traditional host. As the crowd dispersed to avail itself of Nemar's generosity at the food and drink vendors, Jaheil proclaimed his own apprei host to all the threx riders. I saw among those who still lingered Nineth and Pijaes, and also Liuma, making her way toward Chayin and Hael, who stood together apart from the rest.

This angered me. I went to Jaheil, where he stood talking with his own dharener. I informed him within Chayin's hearing that I was off to meet with the Menetpher who had been second. His lips curled in disapproval, but I cared not, for I saw over his shoulder Chayin's face, and it gave me great satisfaction.

"Before I go," I said to Jaheil, "I would introduce you to a tiask who has long admired you from a distance, but would rather suffer on an empty mat than importune."

"Where is this virtuous tiask?" Jaheil demanded, and I pointed out Nineth, who had bedecked herself all in red for the approaching festivities.

Jaheil hitched up his sword belt and licked his lips and put his arm around my shoulders in a companionable fashion.

"Let us go and meet her, then. I am sure that she will find my attentions well worth the waiting."

"Do not tell her I told you," I cautioned, "any more than that she desired to meet you." Jaheil agreed that he would never do such a boorish thing, and I introduced them, and the great tiaskchan seemed almost delicate next to Jaheil's formidable bulk. As I left them together and slipped out into the crowds, I caught a glimpse of Chayin, between Hael and Liuma, with a trapped expression upon his face.

When I was almost among the food vendors, I heard a disturbance behind me. A hand came down hard and spun me around. Chayin stood there, breathing heavily, his fingers digging into my shoulder. Upon his other arm he had draped my cloak.

"I told you to attend me after the race," he snapped. His fingers dug harder. Hot trills of pain ran down my arm. I regarded him levelly.

"You were busy. I would have seen you when your duties were less pressing."

"So you fill your time with whoever is handy? Once a saiisa, always one." The word is a demeaning term for coin girl. "Crying over a crell upon Jaheil's shoulder is not even enough for you, is it?"

"Let me go." People stared at us, some openly. "Give me my cloak." He did, his anger falling in upon itself when it found no mate in me.

"Walk with me, if you have the time," I suggested further, my mouth dry. "We will drink together with the Menetpher." I busied my trembling hands upon my cloak.

"I find myself with an early finish to my business," he conceded. And we walked side by side, without touching, through the milling crowd, searching the wounded Menetpher.

"Hael says that though triumph has attended us, its equal loss is upon the way."

"It is his hest, and not the sort, of which he speaks. He tries to bring his will into the time. I felt it on the track. He learned much from the helsar. He has Tar-Kesa behind him, and the loss he seeks is of your life and mine."

"You give him more than he has."

"Or you give him less, Chayin. I hope you are right. I wish we could leave now." I looked up at the midday sky. "I have fulfilled my part of the bargain. The rest is up to you." And I spied the Menetpher and put my hand upon the uritheria that curled around Chayin's arm.

"There!"

He nodded, and displeasure lurked at the corners of his mouth. "No more than an enth," he cautioned me.

I bowed to his will in that, and started a rather awkward conversation with the Menetpher, during which Chayin sat silent between us, arms folded.

The mask upon my face was stiff and hot, and where it lay upon my cheeks the skin burned. I clenched my fists, that I might not tear it from me and scrape away the abrasive grit beneath. But I did not, because of Chayin.

We exchanged neutral small talk in the dust-heavy heat of the midday among the throng. One skin of kifra was sufficient to wash away the jiask's discomfort before his new cahndor. Even Chayin's contentiousness was soothed, and he unbent his hauteur enough to recall certain anecdotes which he shared with the jiask, who, if he had expected a more intimate encounter with me, hid his disappointment.

Well within the enth, Chayin deftly extricated us from the Menetpher's company; thus I had no chance to impart any subtle warnings or delicate forecasts to the jiask, nor could I use my presence to protect him from the retribution I knew awaited.

Nor did I have the opportunity to further nurture what might grow between Jaheil and Nineth, for Chayin confined me to his apprei. "For my own protection," he incarcerated me there, with a score of guards set to my safekeeping, directly after we had taken leave of the Menetpher. There did I eat and drink and while away the time combing my hair with the apth-tusk comb he gave me.

I might have taken the turning that would have healed the growing rift between us then, but my emotions entrapped my tongue, and I could not. I merely took his gift from him and went to sit wordless under the oil lamp.

He came and squatted down before me.

"What are you trying to do?"

"Behave like a respectable tiask, as you have ordered me," I said. He got to his feet. The hurt I had caused him washed over me, reflected through the helsar and my own reading, along with his desire and confusion. But I did not confide in him, and he used his anger against me, another brick in the wall built between us.

When he left me there and went to his evening's duties, the veil fluttered around him. Even then I did not, as I might have, pluck it from about him with the dozen words of truth I held within me.

Once I went and unlaced the flaps to see if he had truly set a guard upon me to keep me there. Two jiasks politely refused me exit, their countenances cold as the winds of Santha.

Somewhat later I heard low angry voices, and I peered through the laces, to see Hael arguing with my keepers. Whatever the subject of debate, he did not prevail, but stalked off into the first-dark gloom. I went then and lay by the stanchion where Chayin had secreted the helsar. I curled my body around it and rolled into the open arms of sleep, to be dragged roughly from their comfort near to sun's rising by Chayin's half-drunken ravings. It seemed that what I had feared had occurred, and a number of vengeful Nemarsi had descended upon the Menetpher who had struck Guanden with the whip, and given unto him some few strokes of a similar lash. Seeing this, others entered into the brawl, and still more joined in to restrain them. Three lay dead and forty injured when the fighting was done.

Chayin's wrath knew no bounds. He shook as he told me in language I had never heard him use what had occurred. He cursed Menetph and Hael and the badly injured Menetpher, and even those who had so inconveniently died were not safe from his foul imprecations. As he denounced each faction in turn, he kicked and threw whatever came hapless into his sight. Thrice I tried to calm him, only to land upon my belly amid the cushions where he threw me. On the fourth attempt, I convinced him to sit, and then at long last to lie upon his stomach, while I rubbed the knots of anger from his back until his breathing eased, until the muscles no longer twisted under my hands, until he slept at last.

Stalking

The ebvrasea, alone, posited upon the green square of overriding purpose on the board of manifestation.

His wings beat upon the wind from the abyss.

His sharp eyes discern his prey, and they are not clouded by doubt or self-division.

The ebvrasea fills his belly without compunction. He knows not morality, for he is its embodiment.

Once initiated, stalking will not be denied.

Stalking is assiduous.

Stalking culls the weak from the strong. In both hunters and hunted does it perform this function of nature.

Stalking tests its own strength.

Stalking is both method and purpose. It realizes itself without judgment.

Stalking would not be other than it is, and therein lies the key to its success.

Adjuration: If the stalker, upon the trail of his prey, is in turn stalked, he may choose *to continue, that by feigning ignorance he who stalks the stalker might reveal himself. Survival is both the goal and prerequisite of stalking. Stalking is always ready.*

Before stalking, who can stand but those who also stalk?

—excerpted from *Ors Yris-tera*

VI. The Ebvrasea

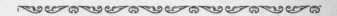

   The screeling cries of pandivvers feasting kept
time to the threx' hooves as we passed between the
last appreis set upon Frullo jer. In the ruddy glow of
sun's rising I could see them wheel and dive above us
amid clouds of wirragaets, ultimately visible as a dark
mist upon the air. The tiny insects were everywhere;
we had been long apprised of them. We breathed
them. We blinked them out of our eyes and flapped
them from under our cloaks as the threx sped across
the ever-hillier barrens toward Mount Opir in the
west.

   Had I been willing to swallow a thousand of
them, I would have asked Chayin what had brought
them out in such numbers. They died by the millions,
crushed upon us as we rode. The cloud of them was
neras across, fading only with full daylight.

   One of the plain-leathered strangers had come to
guide us. He said no word, but sat upon his brown
threx with his helmet-cap masking his face, awaiting
us. We followed him upon a circuitous route perhaps
twenty neras. The ground began to roll, and then we
were met by five of his brothers, all dressed alike in

deviceless northern-style breast armor. There was another there, and that one was Lalen gaesh Satemit.

I had expected words from Chayin upon this account, but I soon realized that he did not mark the man before him as that crell whom I had freed. I did not feel the need to enlighten him. We rode among those taciturn men without a rest or a word spoken until well past midday, over stubbly tundra and progressively more difficult terrain. Larger and larger harinder bushes clumped in breaks before us, their thorny brambles scraping tithe from our flesh as we thrust our way through them. In the later day we turned into a dry stream bed and followed it up into the foothills of Opir.

The air became noticeably cooler and blue-shadowed with the bulk of the Yaicas around us. Small needle trees grew here, and strands of stunted southern thala struggled with their chancy hold upon the slopes. Just out of a copse of almost respectable trees we came upon a small clearing where the smell of the air was suddenly so rank I found myself gagged and choking. Guanden leaped and snorted, and I suppressed a moan as I put more strain upon my battered arms and shoulders to hold him.

One of our guides urged his mount over to Chayin's. All the men held their threx with difficulty. Three were fitting arrows to strung bows that had been slung from their saddles.

"With your permission, Cahndor," said the one who seemed leader of the men, when he saw Chayin's drawn sword, "we would dispatch this apth from a safe distance."

Chayin considered this gravely, while under him Saer twitched and shivered. Even that calm-tempered and sensible beast was discomfited at the smell that reached him. The men had fanned out in a circle, their threx' rears toward Chayin, and I and the man with ready bow beside him.

"You may do what you will," said Chayin. The killing of apths is tightly regulated in the Parset

Lands; all apths belong to the cahndors, who are accountable for their use to Tar-Kesa.

I scanned the trees. I had never seen one.

There came to our ears a great cracking of branches and a guttural squealing. The apth crashed into the clearing, incredibly fast for all its enormous bulk. A red threx screamed in terror and walked backward upon its hind feet before that hairy, huge-tusked head with its short square snout and tiny red eyes. The rider of the retreating beast leaned over his mount's shoulder. His bow thunked, and the arrow penetrated a hand's length into the apth's side-set left eye. Then the other riders were upon it. It reared up on its short stubby legs, its humped neck quivering with barbed, feathered bolts. Streaming brown blood, the thing wheeled and charged leftward, that it might impale a tormentor upon those curved tusks, tossing it in the air and gouging again and again the soft underbelly of its victim with thrusts of its powerful neck.

An arrow lodged in the apth's water sack, and the crested hump deflated before my eyes. The apth, screaming, blinded by its own water, took a fatal arrow, just below those oversized jaws. It went to its knees and laid its tiny head between them. Only its tail twitched. Then that too was still, and the thing was dead.

The stench, coming from offal stuck to the huge beast's hairy coat in thick chunks and rotting gore splattered there from the death struggles of previous victims as the apth tossed them about in the air, was truly unbearable. Not even for the trophy of those man-long tusks could any stand it long enough to dig them out from their sockets. We left it there, waiting only for the men to retrieve those few arrows still unbroken that bristled in the apth's thick hide.

My stomach rumbled angrily, turned numb as my backside from the unrelenting pace, and still we climbed. Through the uncertain light of dusk and on into the dark with no stop, even to rest the laboring threx, did we assay the treacherous slopes of Mount

Opir. The air was thin and clear, and Wirur the winged hulion rose twinkling and fully visible in the sky. The just-waning moon spewed a cold and silvered light upon the trail. To my right a sheer archite face rose up, and upon my left was a sudden drop into black-shadowed crevice. We went single file. I held my breath against the wind that tugged and pulled at me and set my cloak abillow. Soon the crevice was replaced by another cliff, and we picked our way along the bottom of the chasm formed between them in pitch dark. I looked straight up at the tiny slice of visible sky, and saw only the north star Clous. Then that was gone, as we went under some natural bridge. I heard Guanden's feet splash, and realized that a stream coursed its way through the cavern. An ebvrasea screeched, and another answered. Our arrival had been announced.

We stood upon a ledge that sloped gently down into a valley limned clear in the moonlight. At its center, the stars were reflected back into the sky from the calm mirror of a mountain lake. Perhaps twenty neras around, the valley was bounded by rock upon all four sides. Mount Opir towered over the lake in her belly, glittering like a woman at feast of conception with the ice that mantled her regal head and shoulders.

As the threx assayed the twisting downward trail, I made out low, clustered shelters upon the valley floor. We did not go toward these, but took a sharp turn left, along one sheer cliff wall.

Only when we were upon them and dismounting did I notice the squared-off openings that entered into the cliff walls themselves. Old, even ancient, must be these cliff dwellings; not since before the rebuilding have we of Silistra made use of the terrible forces needed to hew those huge rectangular edifaces from solid rock. Such square and ugly architecture as this squat giantism had nothing of Parset or even gristasha culture about it.

My speculation was cut short by the appearance of two men with torches, who conversed in low tones with the leader of those who had brought us. Though I had seen no sentries, I had no doubt that the Ebvrasea's nest was near to impregnable to those uninvited. Everywhere my eyes found unscalable cliff face. The men separated, Lalen of Stra going off with two others. He made a casual gesture of farewell. One with a torch, he who had asked Chayin for permission to kill the apth, motioned us to follow.

We did this, I looking over my shoulder long enough to mark the direction in which they took Guanden and Saer.

Down a torchlit archite passage, glassy-smooth and geometric, our guide led us. The torches were set upon stands on the floor. I was later to learn that this was done because the ancient passage rock had been treated with some substance which made it impervious to hand tools. At intervals down the passage's length I saw such diverse items as fresh threx dung and long-dark power lamps, some broken, with wires hanging down from them like fossil slitsas. Also I marked upon each passage numbers and legends in pre-hide Silistran, their messages unfaded through countless years. Like ghosts they spoke to me: "Med. 1," "Surg. 2," "Power Aux.," "Master Air." I noticed at intervals upon the walls visual displays whose colored graphs still shone brightly, ever shifting. A practiced eye could, from those displays, gauge how many were in the passages, where they were located, even when and where they had entered. This answered one of my questions—why there were no signs of habitation other than human and threx. The doors were air-scanner-controlled, programmed from some central source to admit only certain life forms and attendant matter through polarized molecular barriers that must still exist in every doorway. I sniffed the air and belatedly realized it to be the clear, sterile air, temperature-regulated, of mechanical processing. I was struck with wonder that such a place yet existed, functional, above the ground; and more, that the Day-Keepers had not claimed it.

We turned down a corridor that was not archite green, but a sterile white. It said "Admin. 1–5," "Comm. Inter., Intra." As we passed by the many cubicles upon either hand, it became obvious that the Ebvrasea was using the small rooms in this area as stables. Makeshift rope barriers ran down its length, and curious threx stuck their heads over the ropes and peered at us as we hurried past.

Another turning found us again in a natural archite passage, in the center of which was a threx with three men attending her. She was hobbled, and one of the men had his arm up the beast's rectum to the shoulder. He pulled it out and peeled off the shoulder-high glove of translucent denter intestine as we approached them. I put Chayin's bulk between us, suddenly cold and trembling. Would the time match my hest?

"She has doubtless settled," the Ebvrasea assured the others. The sound of his voice dazed me helpless. If I could have spoken, I would have called his name. If I could have moved, I would have run to him. I stood frozen, behind Chayin, my tiask's mask upon me.

"Take her back," he ordered, in northern Silistran, running his hand down the threx' rump as he turned to face us. We might have stood in the halls of Arlet, so unchanged was he, in a worn tunic of leather, with just a knife slung upon a parr belt at his hips, but that no chald lay there beside it. His tanned face broke into a grin when he saw the cahndor.

"Chayin!" Sereth clasped him in his arms, and as they embraced, his gaze fell upon me. His face, more tired and lined than I recalled it, drained white, all but the scar that traced its length, which turned livid. Icy cold chased the pleasure from his dark eyes. Not even a moment had it taken him to know me, though I was bedraggled, masked, and dirty, wrapped in Estrazi's cloak.

He released Chayin, who moved uncertainly from between us.

"I—" Chayin started, but Sereth's sharp gesture cut him off.

"I appreciate that which you have done in my behalf. I would speak with her alone. Go and get settled in my quarters. We will join you." His voice was a whisper from the abyss. He jabbed a finger at our guide. "Install the cahndor, and see to his wants." The man hurried to obey. Sereth leaned against the archite wall, his arms folded over his chest, his eyes shadowed by the mass of brown hair that fell across them. I remembered the silky feel of it from another time, when he lay all covered over with dust, unconscious beneath the Falls of Santha. I did not move. I did not speak, though my mind told me to go upon my knees to him and beg forgiveness.

After a time he dropped his hands to his sides, and the chaotic rolling of events ceased to deluge me through his memory.

"Come here."

Woodenly I walked the few steps toward him and stood so close I could see his nostrils flare as he breathed. He raised his hands to my head and removed the mask from my face. His fingers touched my cheek, my eyes, and when they came upon my lips, I kissed them. Our eyes met and held.

"Have you no greeting for me after so long?" he asked softly. His arms went around me, pulling me tight to his chest. He buried his face in my hair. I wished that it was clean and sweet-smelling for him.

Then was my hest full upon me. The pattern of light and dark on his worn circlet armor, the smell of him, the feel of those arms about me, his warm moist breath against my neck—all were as I had waited so long for them to be. And owkahen—the time coming to be; I knew it not. This did not trouble me. I partook of his strength and was not afraid. Everything I had done to stand thus with him became as nothing. My paralysis left me.

I breathed his name, and the taste of it did me good. His hands ran up and down my back, tangled in my hair, confirmed the need in him for me. I closed down my sensing as best I could. He relived his pain and could not share mine. Waiting for him to come again into the land of words, I pressed against his hardness, content.

"All this time," he murmured, his lips against my ear, "I have lived Celendra's lie, though something in me knew it false. I thought, too often, that I had indeed gone mad. Though there has been much madness, I hold you—proof that such was not of my making." He brought his face down to mine, so close that his breathing was a gentle breeze upon my cheek. "Where did you go that day? Where have you been all this time? And what brings you here before me at the side of my only ally, with his sign of rank upon your breast, garbed tiask, even to the chald of Nemar upon you?"

"I had to come to you. Since my return to Silistra I have been about it. I have my own questions. If you will have me, I will stay here with you. We can take our leisure at the answers." So simply did I throw my will against my father's. Though by Estrazi's word Sereth was not for me, I disclaimed his rights upon me.

"I have nothing to offer you. Even my life is uncertain."

I touched him. "You have all that I need. Chayin said you would kill me. I came here, knowing that, preferring death at your hands to life with another," I pleaded.

Amusement tugged at the corners of his mouth, danced in its old place deep in his eyes. "I might still kill you. Women have been couched to death before." And then it left him, and his voice turned toneless. "I thought I would, should I ever have the chance." His hand traced the curve of my neck, finding there the thick gold links of the uritheria medallion and drawing them tight about my throat.

"What of Chayin? Where does he stand with you? I need his good will."

"He brought me to you and left me in your hands, thinking you would harm me. He loves you, not me."

"I know that," said Sereth darkly, releasing me. "Let us join him." He pushed me gently down the corridor.

I was content to walk beside him.

"It is good to look upon you."

"Chayin said you keep no women about you," I replied, as we entered a passage, free of torches, where the ancient ceiling lights still functioned.

He shrugged. "I have been known to belt on an appropriate chald and venture into Well Oppiri when my need is strong enough. For a while I took an occasional captive, but the quality of captives is not as high as when we first hunted them. Near the lake there are coin girls among the camp followers, for what they are worth. I developed higher tastes in Arlet than an outlaw's life can sustain." He tossed his head, shaking the hair from his eyes. He wore it longer now, almost upon his shoulders. His hand reached under my cloak, and his questing fingers found the fading ridges of scars there.

"Where did you get these?" he asked.

"I, too, have led a different life from that to which I was born. I am no longer the soft and pampered Well-Keepress you knew. I have killed two men, and a tiask thrice my size, with my own hands. This chald is no gift. I am tiaskchan of Nemar."

"I will keep in mind your fierceness," he promised. "But you cannot be tiaskchan and outlaw both."

"I will give it all up," I said airily.

"Not quite yet," he replied, turning into a corridor of some dark brown material that had actual doors spaced along its length. Before one of them he stopped, and the door slid open of its own accord. Within, Chayin started to his feet, crouching there, frozen.

"Did you . . . ? What did . . . ? No. I see you did not," said the cahndor of Nemar in faultless Silistran.

"Kill her?" Sereth laughed. "Not yet. Would I do such a thing without inviting you?" And he strode across the chamber and rummaged in a wooden chest in one corner.

I stared around me, at this strange and ghost-ridden chamber whose walls were ever changing color. The art of a long-dead age reached out to calm me. No windows broke the walls' expanse. The floor was soft as tas-suede, resilient, tiered in what seemed random sequence, except that the raised areas were different tones of that same neutral. Anachronistic against those walls stood Arletian wooden racks bristling with sword and shield and spear, helmet and armor and five-lashed stones, and even a number of large pelts. Sereth closed the wooden chest and turned to me.

Upon one loam-colored tier in the middle of the room had been dumped my saddle and Chayin's. I found myself standing over them with no memory of crossing the distance from the door. The helsar reached out to me, demanding, rolling softly. My face, shoulders, and arms slicked and flushed, as if I stood over some raging conflagration. In a way, I did. It took all my attention to back away from that blaze.

"What?" I said when I could, from where I found myself sitting upon the floor, Sereth standing over me. Behind him the light from the walls shifted softly. The ceiling was dark with a likeness of night clouds upon it. The room knew it was evening. I had no doubt that in the day one might look up and see the semblance of greening sky. Through the helsar I sensed its gladness to have within it once more eyes to rest upon its work. I pushed the room-consciousness away with a shiver. Did the ceiling count the days and nights, all those centuries when none had dwelt beneath it?

"Choose one!" Sereth repeated. "They are as exact as the best weaponsmith in Yardum-Or could make them. I have held them for this moment a long while."

"And you still say you did not know I lived?" I

wondered, taking the two parr-wrapped bundles from him.

"I did not know it," he maintained.

"The truth of that being that you know not what 'knowing' feels like." Chayin made my point for me in a wry voice as he came and knelt beside us.

I unwrapped the bundles, and laid upon the sand-toned floor two stra-hilted gol-knives. They were without ornamentation but for a small red gol-drop embedded in the butt of each hilt. I hefted them. They snuggled against one's palm, the same. They balanced in the fingers, the same. Each was perfect, eloquently simple. I recollected how he had come by those two priceless gol-drops, in the gollands above Arlet. My eyes misted unaccountably. I took one and handed back the other.

"Tomorrow we will go together to my fitter and have sheaths made," Sereth said. It is considered a bad omen to give a virgin weapon in sheath.

"First, that which is first, Sereth," I declined. "I must take the helsar's teaching. Even tomorrow might be too late, but I would spend this night with you both. It is very strong now, and I am weak. It might come to pass that I cannot shatter it." I paused, not knowing what else to say.

"What is a helsar?" Sereth asked, his eyes narrowed into slits.

"If you cannot shatter it"—Chayin touched my arm—"might you not return the way you came?"

"If I cannot, and I lie there still breathing, upon the fourth day you might do whatever comes to you to arouse me." I took Chayin's dark hand in mine, and turned my head to meet Sereth's anxious eyes.

"In these matters, take Chayin's lead. As to what the helsar is, I am not sure. The fathers know, but they are not saying. You remember the cowled one?"

"How could I forget?"

"The name of that being is Raet, and his world, upon which I found my father, is called Mi'ysten. It is a beautiful and strange place, where natural laws and time itself combine differently. The Mi'ysten have great skills, but not so great as the fathers, who created all we know as time and space. I have heard it said by Mi'ystens that the helsar is drawn into being by the disturbance one causes when first learning to move between the planes, and the attendant rubbing together of the edges of different continuums. That does not explain where the pieces go when they shatter, or why. But it would explain how I came by it. It followed me back from there, one time when I went to see Estrazi upon the wings of uris. I cannot do other than work my way through it, for in this place its very presence is a danger."

"What do you suggest we do?" Sereth said, uneasy. "I am not anxious to cross paths with this Raet again. Although some would say I have little to lose, I would retain what there is." He leaned back against the loam-colored dais, crossing his arms over his chest, slid down on his spine.

"Only what I have asked you: watch over me while I deal with it. It is my problem."

"Who is Raet?" asked Chayin.

I sighed, and shook my head. "It is a long tale. You and Sereth each hold a part of the puzzle. Compare them. I think you will find that Raet and Tar-Kesa are one."

Sereth put his hands over his ears.

"Enough! I am a simple man. I want no contest with gods!" He looked at me, his eyes imploring me to tell him I did not bring Raet's influence again upon him. I could not. There was a long silence, broken only by Chayin digging at the flooring with his knife. It remained unmarred by his attack.

"If you are afraid," I offered, in a whisper, "I will leave here, this moment."

"Were I not afraid, I would be a greater fool than I am," he said. "Now that I have you back, I am not letting you out of my sight." And he got to his feet. "I am hungry. Here on Opir, one must go to the kettle. Let us do so." He held out his hand to me.

As we walked down the hall, he questioned Chayin about what had occurred at Frullo jer, and the race results came out. Sereth was suitably impressed by my victory, and I promised to show him Guanden after we ate. Also did we relate to the Ebvrasea what had passed between Nemar and Menetph and M'ksakka. When he heard what Chayin had said to the M'ksakkans, Sereth's laughter rang through the corridors. When he related our encounter with the Menetphers upon our stolen threx, I, too, felt the humor of the situation. When finally we turned into the kettle chamber, Chayin was just describing to Sereth how he had killed Aknet and become cahndor of Menetph, in the process bilking Celendra out of her considerable heritage. Sereth collapsed onto a bench, holding his middle. Tears of laughter ran down his cheek. My own sides hurt, and I was sure my face would crack from the grin upon it.

"Oh, I would have been there to see her face," Sereth chortled.

"I would wager if you had seen it, you would also have seen M'ksakkan faces," I projected.

"You seem to have done most of that worth doing without me," Sereth objected, wiping his eyes.

"There is still Astria and Celendra," Chayin reminded him. "And, in truth, M'ksakka."

"And Estri to help us. We can reinstall her, perhaps. Would you like us to avenge you upon the killer of your uncle and usurper of your Well couch?" Sereth offered gallantly. I was glad the room was empty. As I walked over to the huge kettle bubbling on the sunken mid-room hearth, I wondered for what purpose the shallow pit had been intended.

"I think we would be acting in accord with the law within, to do such a thing."

I filled three bowls with a huge iron ladle and took them to a plank table. The walls here were dark green, and the floor paler archite. When we went to sit down, the light above us brightened perceptibly. I shivered. "But I would not be reinstalled in Astria, to await whomever Estrazi sees fit to send me. I will go, but not for Astria. That which has been lost, cannot, in this world, be regained." Only after did I realize I had quoted Carth, who was in service to the dharen. Chayin knew; his eyes sought mine.

I was surprised at what I saw there, though I should not have been. The time had come to uphold him, and reality was less painful than his preconceptions of it. He seemed released, calmly attendant upon the moment at hand. And his calm sprang from his foreknowledge, a taste of which set me back, cowering.

Sereth was relating the story of a narrow escape he had had when picking up the knives he contracted in Yardum-Or.

"If you keep roaming the cities in dead men's chalds, Sereth, one of these times you will not return," said Chayin.

"If such were not my practice, you would not be here to chide me about it," Sereth replied, something in his manner reminding me of his bearing before his men in Arlet's hostel. I felt lonely, uncomfortable. Love between men is something that excludes a woman as nothing else can. I tried to determine what had gone into the making of the brown glop in the bowl. I could not, but I would have laid money that such food had not been cooked by a woman. I regarded them from under my hair. The two of them looked like death dealers before whom Raet might rightly falter. A part of me took a great joy in that sight. It wanted no assignations, yet it did not disdain such tools. Not Estrazi's will, or Raet's, or Sereth's will would I do, henceforth, but my own. I tossed my head and made a satisfied sound. I sat a little straighter, shoulders back, breasts out.

"What?" asked Sereth, handing me a bladder he brought to table.

I saw clear and real, obscuring Sereth's face close to mine, that seven-cornered room. Not truly seven-cornered, I noticed without surprise, but with *seven*

corners. Portions of seven different rooms, coming together to share a space in the middle. Each of the gold-
glowing men stood in his own alcove; behind each was
a window, and the countryside framed there in each
window was too diverse to be any one place upon Silistra. This was Silistra: I saw a snowy peak, a glistening
lake in warm sun, rolling field, deep forest. The seven
men looked across the jumping flicker of the central
space at each other. Under the flicker a certain symbol danced, actually seven symbols in seven rooms oc-
cupying the same space-time congruently. I went to
look closer, thinking they could not see me. One
leaned forward, his eyes unsurprised. Ice. Miles deep
within, a glowing redness took note of my presence.

Then I saw Sereth. I leaned against him, not
hearing, a time before I could think. Chayin's breath
was upon my cheek, his fingers at my wrists.

"Did you see?" I asked him. His face swam before
me.

"No, but I knew what it was. I think you cannot
wait any longer. If you do not go to it, it will surely
come to you."

"You are right," I admitted, clearing the hair from
my face. I stood up. "Though I would not do it now, I
will be just as reluctant tomorrow." Sereth, his face
tight, picked up our bowls and deposited them in a
barrel of water, wordless.

"Do you have your uris pouch, Chayin?" I asked
him as we retraced our steps to Sereth's chamber.

"Do you think it wise to use it now?" he objected,
but handed it to me. I unstopped it and touched my
tongue briefly to the liquid within.

"There is no wisdom," I answered him, "only
more or less successful overlays upon what is real." I
handed Sereth the uris pouch. He shook his head in
refusal.

"Then what do you seek in the helsar, if not wisdom?" Chayin demanded as the door to Sereth's
chamber slid aside to admit us.

"Power, that I might defend myself against Raet.

Weapons, if any be there. Tricks of a new trade whose name I do not know, and whose purpose I can but dimly sense." I went and took one large brist pelt from Sereth's rack and spread it upon the floor. Then I stripped off my boot and breech and band and piled them neatly in a corner. Sereth leaned against the dais upon which the helsar rested in my saddle-pack, oblivious of it. Chayin paced back and forth the length of the chamber.

I took the Shaper's cloak and spread it over the brist pelt, that I might slide under it. Though the room was warm, it was not warm enough to chase the chills from my flesh. Where I went, flesh could not yet follow me, but must rest in icy stasis; I would need both coverings. I fussed with my makeshift couch, smoothing wrinkles and evening corners, until I could put the moment off no longer. I went and kissed Sereth where he rested against the dais. His body was stiff against me.

"Take care," he said. I smiled a smile that had no reassurance in it, and fumbled in my saddlepack with clumsy fingers for the helsar. I felt the sueded leather that bound it. It reached toward me, and I barely restrained it. By the thong I carried it, dangling, through the mist that sprang up around me to the resting place I had made. When my feet felt the cloak and pelt, I got down upon my knees and plucked at the knotted thong. I could barely see, so heavy was the fogging around me, but when the thong fell loose, I saw the helsar. It blazed blue-white, blinding, thrice its former size. The filaments spun whirling within it, pulsing. The room around me was a great blur, a prism, a prison. I felt my way between pelt and cloak, the helsar molten between my palms. My feet were shards of ice, my legs frozen stiff even as I tried to draw them against my chest for warmth. I saw Chayin's face for a moment, mouth moving, and from that mouth came curling flames of sound, unde-cipherable. Beside my head the helsar pulsed, and the rhythm drew my eyes to the filaments, and the filaments drew my spirit out from my body. I stood between them, and I was no longer cold. They were fourteen, and they spun around me. I let them go unchecked for a time. The place was all alight, and that light sang to me, a soft song. The spinning filaments hummed the harmonic. All was mist enshrouded, and I knew that mist for my sustenance, and partook of it. The molecules I breathed each had a name, nature, and awareness, and the introductions between us were lengthy. Golden became my feet, for I had feet. Striated armies of mist-chain became my arms, for I would need arms. Between my breasts a great sun flared white-hot, and filled the empty expanses of my new form with light. The strands of my hair flared out from my head and did my will upon the filaments that whirled all around me like swords flashing.

And we did battle there, standing upon nothing, in the light. A great wrenching pain from left of my head stopped the first filament, the second, the third. The fourth tore a thousand strands of my strength from me by the roots. It drove toward my heart. I caught it with my golden hands, and it charred them to flakes of ash. But I stopped it, and with my stumps I fumbled it to its place. Pain taught me its rule in the universe. I screamed and screamed, and the sounds of my mouth twisted in flames around a filament, and hardened there, imprisoning it to serve my will. I rubbed my stumps against my eyes, and I laughed, and my laughter froze the next into silence. I had another. Gloating, I turned to the next. Shocked, it retreated before my will, and I had half the arc I sought. I breathed a sigh of relief that danced before me, jester in my court.

It cavorted and rolled, diverting me before I realized it a trick, and a filament skewered me through one ear and out the other. Upon my knees—did I have them?—I began to slide. I needed no ears to hear the derisive victory chant of the filaments. I threw all my being again into the strands that stretched light-years from my head, and hung by their grip upon the conquered filaments above a pit that held such apt and personal terrors as could only have come from my own mind. Seeing this—that it was my own fear that threatened me with extinction—I assayed the journey upward. I pulled myself by stumps and teeth along the strands of my own hair: welcome pain, keeping me conscious. I climbed through walls of slitsas, writhing, through infirmity of age, upon wizened wrinkled limbs, through voidness, where my lungs imploded and I drowned without them. I discarded the form when the cold between the worlds froze my eyeballs between blinks and they fell in icy dust upon my fleshless cheeks.

Only then did I begin to see. Freed of flesh-need, I hung there, and the rhythm key to the remaining filaments, which was always within me, came to my sensing clear and strong. With it, I fashioned a framework, and another form, so vast it encompassed all that was, is, and ever will be between two atoms of its being. I raised what was not a hand, and from it created a platform. Upon that platform I stood upon no legs, and with the lightning from my non-eyes did I cause the last seven filaments to do my will. The arc around me shivered, settled, became a path.

A new form was needed, and I made one. My dozen legs carried me tireless upon the glassy surface of the path, claws clicking my three-chambered heart's complement. At my left and right, time displayed itself, scene upon scene, lifetimes flicking by me. Occasionally I turned my stalked eyes backward to follow some drama of temporal interest. But not once did I slow my pace. I would not fall into that trap. My loins burned with need, exacerbated by the rubbing of my depending sex organs against my hidmost legs as I ran. Off in the distance I saw another, whose eye stalks were a sensual fuchsia, and whose invitation trumpeted clear to me across the vermilion plain. I snorted my answer. With it, out of my mouth came the smoke and flame of my passion. But I would not stop. I came to the end of the path and did not falter, but launched myself across the yawning gulf upon the wings of need.

Down into the chasm I glided, regulating my descent easily. It was a simple matter to allow the ground to draw me. Gravity held no sway here, where conception ruled.

Awaiting me there were seven beings, whose shapes were diverse and merely an expression of choice. I altered to an upright form, with vocal cords for speaking, as is polite in that land.

"You are late coming," remarked the first, whose skin suit was a universe forming.

"How long have you been awaiting me?" I asked.

"How long ago was this moment woven into the everpresent? Since the conception of creation, when self-differentiation of One created Interchange and together they begat Time. Not long," said the second.

"What dost thou seek here?" said the third, who bore the semblance of an iridescent-winged slitsa, and crossed his six arms across his breast.

"Do you not know?" I asked, incredulous.

"He is supposed to ask," said the fourth impatiently, twittering his pale tendrils together. I cleared my throat, fascinated by the image thrown back to me from the reflective doorway that appeared behind them.

"I seek my heritage, that which has been saved for me."

The sixth gave up a sigh of satisfaction from a mouth which could have swallowed Silistra for a tidbit. "You are she. Would you settle for half?"

"Would you? I am my father's daughter."

"His skills in you are long atrophied, buried by assumptions. Audacity must be companioned by responsibility, would the Shaper's daughter shape," intoned the seventh, and he waved his hand, which was followed upon its arc by the sights of a different place.

I spent so long there that the entropy inherent in the sequentiality I instituted to absorb what I was learning wore three bodies from under me. One was destroyed while still exploring the worlds of simple sorting; that which exists in time and space regulated by reigning natural laws.

The second crumbled from under me while still about the skills of the hest; of bending and twisting natural laws to serve the will. While in that form I learned to adjoin and weave times together, and to bring into being certain chains of events without regard to inertial backlash. I should have stopped there.

But I built a third form, by far my finest, and traveled by the side of my seven teachers into the domain of creation; I learned to suspend natural law and put my own will in its place. There did I find the weapons with which I might oppose Raet. There also did I learn reverence and constraint, and the laws by which such actions are governed. But it was hard and heavy upon me, and when the third form crumbled from beneath me prematurely, I was not willing to make another. Burdens of power, shackles of freedom, did I carry out of that last place. I had reached my limits before reaching the end. It was enough, I thought.

Since I could do no more, my teachers agreed with me. That small sphere I managed, upon the outermost edges of inhabited space, spun lonely. There was no life upon it. I had shrunk back from that last task, refusing the responsibility I must bear to life of my creation. But I promised my world I would return to it.

I took leave of my teachers then, in a form close to my Silistran one, and went upon a vainglorious and precipitous journey. I searched out my father where he was resting.

I found it necessary upon my arrival there to expand my lungs and the chest cavity that surrounded them, and convert their nature. And I walked into the sea that lapped redly at a pinkish shore. And the nature of that sea did not eat the flesh from my bones, for I had changed it also.

I found my father nibbling choice vegetation from the murkish sea bottom, his great red head half-submerged in muck. He was not pleased to see me.

"Since you have learned enough to come here"—his wave-words sounded against my ears—"why have you not learned enough to know better than to do so? I come here for solitude."

"There is no respite from one's own creations," I reminded him, puffed with my new knowledge.

"Speak then," Estrazi said, sitting his considerable bulk down like some huge boulder dark upon the sea floor. Bubbles came from the corners of his mouth. I caught one as it tried to rise to the surface, and turned it into a mirror, upon which I projected that which concerned me.

He watched it solemnly, his lidless eyes unblinking. When it was done, he bent his head once again into the muck. When he raised it, his jaws dripped with brown plump weeds. He chewed a time, ruminating.

"What you showed me," he said at last, "differs quite markedly from what I had intended."

"Then stay Raet's hand from my world."

"Your world, is it?"

"I was born to it, my flesh is of its soil. I must protect that which I love."

"Do that which I desire. In time you will come to see things differently."

"No. There is no validity in self-fulfilling prophecy. I must do that which is right in my sight. You will use me against him no longer."

His mouth stopped its chewing. "How do you know that this very rebellion of yours is not my will? Have you joined with those others of like mind near you?"

"Not yet, but I will do so."

"If you survive, send me a message, and we will meet again. Now, leave me!"

And his command was such that I found myself

flung upward into the baby's cheek of that world's sky, past it, into the dark between the worlds.

Only away had Estrazi flung me. I ended there, in the darkness where potential unrealized is banked. That which does not happen goes to this place, and is reabsorbed into the ever-forming now. There, alone, growing faint, did I learn the consequences of power, and the price paid by those who seek it. There is no fixed future, the darkness whispered. There is no omniscience; nothing is sure, it said as it devoured me.

And I may never know if Estrazi realized his mistake and extracted me, or I escaped by my own power. I was almost not, when an answer crept to me and warmed me in the cold. That thing in me that would not sleep snuggled warm against it. Shatter the helsar, it suggested to me, and you have confirmed yourself in the real world. Will it here, and yourself there. That which is cannot be in two places at once. Trade with the dark. Try.

I tried. I took what self I had and set it spinning, that I might reach all directions. And the spin gave me coherence. No one had ever spun here before. No one had ever refused oblivion, even retained self long enough to conceive such an act. I was. I spun my laughter in nothing's face. And the helsar heard me. I drew it, desperate. It flared the whole of ever-dark nothing light at its entrance. I was blind in the after-glow, caught up in someone's arms like some small child.

I knew he rocked me slowly back and forth. I breathed flesh upon the air, warm moist lifesmell. I heard my heart. My legs were prickled with fire. My feet did not feel. I found my eyelids and caused them to open. It was Sereth's room I saw, but Chayin who held me. The room was night-lit. Sereth slept, his head upon his arm, his rest uneasy, nearby. Chayin rocked me softly, his chin resting upon the crown of my head. The helsar was not in my sight. My mouth was very dry.

"I am thirsty," I said to him, with enough effort

for a shout. I produced only a croak, but it was sufficient. He looked down at me, and I smiled at him.
Perhaps he thought he dreamed. He touched my face
with his hands; then he called my name and crushed
me against him. Sereth, as light a sleeper as a hulion,
was crouched there beside us. I tried to reach out a
hand to him. It fell short, but he caught it in his.

"I thirst," I tried again. My legs would not respond to me. They seemed dead. My hand in Sereth's
trembled violently.

"Get it," Sereth ordered, and Chayin, who de-
ferred to no man, laid me down upon the Shaper's
cloak and went to do Sereth's will.

I tried to maneuver my thick-furred tongue. It remained, despite my best efforts, recalcitrant and unwieldy. Sereth knelt over me. He put a finger to my
lips.

"Be silent," he said. His strong, sure hands
kneaded my legs, and I found voice enough to moan
as his ministrations brought my muscles awake.

"I know," he said, not ceasing his work. His hands
had reached my thighs. "I was once, after a severe
miscalculation, bound in one position five days. Truly,
this is the least painful way." And when I could, I
flinched from his touch.

"Good girl. Now, sit up." And I did that, too, that
I might be as brave as he thought me. I bit my lips
until I tasted my own blood, but I got my legs under
me.

Sereth grunted and sat back on his haunches. A
smile played on his lips, his eyes prowled me, returned to meet mine.

"There will be no more of this," he decreed. "I
have thought long about what to do with you. You
came here, seeking my protection, my help, perhaps
another thing from me." And he was not now smiling.
"I demand and receive unquestioning obedience from
those who follow me. If you join them, I must have
the same from you. You do not want Astria, you say.
What do you want?"

"To serve you. My life is your will. I want nothing more," I managed. I wished he had waited until I had my wits about me. I closed down my sensing, pushing away that which I would not see. If it was so short a time I would have him, then that time was all the more precious.

"If you give yourself to me, it must be fully. Your body and mind, and the skills thereof, must be mine to do with as I see fit. I cannot accept less. I do not explain to my finger why I want to scratch an itch; it is mine. I do not allow that which is mine to risk itself upon its own initiative. Under these conditions, and these alone, will I accept you. Otherwise, go back with Chayin, for he would have you upon any terms." So did Sereth crill Tyris speak to me, in his way, of love, in his coldest voice.

"I expected no different, nor could I settle for less. I am yours upon your terms, upon any terms, without question. It has been so, in my heart, a long time." It was the best I could do. I supported myself with my hands, sitting there. I wished he would touch me, hold me. He did not. He looked at me a time, pensive. Then he nodded.

"Take that off!" He meant the uritheria medallion. With some difficulty, for it was tangled in my hair, I did so. I looked at it in my lap, and my copper fingers seemed to glow and flicker as I handed it to him.

"You will renounce the chald you wear, and give back to Chayin all that he has given you." I nodded mutely. "And you will speak to no one, especially Chayin, of whatever you might have gained from the helsar." Almost, I objected. But I saw the testing in his narrowed eyes and kept silent. Let him make his arbitrary rules.

"Let us see if you can walk," he said, and lifted me to my feet, supporting me as I assayed first one step and then another. The door slid aside, and Chayin entered, a bladder slung over his shoulder. He, like Sereth, wore only brief tas breech. He hesitated in the doorway a moment, then stepped through. The panel slid shut behind him. He walked those few steps to where we stood waiting, his rana-colored skin giving some eerie cue to the room walls, which chose to mimic him, rhythm and tone.

"Here," he said, and handed the bladder to Sereth. His eyes on me were like some wounded animal's. Sereth held out the uritheria medallion. Chayin took it, expressionless, and put it around his own neck. Sereth held the bladder to my lips, and let me only wet my tongue. His arm tightened around my waist, his fingers twisted in my Nemarsi chald. Again he gave me drink, and this time my stomach seemed filled by the single swallow he allowed me.

"Did you find what you sought?" Chayin asked, as again Sereth impelled me to use my legs as best I could.

"I found the sounding board of an instrument that might someday play that music which holds the spheres in harmony. But I must learn to play it. The theory is not enough. The practice, the skill, might sometime be mine," I said.

This answer, I felt, met Sereth's conditions. My sidelong glance at his face confirmed it. He had put, however, his restrictions upon what I could say, only. About what I could do, he had said nothing. Then did I give Chayin the one gift I had for him, in such a way that my anonymity was protected; I banished his affliction from him. Sereth knew no more than that I again leaned heavily upon him. Chayin, pacing us silent on my left side, knew not what I did. But I knew. It was enough.

"The helsar disappeared, around sun's meal this day. Did you shatter it?" Chayin pressed me. I sighed, and the shifting of the time was not lost upon me. For a moment I wondered if perhaps I had come back to a different now from that I had left, but I shook the feeling away.

"I do not know," I lied, not meeting Chayin's eyes. I turned, instead, to Sereth, that he might help me. But he only took his arm from my waist. He stood, watching me, waiting, hands upon his hips. I wavered upon my feet, unaided.

And then I told Chayin, as I had agreed, that I would give back the chald I wore, even though it meant going back upon my word, and also all that he had given me.

And he seemed not at all surprised, only subdued and solemn.

"All but Guanden, I will take. If you truly do not want him, give him then to Sereth. And this"—and he crossed the room in three strides and dug in his saddlepack, returning to us with a volume bound in the green-patterned hide of slitsa.

"I must divest myself of all possessions," I objected.

"You may have the ors," Sereth said softly, "and I will take the threx in safekeeping for you." I looked at him, grateful.

I took the *Ors Yris-tera* into my hands. Then I reached up and put my arms around Chayin's powerful neck and kissed him. His answering embrace was light, restrained, his lips upon mine dry and passionless.

"There is only one thing that saddens me," he said, holding me away from him, his hands upon my shoulders. "That you hold your word—and the chald of Nemar—so cheap." Then he took his hands from me and drew his gol-knife, and before I could move, he had sliced from me the chald of Nemar. I heard the tinkle of the split links as they fell from their strands to the floor. Then he reached into his breech and threw something down beside those links. It rattled as it struck, and lay still, shimmering in the dim light. I looked down, at my feet, upon my Astrian chald.

"Take it," hissed Chayin.

It pained me that he had so misunderstood. I saw Sereth's knowing smile, oblique.

"It is mine no longer," I demurred. "It is not only the chald of Nemar I have put by me, but chaldra. It does not serve me to carry the weight of chaldra." I saw the membranes snapping, agitated, back and forth across Chayin's eyes.

"Have you no honor?" he demanded.

"Do not talk to me of honor. It is a foreign thing to me, and one too easily taken up and put down. I am a woman. I know nothing of honor. I know only survival. Honor is for men. You, a man, took what fantasies of honor I had from me!" I spat back at him.

I turned to Sereth, for he understood. My eyes implored his for help, but none was forthcoming.

"Chaldra was everything to me once, for I thought it right and just and obtaining to the law within. Now I have lost it." I stared down at it; at the Well-Keepress' strand nestled there among the others, and at the red strand—due for changing—of the chaldra of the mother. Red indeed had been the deeds done to discharge that one; both before and after. Now it would never be changed.

Sinking to the floor upon trembling knees, I reached out and touched the chald. I ran my fingers in it, this one last time.

"Get up!" Sereth ordered. I did, leaving the chald there. "We must keep those limbs moving awhile longer." He beckoned me. I went to his side. His narrowed eyes assessed my body, his supporting arms propelled me to the door. "You want to know how you lost Astria. You might simply have asked. I will tell you." His voice was hard-edged, stra-cold. "But first we will walk you to the lake and back; there you will bathe. Then we will eat." He motioned Chayin to also support me, for my muscles had taken a fit of trembling; tetanus after so long, unmoving. I wavered upon my feet.

I pressed my arms against me, crossing them over my chest, that I might stop the tremors that shook me. My palms upon my arms found the skin there dry and flaking, as if by fever. Everywhere I touched myself, that skin that had been darkened by the sun of Nemar came away, a powder, and beneath it the new skin was lighter. In some few places it glowed, hot copper in the uncertain light. I needed a bath.

"Let us go to the lake," I agreed. "But I am not hungry."

"You will eat," said Sereth, as the door slid aside and we walked, the three of us atangle, the corridors of his keep.

"If you insist, but I am not hungry."

"I need not insist. Nor explain. You will obey me, without question." And I bent my head and said nothing, for I knew that I would, in all things, defer to him.

I watched my bare feet, between theirs, pass upon the archite floor. He had left me no choice. Sereth knew me, perhaps as no other man ever knew me. I walked with great attention, conscious of my body, furious at its feeble response. As best I could, I straightened my shoulders and tightened my flanks under me, that my movements might be once again graceful and pleasing. I had not walked so in a long time, and I felt the outcry of certain muscles as I brought them into play. In Nemar, I had adopted, perhaps unconsciously, the tiask's mainly strut. Here such would not do, and Sereth, ever watchful, saw, and smiled to himself, reaching out a hand across me to touch Chayin's arm, brushing my breasts as he did so. My nipples rose to that touch. My body had not forgotten his.

"It is as I told you," said Sereth to Chayin. And Chayin looked first at me, assessing, and then across to Sereth.

"I see it, but I do not believe it. And I certainly do not understand!" We crossed into the white corridor.

"She was well-trained," said Sereth, grinning. "But you spoiled her. She lost perspective. She needed only to be reminded. If the man does not sense himself male, the female cannot sense herself female against him."

"In Nemar, it is different." Chayin pondered.

"Indeed it is." Sereth laughed. "Treat a woman like a man, and she will do her best to become one. If you want a woman, and she thinks herself a man, you must remind her." He spoke as if I was not present.

"But Liuma is not like that. She is . . ." Chayin objected, struck wordless.

"Pregnant with your child," Sereth finished his sentence for him. "Even if she were not, she is yours by law. By any man's law! Would you give up a prized threx to another because under his hand she was gentler than under your own? You would not. What difference, then, with a woman? The flat of your hand is sufficient upon a threx, and upon a woman also. I tell you, you should take her back! One does not give up what one still covets, surely, even in Nemar!"

Chayin flinched from Sereth's words. Then he looked again at me.

"It seems to be my habit," he admitted, "to give up what I most desire. I gave up Liuma, and Menetph, and this one, too. Perhaps you are right, perhaps I should take back some of what I have given.

"Looking at her, I can see that I never really had her. I did not first agree, but this"—and he touched my still-erect nipples, and ran his hand down me—"shows me your truth. I will have my choice, and my chance, soon enough, if what Wiraal and Pijaes say is true."

"The choice, and the chance, are yours alone," Sereth said.

"And what," I demanded, "do Wiraal and Pijaes say?"

Sereth and Chayin exchanged looks in silence.

"Tiasks speak first in Nemar," Chayin pointed out, grinning, though he tried not to show his mirth.

"But this is not Nemar, and she is no longer tiask," Sereth rejoined, as we turned the final corner that led out into the hidden valley that was the Ebvrasea's.

The night sky was cloud-covered. Beneath my

feet the grass was slippery with moisture. A fine drizzle fell steadily.

"Still it rains," Chayin wondered in a portentheavy voice. "It has rained since you fell under the helsar's spell." His grasp caught me as I slipped upon a hidden rock and pitched forward.

"Doubtless," I answered, "it often rains upon the slopes of Mount Opir." My embarrassment at my clumsiness flushed me hot. I was glad they could not see it in the misty dark. The moon, close to third phase, dived in and out of the clouds like some grinta fish skimming the Embrodming Sea.

"It has rained, these four days past, upon not only the mountains, but upon Frullo jer as well. It rains, perhaps, upon all of Nemar. It is an uneasy omen. Never in my lifetime has it rained in the pass Amarsa. The uris will rot, for the ground rejects this untimely torrent. Hael—"

"Chayin!" Sereth's warning cut him short. So there were things that Chayin, also, had been constrained by Sereth's will not to discuss with me.

"Hael has roused many among those at Frullo jer against you," I said, that Sereth might have the proof he sought by his constraint. They stopped in their tracks, as one man. The moon broke through the clouds, backlighting them. It shone back upon itself from out of the lake, down the slope from us. "They will rise out of the desert and strike you upon the plain of Astria, under the banner of Tar-Kesa's will. Thus does Raet move against me. Chayin, you must choose where you stand—your father has turned upon you!" And neither spoke, not even to reprimand me for my outburst.

"Sereth, you also must make a choice. If it is your pleasure to set Celendra groveling at your feet, do so knowing what will follow. If you war with Day-Keepers, it is a doomed battle. I must know your will aforehand, to do it."

"There is only that which one chooses, eh?" Sereth said. "As you say, it is my pleasure to set Celendra at my feet. Since Chayin killed Aknet, it is also necessary for him to lend a hand. Celendra will not rest until she has her revenge, and she can call all of M'ksakka to her aid. She holds Dellin so tight he has lost the ability to think." And I winced, in the dark, at the mention of Dellin, who once in my ignorance I thought I loved.

"Day-Keepers war with me, not I with them," continued Sereth, squatting down to tear up handfuls of the wet grass. "We must strike first. If the Day-Keepers would allow Celendra to come to rule in Astria through murder and guile, if they would do what Hael has done, what Vedrev did, then it seems to me that someone must stand against them." He looked up at the sky, squinted at the moon. "And if all this is simply peripheral to some struggle between you and Raet, that does not make it less real. As many would die, were neither you nor your god-friend involved." He tossed his head, threw down one last mangled handful of turf, and straightened up.

Sereth crill Tyris set his hest, and cared for nothing less. He had known, all along, what it had taken me so long to learn. Even against Raet, he would not give it up. I reached out and touched his arm.

"We will need a multiplicity of plans, to fool a forereader," I said.

"How many?" Chayin asked, with implicit assent.

"Five, say. Enough that she sees only the outcome—her downfall—and cannot determine how it will come. We must make her doubt her own sensing. We shall give her a taste of forereader's disease." Chayin laughed at this, and Sereth swatted my rump and pushed me gently toward the lake.

"Bathe, little monster. I would have you clean enough to couch before morning," he commanded me.

The water was very cold, colder-seeming because when I jumped back after testing it with my toe, Sereth picked me up, waded in up to his own hips, and dropped me cruelly into the icy lake. Laughing and sputtering, I pulled his legs from under him, that he might join me. We played thus, until I saw Chayin, sitting upon the bank, alone. The rain stopped entirely while I bathed myself, scraping away the dead skin with handfuls of fine bottom sand.

"Do my back?" I asked Sereth.

"Kneel down, then," he said. I did, my knees in the soft sand, and his hands worked knowingly upon my back, kneading sore muscles expertly.

"You are couching him, are you not?" I asked him.

"Yes," Sereth said, toneless.

"It is a common thing in the south," I said. He rinsed his hands in the water, and turned toward the bank, where Chayin waited.

"It is a common thing," he said, offering his hand to me.

"I would consider it a great courtesy," I petitioned him softly, "if you would leave me out of what transpires between you."

"Why, Well-Keepress?" I tugged on his hand, that he would stop. He pulled me forward.

"I could give you a child, this night. I would want no doubt as to its sire."

And then he did stop. I spoke those words upon impulse, unthinking. It was not in my plan, or my sensing. And yet I wanted it, though it would change all that was to be.

"Could you?" he demanded.

"Yes." I did not say that I now had that choice, anytime, with any man. As Estrazi had said to me long ago, one must but direct one's organs to do so.

"Could you take some precaution against it, then? I want no such thing. I would not bring about a child I might not live to succor."

If he had struck me full force, he could not have hurt me more. And what could I say to him? That I could protect him? If it came to be that I could, and he knew it, at that moment he would be lost to me, as surely as if by his death. I was, though I knew him right, much shamed by his rejection. Although I had thrown off chaldra, its values were still within me. The Ebvrasea, it seemed, had truly shed its conditioning.

Sereth, already upon the bank, had his arm upon Chayin's, and they spoke together in low tones. I regarded the sky above me, and hastened the clouds' clearing. When I ascended the bank, some little ways away from them, the north star Clous twinkled brightly. I lay down upon the wet grass, spreading my dripping hair about me. Wirur, the winged hulion, watched over me from out of a clear sky. I went to do my hest, my first with my new skills. Upon the grids of force that hold the seven universes forming, I rode, past those whose thrumming guardianship keeps the primal order. I showered in star's breath, moving ever back from the timetracks, that I might see truly. One cannot move in time, for time is within mind. What we apprehend as empty space abounds with mind. At that place where all is congruency, I stopped, and turned to see what conceptions existed there; whose will had preceded me. Upon a place that glowed and pulsed from the strain already on the time, I built still another conception. I could not excise the color pulses from the Astrian sky, nor the corpses ever crawling upon that bloody plain. I forced what existed to my will, and finally saw there a kind of victory. Sereth, I could see, and I did what I might to protect him. When at last I could hold us together, unscathed, in my vision, there was a snapping of the time, sharp as a slitsa's tail, and I found that I had bridged a gap, and locked my will into another, far larger conception. Not what I had hested, but bound to succeed. And so deft was the hand that laid that hest, I could not break the link. I bowed my will to that power, which I had previously only sensed.

I sighed, and sat up under the Opirian sky. Sereth was surely served, perhaps even saved. And since I had not taken time to deal with the seven-cornered room, I put the thought of it away, that I might concentrate upon what I had done. Lastly, before I went back to the men, I checked my weapons, those I meant for Raet. I looked up at Wirur, and took the constellation's measure. If such a battle was truly to be, I would be ready.

And I reveled in my mortal flesh, as I got up and went to sit with Sereth and Chayin, almost twins in the moonlight, and that Raet could not sustain himself in such a body. I had seen the best he could do, under the Falls of Santha. Upon his world, I had been badly disadvantaged. Here, he would take the burden. Nonsequential structures cannot exist, as we know it, in three-dimensional time and space. Raet's power here would be lessened, so much of it turned to simply staying. The need of time-space to spit him out of it might be turned to my advantage.

"What," said Sereth, for I had been long still and silent, "are you thinking?"

"That of which you have forbidden me to speak," I answered.

"Then do not speak of it," he said, and got to his feet, starting back up the slope without another word. Chayin and I scrambled, silent, after him. Once, when I stumbled, the cahndor steadied me. He smiled at me, and tousled my wet hair. A wind sprang up and circled the lake like some trapped animal. It raised the cold in me, and I was glad enough to take shelter from it in the always perfect mildness of Sereth's ancient keep.

We had a saying, in our wellwomen's training: "If you desire something from a man, tell him you do not want it."

"What I need now," said Chayin, rolling to his back, "is some real fear and loathing."

"Indeed?" Sereth propped himself up upon one elbow. "There is, among our admittedly meager selection of captives, one blonde daughter of a wealthy parr-breeder. She enthusiastically fears us, and her loathing is hardly feigned."

"I will have to wake her up." Chayin grinned, fastening his breech about him. He also took his sword belt and strapped it on.

Sereth regarded the sword belt. "She is not dangerous. You can encircle both her wrists with one hand, easily." He sounded mildly reproving. Giddy, I felt like laughing. I restrained myself, barely, pressing my head against Sereth's thigh.

"I want to make a strong first impression. Where will I find her?"

"Past the white corridor, straight three, left at the fourth. Ask the man on watch for her. Tell him what I told you. There are three empty chambers just left of this one. Take your choice." Sereth's fingers played in the hair about my neck as he gave Chayin tasa.

I traced a scar, one I had noticed immediately, with my lips. It went from just left and below his navel, crosswise, down his flat belly, was obscured by the hair there, to show again, trailing off across his right thigh. It was not new, by any means, but it had been deep, and in a hard place to take such a heavy cut. The darker ridge of it was as wide as my middle finger.

"How did you come by this?" I asked him, laying my head upon his stomach, my face toward his. I saw him through a forest of gold-brown hairs, some short and curling—his; some long and straighter, and tending toward bronze—my own.

"They sent Ganrom against me." I was sorry I had asked.

I said so.

"No matter. They sent him against me, and I killed him. He sponsored me for the Slayer's chain. He was a good man. But it was his chaldra to come against me." Sereth shrugged, but his hand was rough in my hair as he pulled me up to lie sidewise against him, his arm around me.

"Why would they have sent him . . . ?" I was aghast that the Day-Keepers would set one man upon the other, when all knew they were like brothers.

"They were thus surely rid of one of us. Strange

moves, they made, to trap me. That is not the strangest, but only the most costly." He rubbed at his groin, remembering. And I saw what he remembered, and his pain, and the long angry months of work upon his stiffened side. He mourned Ganrom's loss, but not that he had killed him. In his remembrances of the fight between them, upon some black lava rocks, was mixed a certain satisfaction, a quiet triumph. I shivered and withdrew from his mind.

"Now, you tell me something," he said, drawing me closer. Unconsciously, I had pulled my body from him along with my sensing. "Tell me how it was to be crell. How you felt. Chayin told me what he did, what he knew. You tell me the rest."

So I did that, puzzled, and under his urging I left nothing out, lest I leave out what he wanted to know. He listened attentively, interrupting me twice only.

"I have neglected to thank you for recruiting him," Sereth said, when I told of the crell Aje—Lalen gaesh Satemit. "Men of his skill pass this way infrequently."

And again, when I spoke of the crell whom not even Besha dared call anything but Carth, who said he was agent of the dharen of all Silistra—again did Sereth interrupt me, asking me to repeat everything concerned with him.

When I mentioned that proof I had seen during my Parset enchalding, the tapestry with the likeness of Raet upon it, Sereth withheld comment.

"You, of all people, know I am not mad," I pressed him.

"I never thought you were," he said softly, his lips against my ear. "What do you wish me to say? If he would face me, as a man, with a sword or any other mortal's weapon, I could fight him for you. I will fight his minions, be they fleshly, until I drown in their blood or am buried under their corpses. I will surely fight Hael. He is a man, like any other. But more than that I cannot do." He kissed my throat, and rose upon his elbow to peer down into my face.

"Think you," he asked me, "that it will be enough?"

"Doubtless," I assured him. The light played tricks upon his face above me. I raised up my head until our lips met.

"I think," he said after a time, "that you lie. That you do doubt."

"Not you, but myself, do I doubt."

He grunted, and lay down once again. I nestled against him and watched the room-flicker play upon the hollow in his throat. I was sure now; the ceiling was lightening. Outside, it must be nearing a new day.

"What will you do with Celendra, when you have her?" I asked him.

"I have not decided," he said. "Perhaps I will give her to Chayin. I owe him a woman."

"Surely you jest!"

"Why? Should I kill her, but let you live? A woman is dangerous only when she commands men. She will be safe in the crellpits. Even you could not escape them. He can kill her, if he wants to. I am no woman-killer."

"I think you hold her too lightly," I said, angry, though I knew not why. He sensed it, and turned silently, to smooth the fury from my body, knowing that my mind would helpless follow. And that made me more angry, for a brief time. Then that was gone from me, and I but moved under those hands that had taught me my femaleness, and I found that they had still more to teach.

I dozed under him, after, until awakened by one of his men, standing frozen over us.

"What is it, Idrer?" Sereth said, rolling onto his back. Only then did I recall the large, heavyset, black-haired Slayer I had first met with Dellin upon the road to Arlet. He had been of Ganrom's band. He nodded to me. I smiled back stiffly.

"A large number of mounted riders approach us." His voice held ill-restrained unease.

"Jaheil and Nineth, probably," I opined. "Chayin

invited Jaheil, and gave him the route, should he choose to follow it."

"Why was I not informed? Get Chayin, he is in one of the empty chambers. See if he expects anyone. Have him in the screen room when I get there. How many do you make them?"

"Forty to fifty. They are still far."

"Mount fifty, and have them wait at the cavern mouth. They need the drill. Move!"

Idrer was gone, charging the door, which barely slid from his path in time.

Sereth took up breech and sword belt.

"If you are coming, bestir yourself," he ordered me. I got up, looking for the clothes I had brought. I could not find them. "Here." Sereth threw me a bundle, and I unwrapped it and sat awe-struck above all that had been in Issa's saddlepack upon the trail to Santha. While I still hovered, staring, at the breech and band and tas-wear and combs and plump coin purse that had been mine, he threw down upon the pile the stra-hilted gol-knife he had given me, and after it a sheath and belt.

"Hurry, or you will miss the wonders of this place at work." I was in the breech and band, with the knife in sheath belted around me, within a dozen breaths, but still I had to run to catch him, striding down the hall. He entered three cubicles in turn, but Chayin was within none of them. The last, however, showed signs of recent use.

Sereth grunted, satisfied.

"What wonders?" I asked him, as we entered the corridor "Comm. Inter., Comm. Intra." He smiled bleakly and pointed at the legend upon the wall. We stopped before a door. Like the other doors in this section, it bore a pre-hide Silistran label.

" 'DAS.' What is that?" I asked.

The door slid aside and I saw what Sereth's answer confirmed.

"Direct Access Screening. Whoever built this place was concerned about who might be coming to

visit." I saw a very odd-looking console, with no fad-
ers, and what seemed to be a large assortment of
light-emitting diodes, all blinking. Sereth began moving his hands over them, and I realized them to be
light sensors of some sort. It looked easy. All the room
lit up with views of the slopes of Opir, except for the
wall behind Sereth's back. In places the images were
not sharp, but hazy.

"That is a large blind spot, after going to so much
trouble," I remarked. One quarter of the slopes, north
to northwest, had no surveillance.

"Those eyes saw, once. It is broken, and I am not
mechanic enough to fix it, nor do I have the part. It
would take a Day-Keeper, and I am hesitant to call
one." He grinned, his eyes upon his hands, which
flickered across the board; low, high, pause, but never
did he touch the console's surface. The countryside
loomed closer, closer.

I saw in Sereth's face that absorption of man with
machine that had brought the culture whose remnants
we used crashing down upon its creators. His hands
flew upon the panel.

"Look," he said. Truly I had no alternative, except
the blind eye behind us. He showed me the thing's
skills; it produced a number of different viewpoints,
even one of the empty sky. Then he laughed, for he
saw them. And again his fingers slid upon the empty
air above the lighted console. The magnification increased, and the moving mass ascending the slopes of
Opir showed itself composed of threxmen. Sereth
grunted. I heard the door. Chayin and another, Idrer,
entered. One final time did Sereth play upon the
panel, and we saw before us Jaheil's party.

"Well?" demanded Sereth, turning from the screen,
leaning stiff-armed against the console. He did not,
then, know Jaheil. I struggled with the image, searching to see if Nineth was among the riders, as she
and I had pacted.

"It is Jaheil, and I did invite him," said Chayin,
relieved, surprised, and obviously pleased. "But he

said he would not come." He peered closer at the screen. "It seems that the cahndor of Dordassa found not only a yra of jiasks, but recruited some of my own tiasks, also." And his eyes upon me let me know he saw my hand in that.

I grinned at him. Sereth looked between us.

"That is all I need!" Sereth said very quietly. "More tiasks. Where am I going to put them?" He caressed the board into darkness. The images did not fade; they were simply gone, the room suddenly acquiring walls of milky gray.

"Seems to me," said Idrer, who seldom spoke, "that they'll find couch to suit them, as did the first batch. Those tents of theirs lasted half the first night!" He was smirking. I had wondered about that, when I went to the lake. There I had seen no appreis risen on the grass, no sign of the forty-two Parsets Wiraal and Pijaes had brought. I wondered what couches the tiasks had found—outlaws', jiasks', or one another's.

"We had twelve wounded," reminded Sereth, "before they settled down."

"Twelve you heard about," muttered Chayin.

"Do you want me to recall the fifty mounted at the cavern's mouth?" Idrer asked.

"No. Send them out to meet this Jaheil, cahndor of Dordassa. Have them mind their manners."

Idrer snorted. Sereth eyed him bleakly. "Then have them pretend. I will have no infighting!"

When Idrer left, still chuckling, Sereth darkened the room itself. "Old habits die hard, with us all," he said, touching me lightly. "Your friend Lalen hamstrung a tiask the night before last. Something about an old debt." We left the darkened room, and the corridor light seemed very bright.

"I miss your meaning," I said to him.

"I might like his sword beside mine."

"I would count him as a friend, nothing more. But we have no bad debt between us, if that is what you want to know."

"Something like that," he admitted. "Chayin, what say you?"

"I hardly know him. There are many crells in Nemar."

"That is my point," Sereth said, serious.

"Ask him." Chayin shrugged.

"I will. What of this Jaheil? Do we need what is now close to one hundred of your men—and women—for this? I had thought more like fifty."

"Let us see what Jaheil knows that we do not, of Hael and what he plans. Jaheil's sword is worth ten lesser blades, his loyalty unquestionable."

"I see," said Sereth, and took a turning that would lead us to the kettle room. "I want a map from you, Estri, of Well Astria, every room and passage."

"And the tunnels beneath her, perhaps? Would you have any interest in such as secret passages, or long-forgotten access to the undertunnels from above?" I asked him.

"Anything you think might be of interest," he answered me, thoughtful. "We also have access to those tunnels here."

"So I assumed," I said.

"You could never get a threx down there."

"Are your men so far removed from the Slayers' ways that they can no longer fight upon their own two feet?" I wondered.

"Whose sortie is this, yours or mine?" he growled, but pulled me against him as we turned into the kettle room, crowded with men at sun's meal. Many stood with their bowls in hand; so full was the archite green chamber that they could not sit.

"Yours and Chayin's," I retorted. "But I am your instrument, and must perform creditably." Chayin laughed, raising his hands as if to defend himself.

"Not me! The ebvrasea, upon the square of overriding purpose, uses the threx and man to his ends," he informed me. I made a face and stuck my tongue out at him. "Hael is not here to keep us abreast," he added. "You should read the *Ors Yris-tera*." We took up bowls from the pile of them in one corner and got into the line waiting to be fed.

"I do not need to—I have you for my daily dose of obscurity," I answered him, as we all took three steps forward, then stopped with the line while another was served. Sereth's eyes roamed his men, acknowledging individuals among them, speaking now with one, now with another as they drifted to him. I wondered how he kept them all straight, and their concerns matched with faces. It was a strong bond between him and these men, who had left so much behind upon principle.

He excused himself from us, handing me his bowl, and crossed the room slowly, for everywhere men's hands reached out to stay him. And he would wait patiently and answer each one, and smile or touch, and then move on. And I saw whom he sought, before he reached him. Lalen, sitting cross-legged with the room's far corner at his back, hunched meditatively over his bowl, his large blond head bowed.

Sereth threaded his way toward him, crouched down. I found I could get a good sense of what passed between them; Sereth's direct questioning, Lalen's level, thoughtful answers. When Sereth rose, the massive blond rose with him.

"I believe," said Chayin when they reached us, "that we have never really met," and he held out his hand to Lalen, who took it in his larger, pale grasp almost shyly. He wore no longer the Parset clothes I had bought him, but had availed himself of Sereth's fitters' skill.

"It is good to see you, Estri, where you wanted so desperately to be." He turned his gaze upon Sereth. "In the shock of first bondage, she was most concerned with you and what had befallen you. I found such loyalty remarkable in a woman." And I flushed, embarrassed, wishing I had never bent my hand to free him.

"And you," I rejoined, "in a position more suited to your skills."

"I did not mean to offend you," he apologized, his pale brows raised.

"Then in the future, be more careful with what might be offensive." And I found I had learned that manner of Sereth's of putting menace and chill in a lowered voice.

"Stop it, you two," Sereth enjoined us, terse. "Friendship, indeed!"

I turned away, and found myself before the kettle master, who served me a portion. It saddened me to see the bitterness toward women Lalen carried. I doubted that I would ever understand a man's sense of fitness. I resolved to be careful of him.

While we ate, standing, Sereth questioned the larger blond man of Carth, who had been upon the same chain. Lalen knew little. But he knew other things, he said, from the crellpits, that might be of interest. Lalen then asked Chayin, point blank, if he should refrain from speaking lest the cahndor be offended. The cahndor bade him speak. It seemed that the romance between Hael and Liuma, built for the seas of adversity, foundered upon the shoals of triumph; their secrets had poured raging from Liuma's mouth in a final effort to extort control upon Hael, suddenly uncontrollable. The amount of detail Lalen held within him of Hael's actions gave them, then and there, their first plan. Chayin allowed that, since only a few men were needed, he would set Wiraal's yra off by threx, this very day, to see to it. Celendra could not refuse to serve them, for as long as they paid well-price, they must be couched. If I had been Celendra, and so soon after the death of my father a whole yra of the conqueror's jiasks appeared at my gate and made known their intention to stay, I would be nervous. And when those men made it clear that they awaited others, I think I should have, if I were Celendra, broken out trembling. And rightly so, for upon the second seventh of Amarsa, one set from this day, the two of Wiraal's men, who would have reserved and couched the Well-Keepress the night before, were to do three things. One of those things necessitated delaying Wiraal's departure until I could draw up an appropriate map. We hastened to Sereth's quarters, where I made a fast sketch, which Chayin took from me, that he might start Wiraal upon his way, and be back in time to greet Jaheil.

"I still do not understand," I complained to Sereth when Chayin had taken leave of us.

"Nor I," admitted Lalen, leaning against the color-swirl wall of Sereth's keep.

"Good. Then perhaps Celendra and Hael will not understand. One good plan is about all I can manage." Sereth leaned over my shoulder, where I worked upon the floor at a larger, more detailed map.

"Celendra has a number of Nemarsi in her Well, and she cannot get rid of them until they move against her. They let it be known that they are expecting reinforcements. Celendra demands Slayers' aid, against what she will then be sure is a plot to fall upon her from within and without. To move against Parsets, the Slayers must have Day-Keeper authority. I wager they will get it, about the time Hael comes storming, battle-ready, across the plain, that he might catch Chayin upon his way out of a ravaged Well Astria with Celendra. All Parsets look alike to Slayers. Neither force is likely to wait to be introduced. The Slayers fall upon Hael's men, thinking them to be us. We, meanwhile, have come up through the undertunnels. We free Wiraal's men, if they need us. We overwhelm those within the Well. We go back into the undertunnels, with Celendra, and whatever else we are pleased to take. Hael cannot possibly survive."

Sereth fell silent. Lalen rubbed his chin with his hand. Then he whistled softly between his teeth.

"What if Hael decides to hide in wait, or is late arriving?" I asked.

"From the rear, certain of my men, who excel at such skills, will provide stimulus, if it is needed. We might even, if it is necessary, give Hael a few threx riders to chase." Lalen was now nodding vigorous agreement.

I finished my map of the Well and sat up as Sereth's eyes caught mine.

"It is, of course, only a plan," he said.

"I had the impression," I remarked, "that Chayin wanted to confront Hael personally. Has he agreed to this?"

"Yes, with certain contingency schemes."

"Then, though it does not match my sorting, I cannot gainsay it." I handed him the finished drawing. Lalen cleared his throat, restless. Sereth's eyes held me bound in ice.

"You trust his judgment, where you will not trust mine?" He spoke barely above a whisper. I leaned over and touched his face, where the muscles jumped in his jaws.

"No. That is not what I meant. I know too little to have a valid opinion, that is all. You have not even told me how Celendra came to rule in Astria."

"That is true," he said. Lalen rose and wandered the keep's expanse, stopping long over Sereth's racked weapons, his unease evident in the set of his frame.

"Was she this contrary, even as a crell?" Sereth asked him.

Lalen turned to face us, the taste of a smile upon his lips.

"Even as a crell," he confirmed.

"And how was she as a woman to you?" queried Sereth in a careful, even voice.

Lalen laughed. "Contrary also. Stiff and contentious. I was to breed her, and she would have none of me. The crellkeep had to all but stand over us. I thought her just untalented, but that cannot be true. She kept Chayin's interest. She has yours." He bent his blond shaggy head and picked something off the floor. It was my Astrian chald.

"I have always disliked blonds," I said apologetically. Untalented, indeed.

Sereth was amused. Lalen inspected my chald,

and I saw that the weight of it was not lost upon him. With a twinge, I reminded myself that I no longer bore that weight.

"She was your mistress for a time, was she not?" Sereth asked him.

"Yes," said Lalen, and threw the chald casually onto the rack against which he leaned. "But only nominally," he added from under his pale brows, the words a growl in his throat. I wished I were elsewhere. What had Sereth to gain from this?

"How can one be 'nominally' enslaved?"

"She was busy with Chayin. I . . . She . . . I do not know what you want me to say," said Lalen, his head hunched between his shoulders. "I was hurt, convalescing. She neither used me nor abused me. She set no work upon me."

"Then she was a good mistress?" Sereth continued his inquisition.

"Yes," said Lalen, every muscle in his body taut.

"But you do not feel indebted to her for that?"

"No."

"Stop it!" I demanded.

"Be silent!" Sereth instructed me. "You do not, in fact, bear any debt to her, though she freed you, though she directed you here, into a situation that suits you."

"She did what pleased her!" The words burst from Lalen's tight lips.

"If I asked you to take your sword and kill her now, would you do so?"

"Gladly." Lalen drew his blade, and the shifting wall colors played upon it.

I froze where I knelt upon the floor. Lalen moved purposefully toward me. In three strides he would reach me. In two.

"Wait!" snapped Sereth, rising. I looked up at them, at the blade poised in Lalen's pale grip. "Sheath it!" Lalen did as he was bid, shaking his head back and forth as if to clear it.

"Thank you," said Sereth, and touched the blond

man's arm. Their eyes met. "No man," said Sereth to me, "would behave any differently. A man whose life has been in a woman's hands can feel no gratitude. He does, however, feel other things." He turned to face Lalen.

"Can I put you, in the face of what you feel, to protect her?" he asked.

Lalen stared at Sereth. "I seek your service," he said finally. "In truth, I did not know the bitterness in me until you bade me kill her. How sweet the thought." He laughed, without humor. "I will keep her alive for you."

"I have no doubt that you will," said the Ebvrasea. "Make your gear ready. You will leave with us, mid-meal tomorrow. I will find you, if I need you before then." And Sereth walked Lalen to the door.

I still knelt where I had crouched under Lalen's blade. My limbs shook and my mouth was fear-fouled.

"I hope," said Sereth, squatting upon the balls of his feet beside me, "that you took my meaning. He is a good man."

"I took it," I said numbly.

"Now," he said, stretching himself out upon the resilient floor, "if you wish, I will tell you how Astria went from Jana's hands to Celendra's."

I lay against him as he talked to me of Astria. I hardly listened. My tremors and fears would not leave me. I learned that my name had been written upon the Day-Keepers' Roll—that I was legally dead. Jana's name appeared there also, for it had been more than the two years required since she had disappeared. Celendra had simply demanded the Well, as ranking keepress on the planet, directly after my uncle Rathad's death. That death, Sereth said, could not be attributed to any violence, nor was there sign of any unfair play. He had not been ill, he had simply died, leaving none of our blood in Astria. Celendra appointed no adviser, but attempted to run both Port Astrin and Well Astria herself.

"Astria," he continued, "is much changed. Celendra has brought in every star trader's device she could imagine. It is said they have pleasure baths there now, where one floats without getting wet upon innumerable founts of some special water. Port Astrin is surely the blackest hole upon Silistra."

"M'lennin must be thrilled," I said, hate rising to temper the fear in me.

"M'lennin is upon M'ksakka. Dellin is Liaison First, and has been since Celendra took up Astria." I sat up, and he narrowed his eyes at me. "He has taken the Slayer's chain," he continued. "Are you upset?" he asked, and then sat up also. I scraped away my hair from my face, wondering when I would have a moment to tend to it.

"No. I just thought of something. If you have him in your plan, as you intimated, and he resides in the Liaison First's keep, I could be of help. There would have been no reason for them to have excised my print from the computer that sentried that place. I can walk in there whenever I want. The doors will still respond to my hand."

"You are upset," he said, pulling my hands as they worried a snarl at my neck. I shook off his grasp.

"Yes," I admitted. "I am upset. That demonstration of yours upset me. The past does not upset me. I do not care about Dellin. I am frightened by what you showed me."

"It was merely instruction into the nature of men," he said gently, raising my face to his with a hand upon my throat.

"And not a warning?" I asked.

"We have been close upon such a situation before," he admitted, and I knew he meant that time below Santha, when I had bargained with Raet for his life.

"Do not bind me this way. I must use what little skills I have to defend myself."

"Someone must." He answered only my first statement. I was totally at a loss. What I had done in his behalf, I could not undo. Nor could I forever keep from my skills, or keep him from knowing. I got up and roamed the room, telling myself that I had so little power yet, my worry was premature. I made one circle of Sereth's keep, my right hand trailing upon the hilts of his racked weapons as I passed them. His eyes followed me as I made a second circuit. It is often my need to move when I think. I ran my fingers over the worn hilts that shone with the softness of metal in frequent use. They seemed ready to jump to my hand.

"Where is the cloak I wore when I came here?" I asked evenly, at a great cost. I stopped still, my arms crossed around me, waiting.

"In the chest." His voice was frankly puzzled.

I got it from where he had neatly folded it, and carried it near to him, spreading the plain-looking brown width of it upon the browner floor. Taking the stra-hilted knife he had given me from its sheath, I knelt upon the cape. Sereth rolled to his side and propped his head upon his arm. I glared at him. He grinned widely. I cut away the stitches that bound the brown cloth around my father's cloak, working carefully around the starburst clasps, first one, then the other. When every stitch was loose, I lifted the top layer of brown material, and the Shaper's seal glittered like the stars in the keep's shifting light.

Sereth was up on his knees beside me. He leaned over the cloak, running his hand upon the cool-feeling scintillant spiral. He knew that sign. He sat back upon his heels, silently questioning.

I took the edge of the cloak and with it wiped the dulling agent from the sunburst clasp. Then I backed off it and took the black cape in my hands and swirled it over my shoulders. I fastened the chain between the clasps.

"This is my couch-gift to you," I said solemnly. "But you must know what it is about. And you must accept, and not be angry. Promise me."

"I promise," he replied.

"Take up a blade you would not mind losing, and strike me anywhere the cloak covers me," I directed him.

"Estri—"

"Do it. I will not be harmed."

"I will not."

But in the end, he did go and find an old, much-seasoned weapon, whose blade bore numerous nicks and chips.

He stood before me with it, hefting the hilt meditatively in his hand.

"You must strike with some little force," I demanded, looking up at him with what I hoped was confidence.

"You are sure?"

"Doubtless."

"There is no other way?"

"It might only work with a person inside."

He shrugged, and brought his arm back and down so fast I could not have dodged it if I tried. I felt it touch, and a sort of a mild shock. The blade, like the one I had tried upon Chayin, shattered into tiny fragments, and for a moment they hung in the air, motes of metal dust. Sereth's hand, the hilt still in it, glanced my shoulder. What he held, when he recovered himself and looked down awe-struck, was but the stub of a hilt, only the amount enclosed in his fingers. He balanced it upon his palm a time, staring.

When he looked up at me, it was with a boyish, excited expression I had never seen upon him. I had been afraid that he would be angry, that he would refuse it.

"That kind of help," he said, "I will gladly accept."

I took it from my shoulders and handed it to him. He would doubtless need it. I, surely, did not. The protection I sought was not from steel or gol. He took it from me, and put his arms around me. I was content, even happy. I pushed away all else, that I might remember what passed between us unshadowed. But the shadows of the future always cloak the past, and in doing so, change it.

He looked well in the Shaper's cloak, though he took it off almost immediately and replaced it in the wooden chest. It seemed to me, in my wishful thinking, that he looked almost born to wear it. But Estrazi had told me: Sereth was not for me. Yet I set my hest against him. I took those moments to reinforce what I had done, to make a bastion against the chill winds that whined shrill songs in my ears.

"You are sure," asked Sereth, crossing the room to slide aside a hidden panel by the door, "that you do not need it?"

"I am sure," I said.

"This," he said, closing the panel, "is my couch-gift to you, and one for me as costly as that cloak to you. We have an enth, alone. None will disturb us. I would speak seriously with you." And with that he came and sat opposite me, his back upon the dais that still bore my Parset gear.

"First, briefly, about Lalen. He has been, a good number of years, a slave. Such can do strange things to a man's mind. I had to see what he would do. I wanted you to realize, also, where such a man would put you. If he falls, in your service, you need not even blink. But I think he will not fall. He will protect himself. A man must do that, first. His hand will be stronger, his head clearer, than perhaps even mine, for it is his only task to see that you live." He slid down upon his spine and looked up at me.

"I see," I said. I knew that look upon him. I waited.

"When I met you, my life was settled. I had, in my own eyes, success. I had women, children, land, threx. Position and power—all a man wants. I had the Seven's sword.

"I misjudged some few actions, and I lost it. When I drew upon Vedrev, I had no clear thought. And when I found myself with so many swords in my service, it was too late. I did not want this." He waved his hand. "Alone I might have gone to Dritira, or Gal-esh, and made some new life. I cannot leave these men, who left so much for me."

He took a deep breath and blew it sibilantly between his teeth.

"I speak to you of this with some difficulty," he said finally. "I have always kept my own counsel. This is a precipitous life, with no clear purpose, or any proper ending. We are marginally safe in the Parset Lands. Elsewhere . . ." His voice trailed off.

"When I conceived plucking Celendra out of Astria, it was a simple undertaking. Something to fill the time, I thought it, and another small strike against the Day-Keepers who continually harass me. I wanted Chayin's Parsets to hide among, and we would have walked in there and taken her out from under their very noses." He smiled wanly. "However, things are greatly changed. All has become very serious, and the dangers are no longer slight." And his voice turned even softer, and I leaned forward to catch his words.

"You must decide what you would do if I do not survive this. And consider, that if I do, there is always the next time. Chayin and I will doubtless come to contest over you eventually. Men can share anything but love of a woman. Should, for one reason or another, you pass again into his hands, I would, were I you, rest there content. In many ways, you two are a more likely match. And one could do worse than Nemar."

I found my vision badly blurred, and I pulled up my knees and rested my head upon them.

"I am not doing this right," he muttered, suddenly standing. He put his hand upon my head, and I leaned against him, my face pressed to his leg. "I am no provider," he said in a whisper. "Behind me I left four women, three children, and a grandchild whose sex I do not even know. Before me is only conflict. And someday, death at a stronger hand. And I was content with that, until you came here. I am no longer content." I watched my tears run down his thigh, over a bare area worn free of hair.

He pulled my arms from about his leg and knelt down to take my shaking shoulders in his hands.

"You must understand. It is not a good thing, when a man who wields death comes to hold his life dear. It weakens. In my weakness, I fear for you." He sought to quiet me, but I would not be quieted for a long while. When my convulsions ceased, he still held me, whispering things he had only before said to me in the heat of passion.

And then he asked me about the cloak. I told him all that he wanted to know about it, and about Estrazi and Raet, though it discomfited me to do so.

At the end of it, I begged him excuse me, that I might walk awhile alone in the corridors, until I found myself eased.

He went to the door and slid aside the panel and played with it. The door, so instructed, opened. He kissed me lightly upon the forehead. I walked past him, wordless.

After a time, wandering aimlessly, I came upon Chayin, who was alone. His expression told me how I must look—red-eyed and swollen-faced and bedraggled. He leaned his arm upon the wall, between two of the torches that lit the passage.

"Do you have your pouch?" I asked him, after enduring his wordless scrutiny. I could not have passed by him; he commanded the corridor.

"He does not want you to have it." His face seemed dark after Sereth's, in the flamelight. But he got it out and tossed it to me.

I tasted uris, the first time since I had awakened. It was an intensely pleasurable experience. My nerves steadied, my anguish receded. I did not toss it to him, but brought it, and handed it back. He looked down into my face; his fingers traced the tracks of my tears down my cheek.

"He is not as you expected him to be, is he?" he said, gentle.

I shook my head against the tears that again threatened my sight.

Chayin drew me to him and held me. I sensed him exploring my memories, but did not move to stop him. "It is almost over," he said to me. "You can be strong this little while longer. Soon, all will be very simple. The new time brings with it a different balance. I have thrown the yris-tera again. Everything, it seems, has a solution." He put me back from him. How quickly he had grown strong, freed of his affliction.

"It does not seem that way to me." I sighed.

"Only because you are so busy appearing less than you are." His eyes held dark concern for me. "The ending of that, too, comes fast upon us."

"I must get back," I said, to extricate myself.

"Go, then." He flashed his bright smile. "Do not worry," he called after me. "When you need me, you will not have to call."

VII. The Liaison First

It was shadowed and musty in the undertunnels, with only a scant bowl of light here and there above the central channel, which ran unending to the limits of sight. Off it branched other tunnels, strings of light, six of them. A gray place it was, and full of ghosts. This was Day-Keepers' domain, or should have been. The glassy gray floor was slippery under my booted feet. I turned to watch Sereth, in an alcove set into the tunnel wall. Chayin, garbed as I in the weapon-concealing brown leathers we had worn from Frullo jer, peered over Sereth's shoulder. I moved my left leg, heard a clink, and bent down to set the razor-moons better in their sheaths. Lalen, leaning, insolent but alert, against the smooth glassy wall, watched me. He, as Sereth, wore circlet armor, and each of us bore weapons enough for three. I hoped we would not need them all.

"But where are we going?" I had asked him, for I had been excluded from all their final planning.

"To pay Dellin a visit," Sereth had answered. It was Amarsa second second. Wiraal could not possibly reach Astria by threx before second sixth.

I shook my head in wonder at the Ebvrasea's in-scrutability. A sort of grating sound bounced around the undertunnel, and a section of the channel flooring withdrew into itself, revealing another level beneath. Up from those depths came a silver oblong shape, most reminiscent of a M'ksakkan hover. When three-quarters of its rounded, windowless bulk was above the surface upon which we stood, it ceased rising. I heard the metal screech again, as the channel floor closed itself up.

Sereth laughed softly, and I glanced over my shoulder to see him darken the alcove. As he stepped from it, it closed behind him, leaving no sign that any-thing other than featureless gray wall had ever been there. He touched a small box in his hand, and there was a humming sound.

Lalen, with a soft exclamation, pushed himself away from the wall. Chayin, at Sereth's right, came and turned me by the shoulders. I knew what I would see. Almost, I resisted. Then I let him turn me. The oblong metal sphere lay open to us, inviting. It looked, from where I stood upon the platform, much like the keeps above our heads.

Lalen came up behind me, peering over our shoulders. He, too, felt uneasy here.

"Come, you two," said Sereth indulgently. "It is perfectly safe. Certainly safer than any threx."

So I let him coax me to jump across that yawning gap, a full two hands' widths, and onto the resilient loam-colored flooring of the oblong's interior.

When we were, all three, within, Sereth followed and touched again the lighted box he held in his palm. A tremor came up through my boots. We were moving. I was glad that I could not see the tunnel, around me, speed by. Sereth put the tiny box in his pocket-belt. Then he motioned Chayin to him. I eyed the seats circling the wall.

"I want you to know how to guide it, in case," I heard him say, as Chayin bent his head over a panel Sereth's knowing fingers exposed to view.

I went and watched also, that I might keep my mind off the tons of mountain over us. When I knew I could, if need be, make the craft obey me, I went and tried a seat. I found, as had Lalen, who lounged stretched out upon the floor, that those seats were made for smaller, shorter frames than even my own. Formed, as they were, for diminutive rears and child-length legs, I could not find comfort in their support. I, also, sat upon the floor, taking from my belt the slitsa-covered ors Chayin had given me. I saw that he had folded back the tips of certain pages. By the time I had read each indicated page and smoothed back all the markers, we were there.

"Here we are," said Sereth, the first words he had spoken in enths. Somehow none of us found it easy to speak, encased in our ancestors' legacy.

"Where is here?" I asked, slipping the book in my pouch. I wondered what they would think, those forgotten ones, of the use to which we turned their handiwork.

In answer, Sereth, disdaining his tiny box, played upon the craft's panel. The wall upon my left slid aside, although I was sure we had entered from the right. Thusly exposed was a tunnel the double of the one we had left neras behind; gray and glassy and featureless.

"Hurry!" Sereth ordered.

Chayin went first, and turned when he stood upon the platform. The space between platform and craft was a good stride across. Sereth pushed me gently toward Chayin, who extended his arm to me, and I jumped it. Then Lalen crossed over, giving the chasm no notice.

Sereth leaped through as the wall of the craft started closing. Even as his feet hit the platform, the craft began to sink beneath the channel, and when it was gone, the channel flooring, soundless here, slipped into place leaving no visible seam.

We stood there, in that pressing silence, regarding

each other. Our breathing seemed very loud in that emptiness.

"Where," I asked, "are we?"

"Let us go see. I put us within a nera or two of the Liaison First's, but we may be farther." Sereth put his hand upon the wall, carefully judging the level, and walked toward his right. Chayin mimed him. I stood watching until Lalen's hand urged me to follow. I turned and glared at him, but I went, after I shook his grip from my arm.

"Here," said Sereth when we had walked perhaps a half-nera along that gray same-seeming platform, and a portion of the wall fell back, revealing recurved stairs of well-worn archite. A paucity of ceiling globes gave the stairwell shadowy menace.

When we were all through the hidden door and stood upon the stairs, Sereth turned to Chayin.

"Close it," he suggested. Chayin felt along the right-hand side of the door. It slid shut with not even a scrape, and semidarkness closed upon us. My ears felt as if I had changed altitude too rapidly. I swallowed, and waited for my eyes to adjust.

"Move," hissed Lalen, ever behind me. I sighed and followed Chayin and Sereth, taking those shallow stairs two at a time.

It was a very long and winding stairwell. I climbed behind them so long there was nothing in the universe but stairs, and the effort of raising one's aching thighs to take them. So hypnotized did I become that I crashed into Chayin and Sereth where they had stopped at the stair's head, as I stumbled for a stair that did not exist.

"Quiet!" Sereth hissed. Chayin's arm steadied me where I straddled two steps, for there was no room upon the top one.

Sereth caused that wall, also, to move aside. The light of sun's setting upon the Astrian plain flushed redly over us, spilling down the stairs behind. The sight of it caused me to gasp. We were, truly, upon those plains where I was raised.

I pushed forward between them.

"Look you, Sereth, Chayin." And I pointed south-east, where Astria sparked and gleamed upon the ho-rizon, her towers arcing prisms into the blazing sky. I stepped out upon the ledge, which had kept its secret so well from me. I had played upon this hill, among these boulders, as a child. I had roamed here, often, with Santh.

"No wonder one never sees a Day-Keeper upon his way anywhere," I breathed.

Chayin laughed. "Except Hael," he amended.

"Will they not know we have used their ferry?" I asked Sereth.

"I doubt it. They do not count that craft among theirs. Nor, to my knowledge, have they used those tunnels I took." He looked around. "Move," he said to Lalen.

Lalen moved, and Sereth showed us all how to control the stone door—by a sensor under a stone panel that slid to a special touch only. He bade us each try until we had made the door obey us. By then the light was almost gone from the sky.

"Is that the Liaison First's?" he asked me, point-ing to the distant squat structure just taking light for the evening. It hulked there, all star-steel ugliness.

"Yes," I said, remembering how miserable I had been within it, at M'lennin's hands. "Are we going to walk right in?" I queried him.

"Right in," he affirmed.

Chayin stretched. The uritheria medallion glinted balefully at me from his chest. He had his cloak thrown back, rubbing that old shoulder wound that often pained him. "Let us start, then. I would walk out this stiffness."

We started. I judged it to be seven neras, over easy ground. The moon, third quarter and failing, was not yet risen when we stopped, so close we could see the outer court gate and the red-glowing palm-lock within. We shared a bladder of water, ate some pounded denter. The men played with their gear.

"Just walk right in?" I asked.

"Get us through the gates, yes."

"There is manual override," I said thoughtfully.

"Why would he override a welcome visitor?" Sereth said.

That was true; the keep would announce me as one in its data bank. No alert. Dellin might not even bother to monitor the door at all. M'lennin had often not bothered.

Sereth, Chayin, and Lalen donned the soft-capped Parset masks they had brought.

"Just let him see you," said Sereth. "Once he sees you, he will have no thought of us. Remember, you are surprising him. It is likely he does not know you are on the planet."

I smiled, and as we had agreed, I unsheathed the knife Sereth had given me and took first blood with it upon my own arm. I winced at my hand's work. The scratch, long and just deep enough, bled copiously. I shook some of the blood upon my clothing as it ran down my arm onto my hand.

"Let us go. I could bleed to death." And I walked beside them until we were close to sensor range, at which time Sereth and Chayin made as if to support me, and we lurched hurriedly along, Lalen guarding the rear with nervous strokes.

"If this does not work," I whispered, "what will we do? What if he has guests? What if he is not here?"

"Be silent. Look hurt. Stagger," ordered Sereth.

Then the sensors had us, and we were all silent. The lights in the outer court rose brighter. We had been announced. I slapped the palm-lock, and the door slid aside. We clattered up the three steps, and as the door slid soundless closed behind us, I heard a commotion. Chayin drew his blade. I reached into my boot as Dellin careened around the corner, two men behind him. I threw the two razor-moons, one to Dellin's right and one to his left. He was half-dressed, unarmed. One man screamed. Someone grabbed my shoulder, and I was upon the floor, behind Chayin and Sereth, with Lalen straddling me, blade ready.

"Estril What?" I saw him understand, stop dead, raise his hands and clasp them above his head. One of the two Slayers was doubled over, the razor-moon deep in his gut. I wondered how I could have missed the second man, who held his sword wavering, crouched upon the landing leading back into the reception hall.

"Put it down," I heard Sereth say. The man looked around, turned, sprinted up the steps, down the corridor. Chayin leaped after him, scooping the razor-moon from where it lay in the passage. Moments later, I heard a scream.

Through Sereth's legs I saw Dellin eye the wounded, groaning Slayer's sword.

"Let me go," I begged Lalen, who still stood over me. He wrapped his free hand in my hair.

"Pick it up, Dellin," invited Sereth.

"You will kill me."

"Not immediately. Pick it up, Slayer." And Dellin did. Chayin appeared at the top of the stairs, his arms crossed over his chest, and squatted down to watch.

Dellin hefted the blade, slick with its owner's blood, and took a step toward Sereth. Sereth's blade flashed an instant after Dellin's attacking stroke. The sword fell from Dellin's grasp and skittered across the star-steel floor. Dellin clutched his hand against him, staring at the offending weapon, unbelieving.

"Try again," Sereth suggested diffidently. "We all have our off days."

I leaned forward, but Lalen pulled me back by the hair.

This time Dellin grabbed up the blade and lunged with it in both hands at Sereth, holding the sword as a spear. Sereth simply was not there, but beside him. The Ebvrasea's sword whickered through the air, and Dellin's blade skittered almost into my hands. Dellin went to his knees, and Sereth neatly knocked him senseless with his weapon's hilt.

He stood over the Liaison a moment, then reached in his pocket-belt and manacled Dellin's large wrists behind him with heavy Nemarsi wristlets. That three-linked style is unmistakable to any who has ever worn those obdurate steel bands.

I found myself rubbing the small bones of my own wrists, remembering the sores steel chafes upon them. Dellin's black-haired head lay still. I recollected another time I had seen Sereth knock a man's blade from his hand upon the first stroke. I started to get to my feet but Lalen wound his grip tighter in my hair.

Sereth was bending over the wounded man, his booted feet in a pool of blood. He pulled the razor-moon from the Slayer's middle and turned away. He shook his head.

"Your turn," he said to Lalen, indicating the badly wounded man. "I will watch her."

I went to Sereth and hid my head against his chest while Lalen dispatched the man I had mortally wounded. I had to step over Dellin's unconscious body to do so.

"Next time," said Sereth, "you will dispatch your own wounded." He pushed me away from him and bent to Dellin, the gory razor-moon still in his hand, wiping it clean upon the unconscious Liaison's clothing.

"That is formal garb," I remarked, looking at Dellin, his hands behind his back, in his black breech with the gold banding, his white tunic colored with the fallen Slayer's blood. Dellin had gained weight since I had last seen him. His form, always carrying too much muscle for my taste, had that unhealthy softness about it of a man just running to fat.

Sereth handed me the razor-moon, and a shadow fell across us, where we knelt over Dellin on the star steel. Chayin loomed there, holding the second razor-moon.

"Perhaps we should wake him, and find out where he was going. None of them, it seems, are going to get there, and my man has lost the ability to answer." Chayin had that kill-smile upon him.

Sereth squinted up at him. He nodded.

"First, we must make sure that we have no visitors. Estri, can that be done?"

"Third door on your left, around that corner. When last I was here, the room was blue. From there you may program the doors as you wish."

"Come do it. I am not familiar with M'ksakkan devices. Lalen! Bring the Liaison." And he did, with some difficulty, for Dellin was almost as large as he.

So we came to stand in that blue room, which had been M'lennin's most private quarters.

Lalen, with a grunt of relief, dropped Dellin's deadweight to the iridescent Torth pelts. Chayin's eyes roamed the keep, impressed with all the off-world opulence. Still did the strung-ruby draperies from the looms of Pliatus, half a galaxy away, adorn those M'ksakkan crystal windows. Still did the wistwa desk, carved from the creamy bones of the great sea beast of Oguast, dominate the room. Dellin had not changed a thing. Even M'lennin's ragony pipes sat in their display rack upon the desk's top.

I went to the room's one blank wall and slid it back, exposing the master board that ruled the Liaison's keep.

I showed its workings to Sereth, who was quick to learn. I remembered the first time I had seen that blinking plethora of lights and switches. I showed him the patch bay, and how it could be used to route any function of any input module, and the logic of the system was not lost upon him. Truly, the board had only five capabilities: communications, in-house and out, programmable function of its automated services, duplication of inserted material, and visual display. But each function had widely variable parameters, and the combinations of effects available neared the infinite.

By the time Sereth had wiped from the data bank

all entry prints and fed our own into it, the Liaison First was groaning softly.

I heard the clink of his manacled wrists as they discovered their bonds. He moaned again, and would have rolled to his back, but Lalen's foot thudded audibly against Dellin's kidneys. He made a tiny mewling sound and turned his head toward us.

"Lie still, M'ksakkan," Lalen commanded. The Liaison's face was beaded with sweat.

Chayin, disdaining the steel and sueded chairs, crossed his legs under him upon the Torth pelts, his knees near Dellin's head.

"Would you like to sit up?" he said pleasantly to our captive. Sereth stepped back from the board, taking from his pouch a length of braided leather.

Dellin did not answer.

I went and knelt beside Chayin, where the Liaison could see me.

"Do what they say," I advised him gently. His gray eyes sought mine, accusing. He was breathing heavily, and I almost reached out to touch him. Instead, I twisted my hands together in my lap. This man, whom once I thought I loved, had betrayed us.

"Estri," he whispered, "help me." Sereth, Lalen, and Chayin removed their masks.

"I will do what I can," I said softly, leaning forward. I saw Sereth turn his face away, to hide the smile upon it. "Obey them, and perhaps you will live."

"Sit up," Chayin said again, and this time his tone was not gentle.

As Dellin struggled to get his legs under him, Lalen leaned down from behind and twisted his fingers in Dellin's black hair, pulling him savagely up upon his knees. Sereth knelt behind him and looped the leather around each ankle in turn, threading it, before he tied the ends together, between the manacles' middle link. Dellin sat upon his heels, most effectively restrained.

"Let him go," Sereth commanded, and Lalen released his grip in the Liaison's hair.

Sereth walked around his prisoner once, slowly. His arm flashed down twice, ripping first tunic, then breech from him. The sound of the material tearing was loud in the silence. Dellin, naked, trembled visibly. Sereth stared at him, hands upon his hips.

"What do you want from me?" Dellin begged.

"Some answers. If they suit me, then I might allow you to serve me. If your service pleases me, we will see about the rest," Sereth said, very low.

"Anything," the Liaison First whimpered. "Estri, tell them. You know me. I will do anything!" He pleaded. I said nothing. It is discomforting to me to see a man grovel.

Chayin laughed his harshest laugh. Lalen squatted down where Dellin could see him, crossing his massive arms. Sereth took out his knife and cleaned his nails.

"Sereth, please!" His eyes were desperate. "I did not mean—"

"Who were those men? Where were you bound?" Chayin snapped.

"Gerin and Faer, of the hostel. They . . . stay with me. We were going to dinner, with Celendra, in the Well." The words tumbled from his mouth, so anxious was he to please. I wondered how I could have ever felt anything for him.

Sereth nodded.

"You will call Celendra. Tell her that you and your boys"—his voice snapped like a huija—"have been detained." Dellin bobbled his head in acquiescence. The sweat ran in streams down his corded neck.

"What could keep the three of you here, inaccessible, for a set's time?" he demanded.

"I do not know," said Dellin, after a silence, fearfully.

"Think of something," Chayin advised, shifting his dark bulk enough to draw his gol-knife, "or I will feed you your own eyeballs, one at a time. If by then you have no answer, I might find more work for my

blade. There are many parts of a man that may be
removed." He eyed Dellin's maleness suggestively.

The color drained from Dellin's face. He called
upon the gods of his mother, just before Lalen's blow
bent him double, gasping. I saw the tears in his eyes,
turned my head away.

"Have you a thought?" queried Chayin.

Dellin had a thought.

"Contagion," he moaned. "Sometimes . . . hot
experimental medicines . . . come through here . . .
I could call her, tell her that. Tell her we are ill, and
must stay isolated until the keep cleans itself and the
sickness passes out of us."

Chayin got up upon one knee and took Dellin by
the hair. Lalen, behind, held him steady as he writhed
in terror. Sereth merely watched, until the touch of
Chayin's gol-knife upon the Liaison's cheek tore a
scream of terror from his throat.

"Hold," said Sereth. "I cannot believe," he said
softly, "that such as you can wear the black chain."
And with that he bent and cut from Dellin the Slayer's chain, and threw it across the room. Dellin, held
immobile, could only tremble.

"I will not free your hands. Call her. And take
care she suspects nothing."

I saw cunning flicker upon Dellin's face.

"You must do it from the desk communicator, else
she will see us also," I said, and his feral look was
replaced by hopelessness.

Lalen unbound Dellin's feet, and pushed him,
stumbling, to the steel and sueded chair behind the
wistwa desk. There he rebound the Liaison's feet to
the chair's legs.

Sereth motioned to me, and I readied the small-
screened desk communicator. Dellin had to give me
the call codes; when I ruled in Astria, there was not
one machine in the Well.

I motioned the men back from him, that they not
be caught in the wide-angle viewer. Facing Dellin,
behind the desk, I leaned over and punched up Well

Astria. As I did so, my queasy stomach was settled by the hatred rising in me. Call codes for Astria, had they? Not for long!

I jerked my hand back, out of sight, as the red light upon the tiny console came on.

"Celendra!" snapped Dellin, his face anguished, to someone we could not see from behind the screen.

And then I heard her voice, soft velvet, as I had remembered it. In my mind I could see her, dusk upon midnight, imposing. She was not pleased at Dellin's message. Her voice grew petulant, and she demanded to know what ailed him, and how he dared, with his clumsiness, interfere with her plans. For a moment I thought she might sense us. Sereth raised his eyes from nails, and his gol-knife to a ready position. Dellin found art enough in him to placate her. His obsequiousness sickened me. Finally, with a vengeful curse upon his manhood, Celendra broke the link from where she sat in Astria.

I let out the breath I had been holding and slapped the off switch.

Chayin chuckled in satisfaction. Even Sereth smiled. Dellin did not, but slumped in the chair, despondent.

"What," asked Chayin, throwing one leg over the desk, "did she mean when she asked you if her will had been done?"

Slowly, miserably, Dellin raised his head. His face was contorted. He licked his lips.

"If I tell you that, you will surely kill me," he rasped.

"It is not a question," explained Chayin patiently, "of whether or not we kill you. If I were you, I would crave death. It is merely a matter of how long it will take you to die." And he leaned forward until he peered into Dellin's face. "In Nemar, we can keep a man alive a long time. Be assured that you will tell us everything. In fact, you will beg to do so. When you have left no eyes with which to see, no tongue with which to speak, no fingers with which to hold a writing instrument, you will take that instrument in your teeth, to write for us that which we would know. If you still have mind by that time. Do not doubt me, M'ksakkan, I have had a great deal of practice."

Dellin closed his gray eyes, and his lips moved silently. I turned away from the sight of him, my own hands trembling as I put them to my head to cover my ears.

Sereth watched me coldly. His lips twitched, and he held out his hand to me. I took it in my icy, sweat-drenched grip, and leaned faint against him.

"Perhaps," he said in my ear, "you are not as fierce as you thought."

"Let me go and shower."

"No." His tone let me know appeal was useless. I put my cheek against his shoulder.

"It is one thing," I whispered, "to kill an enemy. Have pity. I once couched him. I cannot stand and watch this!"

"Would you rather help? It would give you something to do."

I turned and ran from him, from Chayin and Lalen and Dellin, whom I once loved. I ran, and the doors made way for me. Into my old keep I stumbled, and through it, until I stood shaking behind the wash-room door. Only Sereth's laughter had followed me. I sank down upon the cool tiles, sickened.

When I could, I got up from the floor and stripped. Then I let the hot needle spray calm me, leaning against the shower wall a long time.

Dripping puddles upon the tile, I combed the snarls from my hair very slowly, seeking the simple, thoughtless labor of working the strands free, one by one. It hung smooth and snarlless over my hips, raining drops upon my thighs, when Chayin at last came to fetch me.

The door slid aside, obedient to his identity. Dark and savage he seemed, framed against that room full of star things. It came to me, looking at him, that he was doubtless capable of doing just what he had threatened to Dellin, or to any who opposed him. He had grown strong since I lifted his affliction from him. It had been so simple. He scrutinized me slowly, leaning in the doorway.

I put down the comb, dressing wordlessly, turning away on the pretext of applying salve to my self-inflicted wound. Chayin, cruel, powerful, crouched upon the moment in my sensing. He would take what he could, when his time was right. He caught me there, searching the source of his strength. I withdrew as he moved toward me; backed away until I could back no farther. The wind from the abyss pebbled my skin.

"I did not know you had that skill." My voice trembled. He pressed me back against the wall.

"What were you seeking?" He ran his hand down my face, touching my throat.

"Is he dead?" I asked faintly.

"Not yet. He is less a coward than he first appeared. Sereth wants you there; he feels your presence might aid us. But that is not what you sought in me." His hands closed about my throat, I found it necessary to raise my head. His thumb pressed painfully into the hollow below my ear.

"If you ask, I might tell you. Do not seek me that way again."

I gasped his name. His grip loosened. The membranes snapped once, back and forth, across his dark eyes.

I did not ask. I did not have to. The veil served him; he saw and was not afraid.

"Sereth wants me there," I reminded him. He smiled, mirthless kill-smile.

"He will wait this little while longer." I serviced him while he leaned back against the wall, silent. It was a thing of moments, of a man's simple use of that which is available to him.

I shivered, upon the tiles, and shook out my hair, which still dripped. He arranged himself in his breech, regarding me oddly.

"Have you read much in the ors?" The uritheria glared at me, golden, hostile.

"Only that little, while we were in the undertunnels," I replied.

"You should read it." He crossed his arms, and the tattoos upon them slithered.

"What did Dellin tell you?"

"Not what we wanted to know. Yet." And he pushed himself from the wall, turned, and strode down the hall, without waiting to see if I would follow.

I ran and caught him. He gave me a sidelong glance. The whites of his eyes gleamed.

"Chayin . . ." I touched his arm, that which bore the winged slitsa wound around a Parset blade. "Let me have your pouch."

"He does not want you to have it. He is right. You grow dependent."

"You use it!" I flared.

"I know how to judge its use! I said no, once . . ." He stopped. We were before M'lennin's quarters, where Sereth held the Liaison First.

"This is no arbitrary decision upon my part," he said. "You strain your body with your mind's demands as it is. Can you not get the help you need from the helsar's teachings, from your own hesting?"

"There is no one truth, no one hesting. A number of powerful minds have invested in the point of time we approach. I am surely not the strongest. The strain upon the moment is fantastic, the result, to me, unknowable. I doubt if any know it. Even Estrazi, who made this whole world, cannot foresee everything that occurs upon it."

"The ors knows," he said positively.

"Does it know whether or not I will live? I see only so far, and then there is nothing." And I spoke my fear for the first time aloud.

"It knows," he said. "But perhaps it is kinder if your mind holds certain things from you. You will not die in this battle." And he pushed me toward the door, which opened obediently.

I saw Dellin.

He was slumped over, still secured to the chair, which the men had moved back from the desk. There was no blood upon him; he was unconscious. Sereth lounged upon the wistwa desktop, one leg thrown over its creamy expanse. He twisted around as we entered, and again I was struck by the animal ease of him.

"It took you long enough," he said. "Come here!"

I went to him, and he put his hands upon my arms.

"Perhaps you can get him to tell you what he will not tell us."

"Let him be. All that is left to any of us is to do what the time demands. Celendra can get no help against what will be, any more than you or I."

"You cannot know that." Sereth's grip tightened upon me. "I cannot make decisions on the basis of riddles. Do what I say!"

Anger rose in me, born of Chayin's offhand use, slapped into life by Sereth's contempt. "I will, but it is time wasted. You have done enough to him. He cannot harm you; what he knows cannot harm you. Whatever seeds he and Celendra have planted will not bear fruit."

"I must know what Celendra meant, and why he keeps back that knowledge from us."

"Have Chayin ask the ors. Either you believe me, or you do not. In the end, it will be the same." And I jerked my arms from his grasp and went to Dellin.

I took his black-haired head in my hands and lifted the deadweight of it. He breathed unevenly. Kneeling, I brought his face, slippery with sweat, close to mine. I could see the swelling and darkening of their work upon him.

"Dellin," I called him softly. Then again. I could feel him give up his pretense, his refuge. He opened his eyes, and I saw suddenly the trapped animal, who

would gnaw its own leg off if it could. But even that
had been denied him. It took some time for him to
know me.

His eyes focused, and his swollen lips moved. I
asked for water, and Sereth sent Lalen, all this time
squatting in the corner, to fetch it. When he had done
so, I gave him drink. He winced. There was a lot of
blood in his mouth, and more when he coughed.

He squinted at me, as if from some great distance.

"What is it?" I whispered to him. "Tell me. I will
not let them hurt you again." I wondered if he knew
that they would not have to hurt him again. I brushed
my hand over his neck, up against his ears, and found
my fingers, when they came away, dark with his
blood. Then I knew that he did know. He was loath
to die here upon Silistra, so far from all he loved. And
I saw us as he did, barbarians all. What brought an
ache inside me was his confusion. He did not understand. And he wanted desperately to understand for
what he was dying. I had, for him, no answer.

"Estri," he mumbled through his broken mouth,
"help me. I hurt." A spasm of coughing wracked him.
I closed my eyes and held his head against my breast,
and his injuries came clear to my sensing. Without
thought, I sent what I could of strength and healing to
him; what small skills I had did their work. I demanded more.

Dellin raised his head, and his gray eyes were
clearer.

"I will not let them hurt you," I promised, helping
him as he tried to straighten up. His eyes flickered
from Sereth, to Chayin, to Lalen against the far wall.
He took a breath that rasped and gurgled in his chest.

"Let them say it." He formed the words slowly,
with great effort.

"Sereth, tell him."

He did not, but slid off the desk, putting his arm
around Chayin's shoulders. They spoke in low tones,
and finally both came to stand before Dellin's chair.

"If you tell us, and cooperate, we will let you live. What has been done can sometimes be undone." His hands were upon his hips, voice flat, cold. "You have my word. I could use you, in case Celendra has to call you again. We will leave you here when we leave. You will, of course, be bound, but someone will find you eventually. That," he said, tossing his head, "is the best offer I am willing to make."

Dellin stared at them a time; then he nodded, wincing at the pain of movement.

"Celendra has asked," he said slowly, "for certain aid; M'ksakka sends it." He stopped, fearful. "Two warships, that she may revenge herself upon her father's murderer." He coughed. "It is complicated. I could try to stop it." He slumped in the chair, helpless, waiting.

I wondered if Dellin knew that very man stood before him, and decided he did not. Chayin's face was emotionless. Upon Sereth I saw another expression, as if he had expected this, and had been upheld.

"When you feel well enough," the Ebvrasea said, his voice a knife upon silk, "we will see that you have a chance to call them. Think upon what you would say."

Dellin nodded, and a spasm of coughing wracked him once more. Chayin took the uris pouch from his belt and handed it to me. I recollected, as I unstoppered it and poured a huge amount down Dellin's throat, how much it had strengthened me in the desert. I contrived to spill some upon my hand as I passed it back. Chayin saw, but only smiled. I licked my fingers, that place between thumb and first, and was myself greatly strengthened.

"Estri!" Chayin's voice snapped. I jumped to my feet, guilty. "I am hungry. It must be past time for a meal." Only then did I realize that he could not read the clocks here, all Bipedal Standard. I almost laughed in relief that he would not chastise me.

And we left Dellin there, with Lalen to guard him, and went into the Liaison's kitchen. There I fed them both by hand, disdaining the menial robot blinking ready in its alcove. The thought came to me that I should have built a fire in the midst of the M'ksakkan marble, if I were truly as Dellin saw me. While I worked scavenging a meal from Dellin's stores, I set my healing upon my own wound, to test my skill.

When I handed Sereth and Chayin their plates of parr and narne, and served them the excellent kifra Dellin stocked, the scab, dried and white-edged, began to curl up from my skin. I scratched it, for it itched me. The scab came away, revealing new copper skin underneath, hardly darker than elsewhere upon my sun-bronzed arm. I smiled to myself, as I took two of the plates back to Lalen and our captive.

Lalen took his meal from me, surly and taciturn. He set the plate upon the wistwa desk and fell upon the contents with relish.

"I will not feed him. I am no nursemaid," he said when I set down the second plate and turned to leave. "Nor will I release him to feed himself."

So I fed him, as best I could. It was not easy for him to eat even the softer foods I had intentionally brought. He did, however, drink the goblet of kifra down to the last drop. Over it his eyes met mine; under those frank straight brows of his they seemed steadied. He sat straighter, his spasms had left him, and the blood upon his face had clotted. Lalen, finished with his plate, watched us, glowering.

"You will live." I said my first words to him as I rose to leave.

"Do not talk to him," Lalen snapped.

And I turned and left, silent, lest Lalen take out upon Dellin any temper I aroused in him.

As I reentered the kitchen, muted, angry voices greeted me. Sereth leaned against the steel oven.

"We have no option. We must wait and see what Celendra does. She will keep Dellin informed, you can be sure. I would not move from here until she screams for help. When we hear that Wiraal's men have arrived, we will leave here, and not sooner."

"But the M'ksakkans—"

"What can you do? Call a Day-Keeper and tell him that while beating information out of a Liaison you have stumbled upon this unlikely plot? Think, man!"

Chayin paced the floor, stalking he knew not what. He slammed his fist hard into the menial's blinking panel, killing it. Its machine's breath poured from it, dark with death, bearing an acrid odor. Chayin stared at it, then turned. He saw me.

"There is nothing we can do," he said to Sereth. "Nothing at all." His black eyes, far behind the veil, pinned me still, my back pressed against the door. Then he looked away, at his hands in their tight fists. He opened them, spread his long dark fingers. "It is just that I am not one to sit and wait. I will take the watch of him with Lalen." And he strode to the door, pushing past me as it opened for him.

Sereth rose, too, and came toward me.

"You should eat," he said, and rather than disobey him, I ate.

"Chayin said," he remarked as he watched me pick at my food, "that you must have gained great weapons in the helsar. He wonders why you do not share them with us." His tone was only level. It was his eyes that froze me, a chunk of denter halfway to my mouth. I had sensed Chayin's testing. I put down the food, pushed my plate away.

"Could you stop me, as Raet once did?" he questioned. "Could you imprison me in my own body?"

"Yes," I whispered. "I could do that."

Sereth slid down into a chair. He brushed his hand across his eyes.

"What else can you do?" he demanded.

"A great deal, and very little. Do not make me show you. I crave this last normalcy, before all goes once more insane. It is just a little to ask."

"What do you fear?"

"Once I open to my strengths, what will I be? Whom may I find to talk with, to love? I would not be so different, so alone, as I will surely come to be. Would you still want me, upon my sufferance? Knowing that by whim I could reduce you to component atoms, would you rest easy in my arms? Would any man?" I pushed away and rose, walking to the man's-height crystal window. Sereth was silent.

"Whatever weapons, the strength is in the wielder. Do you need no practice, no work upon these skills?" he asked at length.

"I save what I have for my moment of need. It could be that I am wrong to do so, but three days' practice will not even the odds before the millennia Raet has had to hone his skills."

"Show me something," Sereth insisted, watching me from the chair. I shrugged, hopeless.

"What if I tell you a thing? Celendra will not call until the evening of Wiraal's arrival. She is angry. She waits for Dellin to call her and apologize." I turned to face him.

"Show me something," he repeated, implacable.

I sighed and brushed my hair, now dry, from my eyes.

"Watch, then." The menial robot was, dead as it was, only a junk heap of useless parts. I pointed to it, then lowered my hand. The metal burst into heatless flame, fierce and bright. It was simply a matter of creating an envelope around that form, an envelope of different natural laws, in which metal and glass and rubber became unstable elements. When there was nothing in the alcove, I raised my hand again and erased the pocket of alternate space I had created. It was neatly done, for a first try. I sensed no leakage. Sereth's eyes upon me were a stranger's.

"And what else?"

"Anything. Name it," I said with a sinking feeling.

"You say Celendra will not call. Make her call." Obedient to him, I closed my eyes to do so.

"Wait!" he snapped. "I just wanted to know if you could. Have you done such with me?"

"No," I whispered, agonized.

"Chayin said he felt you in his mind, that you did things to him he does not fully understand. Is this true?"

I sank to my knees upon the M'ksakkan marble. "Yes." I barely formed the word, wretched, staring at the veins in the stone.

"Get up! Come here!" I went to him, where he had risen. He stared down at me. "You want normalcy? I will give you some. And we will see if the bonds I have upon you are strong enough. Go and make yourself ready. I will come to you, when I choose."

I turned, mute, to obey him.

"When I open that door, I would see you kneeling by the couch, suitably adorned."

I felt the flush upon my skin as the door made way for me.

It was a long time before he came to me. Time enough for my knees to turn numb and cold. Long enough for me to reflect upon what bonds he meant, and to learn that they were strong indeed.

When he did come, he himself tested them upon me.

"Please," I begged him, my body arched, sweating, under his hand.

"Where are your formidable skills now? What are they?" he demanded sternly.

"Nothing. They are nothing." He touched me upon the belly, and I moaned and sought him, my lips upon the inside of his thighs. I kissed him, bit gently, pleading, helpless, crell to him and my own body's needs.

When it pleased him, he took me, and I wept under his thrust.

"Whatever else you are," he said, crouched above me, wiping the sweat from his upper lip, "you are still a woman." And his hands would not let me rest. I tried to roll away, exhausted. His white teeth were sharp and strong upon my breasts.

"And do you know your bonds now, little crell?" He laughed low.

I knew them. The gift of a night alone was not wasted upon us. Those moments glow in my mind, each rich with the savor that only life-risk can impart. Crell under my master's hand, I was suddenly wealthy. Opulent is life, in the light of such freedom as comes with submission to a man who will accept no less.

I lay long after he slept, thinking. His arm thrown across my breasts, he dreamed and muttered in his sleep. Sereth and I had pegged an evening of time together in that room I had fitted to my taste so long ago as M'lennin's couch-mate. How I had hated him. I had also first lain with Dellin here, upon this couch made by Astria's own master. Celendra, surely, must use this keep. I envisioned her, black and supple, sinuous upon the silken covers that had been fashioned to my order. Then he awoke and chased all thoughts of her from my mind.

The next morning, Amarsa second third, Dellin sent his message to M'ksakka. Intra-, rather than inter-space, it sped, as the M'ksakkan ships do in the great void. But such can be done only at certain points in the cosmos; the message would rise up and out, lasered, for more than a light-day before it passed, instantaneous, around 160 light-years of space. We would not get an answer before Amarsa second sixth, when Wiraal was due in Astria with his jiasks.

We waited. Chayin, desert stalker, strode the confines of Dellin's keep. He paced and paced, and drew ever more distant.

Sereth, perhaps from his Slayer's training, rested content. He waited for Celendra to call, patient, sure. He watched Chayin. They worked their skills together, well-matched, that they might keep their sword arms loose.

Clouds drove the humor from Sereth's eyes, as the

days passed. Often he stretched his lean form upon
the floor in the room where Dellin was kept, smoking
the Liaison's danne in a ragony pipe, meditative. He
would talk to Dellin without rancor in those times, as
if the two were together again in Arlet, as if Dellin
were not his prisoner, not beaten near to death, not
bound to his chair. From Dellin, Sereth extracted all
that he wanted to know, while Chayin paced and
snarled.

Lalen came to Sereth once, where he lay there
upon the iridescent Thrah pelts, and asked after his
blade gruffly, that he might have something to do
with his hands. The blond-haired man had honed every edge he owned in turn, until they would each slice
a hair from the strand's weight alone.

Sereth, who never left such things to another,
gave up his gear to Lalen.

The hands crawled upon the M'ksakkan clocks.
The B.F. date changed sluggishly. Celendra did not
call.

Sereth brought Chayin to couch with us, that he
might bridge the gap he felt growing between them.
At sun's rising, Amarsa second fifth, I woke to Chayin's arm upon me.

"Get yourself elsewhere," he whispered to me. "I
would be with him a time alone."

Sereth's stiffened form let me know he had
heard. Once I had wakened him with a single word,
spoken in sleep. I leaned over him, kissing the nape of
his neck before I rose. He made no move.

The door closed soundless behind me. I stood
alone in a corridor of angry memories. I wandered it
for a time, my eyes stinging, my face both dry and
tingling from lack of sleep. My feet brought me to the
kitchen, and I drank rana until my eyelids would stay
open of their own accord. It was second fifth. Today
she would call.

I watched the sun's rape of the night through the
window. I sensed the nature of what concerned

Chayin. It was a private thing, between them. I did not seek to intrude further.

By mid-meal, Celendra still had not called. I prepared food, brought it to Lalen and Dellin. I brought also servings for Chayin and Sereth. Their denter cooled upon the plates, the blood and fat congealing on the meat. I read the ors, smoked danne, stretched out upon those alien dead beast's skins.

Khys, I thought as I closed the book, might be better understood in another translation. I sighed and put the Parset volume aside. The test of its augury came fast upon us.

Dellin's eyes were on me when I looked up. We had not spoken since I had assured him of his life. Perhaps he, as I, felt there was nothing to say. Lalen had eaten, but he had not fed the prisoner.

"Thank you," said Dellin to me when I brought him the cold food and fed him, bite by bite.

"Thank Sereth, that you live to eat," I said icily. I heard the manacles upon his wrists clink.

"Estri, please."

"I do not want to hear it," I said, thrusting a large enough bite in his mouth to silence him. The door slid aside. Lalen rose.

Sereth wore the Shaper's cloak upon his shoulders. He had not done so upon the way here, but wound it around under his leathers. He avoided my eyes. Whatever had passed between him and Chayin, he was not at ease with it.

Chayin walked to the desk, where their food lay, and touched the coldness with his finger. He also had taken time to battle-dress. He even wore his high boots.

"Doubtless, you can do better than this, Estri," he said to me, giving the slab of meat a desultory prod. Chayin was greatly eased. He even smiled.

So I took the meal I had made them and threw it away, and made another. I served them, with exaggerated crellishness, where they sat talking together, near to Dellin. They took no notice.

When they had finished, Sereth went to the master board. He had just activated the visual display when the call code sounded. He slapped the board quiescent and dived out of range as Chayin jerked Dellin's chair before the desk. Kneeling beneath the desktop, out of sight, Sereth drew his blade with one hand, and reached up to activate the receiver with the other. Chayin stood upon my left, Lalen upon my right, though I had not seen him cross the room.

"How are you feeling?" purred Celendra's voice. The light her image threw flickered across Dellin's half-healed face.

"Better," he managed.

"You look terrible," she said sharply.

"I passed out in the hall. I will be fine." His eyes watched a face we could not see. I saw him shiver. Beneath the desktop, Sereth's blade rested naked between Dellin's bound legs. "What do you want?"

"Just to see if you were ill. I see you are ill. Have you any word?"

"No," croaked Dellin.

"What?"

"No word from them. But do not worry."

"That is easy for you to say," Celendra snorted. "You see no more than your hand before your face. I want you to call me, tomorrow mid-meal. I have great unrest. Perhaps by then you will be well enough to leave your couch." And she broke the connection without even a tasa.

Dellin slumped in his bonds, white-faced.

"So"—Sereth laughed—"Celendra called him upon your schedule, Estri. To see how he was feeling." And his laughter infected Lalan and Chayin. I found myself smiling. The jiasks would get there tomorrow, and we would be informed by Celendra of her exact reaction. We did not even have to wait for her to call us. She had ordered Dellin to call her! Chayin hugged me against him. For a moment I was eye-to-eye with the uritheria on his bicep. It leered at me. Then he let me go.

Sereth went and again set up visual screening, that we might see any approaching us. The day was exhausted before he turned away from it.

"Let us take a walk," he said, stretching. "I am stiff from sitting." He led me unresisting back down the hall of marble, into the corridor of star steel, down the steps into the outer court. The extravagance of Astrian dusk turned him as copper as I. I sniffed the air, sweet and clean after the keep's alien odors. It caressed the skin, told stories of the life it carried. I breathed summer sarla and narne bloom, and the pungent ripeness of this fertile land whispered all around. As I watched, the constellations made their stately entrance into the newborn night. Yellow criers took song, while swamp kephers kept the time, and a hundred species, waking, hummed and buzzed and whistled.

Sereth's hand was cool and reassuring on my waist. My father's cloak rustled upon his shoulders. Through M'lennin's fastidious gardens we circuited. The second time around the outer court, he pushed me gently to the grass within a circular harinder brake. We lay there long, looking at the stars.

And that was where Lalen, breathing heavily, found us.

"Dellin speaks again with the woman. Chayin sent me for you." He said this last to empty air; Sereth was gone, running. Lalen reached down and lifted me like a small child and half-dragged me beside him. He was, I reminded myself as I struggled to pace him and retain my arm, responsible for me.

"Let me go!" I demanded as I stumbled while he impelled me up the steps. "I warned you." I sighed, and caused his grip to drop from my arm. I walked up the stairs, and he made way for me. I smiled to myself as he fell in beside me. His consternation was evident. He did not ask, and I did not enlighten him.

"What, exactly, did she say, from the beginning?"

Chayin recited it for us. Wiraal had arrived early. Celendra could do little else than serve them. The significance of a visit by so many Parsets was not lost upon her. She demanded his aid, and he referred her to the Slayers, to her own Day-Keepers. She fumed. Dellin pointed out that he could not be implicated in the disposal, out of hand, of twenty-two Parsets, at this moment. He suggested she bide her time until the ships came. She snarled at him. Chayin's dark face bore a huge grin as he dutifully repeated every curse. In the end, Celendra had agreed. After all, Parsets are men, like any others, she had acknowledged. With that profound statement, she had broken the link.

Sereth was not pleased. Wiraal was too early to suit him. He knew Celendra. He had timed the arrival of the jiasks in Astria with that of certain other sections of his total force.

"It is too long between," he said softly. "We will have to go in there now, take her, keep her there, and quiet, until Jaheil and the tiasks arrive. I do not like it. I cannot give her enough time to figure things out." He slammed his hand upon the desk.

"Chayin! That man of yours needs a lesson. 'By' is not the same as 'on.' If he were one of mine, I would do without him."

The Viable

The woman, alone, posited upon the gold square of prime mover, on the board of catalysts.

Though her legs tremble, she is supported by what comes to be between them.

One who submits to the bidding of the First Weather is upheld by gale and breeze, and the very mountains make haste to provide her a resting place upon their summits.

The weak is surmounted by the strong, and thus comes to contain its strength.

Only that which may be conceived can be done. It is necessary to prepare expectation concomitant with the fruitfulness of the time.

Adjuration: That which is born to fill a need is always strong enough, for the demands of the time provide helpers as they are needed. The principle of replication is raised here to its purpose. What profit to that force, if in its hour it quails and trembles? The seed when placed finger-deep in warm loam, commences the duty for which the time has prepared it. Though it may tremble when first it *is buried in the earth, shut away from air and light, it knows its purpose. So must it be with the Viable. The seed does not draw back from the cracking of shell or the putting forth of blind shoots, lest it should lose them. The seed knows that to reach the light once again it must thrust upward until it breaks the surface asunder, and that at that moment of success it will be other than that which undertook the task. The seed does not fear the loss of its seedness, but recognizes the transformation as its destiny and goes to meet its fate with confidence, for within it is the conception of rebirth.*

—excerpted from *Ors Yris-tera*

VIII. Well Astria Revisited

We stood knee-deep in the sewers that feed into the Litess. Above us was Well Astria herself, open, vulnerable. She was a high-couch woman, not built to withstand siege. Below us were the undertunnels through which we had come here, unobserved.

We had left Dellin, bound and gagged, in his outer court. The Liaison's keep we sealed. It might stay sealed forever, as we had erased all entry prints from it, retroactive to our exit. The building had no friends, and would open itself to no one. None would make use of the tools within, at least not for a long time.

Our makeshift plan was much changed. Chayin had taken a different route than we, and by now he had surely bought his well token and reserved Celendra for this night, as Wiraal was supposed to do the next evening. He would be moving among his men, in the common room, spreading new orders. If he had found Celendra, he would be, even now, with her in my own chamber, where the ceilings had been muraled by the finest gol-etchers upon Silistra, and the sky came tinted through the translucent roof.

I sighed, and wrinkled my nose, wishing I were Parset and could fold my nostrils against the smell.

As a child, I had not been bothered by the smell. These watery, phosper-mold-covered stone conduits had been my refuge, my secret world. I ran my hand along the stones, seeking. One did not waste gol upon sewers. I recalled the raft I had assembled here, piece by surreptitiously acquired piece, on which I had poled my way through my fantasies when so young the sluggish water had been waist-high upon me.

We could probably have taken the stairs just behind us, and walked Astria's back corridors unobserved. I judged it between eighth and ninth bell, busiest enth of the evening in any Well. The girls would be in the common room, bedecked, awaiting their patrons' pleasure. The dining, drink, and drug chambers would be filled. It was the choosing hour.

Know you Astria? She is not as Arlet, where Liaisons' and Day-Keepers' school and Slayers' hostel all exist within the outer walls. All that we need is brought to us from our dependent city, Port Astrin, south from here, where the Litess meets the Embrodming Sea. Between Astria and the port, upon the easterly banks of the Litess, lie the Day-Keepers' school and the Slayers' hostel, at a distance of some sixty and seventy neras, respectively.

I did not take us up those stairs, which would have led into the couching keeps. My fingers found what I sought at the level of my shoulder. I could barely make it out—the first stra rung of eighty, set into the stone, limned faintly with moss.

"Here," I said, and my voice echoed back to me. Sereth's hand touched the rung. I could feel Lalen's bulk, ever behind me. "At the top is a stra trap, which may be lifted. These crawlways exist only in the older buildings. They are seldom used."

Sereth swung lightly up the first rungs. High above us, twelve floors, lay the Keepress' chamber, in the oldest and highest tower, which was once the whole Well. Now the Well curled around, her gleaming towers much multiplied, encircling a nera of open ground, but still was the first business of Astria pleasure and replication, carried on in this tower alone.

We climbed. I counted the slippery rungs. Once I lost my foothold, and my heel struck Lalen's head as I hung by my hands' grip. His fingers grabbed my ankle, steadied my weight, guided my foot back to the rung. I pressed my face against the cool stone, thinking of the fifty-rung drop.

When I had gained the seventy-first, Sereth lifted the trap. Light poured in through the opening, blinding after enths in the mold-lit dark. There should have been no light there. I scrambled the remaining rungs, disdaining caution.

Sereth's hand reached down. I took it, and crouched beside him in the crawlway, bright with strung power globes and filled with cables like huge black slitsas upon the gol. I looked around in wonder. Astria was much changed. Above me were pipes of stra and copper—the plumbing that had been once the primary reason for these passages.

Sereth must have read my face. He pulled me gently away from the trap as Lalen's head appeared in it. The two of them lowered it soundlessly into place.

"The Keepress' chamber," he reminded me gently.

"The Keepress' chamber," I repeated, dazed. How dare she string lights in my crawlways? And for what conceivable purpose? Every torch sconce in Well Astria was a precious stone, sculptured by a master's hand.

Sereth pushed me, hardly more than a nudge. The glare of the naked globes did ugly things to his skin and to the scar upon his cheek.

I shook off my feelings, and, half-crouched, led us down the crawlway. I found my smallness an advantage; the men had to go on their hands and knees, slowly. Lalen's shoulders brushed the walls. I took us up an ascending passage, then right upon level surface, then again right into a sloping, curving tightness that would lead, directly, to my old keep. Even in the olden days of this tower's building, when we were so few and fresh from war that none would raise hand to another, it was thought that the Keepress might need her own exit.

It was slow going. My knees hurt, and my palms stung. Lalen cursed continually the close walls that abraded him. When we reached the passage landing, a small level space before a wall of amber gol, the stra door set into it was locked tight from the inside.

I sat between them, where they huddled upon the landing. The door was crouched-woman-sized; I hoped Lalen could squeeze through it. We waited.

After a time we heard voices beyond the wall. All that could be told from them was that one voice was male, the other female. Sereth, needlessly, put his fingers to his lips. Lalen drew his gol-knife.

The voices changed their tenor, grew faint. Perhaps a quarter-enth passed. I shifted my weight. Sereth hissed at me.

At that moment there was a creaking, and the low stra door was swung back from the inside, exposing a Parset rug that did not belong there. Crouched upon it, peering at us, was Chayin. Torchlight flickered over his hugely grinning face. She had had the grace to leave the sconces, then. I crawled through first, at the cahndor's wordless invitation, wondering what had become of my white-upon-white floor tapestry, that one I had commissioned in exotic Galesh.

Then I saw Celendra. In mid-crawl, I saw her, and rose up on my knees. She lay upon that red mat she must have brought with her from Arlet, all bound up in her Arletian love chains. They are women's chains, strong enough, yet light. They would not chafe her black and shapely wrists like crell chains. Objectively, I admitted that she was very lovely, lying there, bound and gagged with her own thigh-length black hair. Chayin had balled a great wad of it and forced it into her mouth, taking more of her silken mane and binding it across her mouth, then tying a great knot at the back of her dusky neck. Her gold-green eyes stared over her gag, terrified. I did not blame her. Chayin can be truly terrifying. He had bound each hand to her ankles, between which she had a handbreadth slack of links, as is often done with pleasure chains. She was leashed to the foot of my Astrian couch, on six links of tether.

It struck me funny. I knelt, laughing softly, until Sereth pushed me out of his way. I fell to my side and lay there, smiling. When Celendra saw him, she closed her eyes. Trembling, she bowed her head to the extent her leash allowed it.

Lalen squeezed through and closed and locked that half-door, his quick eye even replacing the rusty curtain that Chayin had thrown back to expose it. Chayin, who sat now upon the rumpled couch covers, was fully dressed. In his hand he held a braided strap, of the sort with which Parsets discipline women. Wide it is, and not fearsome in itself. Wielded by Chayin's strength, by a man's strength, it was a very terrible instrument indeed. I recalled the feel of that strength when I had displeased him in the desert. I looked around. I might have been in Arlet, rather than Astria. Celendra had brought all her accouterments with her. She had played at submission a long time. But now she shook with fear. She would find out how the reality differs from the fantasy. She moaned softly. She would moan often, as a crell. She did not know, of course, unless her forereading had told her, that she would be crell. I found it satisfying. There is never ease between beautiful women. I took pride in my position of high favor with these powerful men, and joy that she was not so favored. I stretched out upon one hip and crooked my leg. I was no longer angry. Celendra would get exactly what she deserved.

"I bought her token from Wiraal, and one for tomorrow night, also. I paid, even, a deposit for overage, that I might have her undisturbed from now through the morning of second seventh. The fee was exorbitant. She was flattered, and so should she have been. I have better cleaning threx stalls in Nemar. It was hard for me to believe," said Chayin, grinning broadly, his face turned so she could not see it, "that this was truly the Well-Keepress, when I found her. I told her I would have no lesser in my arms. That is the truth. I think I have never had."

Sereth had walked around Celendra and was leaning against the window. When I lived here, those windows had no M'ksakkan crystal in them. The room was all reds, browns, and blacks. I looked up at the ceiling that was also roof to this tower. That, at least, was unchanged. Once a year, the stars lined up with the etchings of the constellations. It is a glorious sight, upon the anniversary of the Well-raising. This night, it was not unlovely.

I went to Sereth, thinking to give solace. His face was against the pane, his shoulders hunched. Only when I peered up into his eyes did I realize I could not give it.

I reminded myself that this woman had birthed him his only son. That in her, he saw Tyith, and what she had done to him in revenge for the boy's death. That she had known Tyith would die, I did not doubt. What lay between them, that a woman would sacrifice her own son to destroy the man who had brought that child upon her? I touched him, wordless, and to my surprise, he took me under his arm and laid his chin upon the crown of my head. I felt the stiffness leave him. I kissed the hollow in his neck, running my tongue there lightly.

"Be silent in this," he whispered to me, "unless I ask you to speak, no matter what is said." He looked down upon me sternly.

"I promise," I said, and a smile touched him. Forever he was silencing me, and forever I disobeyed him, without meaning to do so.

There was a sharp, muted sound, the sound of lash upon flesh. We both turned. Chayin struck her once more upon the back. The leather hissed, parting her skin. She lunged upon her tether and presented her buttocks to him. He greeted them with a restrained stroke. Welts rose high and angry upon her black cheeks.

"She likes that," said Sereth dryly. "Do not give her too much." But those devastating, knife-sharp blows were not to Celendra's liking. She wriggled and cried out around her gag. Chayin, for all his punishing savagery, was very careful. And I realized he did not use his full strength upon her. He struck always as men strike women, judging, giving quarter, and even that was too much for her. Huddled before him, her neck stretched to the tether, she seemed smaller than I remembered her. Chayin put down the lash.

He leaned over, twisting her head back. The couch creaked with the strain as the leash hummed taut.

"Do you like that?" he asked her, his face close to hers, shaking her head back and forth. She made noises around her gag. There were tears in her eyes. "Blink if you like being whipped." Celendra did not blink. "Good," grunted Chayin. "You are not supposed to like it. When you are crell, you will bring me the lash in your teeth, upon your knees, begging."

Celendra struggled wildly. She was half Parset, and she knew, better than I had known, what it meant to be crell. Chayin arched her back by the hair until she lost her balance and fell heavily, her body held off the ground by the collar and leash.

"Estri, Sereth, come sit here." I ran my palms over my face, that I might smooth away any shadow of my mixed emotions. I went and sat by Chayin, where he patted the couch beside him. Celendra's knees were at Chayin's feet. Sereth came and sat near me. He looked down at her, his face cold. She met his eyes, pleading, shaking her head to and fro; little strangled noises came out of her. I put my hands around Sereth's arm, leaned my head against it. Celendra watched me. I smiled politely.

"We have not been," said Chayin to her, "properly introduced. I found it served me to fabricate a name," he explained to Sereth, who needed no explanation. "Jasrey aniet Saer"—he grinned—"is the name I used, if you have need to call me by it."

"Son of a threx, are you?" Sereth laughed. Celendra looked between them, horrified, understanding. "Let me introduce you two properly. Celendra Doried bast Aknet, meet the man that set your father about the chaldra of the soil; Chayin rendi Inekte, chosen son of Tar-Kesa, cahndor of Nemar, cahndor of Menetph."

Celendra found strength in her to renew her struggles. Chayin kicked her casually in the diaphragm. She choked and coughed and finally knelt quiet, her head down. Tears fell upon her breasts, ran off those dusky nipples, raining down upon her thighs and knees.

"Stop it, crell, or I will give you a beating worth such a production!" Chayin snapped, irritated. Celendra sniffled. Her shoulders ceased heaving. She straightened perceptibly.

Chayin ran the length of braided leather back and forth between his long-fingered hands. Celendra watched the motion, hypnotized. If she had been a man, it would have been the sharp-fanged huija he used upon her, and her back no more than shredded flesh upon exposed bone. I had seen it. Celendra had not. The welts she bore were nothing. I knew. She did not know. I shot a glance at Lalen, sitting cross-legged before the rust-toned curtain, drawn sword on his knees. Lalen, I saw, also recollected what it was to be crell. His stony face showed his contempt for her, she who did not know.

"That is better," said Chayin. "Straighten your back. Pull your stomach in. Throw those breasts out." With each order, he slapped the leather loudly against itself. She was quick to obey him.

"Celendra . . ." Sereth said softly. She flinched as though she had been struck, and raised her face to his. "We know about your arrangement with M'ksakka. Your friend Dellin lies bound and gagged, helpless in his own keep." Celendra shuddered. Her head bobbed. Her shoulders sank, and she slumped. Chayin brought the coiled lash down hard across her breasts.

"I told you to sit up," he said. She sat up, her eyes upon Chayin's hands. She had begun to sweat. Little beads of it broke out upon her forehead, between her breasts.

"I have given you to Chayin. Do you understand that? So sure were we, so easy was it to take you, that your fate was decided a set before you fell to us. You have been a crell this whole time—Chayin's possession, only you did not know it. Now you know. You, by my will and design, shall be less than a beast of burden in Nemar. I gave you to him. You are his."

Celendra's body pleaded with him. If she could, she would have kissed his feet. She could not. All she could do, she did—widen her eyes and tremble and make tiny noises like some poisoned yit.

"As you may know, there are many different kinds of crells," said Chayin informatively. I thought of those oiled, fragrant girls he had kept at his palace in Nemar North. I thought of the cell where I had been chained. "What your lot is like depends on you. Though you are surely no man's ten, you might keep yourself from the mines. We shall see. I will free your tongue, and with it you will choose for me. You will repeat exactly what I say. You will beg to live, as crell to me."

And he took his gol-knife and cut the hair that bound her mouth. The shorn tresses fell to the floor. He pulled the balled, soaking hair from her mouth. She chose for him then, as I had so long ago. With quaking voice she proclaimed herself crell. She gave her life to another, that she might not die. I felt, for the first time, a twinge of sorrow. Chayin was not playing. He truly did not like her; doubtless he would not keep her. I wondered what her lot would be like in Nemar.

Sereth rubbed his hand up and down my arm. He

touched me lightly on the lips. I started, realized I had been staring.

"Celendra!" Sereth snapped. She raised dumb eyes to him. She seemed stunned.

"I want you to tell me exactly what precautions you have taken against your master's forces. You do not know how much I know. If I were you, I would not lie."

She tossed her head. For a moment I saw Celendra, haughty and regal, who had once said to me that there were not many men who could conquer her, even for a night. Then that woman was gone, and a velvet-soft stranger looked out of those eyes at him.

"I knew it," she whispered. "Each night, I waited. I knew it would come. When they could not kill you, I knew it just a question of time. I am glad . . ." She choked. "Glad the waiting is over." And her shoulders shook, though she kept them well back. Sobs wracked her. Sereth shook his head and leaned back upon the couch, impassive.

Chayin struck her across the face. She composed herself. Her breasts quivered.

She told us what she had done: she had called upon the Slayers, who waited for Day-Keepers' approval. If they got it, any approaching army of Parsets would be dealt with by a contingent of Slayers, who were already preparing. When that was in progress would more Slayers swarm into Astria herself and dispatch the yra of jiasks who pleasured there. Also, she told us what we already knew—of Dellin and M'ksakka—and what she said, we knew was true.

"I want you to call a messenger. You will issue certain orders," Sereth said when she had finished. He still leaned back, nonchalant and easy upon the couch.

"No," she whispered. Hope lit her face bright.

"Do not tempt me," Sereth advised, sitting up. He regarded her, amused.

She shook her head. "If you need me, there is hope yet. No."

"Little fool," he mused, as he got to his feet. He

took the tether and unclipped it from the couch, arching her up until he could hook the clip to the chain between her ankles. She lay there, her body a tight bow, helpless. She had sought to bite him. He was not pleased.

"With your permission, Cahndor?" Sereth paused, kneeling over her, his hand in her chald.

"I have always wanted to see how you do it," said Chayin, leaning forward. "I have seen the results, but never the work in progress."

"It is only"—Sereth grinned—"a matter of timing."

In less than an enth Celendra wrote the message that Sereth wanted. In fact, she pleaded passionately to be allowed to do so. When Serenth's hand came close to her lips, she kissed it. They unbound her hands that she might write it, and then they reshackled her.

She begged that they leave her hands free until she had seen the messenger. Sereth would not allow it. They had seen her thus before, he said. It was only she who saw the difference, only her submission that shamed her, he pointed out, locking her wrists again to her ankles.

Sereth, wisely, gave her no rest from his hands, lest she come back to her contentious self too soon. Over and over he repeated to her what she was to say.

"Should you not hide?" asked Chayin.

Sereth chuckled. "Clump yourselves. Often in Arlet there were more than two in a couching. I doubt it is different here." I saw the flaw in his thinking, but he had bid me be silent.

I was between Chayin's legs where he sat upon the couch, with Lalen curled around him, when the messenger's knock came.

Sereth opened the right-hand door, keeping it between his body and the messenger's sight. Those carved doors had been in my family two thousand years.

The man stood there, blinking. He noted Celendra, expressionless. Sereth closed the door. I twisted to see him better.

"High Lady!" he gasped, and went upon his knees, his forehead to the Parset rug.

Sereth momentarily went blank. I stood, uncertain, half-risen. Then he nodded.

I went and knelt before Ges, whose father's father had been in the service of my mother's mother. I touched his shoulder. He raised misted eyes to me. We were within a year the same age. His open-faced countenance had not changed. His blue eyes sparkled with joy. I offered my cheek that he might kiss it.

"We thought you dead, Estri." He waved his hand around. "Things are troubled."

"More than you know," I said softly. "But I am not dead." I smiled at him. I hated to do it, but the contingency was upon us.

"I need your help," I said to him.

"Anything," he promised. My eyes found Sereth's, for confirmation. He gave it.

"At sun's rising, put upon the door the sign of Feast of Conception, that none may disturb us. Between now and then, find, if you can, every man and woman loyal to Astria and bid them wear a white armband, that we will know them, and fight beside us to reclaim the Well." White and silver were my colors, once the colors of this room, for four generations the colors of Astria.

"There will be many anxious to do so. What of the Parsets?" He did not see, as we had thought such a one would not, that I had no right here, and that what he did would make him outlaw.

"They are my helpers. We will fight Celendra's men, and what Slayers raise hand against us. These messages of Celendra's are our doing. See that they get to the hostel. And more you must do."

Ges, like a trustful tasling about to be slaughtered, nodded. "There are few here who would uphold her," he said.

"Listen to her, take these words of ours from her mouth, spread them, and return."

And Sereth bade Celendra speak, that she might take a hand in her own destruction.

"Tell Rin that the morning is over." She wept. "Do you understand? It is the code we keep for signal. By that he will know." Her voice went from her. Sereth's hand upon her helped her find it. "By that he will know the message is truly from me, that you are my envoy." And the message Sereth gave to Ges, in Celendra's hand, informed Rin diet Tron that she had the Parsets in Astria under control, and that he need no longer keep alert for reinforcements from the south.

"That is all?" wondered Ges. He turned to me, his face troubled. "High Lady, I do not understand."

"Then you must serve me without understanding," I said gently. "Do as I say. Tell no Slayer of what we plan; deliver instead this falsehood. Trust me."

"I do," he said, his huge eyes sincere. He turned to go.

"And do not forget to place the sign of Feasts of Conception upon the door at sun's rising. It is of utmost importance," I urged.

"But who has conceived?" he asked.

"No one. Lie. Work something out with a girl. Just do it!"

Those blue eyes stared through me. He nodded slowly.

"I will talk to Cia. We shall say it is she." Sereth, at the door, struggled to contain his amusement. He opened it. Ges, uncertainly, turned to leave.

"Tasa, Ges!" I called after him. He waved, smiling over his shoulder. Sereth closed the door he had opened, and leaned against them where the two doors met. He let out a long, sibilant breath through his teeth. Celendra lay where he had left her, softly sobbing.

"You should have hidden," growled Chayin. He walked over to Celendra and put his foot upon her. "You make one more sound, and I will fill that mouth of yours too full for you to make a second. Do you understand?" She strangled a final sob. He reached under her and jerked her into the air by the chains, throwing her upon the couch as if she weighed nothing. Lalen barely scrambled out of the way. She lay there, unmoving, fighting for control. Even as she started screaming, Lalen's hand came down upon her mouth. I barely noticed.

I thought of Ges, whom I had betrayed. But I could not have told him. If he had known that the Ebvrasea stood before him, he would not have asked why we sought to deceive Rin diet Tron, First of the Slayers' Seven of Astria. Rin diet Tron, father of Jana, whom Celendra had surely murdered, was a man to whom chaldra was everything. By chaldra he determined the law within, and thus did he live. Though he had been my most-loved teacher, though he had taught me all my fighting skills, I could do no other than deceive him. It was his chaldra to protect the reigning Well-Keepress. He would assuredly do so.

Ges, of course, never delivered his message. Another message went out of Astria, to the Slayers' hostel, drafted by those who apprehended him, by those who monitored our every word and action through the surveillance devices Celendra had installed in each couching keep of Austria. Somewhere, at the end of those cables we had passed in the crawlways, sat Celendra's monitors—those who had sent a man I knew to us as messenger, those who thought that to such a loyal servant we would reveal our plans. And so out of Astria went the message we really desired—that we held the Keepress, that we awaited our army, and most important, that through Celendra's monitors was her safety assured.

Sereth called me to the window where he had waited, silent, more than an enth. Together we watched the lone threxman speeding through the night toward the Slayers' hostel. Though Celendra might do as she pleased in Astria, Rin diet Tron had no receiver for her star toys in his fortress. The rider, speeding, was proof. Celendra, who could speak to any Liaison upon Silistra at the flick of a switch, could not contact a Slayer or a Day-Keeper any faster than a threx could run.

We stood long together, waiting for Celendra's men to do our work for us. Muffled but unmistakable sounds of swordplay came to us from the floors below—Celendra's men, hastening to bind any whose loyalty to her was not sure, before they fell upon us. Celendra heard it, too, and laughed beneath her gag.

To fool a forereader, I thought as Lalen bestirred himself in response to a cadenced scratching upon the half-door at his back, is no easy matter.

Chayin took up his sword, smashing the hilt of it into a small mirror set in the gol beside a torch sconce. Celendra's head turned to watch him. Her eyes widened. She struggled. Two more of the spy-eyes did Chayin dispatch, while Celendra watched helpless, and in through the low door squeezed Wiraal and half his force.

Wiraal's drawn blade dripped redly. He was scratched, and his cape had been torn away. Breathing heavily, he leaned against the wall. Lalen stuck his head into the crawlway, peered around, closed and locked it.

Sereth had Celendra by the hair, dragging her bound blackness across the floor. He threw the Parset mat off the star-bought communicator she had used to summon the messenger. His sure hands woke the machine, readied it to speak to every room.

Only then did he lift his foot from her hair.

"I am going to free that flapping tongue of yours, and you are going to call them off! I want every male and female in this tower in the common room. They will bring with them all their weapons, and pile them there upon the floor. They will bring with them, each one, sufficient chains for their binding, and lock them upon one another, Wiraal will collect the keys. If we find one armed Slayer, one missing key, one fleeing coward, I will kill you." And then he knelt down and took the gag from her mouth, and she knew, as I, that he would, surely, kill her if she disobeyed.

She looked at him a moment, almost smiling. Then she bent her head and gave his orders, and for the first time her voice held defeat. Celendra had met her match. She had lost, and she knew it. She trembled, and her skin seemed gray, and she did not even raise her head when Sereth ripped the communicator apart, though wires and sparks and shards of glass showered her where she knelt.

"How?" she wondered, barely audible. I thought he would strike her. He did not. He squatted down and grinned at her. Wiraal cleaned his sword upon the shining well silks. His men, ten of them, tended each other's wounds. Their talk was sparse and gruff, that of men upon the kill. Uris pouches were passed. Leaning against the window, between two jiasks I did not know, I availed myself of one as it passed. So easy was Celendra brought low, despite all her skills. Knowing her, he had found it so easy. Even her last and most subtle ploy, that of the messenger, he had turned against her. She had orchestrated Sereth's destruction, knowing he would come, knowing even that I would be with him. He had taken the composition from her hands and played it for her, but his own arrangement.

"How?" Celendra begged to understand.

A knocking came at the double doors. Men shifted as one, their weapons ready. Chayin crossed the crowded keep in a dozen strides and cracked the doors. Then he opened them both as wide as they would go.

In that torchlit hallway stood the rest of Wiraal's jiasks. They were eleven, scruffy, bleeding, grinning. Upon their arms were draped necklaces of crell chains, brought with them from Nemar, for which they had not yet found use. They flanked their number in Slayers, whose slate leathers had been pulled from them, and replaced with manacles. Their necks were bound together with locked loops of a single length of thick chain, as is done with mine crells.

"Looks as if you can kill her, Sereth," said Chayin sourly, regarding the wounds upon his men.

"Is there resistance out there?" Sereth queried the room in general, as the jiasks pushed their prisoners within.

"Not since that voice in the air," chortled one jiask. "We started fighting these beforehand, a slight miscalculation. When they heard it, they just threw their swords down. It was the most amazing thing I ever saw!" The jiask shook his head, still laughing. In his humor he had lapsed into Parset.

Sereth put his hands upon Celendra, unresisting, and rebound her. He removed all but the leash and collar, and the wristlets, which now secured her hands behind her back.

Pointing first at Lalen, then at Wiraal and Chayin, he pushed Celendra through the crowd out the door.

Though he had not invited me, I ran to him. He stopped, just in the hallway. Lalen took up his stance at my side. Sereth's cold eyes measured me.

"You may," he said.

The kill lust was upon him, then, as it was upon Chayin, and every male face I saw. Even Lalen, always stern, seemed transformed. Their eye-whites glittered and their teeth flashed. They stood poised there, in that white-gol hallway with its amber floor, waiting for his word to unleash them.

"You may, but stay close," he said again, turning to the crowded room. I reached down and set my razor-moons, that they would leap unimpeded to my hand if I chose to use them.

"You"—he pointed to the jiask who had spoken—"I give you charge. Take half your force and rip out every cable and machine you can find. Do not neglect the crawlways. Be cautious, be thorough. The rest of you, split into twos and check every chamber, a floor at a time, starting here. I want no living thing any-

where in Astria but the common room. If you run out
of bonds, kill them. These few men . . ." He looked
upon the Slayers, those who had once been his brothers. The black strands of their calling gleamed darkly
from the chalds at their hips. "These few men," he
said again, "bring also to the common room. But last.
Make sure they are well secured, leave a guard on
them. Those you find bound by her people, free, and
bring them also."

Behind us, the sea of men began to part, as they
separated the tasks among them and drifted to the
new leader Sereth had appointed.

"He is not whom I would have chosen," grumbled
Wiraal to Chayin.

Chayin bade him be still.

"Here," said Sereth, pushing Celendra toward the
cahndor. "She is your crell. I might need my hands
free." She stumbled, fell upon the amber gol like some
shadow cast there. Sereth looked at her in disgust.
The tether dangled from her collar.

"Sereth, please, no."

"Get up," said Chayin wearily. "I hope we do not
have to go through all this again because you did not
believe it the first time. I have not so long to spare."
He hefted his Parset sword. Celendra got up and
walked meekly between Wiraal and her owner, the
cahndor.

"We must stop at the chamber Wiraal used,"
Chayin demanded of Sereth.

"Why?"

"He left his huija there." Chayin grinned.

"In his saddlepack, I suppose?" Sereth shot back.
"Where else?"

"And that is where all the crell chains came
from?" Sereth asked.

"Would you have bound them with couch sheets?
Where a Nemarsi goes, so goes his saddle."

"And whatever happens to be in it." Sereth
laughed.

"What," asked Wiraal, as we descended the stairs

that wound around the tower's inner core, "is the disposition of these women? I left a beauty trussed next to my gear."

"Do what you will. Only, do not burden yourself with too many. One cannot fit a wellwoman in a saddlepack." We came out upon the second floor, which is all sea-green. I wondered how any girl in this low-priced section could have taken the jiask's interest.

When Wiraal opened the chamber door, I wondered no longer. Lovely and ripe was that brown-haired, gray-eyed girl. She was very young, and it was her inexperience, not anything else, that priced her so low.

Wiraal patted her where she lay, bound and gagged as Celendra had been, upon the couch. "I will be back for you," he promised, and her terrified eyes were huge upon him.

Then he turned to his saddlepack, and as he routed among its contents, I realized that Celendra never had a chance. Wiraal alone could have stood against formidable odds a good long time with that arsenal. He took his huija and shook it loose. The metal teeth gleamed, embedded in that supple leather. He snapped it, cracking, and Celendra screamed.

Chayin laughed, humorless, and took her by the tether.

"I know what I am going to do with you. I am going to have your vocal cords cut. Then I will give you to Jaheil."

Celendra did not know Jaheil. But she knew Chayin, and she quaked. She laid her head upon his arm. She looked soulfully into his eyes. Her pointed breasts pushed against him. She whispered something, placating.

"Perhaps I will change my mind," he allowed, "about the vocal cords. But I will doubtless"—he pushed her from him, jerking her up short by the leash—"give you to Jaheil."

"What do you find so offensive about her,

Chayin?" I asked, as we left the couch chamber and
its bound occupant and headed for the common room.
I was curious. To me, Celendra is outstandingly
lovely, with her velvet skin and her great breasts like
pointed pillows and her wide, curving hips. I am
small, slim-hipped, insignificant compared to her. I
know men find grace in me, in my long delicate legs
and my very fineness, but I have always secretly
wished to be voluptuous, statuesque. It is truly said
that a woman cannot assess her own beauty.

"Tell me," I insisted. "I think she is beautiful. I
want to know."

"Do you, Sereth," asked Chayin, "think she is
beautiful?"

"I did, for a long time," he said quietly. "I had a
sickness for her, once. It ate away at me, and when it
was done, I no longer found her so."

"She is too much a tiask to suit me," said Chayin.
"There is too much man in her . . . something. I do
not know." He frowned. "I just do not want her."

"I think I know what you mean," said Sereth, still
softer. "When I first had her, such was not her nature.
Perhaps it was I who made her as she is. Perhaps just
what came to be between us . . ." Unconsciously he
slowed his stride, remembering. "Before Tyith, in the
very beginning, she was quite different." I saw Celendra's face. I cannot describe it. She stared at her
feet, bare, upon the gol.

And I, too, stared at my booted feet in the silence
that came over us all. Beneath them, the gol floor became steps, and we descended to the common room. I
wanted to go to Sereth, to beg an enth alone, but I
did not.

I have often wished I had done so, lying here, my
thoughts upon him. The future cloaks the past, experience alters it. And memories, I have come to know,
are not the permanent possessions I once thought
them.

We came out into the common room, filled with
shackled men and women. Sereth, in the doorway,

stopped, his eyes searching tricks and treachery. Four jiasks moved through the prisoners, kneeling here, stooping there, checking.

In Astria we have no divisions to our common room, as they do in Arlet. A man knows the girl's price by the color of the armlet she wears. All the furniture, couches and pillows, had been pushed to the sides of the great white-and-silver hall. The bodies were so thick upon the floor that the inset designs of colored gol could not be seen.

Sereth called a jiask to him.

"The wellwomen?" the Ebvrasea asked.

"We are collecting the last of them now."

Sereth nodded. "Separate them into groups— Slayers, wellwomen, customers, Celendra's hirelings. Where are those who were bound when you found them?"

The jiask led us among the throng to a small group huddled unbound near the door to the drug chamber. They looked up at us, fearful. Some were bleeding, most were bruised. In that group were well-women, servers, fitters. My name came from their lips; hands were extended to me. I stepped back. I was chaldless, woman of an outlaw. All my name held for them was a similar fate. These were those whom Celendra's people felt need to restrain, lest revolution come upon Well Astria. If it had not been for the diversion they provided, things might have gone another way. I searched the faces again. Ges was not among them.

I realized, as I stared around me, that I had seen not a single corpse. Though Sereth was outlaw, he was still a Slayer, and doubtless one of the shrewdest of them. Had Astria been taken, truly, by Parsets, these floors would be covered with dead.

Sereth crouched down among them. As one, they stared at him.

"You, all of you," he said, barely whispering, "I will offer a choice. You must consider before you answer. This is not what you think. Estri will never rule again in Astria. Day-Keepers will come here and look for guilt and complicity among you, for they will never believe we did this alone." He looked around him, licking his lips.

"I can bind you and put you with the others. I can leave you free, and you may do as you will. We will be here one day only, and when we leave, Day-Keepers will come. There will be a new Well-Keepress, for we will take Celendra with us. Even now, from the suspicions of Celendra's people, your chalds may be in danger. Your help would be welcome, but we cannot take any of you when we leave." He leaned back upon his heels. Wiraal drifted away from us toward his jiasks.

"I raised hands to a Slayer," said one man in a low tone. "I have nothing more to lose." Sereth's mouth tightened, understanding.

"What was your skill?" the Ebvrasea asked. I saw Wiraal counting heads, and something cupped in his hands—keys to the pleasure chains of Astria.

"I was a fitter, but not for women. Once I worked for the hostel. I made an enemy there. When Celendra demanded an armsman, my enemy saw to it I was chosen."

"Have you any of your work?"

The man raised his head, staring.

"In that pile, perchance," he said, pointing to the knee-high jumble, a man's length across, of confiscated arms.

"Go find some. I would see it." The man rose and threaded his way hurriedly among the prisoners.

Sereth turned back to those whose disposition so perplexed him.

In the end, we bound all but ten, who felt themselves already marked. They troubled Sereth greatly, these men, for eight were of couples, and none, he felt, suited to run with his own renegades. He advised them to elect a leader, take what they wanted of Astria's treasures, and get themselves a good start upon their new lives.

When he stood up finally, his face was tight and drawn.

"There is more of this," he muttered as he turned from them. I pressed myself against him. He patted me absently, then headed toward the far side of the common room, where Wiraal had grouped the Slayers. I would have let him go, but Lalen shoved me after him.

Halfway to them, the armsman stopped him, with a handful of his craft.

Sereth took from him, piece by piece, his work. He tucked in his chin and regarded the weaponer under his hair, as he sometimes does when thinking.

He threw me a stra straight-blade. The weight was perfectly balanced, the hilt snuggled against my hand. I smiled at the man, and handed it back. Sereth's eyes took mine. I could not believe he would consult me in such a matter. His eyes laughing, he handed me a short blade. I examined it, passed it to Lalen, who grunted approvingly.

"Get yourself a threx, and provisions. Pack the tools of your craft. Where you go, you cannot buy what you do not have."

The man grinned, turned, and hurried from the chamber, stopping only long enough to deposit his samples upon the pile.

"Sereth," called Chayin, standing with Celendra next to Wiraal. Lalen had to bodily move me. As I watched the weaponer, it had come to me that he would never serve us; that neither Sereth nor I would ever stand again upon Mount Opir.

"What is wrong with you?" demanded Lalen. I could not speak. I trembled, silent. Then I wheeled and ran through the prisoners, oblivious, stepping upon them.

"Sereth! Sereth!" I grabbed his arm, pulling upon it, dragging him away from Chayin and Wiraal and the Slayers above whom they stood. "Sereth! Hold me, oh, hold me!" And he did.

"We have got to go! Go now. Please. I cannot do it," I begged through frozen lips.

"Quiet, little one." He pressed my head against his chest, his lips close to my ear. "It will be over soon. You are doing fine."

"Please, now. Chayin. Ask Chayin."

"Chayin, come here. Do you know what is wrong with her?"

And the membranes closed over Chayin's eyes, and stayed closed.

"Doubtless," he said quietly, "she has seen it, that which her mind kept from her, which she would not admit she saw." He rubbed the back of his neck. "She wants you to leave, I imagine?"

Sereth nodded. His body stiffened against me.

"Go if you would. If you take her, you will not get far. If you leave her, to do what the time demands of her, you might make it. I would like to say I could return her to you, but I do not find such in the sort." He spread his hands. "It is a decision the two of you must make." And he turned his back to us and walked back to Wiraal.

"What is it?" he demanded. "Why must we go?" And I knew when he said it he had his decision already made.

I pressed myself tighter against him, as if I could somehow stop the moment's passing.

"You will not leave, no matter what I say." I despaired. He kissed my temple.

"That is right, I will not. But it might serve me, to know what you see. Perhaps we can avoid it."

"We cannot avoid it. We are it!"

"You speak riddles, woman." He shook me, holding me away from him. My eyes had no tears in them. I was incapable of tears. I raised my hand and put my fingers upon the deep scar he bore, tracing its length. I fought for strength, and that strong place within me gave what it could.

"No woman," I said to him, "is worth what my price will come to be. When you have said to me what you have said, you must listen to the same. There will come a moment when you might save yourself. You would be a fool not to do so. I will think no less highly of you." And I bit my lip, until salt blood ran upon my tongue.

He tossed his head, bewildered, and smiled a strained smile. "We will discuss it further later," he said, and turned me firmly toward the captured Slayers.

I saw upon Chayin's face what was surely compassion, as we joined them. We were not so far from him that his desert-sharp ears could not hear. He knew, as I, that Sereth and I would not have time, later, to discuss anything. He had known since Frullo jer. I stood between them, Chayin and Sereth, and the cahndor's hand found mine and gripped it tightly. Lalen held Celendra's leash, abstracted, staring at the captives.

"They would speak with you," said Wiraal, gesturing to what was now close to thirty men, chained together by the neck, their hands bound behind in crell chains. "In Nemar, we would shut their mouths, permanently, for asking."

He stood spread-legged before them, his hands upon his lips. The torchlight sparked from the Shaper's cloak he wore. Naked but for their chalds, they craned their necks to see him—the Ebvrasea, past-Seven of Arlet, chaldless, outlaw. Most of them were unscathed. Three bore flesh wounds.

"Who speaks for you?" He asked his question to one he had singled out among the prisoners, one who bore a diagonal wound, bloody, across his chest. His chains rustled softly as he struggled to his knees. The men upon either side of him moved closer, to ease the tightened links upon their own necks.

"Seven—" the man said.

"Do not call me that."

"What are you going to do with us? Surely you would not see us crells?"

"How did you come by that wound?" Sereth asked, deathly soft.

"They came at us in the passage. We had no choice."

"You will doubtless come to regret it. Were you not instructed specifically against crossing swords with Parsets?" I wondered if Sereth's senses had left him. Did he think himself again Seven of Arlet?

"There is the life-right," the man growled.

"Yes," said Sereth, "there is the life-right. I made that choice myself."

The man squinted at him, his eyes searching.

"They are like spirits. I have never seen men so fast."

"They use uris," Sereth reminded him. "And in quantities that would destroy you or me in a few passes' time. Their constitutions are quite different." His voice was softened. "I see no disgrace in what you did, not in taking up your weapons, nor even putting them down. None but another Parset could stand against a Nemarsi. Perhaps," he added softly, "that is why Slayers are forbidden to fight them."

"You would not see us crells. Not you!"

"No," said Sereth, "I did not say I would. I will leave you to your brothers' judgment. May it fall fairly upon you." And he turned his back upon the kneeling man.

"Chayin, can you not take some of this load?" Sereth said, running his hand over his eyes wearily. It seemed to me that the torchlight dimmed.

"I will try. They all look alike to me." Celendra, beside him, surveyed the ruins of her life. I was sure now: sun's rising lit the translucent white gol from without, causing it to seem that the torchlight dimmed. I touched Sereth's hand at my waist.

"The sign for Feast of Conception," I reminded him.

He demanded of Celendra the plaque's location, and sent Wiraal to get it. Upon Feast of Conception, the Well is closed to business, and all present the previous evening are feted, at the Well's expense. It is considered a bad omen to admit any others, although once Celendra had broken that rule for me. And indeed, ill luck had attended us.

When Wiraal returned with it, he went and placed the oblong plaque upon its hook on the great Well door. Until dawn, Amarsa second seventh, one full day from now, the Well tower was effectively sealed off from the rest of Astria. By that time, Jaheil's appreis would have blossomed upon the plain. Sereth and I stood in the great entrance hall, and through the door he caught his first glimpse of the wonder of the Inner Well, ablaze with light refracted from the prismatic towers. Then Wiraal leaned his weight against the great door, closed it.

"This is the strangest fight," he said, resting back against the bronze door, "that I have ever fought. Put a sign on the door, indeed!" His perplexity was obvious.

"Post a guard here, if it pleases you," said Sereth.

"I will. After I find that crell. It is a pity we cannot take them all. When do you think the Slayers will arrive?"

"It is seventy neras from here to there. The rider from Celendra has not yet arrived, will not before midday. If they have their orders, they might move within an enth. There would be the question of how fast to drive the threx—if they would fight Parsets mounted, they could not spend them so freely as the messenger might. It is my guess that they will not have their orders. Rin diet Tron is not a man given to precipitous action."

"When do you anticipate them?" Wiraal pressed.

"Anytime between first bell and sun's rising tomorrow." First bell to sun's rising is a spread of about seven enths—half the short-summer night.

"If they spare their threx. If they do not have their orders. What if they do not spare the threx? What if they do have their orders?"

"Then perhaps the Feast of Conception we have

called will save us. Jaheil, remember, arrives at sun's rising, if not before."

"And Hael, I wager, close behind him," Wiraal said dryly.

"And upon Hael's heels, Idrer and my men. And do not forget the tiasks—Pijaes and . . . what is her name?" Sereth asked me.

"Nineth," I supplied.

"No one," quipped Wiraal, "could forget Nineth. This whole escapade begins," he admitted, eyes dancing, "to make a sort of demented sense." And he chuckled, still leaning against the door.

"I do not relish it, but we must go back to the common room," Sereth said, and Wiraal nodded, pleased to be included in Sereth's "we."

"Tell me of it in the crawlways, Wiraal," I teased him. "How did you lose your cloak?"

"As Chayin projected, we found fourteen of Celendra's hirelings, sneaking upon you. Even did they have a device with them, some star thing, that they planned to use upon the stra to eat it away. I tried it upon a good blade. It works."

"Where is this device?" Sereth asked.

"I threw it in the sewers. That is where we caught them, just coming down the stairs from the couching places. As the cahndor said we would. And that is where I lost my cloak. I needed a new one, in truth."

"Where are the fourteen hirelings?" Sereth asked delicately.

"Where goeth the spirit, when no longer enfleshed?" Wiraal queried him.

"I am sure I do not know," answered Sereth sharply. "I would see the bodies." And I knew he sought Slayers among them.

They were just beyond the common room, in an alcove that was ringed with tas-covered benches, piled upon the floor. I had been wrong when I assumed that none had died this night. There were not fourteen, but many more dead. Among them was Ges, one of six who had died at the hands of Celendra's men.

I leaned down and touched the calm, cool face of Ges, with whom I had grown to adulthood.

As I straightened up, I heard seventh bell tolling. I could not see it, for upon the ground floor of Astria there are no windows, but outside, Astria was rising, all unknowing. Soon the musicians would tune their instruments, the physicians tend their sick, the students of Well Arts attend their lessons, all unaware that the Ebvrasea and the chosen son of Tar-Kesa held the central tower. When they did learn, they would exclaim in wonder that twenty-five men and one woman had done such a thing, had taken Well Astria, at such a paltry cost. The death toll steadied and held at twenty-six. Twenty-six were lost in the downfall of Celendra, and more than six hundred taken captive, on that evening, second fifth of Amarsa.

One dead for each of our number. The coincidence consumed me, wrapping me in its clammy, morbid arms as I stood against the common-room wall, where Sereth had bade me await him. Lalen lounged by my side, ever present, and in his hand he held Celendra's tether. I was careful to keep him between us.

Wiraal had found and claimed his wellwoman immediately upon our return here, and in doing so set a precedent. There would be a distinct widening of the gene pool in Nemar. I, who had adjudged twice a thousand applicants as Well-Keepress of Astria, watched the Nemarsi at their choosing, and I saw that they chose with discrimination, with shrewdness, with that innate wisdom of a man's eyes upon many women.

Astria gets first choice among potential wellwomen, after the Day-Keepers have taken what they desire from the fruit of Silistra's wombs. At first maturity, they test and rate the girls, and make their ratings available to the Wells. From everywhere upon Silistra, excepting the Parset Lands, do women come to Astria. Of all Silistran women of childbearing age, these were the finest. And now they went to Nemar, the pick of them. I wagered some formidable spawn would come of that mixing. Such women would much enrich the Nemarsi.

Many who were chosen, I knew. There is not a great turnover in wellwomen, normally. It takes an average of fourteen years to get one with child. I felt assured that in Nemar it would not take so long. I saw a woman passed over, and another chosen in her place. The jiask's choice had not such momentous breasts as the reject, but she was sweet of disposition, and her bones were neatly turned. I would have done no different, were I he, did I have his predilection for bonds.

Chayin and Sereth, after much discussion, had limited them to one apiece. It was past mid-meal when the last of the twenty-one jiasks had chosen. Chayin took none, nor did Sereth or Lalen. When Wiraal chided the cahndor, Chayin regarded him icily.

"I will have enough to do to look out for my own life, as will we all these next few days. No woman goes out of here until we have victory upon the plain. I will have Hael's head in my hand before any jiask lays claim to his spoils." He said it quite loud, in that roaring dorkat voice of his, and the men, muttering, put their women together upon a single neck chain to await that event.

Further, Chayin demanded of his men that they abstain from drugs other than uris, and that they stay out of the drink room. No women, no danne, no kifra until he rescinded his order. Then he strode from the room. Sereth, from where he stood with those we had left unbound, ran through the captives after him.

If Sereth had not put me with Lalen, I would have gone myself. But Lalen could not leave Celendra, and he could not leave me, by Sereth's order. Nor was he anxious to drag her along behind. She leaned, quiet, perhaps uncomprehending, against the white gol. Understandably, Lalen would not chance rousing her. We waited.

There is only the battle left to tell, and how I came to be here. My memories fade from me as if they were a Parset carpet and someone stood at the start of my life, rolling it up, slowly and with infinite care.

We saw Jaheil's yra's camp upon the plain under the light of the cresent-bound moon. I stood with Chayin and Sereth, upon the Keepress' overlook. We had broken Celendra's M'ksakkan crystal to get out there. It views not the Inner Well, but southeasterly the Astrian plain.

They had been, all day long, absorbed in the details of conquest and impending battle. Enths they had been gone together, leaving me with Lalen, and when they returned, their eyes were shadowed.

The men were tense, alternately boisterous and withdrawn. They ate little. They watered their women. They worked upon their gear. Sereth and Chayin and Wiraal roamed among them, among their captives. Celendra waxed hysterical, and Chayin gagged her once more. He did not, however, put her with Nemar's new crells upon the chain.

I sat long upon the floor by Lalen's knee. I mourned in silence, and the fear passed out of me. Free of it, I started what was my true work here. I cuddled my hest to me, and gave it strength. I sought Hael, and found him close enough. And found Raet, as I had expected.

Cold I was, by that time. I had not blinked in a quarter-enth. Upon the gol before my eyes was the sense of him, a door to where he was, if you will. I gave him civil greeting, in his own tongue. The flame glow licked around his bronze face, those eyes that have suns for centers assessed me, and he gave his cousin greeting. Raet, son of Kystrai, who was a brother of my father, acknowledged me. My father's daughter's brother, great-grandmother Astria had called him when she read my path more than 842 years ago. Raet was that, also; born of the same womb as Esyia, my half-sister. But relationship breeds more than love, when inheritance is concerned. Raet and Esyia had certain flaws in their makeup. Mi'ystens are powerful, but they cannot make worlds, nor stars. They would like to have the space worlds wiped clean, that they might set their own creations upon them. I had made a world. A paltry world, true, but a world. Raet knew. He acknowledged me. Never before had he done so.

I reiterated my position to him. I would not step aside. I called him by the name through which he ruled in the south—Tar-Kesa.

He stated his intent, as was proper. He called me by my true name, that of the sevenfold spirit.

"Upon the plain of Astria, at sun's rising?" He begged my pleasure, as time called us both elsewhere.

"Upon the plain of Astria," I affirmed. The gol was only gol, the door closed in upon itself. My eyes burned and teared.

"What?" I asked Sereth.

"Come with me," he said, extending his dark-tanned hand. "I have something to show you." His eyes were narrowed. Sereth's sharpness had not missed my absence.

I got up, too soon. My numbed limbs were clumsy. He caught me. Chayin stood there, grinning. This time, with Raet, there had been no bargaining, no threats, no offer of quarter. No longer was I flesh toy to him. I smiled to myself, and stood upon my own. If he thought me so much, perhaps I underestimated my chances.

"Slowly," said Chayin, and called me by that name he could only have known from Raet's mouth.

"There is a chance," I said to him, "that one might get hurt, doing such things." I straightened and stood unsupported, brushing my hair from my face.

"Jaheil approaches," Sereth said, looking between us. "I thought you might like to see it."

"I would," I confirmed, and got upon my toes to kiss him. His arms went around me. Over his shoulder I saw Celendra, still gagged, watching dull-eyed.

The three of us walked the halls of Astria together, and those stairs that led to my old keep.

"What of Rin?" I asked, as we gained the fourth floor.

"No sign. And the sanctity of Feast of Conception"—his teeth flashed—"has not been broken."

"And if Rin will not fight Hael for you?"

"Then we will fight him ourselves," growled Chayin. "Those Slayers will only take the edge off of Hael's men, if what I saw here was any indicator."

"Whichever way, if they engage each other, those they kill are that many fewer to worry about. If the Slayers win, we fight them. If they lose, we fight Hael. Probably a little of both," said Sereth, not overly concerned. He fairly quivered in eagerness.

I watched him with a dull feeling as we climbed. Detached, as my power came to call, I found myself empty of thought, silent. Within me there was for the first time a sense of order. All that I had become, poised ready, like a rack of weapons, sharp and fine. I found I was curious, eager, even, to test those strengths that had place only against their like. I tasted kill-lust. It is stronger than uris, and doubtless more habituating.

We strode through the halls, of one mind. All life takes life to survive. They kill their own kind, the survivors. One respects death, as life. There is much after what we know as life, but that is no reason to value life low. The lessons that are firstly given are given here. The foundation must be strong if the building will stand. I did not seek death upon the plain. I did not suddenly come to value my life low. I was only not fearful for it.

With Chayin on one side of me and Sereth upon the other, I walked Well Astria's halls much changed. In my old chamber I no longer craved the past. As the men, only the moment concerned me. That and what could be made from it.

"There," said Sereth, turning me just south of east. I had stepped carefully through the jagged shards of crystal, still adhering to their frame, and positioned myself west. I looked for Jaheil also in the south. He had not come through the Skirr, by Datur pass. He had not come from the southwest, along the treacherous coastal cliffs.

Amused, Sereth turned me, the Shaper's cloak whipping in the night breeze.

"I do not see anything. There is nothing east of here but the Litess and the sea. Both Day-Keepers and Slayers are south of east."

"Nevertheless," Chayin said, leaning close, his arm extended, "there is Jaheil."

I strained my eyes in the clear moonlit night. The plains of Astria swell gently, like some everfrozen sea. I was no Parset. In the full moon I might have done better. In the waning crescent, Chayin had to direct my gaze.

"See them. The light comes back off their metal." And where he indicated, less than an enth's ride, I saw them. Once shown, the mass of them moving, dark-twinkling against lighter dark, was not difficult to follow.

"How from the east?" I demanded.

"We will let Jaheil tell you, mighty seeress." Chayin chortled.

"He did not!"

"Did not what?" Sereth queried me.

Chayin threw a leg over the overlook's hip-high guard wall.

"How?" I demanded of him.

"What other way?" he answered. "Dordassa North is a port. It was much easier upon the threx to trek them to Dordassa North, load them upon barges, deposit them upon the banks of the Litess, and ride them that little way here."

"Barges?"

"It is often done," said Chayin indulgently. "Remember, all but Nemar have usable coastline. The Menetphers, when they war with Dordassa, often ship the threxmen there. Coseve and Itophe wage constant war upon the seas."

A strand of my hair blew up and across Sereth's face. In brushing it away, he pulled it from my head.

I laughed. Nineth was with Jaheil. She, her yra of tiasks, and their threx were not accustomed to barges, nor to water of any kind. I wondered how she had fared in that ride up the coast to Port Astrin, then inland along the Litess. Fresh indeed, would be Jaheil's jiasks and tiasks.

"Whose idea was it?" I asked, a suspicion dawning on me.

"Sereth's," Chayin said magnanimously.

"And where they happened to take land again, I suppose, was a place that would bring them quite close to the Slayers' hostel," I postulated.

"Reasonably close," Sereth admitted. His smile flashed in the moonlight. "Let us go and see what Jaheil has to say." And Chayin nodded, and extended his hand to the Ebvrasea. Grinning widely, as if some great deed had already been done, they traded a six-turn grip. It is a jiask's grip, one of triumph.

They took the stairs of Astria at breakneck speed, like two small boys. By the time we made the common room, I was panting.

"Jaheil arrives," roared Chayin, barely skidded in the door. "Ready yourselves."

The exodus was orderly, smooth, and perplexing. The men, each before sidling silent out the rear door of Well Astria, collected their saddles. These they dragged with them out the door, hoisting them up over their shoulders as they went. They left their threx where they were stabled, in the Inner Well. Also they left there, as Chayin had directed them, their well-women. All but Celendra. She walked meek beside Lalen. Now that the threshold was behind her. Over that she had made him drag her, in one last contentious fit. And then Sereth had spoken to her, a few sparse words, very low. Gagged, she had not answered. But she walked.

Double file we strolled leisurely across the plain of Astria, to meet Jaheil.

The appreis were risen, dawn only two enths away, when we reached them.

The circle of appreis was forty-two, and within them, those of Jaheil, cahndor of Dordassa, and Nineth, tiaskchan of Nemar, were raised. Jaheil's was of splendor befitting a cahndor, though spare enough by his standards. He apologized for the exigencies of war thrust upon him, as he seated us.

Between the encircled appreis and the ring's perimeter I had seen the threx, strung out at lengths upon ropes. I knew then why the jiasks had brought their saddles here upon their shoulders.

As I ducked into Jaheil's apprei, Sereth's back before me, I shivered. Much had befallen me in such shelters. I greeted Jaheil, looming huge and dark in the light of the oil lamp. He sat, dressed all in black, as is his custom, pulling upon his great beard with one hand. Sprawled next to him upon the grass of Astria was Nineth. Nineth, who was so large I had given her Besha's clothing, and whose red-brown skin sheathed muscle enough for most men. Nineth, who raised her hand to greet me, and stopped halfway. Her sharp eyes flickered. I no longer wore Chayin's medallion, nor my Nemarsi chald. Her eyes took mine, haughty. She said no word to me, and lowered her hand.

I took my place next to Sereth, whom Jaheil had seated upon his right hand. And Chayin entered, pushing Celendra before him. He thrust her to her knees before Jaheil. I leaned forward, unabashed, that I might see Nineth's face, and Jaheil's.

"This," said Chayin, prodding Celendra with his foot, "I have brought you as gift." Celendra had her head to the grass. This night, Jaheil had not spread his mats.

"Are we now couch-mates, Chayin?" Jaheil said, straight-faced, in a high voice. Chayin snorted.

"Sit up, crell," Jaheil urged. "I would see you." His fingers fondled his beard, anticipating. Nineth, as well as Celendra, sat up. The tiask's eyes were non-committal, at great cost. Lalen entered, quiet for all his bulk, and crouched next to me.

In all her beauty, gloriously robed in her naked-ness, Celendra sat up. Next to Nineth, she was un-speakably delicate. Her heart-shaped face raised to him. Her huge gold-green eyes pleaded favor from un-der brows like crier's wings. She shifted slightly, that her knees might be together, and her chains rattled. Between her high breasts depended the six-linked tether from her collar. It glinted softly, swinging in the lamplight.

Jaheil looked upon her a time in silence. Chayin's face, standing over her, betrayed no emotion.

"Stand up, crell!" Celendra stood. He had her turn, then kneel again.

"That was thoughtful of you, Cahndor," Jaheil said at last, his eyes twinkling. "I will use her as shield in the fighting, if there is any." He reached over and took her tether, pulled her by it. "Sit here," he invited, putting her upon his ample lap, as if she were a child. Nineth rose and left, wordless.

Celendra moaned under her gag, enfolded in Jah-eil's arms as he explored his new possession. He had not asked why Chayin gagged her, but he made no move to free her tongue.

"Are there more?" Jaheil asked.

"Many," said Chayin, taking Nineth's vacant seat upon Jaheil's left—his rightful place, which he had waited for Nineth to give up.

"You can have all you want of them. They lie there ready, bound, for your men to take, when this is over. This one was the highest of them." He indicated Celendra, enfolded in Jaheil's exploring grasp.

"Again, I thank you," Jaheil said, and rolled Ce-lendra off his lap. She lay there, very still.

"We have some things to discuss, and little time," Sereth said softly.

Chayin inclined his head. Before Jaheil, in this place, he was again the living god.

"Did you do as we asked?" he demanded.

"Yes," said Jaheil.

"They saw you?"

"Doubtless," said Jaheil.

"And they did not obstruct you?"

"Not even a warning."

"Sereth, perhaps they will not, after all, move to aid her."

"Perhaps," allowed Sereth with no conviction. "We should get mounted. Form the tiasks upon the outside. A Slayer will pull his stroke against a woman."

"They may not come," said Chayin. Jaheil looked between them, his brows pulled together.

"Do it!" the Ebvrasea ordered the cahndor. Jaheil's brows went up, then down even farther. Lalen shifted his sword arm clear.

"Position the tiasks upon the outside," said Chayin to Jaheil. "Best men in a center swathe. If the Slayers appear while we engage Hael, you know what to do."

"And remember," said Sereth softly, "my archers, and how far that death can fly."

Jaheil allowed that he had already spread that word.

"Afterward," said Chayin as we rose to find the threx Jaheil had brought us, "go into the Well and allow my men to get their wellwomen. Take what you want; none will obstruct you. If you leave by midday, that is. You must do so. I will not be with you." He took the medallion of uritheria from about his neck and handed it to Jaheil. Bewildered, Jaheil put it on.

"What do you want me to do, Chayin?" he asked, his snarling manner much softened.

"We will, in this battle, have a chance not only at Hael's head, but at two other heads. If we were to have all three, as I think we will, we could unite the Parset Lands. It is up to you to do so. I give you regency in my name. You are the only one fit to hold it."

And his eyes said that he recalled Liuma, regent of Menetph.

"And where will you be?" demanded Jaheil.

"I cannot tell you that. I will be safe enough. In the pass of winter solstice, I will return to you. And we will change what is then, even more." The wind from the abyss sighed in Chayin's voice. And Jaheil saw the veil heavy upon him, and only nodded and held back the flap. "You will return to us," Jaheil added as Chayin ducked under his arm.

"Yes. With certainty." And Chayin flashed his dorkat smile.

Between the appreis, threxmen prepared their mounts. Through them Jaheil led us, to where Saer, Guanden, and Krist, Sereth's black, stood beside his own red giant. Before each was piled his gear. Jaheil had been thorough, I thought as I struggled with Guanden's head. Finally Sereth held his ears for me, that I might get the bitless northern headstall upon him. Upon my saddle, as every other I had seen, was affixed a coiled huija.

"I cannot use this," I said, as I hefted the saddle. I had to strain to get it upon his high withers.

"Then do not use it," Chayin said, from upon Saer's dappled back. Nose in the air, the threx lunged and pranced, cutting chunks of sod from the earth with his steel-shod hooves. "It was the boat ride," I heard Chayin mutter, stroking his arched crest.

"Perhaps I should have brought you Issa," said Sereth critically, watching Guanden's ill-mannered attempts to maim me as I drew tight the girth. I well recalled her, that fair red threx, and her easy ways.

"He will be better, for this day," I grunted, and stepped back from my work. Chayin had Saer calmed. The great dapple stood with his head low. Only his distended nostrils betrayed his excitement.

Behind Chayin, the stars were fading. Between the appreis I could see the first presaging green in the east. And I saw also a certain misting, like a dust cloud up from the south.

I took Guanden's reins from Sereth and touched his arm.

"Look south," I advised. He did, squinting in the dark as if it were already day. He turned back to me, his face only shadow play, and offered me a boost up onto Guanden's back. The threx snorted and squealed, and kicked both legs straight out. I slapped him hard between the ears, and he calmed and stood trembling.

Sereth approached the dun warily, put his hand upon my thigh.

"Stay close to Lalen. Do not try to keep with me. I will be near." He squeezed my leg, and turned to Krist.

Chayin brought Saer up so close that our knees brushed. Guanden four-stepped, and I raised my hand in warning. His rolling eyes saw, his ears flicked back, and he reconsidered, satisfying himself with a defiant squeal that shook his belly between my legs.

I watched Sereth, dark shadow sliding graceful against Krist's blackness, and as I did so, dawn colored his form. It was very still, but for threx sound, as if the creatures of the plain held their breath in expectation.

Jaheil walked his red beast to us, Celendra bound to his saddle by her wrists. He swung up behind her as the first ray of the sun broke over the plain and set his mount's coat aflame. I had been before a Parset in battle once, I recalled. But I had not been bound, and I had been armed. Celendra's gag, and her chald, were no longer upon her.

Sereth swung upon Krist, and that beast only stood, proud and wise, beneath his master's well-loved weight. Sereth stroked him briefly, speaking low to those back-turned ears, then brought him up on my left. Lalen, riding some brown threx, a male of good size, joined us. There were perhaps twenty left within the circle of Jaheil's appreis.

"Shall we see to the fruitfulness of the soil, Sereth?" Chayin broke the silence, his face colored with dawnfire. Not waiting for answer, he wheeled Saer and was gone.

"As best we can," the Ebvrasea rejoined, turning Krist's head to follow.

So we came out onto the plain of Astria, and the forming three yras made way for us through their midst. Once, such a war would have been fought upon Silistra with a hundred men for every one of our seventy-one. In those times, we were of formidable number. Now, in the north, no more than fourteen are ever joined on a commission. Upon the plain of Astria, we were very many, our seventy-one.

Formed, the tiasks upon the outside, a swathe of picked men bisecting the circle, we moved south. Slowly did that circle move. Even slower for us in the midst of it. I counted my breaths, and they were precious. Harness creaked and jingled, hoof falls cadenced my heart. The sky was tiered fire, between clouds like racked blades. Bloody was that sun's rising into the greening sky, like a reflection from the chaos to come.

Hemmed in as he was, Guanden gave me little trouble. As I bent to set my razor-moons, I saw Sereth's sidelong scrutiny. Upon my other side, the right, was Chayin. The cahndor smiled to himself, his body rolling with Saer's stride. Before us was Jaheil's red threx, and Wiraal upon a gray. Behind came Lalen and Nineth, in crackling tension. They had apparently been acquainted previously. I wondered briefly how Aje the crell had fared at the hands of Nineth, tiaskchan. Then I forgot them.

At a place indistinguishable to me from any other upon the plain, Chayin roared his force to a halt. Scattered here and there were some few stands of trees, but none within a quarter-nera. Approximately that distance behind lay the appreis.

In that circle, he held them. We faced every direction, silent, ready. Blades took the sun's rays. The new day sparked off Sereth's cloak, off the Shaper's spiral.

I twisted in my saddle, marking what the men watched in the lightening day. Over the greening plains of Astria they swept, surely thrice our number, a band of dark shapes. Before battle is joined is a time that moves most slowly. One's pulsebeats might be bells tolling enths. We watched them come, at full speed, across the plain.

I remember the smell of the air, heavy with moisture. Of the threx and leathers and steel, and of our battle sweat upon us. My palms wept. I wiped them continually upon my thighs. The hilt of the straight-blade I carried was comforting, warm. I stared at them, at the mist above their heads.

When they were close enough that the banner of Menetph, and of Coseve, Itophe, and Nemar, could be seen, and their threx' hooves roared like the Falls of Santha, Chayin shouted his men ready. And shouted again, as he twisted in Saer's saddle. His desert-trained eyes had detected them, even before the watchful tiasks; Slayers, perhaps a hundred, fell upon us from the east.

Bursting from the circle's forward edge, the tiasks doubled themselves easterly, that they might meet the northern men. Up from west of south came the army of Hael, of Omas of Coseve and Locaer of Itophe, and they were uncountable.

As the first wave hit us, Parsets screaming, threx squealing, the sky turned to deepest night. Blades flashed unseen, men and beasts roared in terror, and the battle was joined. I screamed too, amidst my protectors, thinking I had gone blind. There was no moon in that night, only the stars, glittering cold upon us.

Guanden thrashed and heaved under me, wrenching my arms. I heard the weapons of the out-edged men, whirring. Screaming, the circle split. Upon code word in the darkness, Chayin's force, blind, opened before the slayers, who drove through us toward Hael's attacking throng.

For a moment, all thought flown from me, I struggled to hold Guanden in that shadowy corridor

of death. Behind me surged the first of Hael's van-
guard; before, the oncoming Slayers. "Estri!" I heard,
and searched the voice in the darkness even as I
whirled Guanden from between them. So close did I
come to my ending there, in that battle deafness, that
I saw the eyes of the first Slayers gleam, and Guanden's rear took a glancing sword cut. Into our
ranks Guanden plunged, our people closing around
me. I had time to sink a razor-moon, then another, and
then someone grabbed Guanden's head. I almost cut
the hand away, before I saw it was Lalen.

"There!" he shouted. I went, reining Guanden,
reeling between the fighting men. Out of the dark a
threx' head came, teeth huge and dripping. I closed
my eyes and brought my blade down. It squealed and
was gone. Lalen's threx, upon my left, skittered beside
us, flesh shield. His blade sang above my head; even
did he thrust it between my breasts and Guanden's
plunging neck. To the far edge he headed me, where
Chayin and Hael fought off from the rest, their beasts
upon their hind legs. One glimpse I had, as the sky
exploded in flashing sheets of colored lightning—
Chayin, with Hael's head, Sereth, his blade raised in
mid-stroke, against four.

Then the dark, and a new blinding: light. From
the fiber of the sky it came, roaring a roar that made
men drop their blades and put hands to their ears,
that made threx bolt, oblivious of their riders. Raet/
Uritheria. The height of the highest tower of Astria
it was, flapping great wings translucent in the sky.
Then stronger. Seething noncolored light, the atoms of
creation in it not yet cooled, it opened its great fanged
mouth and turned its singeing breath upon the struggling men. Its clawed feet grabbed riders from their
saddles. Its wings made gales that blew threx from
their feet. I smelled flesh burning. Hair, crisped to
ash, floated upon the air.

Guanden threw me from his back in his terror, as
if I never existed. I lay where I had fallen, oblivious

to the hooves raking the sod around me. I fought for breath.

And found it. Found myself. Rolled upon my back, to see the sky. A shadow fell over me—Lalen, dismounted, his steel flying in my defense. He straddled me. I sought Wirur, winged hulion, great fanged carnivore, where he held court in the sky, and he was there for me. I called my fate, and in my sight between those stars that made him, a million new stars came into being. More, and the battle faded. Bone, for a moment, framework of bone in the sky, and then I was there.

I peered down through my slitted eyes upon the plain of Astria, twitching my tufted ears to the sound of men dying, of roasted threx, of Raet and his cacophony of death. Then I saw him, my enemy, and I breathed breath of acid ice from my nostrils upon the land. I tore myself, with a great wrench of muscles, from the firmament. Behind me, a keening began as what was not time and space rushed through that hole. I growled to myself, at first wing's flap, as my hulion quarters tensed to take spring upon the earth. Those horny pads of mine touched dead and dying, crushed them as they froze to tinkling ice shards.

Raet/Uritheria saw me, raised gory head upon sinuous neck. The men and threx were as yits, upon which we stepped. Uritheria rose up from his play. I opened wide my fanged mouth and jumped for him, ice-breath before me. Meeting flame, combusting. His great leathered wings snapped under my stiff-spread paws. Claws dug into those useless wings, my own flapping for balance. I sought his neck. Closed upon air. Writhing, twisting, screaming, he turned his head, straining, to snap at my throat. I was not truly quick enough. I felt his burning teeth, deep. Enraged, I tore my flesh from his bite and screamed into those eyes. Blinded, the ice crystals that were once orbs glittered upon his scintillant scales. A roar of pain singed me; knives in my ears made me wish deafness. Those great jaws closed upon my shoulder. I twisted back my

head, and bit out Uritheria's throat. He quivered, his
teeth grinding upon my bones. The roaring became a
gurgling, the gurgling a pulse. He did not fall. He
faded. His jaws locked upon me in his death throes. I
stood, looking around me, until those teeth were out
of my shoulder, back where they belonged, reformed
into the space they once had been. I licked my chest.
It pained me. Raet/Uritheria faded, his substance
sucked up by the continuum from which it had been
stolen.

From my great height, calmly I observed the tiny
men, all fallen, upon the place that had been the plain
of Astria. It was a different place; the night-day-sky
here flickered undecided, and sometimes the day was
no Silistran day. Upon their backs and stomachs the
fallen rolled and crawled, the ground heaving under
them. A great circle, some hundred neras in diameter,
had my standing place as center. And beyond it—a
sharp drop—lay the rest of the Silistran lands. And I
knew, thought I had not seen it, that those edges were
sheer and clean, and devoid of life. Whatever had
stood there, stood no longer, destroyed by the con-
vergence of alternate planes—Astria had not come
back to time-space, fully. The hole that with its suc-
tion had brought about this disjoint in time still
wailed. The sky raged with storms of light. The men
screamed and cried and called upon their gods, for
each had been dragged from sequential time. They
cowered, the bravest of them, at the cold. The atoms
of their being had been hurled from one universe to
another, and there is great pain in that returning. I
felt sorry for them. Almost gone was Raet/Uritheria.
In my throat I felt a rumbling growl of pleasure. I
sniffed his presence, what was left of it. A great, concussive explosion filled the sky with white light, then
another, off near the north star. I purred to myself
when I realized how far into space the disruption extended. Far enough. Anything coming upon those
convergent alternatives would be translated into en-

ergy, the constituents of which are the common denominator of life.

I lowered my head, that I might see how they fared, the little ones, when Raet/Uritheria no longer bound me there with his jaws. I saw my body, and it called. With a farewell it could not hear, I let my rightful place, that hole yet to be plugged, take me.

Easier than descending, it was, fitting back into that space between the stars. I licked my damaged shoulder once. My tufted ear tasted star breath, my tail flicked into place. And the keening of the rupture ceased, settling the balance once more.

My shoulder hurt terribly. I tried to rise. I could not move my arm. Pain made my sight grainy with red dots. When I could, I closed my eyes, that they might not burn and tear. And then the rain began. I felt it, falling sharp upon me, bouncing. Sluggish, I tried to think what it could be. Through my pain, I realized only that . . . that I could not think. Eyes closed, the pelting of sharpness upon me, I struggled to my knees, and to my one good arm's support. I wondered dully if I could crawl with only one arm. Then I wondered where I would crawl.

Eyes, open for me! They did so, grudging. The ground I saw, beneath my dangling head. And upon it, a dozen small crystals, glowing apulse on the grass. Helsars. A rain of helsars, as the shifting edges of time-space rubbed each other in their settling.

With what little strength I could muster, I raised my head. The plain of Astria was ablaze with them. Atop the bodies, men moaned and murmured to their wounds. Women crawled about upon their hands and knees. In places, threx stood, four legs spread wide, weaving. And some helsars, I saw, those brightest glowing, had already found their pupils. So many. Enough for the whole of Astria. I began, slowly and without understanding, to crawl through them. It was a hobbled crawl, upon only one arm, over dead and dying, and some who fondled helsars even in their pain. All of these had been where one must go, and returned to claim what they had created there. No helsar attached itself to me. One, and only one, is the rule.

But I did not understand that, as the day came once again upon the plain of Astria. I only crawled, in my pain, among the wounded. The sod, torn up, was muddy with the blood of man and beast, and my good hand was covered with a gory clay. What I sought, I did not know until I found it. All I knew was the ground, still heaving under me. It threw me to my back a dozen times, like some unbroken threx. It made the helsars jitter and dance upon the grass. It made women, even men, cry in fear. That and the wind: deracou, perhaps, is as strong. It ripped at us, pushing the weak down to the ground. It pelted men with helsars; certain men, certain helsars.

My knees were bruised and torn. In my shoulder were great toothmarks; in places my flesh was chewed pulp. At one point I stopped and regarded it. It occurred to me that I must stop the bleeding. I did so, and was too exhausted to do more. Then I crawled on.

I put my good hand upon a dead man's chest, riddled with arrows I had not seen fly. I looked at the face that was not there. I shuddered, seeing the vacant stump of the man's neck. He wore upon him a green device. I stared at it, thinking of why I should mark it. Some of my fog lifted from me then. It was the device of Coseve; more, of its cahndor. And I crawled over the body of yellow-eyed Omas of Coseve, whose head lay nowhere about.

Then only did I seek Sereth. I screamed his name across the plain. None answered me. I found strength to rise to my feet, and stumbled among them, the wounded and the dead. Up ahead were threx, a dozen of them, still standing. I ran there, hoping, crying, calling Sereth's name over and over.

It was by the threx, they were. Chayin, leaning upon Saer, heavily, cut in a hundred places, his cloak gone, torn for bandage. At his feet were three heads, disembodied. A little way from him, Jaheil bent over Celendra. His left arm was in a sling wet with blood. He turned his head at my stumbling approach. The cahndor of Dordassa had no left eye. I screamed, and put my good hand to my mouth, biting it.

For I saw him. He lay facedown on the grass, the Shaper's cloak still upon him. Krist stood with all four feet over him, his eyes rolling, froth dripping red from his mouth. The beast was badly injured. A broken sword hilt protruded from his chest.

"Estri!" Chayin croaked, reaching out a hand to stop me. He staggered toward me, forgoing Saer's support, and had barely the strength to hold me back.

"The beast is crazed. Let him be. Sereth is dying; he would not want to see you pummeled before his eyes." I could feel Chayin wavering. His voice was husked with pain.

"No! He is not! I will not allow it!" I screamed, and tore myself from his grasp. He looked at me, shrugged, and limped painfully to Saer. He leaned there, tears unashamed upon him, watching.

"Krist," I called softly, extending my good hand. "Krist, it is me. Estri. Let me help him. Let me see him." And it was not what I said, but the tone, and my mind-touch, what little there was to spare. Krist snorted and tossed his head. He let his bared teeth come together, cocked his head to me. He extended his great-jowled jaws, from which his reins dangled. I scratched him, as I had seen Sereth do, where neck meets head. He groaned pitifully, snuffled my hand. "Sssh," I told him. "It will be over soon." For that valiant beast, it would be over within the enth.

But he let me back him from his stance over Sereth. At his master's feet, Krist was content to stand, his brave head raised, ever watchful.

I was beside him, upon my knees. His face was to me. With my left hand, my good one, I brushed his blood-matted hair from his eyes. They were open.

"Estri," he said softly. He coughed. "Little one, come here." And he raised his arm, that I might be under it, against him. I saw what wound he had sustained.

"Sereth," I sobbed, "oh, please, no." And I crawled into the shelter of his arm, against his blood-soaked side.

"Do not be sad," he said. "The sun is again upon the land." And he kissed my temple, and his eyes closed. Pressed to him, I shook with loss. I could not breathe; my chest choked me, my guts froze into a tight fist. And I went into him, with all I had. Of my diminished life force, I gave him all there was. I turned him, somehow, and pounded upon his chest, and gave until all I saw were gray shadows before me. Until I could no longer hold my body upright. As I fell forward, atop him, in the grayness I heard voices, somewhere above.

"There they are! Take them!"

And something shimmered toward me out of the mist.

IX. "I Am the Hest and the Sort"

It hurt, very much, whatever they were doing. I could not see. My whole head seemed constrained. Sound other than breathing was muffled, and breathing itself was a great effort. My shoulder, surely, would soon consume me.

A time later, when the pain lessened, I sensed my body, upon something soft. I heard voices then, but no words. With my mind, I tried to get a sense of my surroundings, and shrank back, a scream in my throat. If one had raised up a molten sword hilt, dropped it, and tried to use the same hand again to grasp the red-hot hilt, the anguish might have been similar. A cold began to grow within me as I knew the silence for what it was. I began to assess my damages, needlessly. I felt hands upon me. Nothing else. No glimmer of to whom or what those hands might belong. Deaf, dumb, and blind I was. Those eyes, ears, and tongue that are mind's had been burned badly. Perhaps even burned away.

The knowledge still remained. One cannot see without eyes, though one knows how to see. One must have data to interpret. My shoulder did not hurt at all.

Once before, I whispered to myself, I had been without my skills. Upon Mi'ysten, in the cubes, I had been so stricken. It had passed. I tried to speak aloud, and found I could not. Then I began to remember how I came to such a pass, and shrank back into unconsciousness.

And came up screaming Sereth's name. A hand pressed, muffling, over my mouth. I could not see: a cloth was bound around my head. It came to me that I was supported, upright.

"Will you be still?" I heard. I nodded. The hand was removed.

"Walk, if you can," the voice said. Upon either side of me were hands; bodies, men surely.

Staggering, I tried. The supporting arms kept me upright. There was no pain whatsoever in my shoulder. I could get no sense of where I was, or how long it had taken to arrive here. I saw no sort I could not choose. I merely grabbed tight to consciousness and struggled with my weakened body. Twice my companions changed direction. In those moments, my ears, straining, detected more than three pairs of feet. My need sent to me to try my skills once more—I sought Sereth. The pain was excruciating. I sagged between those who held me. They did not slacken their pace, but dragged me with them.

There was a scuffling behind us.

"Hold still, savage!" I heard. Then a grunt, then only footfalls, and the whisper of bodies moving. My heart lightened. Both voices I knew. The Ebvrasea lived. This place was the Lake of Horns, doubtless. The voice that had spoken was that of Carth. His peculiar lilt was unmistakable. Carth, arrar to the dharen of Silistra, would surely take my part, if he could.

And I understood my blinders. Mere Silistrans do not walk in the dharener's city. The high ones lived here. Those who never go about in the land, those shadowy, almost mythical figures who rule those who rule Day-Keepers, reigned here. And Carth had said to

me: seek him when I came to this place. I had
thought it some special invitation, in thanks for his
freedom.

We stopped. There was motion before me, a moving about. A gentle hint of air crossed my cheek. Then
my guards, for that they were, moved forward. Five
hundred and three steps before they stopped once
again. Their hands were no longer upon me. I stood
alone. I reached up to free my eyes, and none obstructed me.

My first sight was blurry, from lids pressed tight
too long. The room was seven-cornered, of blue-black
northern thala. Light came from tiny fireballs like
miniature suns that floated near the vaulted ceiling.
That ceiling was of hammered gold, soft and ruddy,
gleaming.

I squinted at the figure before me, and slowly it
took focus. I rubbed my unmarked shoulder.

"I am Khys," said the first male of my own race I
had ever seen. His red-gold skin shone softly; his eyes
had the fathers' fire in them. His hair was copper,
thick-waved strands that just brushed his wide, black-
robed shoulders. He wore no ornament but a weighty
chald, within which was woven every strand attainable upon Silistra.

"No," I said, shaking my head. I could not move.
With the barest narrowing of his eyes, he held me still.
If I could have moved, I would have bitten his throat
out. I hated him upon first sight, that intolerably perfect mate for whom Estrazi intended me.

"Yes," he corrected, looking down through eyes as
old as Silistra. He had Estrazi's size and build, but
with some subtle difference. Never would I let such a
one touch me. I would die, first.

"You do not have that choice. Be silent." I had
not spoken aloud. I tried to quiet my thoughts. A
shield was beyond me. I could not move, but he had
left me able to speak. "Little savage, I need not restrain you, if you will restrain yourself."

He looked at me, dropped his hold. Then, only,

could I peer around me and see where I stood. In the center of that strange room, upon the glyph of the Shapers, was I. I saw Chayin, with Carth. And Sereth, between two massive guards. His hands were bound behind. The wound that should have killed him was dressed with clean bandages. Other than that, he wore only breech. He leaned heavily upon his guards, but he lived. I went to him. Carth, who held Chayin, caught my arm and returned me to the glyph's center, facing Khys, dharen of Silistra.

"Be careful," Carth whispered as he caught me.

"Once more," said the dharen when I again stood before him, "and you will have no choice." In pain that sank me to my knees, I struck out at him with my hate. He laughed. Only a muscle near his right eye twitched. A tiny sun appeared between us and floated to the ceiling.

"A threx, when she sees a potential mate, tries to outrun him. You have been outrun. Failing that, she might try to outwit him. You have been outwitted. Escape denied her, she must try his strength. But lightly, for he might be strong enough to destroy her." I had gotten, shaking, to my feet. He knelt me. I did not kneel. He knelt me.

"At the last, if she would live to bear the young that is her purpose, she becomes docile. Consider it. Stay there!" And he surveyed Chayin and Sereth.

"So I have you at last," he said, deep and soft. "The barbarians and the bait." He motioned his men back from us, a movement bespeaking unlimited command, from one long-accustomed.

He turned his fiery gaze upon Chayin.

"What have you to say for yourself, Cahndor? You range far afield with your slaughter. You have looted my best Well. You have killed a dharener." Khys waited, hands at the chald slung about his robed hips. Directly behind him was a dark-curtained window.

Chayin regarded him a moment in silence.

"I did what the time demanded of me. I will do

more, for you will not obstruct me." He held his head high. "These people are under my protection!"

Khys chuckled, mirthless.

"Do not be naive, Cahndor. With Raet no longer in the south, I have no need to tread softly there. Within a pass, there will be no southern dhareners, no temples to Tar-Kesa. There will be Wells, and uniform chaldra. I will have access to those genetic strengths Raet has so long withheld from me. If you rule again, you will do it as my agent. And you will leave here as such, or not at all.

"All of you"—he lashed those eyes across us—"have done more than you know. That you have survived shows you possibly worth saving. You are mine to dispose of as I like.

"Dumb animals, savages, you are. You do not even now know what you have accomplished. You but did my will. I am the hest and the sort. You stand before me with your petty guilts in vainglorious delusion!

"Estri Hadrath diet Estrazi, daughter of the Shaper!" He snapped my breath from me. "You were born where we could not, dared not touch you. Such blood as yours is not wasted upon barbarians! All that has happened to you, your great-grandmother foretold. Even that gave you no insight."

I just looked at him dumbly.

"Perhaps you will never understand," he said pityingly. "Maturing you as he did, demented, depraved, was part of what had to be done. A trap, you were, one Estrazi set to catch gods!"

I could only look at him.

"He set you where we could not touch you. After he had not spread his seed upon Silistra in two thousand years, he came and left one child. He knew it would concern us, and what we would do, up to a point. But I did not, as he hoped, contest with Raet for you. When first I approached you, Raet obstructed me. He had been obstructing me since hide days. It was he who drove us to the hides in the first place!"

His triumph was obvious. His eyes sparked as he talked.

"How carefully Estrazi set his construction. Only such as you could have served. It was his ambivalence that destroyed Raet."

"I do not understand you," I said.

"Not only were you bait for Raet's downfall, you were marked for mine! Should I have taken you, as you were, with those great unbridled strengths of yours, I would surely have fallen to whatever he has in mind for me."

"My father is not as you say."

"We war for the space worlds, little savage. The experiment has proved too successful, not insufficient. We are strong, effective, and different. Our conception reaches out among the planes. Time and space are no longer easily controllable from without. The fathers will not destroy us directly. The moment when we could be unmade has passed."

"He used me to show us worthy."

"He used you to take Raet's interest, to draw him to you. You were his test, and he failed it. Mine too, you are, it seems. But Estrazi will not draw me into his hest."

"You fool yourself," I said softly.

"You speak to me of fools? Do you know even the triumph due you? That Astria abounds with helsars, and hundreds, eventually thousands, will take those teachings—do you know that?"

I bowed my head, staring at the glyphed floor.

"Do you know that you have neatly terminated at the sprouting all our troubles with M'ksakka? They sit and quake, wondering how we destroyed those ships. They will send their apologies. When we allowed them access to Silistra, it was with full knowledge that in your struggle with Raet you would teach them their place." I remembered the two great flashes of light, in deep space near the north star Clous. I shivered, clutched myself, thinking how long ago it was that M'ksakkans had first set foot upon Silistra.

"You will be lauded, as Astria predicted. They will pilgrimage to the helsars in your name. And more. Yet you are nothing, only a tool, almost useless now. Nothing that you have done was other than we planned for you. Both your paltry hest, and your father's, we turned to our purpose."

I looked up at him, tears in my eyes.

"We will see what might be done with you, if something may be salvaged. It is not my custom to waste such blood as you carry in your veins." A chill amusement touched his face, disappeared, leaving only the hauteur.

"Not while I live," I said softly to him.

"You will think differently soon enough, when your mind is cleared of the rot within it." And he turned his eyes upon Sereth.

"Outlaw, you are my greatest problem. I cannot exonerate you of your crimes, much as I respect your abilities. The splitting of those troops, their deployment, the archers at just the right moment, when you reformed behind and out of range—you are perhaps the most valuable of all. But I valued Vedrev, whom you killed."

Sereth raised his head. He was pale beneath his tan, his hair still matted with dried blood.

"If, as you say"—he spoke in barely a whisper—"we did only your will, and served you so valuably, I have certain observations I might make."

"Make them," said the dharen.

"If you sent a hundred Slayers onto the plain of Astria, knowing all would die, if you let Estri stand alone before that power without moving to aid her, if you let Celendra rule in Astria and Vedrev falsely accuse me, then it is not she, but you, who are demented. What you do with me now should be an easy decision. What is one life, to one who spends life like copper dippars?" And he met the dharen's gaze, unwavering.

"You," said Khys at last, "of all of them, most perplex me. In Estri there is a Shaper heritage, Chayin bears the blood of Raet—both of them strong infusions. In you there is only a mixing of low concentration. And yet you stand with them, on firm footing. I might offer your arrogance up as reason for your death. But I will not. I will offer you the arrar's chald, in trade for your name. And justice will be served." Sereth shifted his weight. The chains upon his wrists rustled.

"I do not understand," said Sereth. The arrar, chald of the messenger, is given to so few that until Carth I had never met a man who bore one.

"I cannot pardon Sereth crill Tyris, the Ebvrasea. I might give a man, Sereth, a chance to come into my service. None who bear the arrar may retain ties to their past. They bear every chald given upon Silistra. They must be free of factionalism. Such a man bears only his given name." Tight lines shadowed Khys's jaws as he spoke.

"I could even part with that," said Sereth cautiously. "I cannot say yet. I need time to think."

"You shall have it." He smiled graciously, copper-gold, glorious. I detested him.

"What of my woman?" Sereth asked.

Wrinkles came upon Khys's wide forehead. His arched brows drew together.

"Surely, after all you have heard here, you cannot still delude yourself that you might be allowed to breed such a female?" Even as Sereth's body stiffened, I could feel Khys's restraint flash out.

"Take him," said the dharen abruptly, "where he may rethink his position. You!" He whirled upon me. "Stay there!"

I stayed, upon the glyph of Khys's defiance, on my knees, while they dragged Sereth out. He did not truly struggle, but he did not move with them.

And there were just Chayin and I, and Carth. And the dharen.

"Unbind him," Khys ordered. Carth freed Chayin's wrists. He rubbed them. His rana-colored skin was covered with half-healed wounds. I could see the membranes snapping agitatedly back and forth. I still knelt upon the Shaper's glyph. My limbs trembled uncontrollably, kneeling there in the great empty seven-cornered hall.

"I would ask a thing, dharen," Chayin said.

"Ask it."

"You called me Raet's son? Is that true? And Hael—what of him?"

"He was not, though he would have given all to be. The hate he had for you stemmed from that. He was priest of your father. You had the blood, the skills, not he. Raet realized, when he chose as he did, what tensions could be catalyzed. Hael served him well. I would have a hundred such." The dharen rubbed his long-fingered hands together.

"That is why, then." And I knew he meant the curse his gifts had been upon him.

"When I have a male child from her, you may put spawn upon her also. I would be interested in the get of such a union."

"Chayin rubbed his neck. His eyes flickered. He walked the three steps to me and touched my head. I looked up at him. His face was pained. He squatted down upon his heels and put his hands upon my arms, kneading.

"You know there is nothing I can do to aid you, Estri," he said, very low.

I looked at him, at his darkness, at his distress. And yet, between them they discussed me like some threx in heat. I had no doubt Khys could put an unwanted child upon me. Once I might have obstructed him. No longer.

"Cahndor," I said, toneless, "do what you will. I would as soon your get as any other I am likely to bear. They breed crells in Nemar."

"Estri, please." He pulled me to him, pressed his face close.

"Chayin, if one has no control of one's life, there is left only the way we choose to meet what comes. Put a child upon me, if you will. I will be whatever he has made me, by then. It will not matter. Perhaps I will recollect myself, at your hands." And I did not understand what I said then. Khys did, and he looked at me sharply, his handsome face drawn tight and hard.

The cahndor released me, slowly getting to his feet.

"I would be honored," he said. "Doubtless it would be easier for her than with a stranger."

But Khys was not listening. From his robe he pulled a glowing circlet. Holding it between his fingertips, he came toward me.

"Please," I begged him, kneeling frozen, at his pleasure. He caused my hand to raise the hair from my neck, that he might have ease putting the band upon me. My mind screamed and struggled, but my body obeyed him perfectly, without question.

"Please," I said again. He knelt and closed the band upon my neck. It was tight. He touched it, and it became tighter. Such a band I had worn upon Mi'ysten, that I might not be pulled from one sequential time to another. There, it had been done for my safety. I had thought myself bereft of talent. In the greater silence precursed by the tingling of the band tight upon my neck, I knew I had not been.

"I cannot have you setting such hests. You will set no more." And his fine-chiseled features were devoid of emotion.

"My hand still holds my hair," I reminded him as he rose from me. He let me lower it. I thought I would surely go mad.

Khys smiled. "You will find the band easier. And though I could hold you indefinitely by will, I need not now waste my attention. Your experience upon Mi'ysten had not prepared you for our bands of stabilization. Great power demands powerful restraint."

I touched my fingers to it, and felt the raised pattern upon the warm, vibrating metal. Through that barrier, a circuit breaker, if you will, nothing would pass from me. I could not, as I might have if my strengths returned to me, remove myself from the Lake of Horns. Nor even find some alternate I might bring into the time, where Khys would be less dominant. I might have been tempted to try even that. But now I could not. That tiny hest I had set was my only hope. I clung to it.

"I will not obstruct you," I pleaded, my hands still at my throat. I could not get my fingers beneath the obdurate metal.

"I hear you," he reminded me. "And when I hear what pleases me, I will remove it."

And my hate flared again. Khys laughed. Miserable, I realized, even as I tried to quench it, what hearing he meant.

"Cahndor," said Khys, "my man will show you to the quarters I have had prepared for you. You will find your helsar there. Only acquaint yourself with it. We will take a meal later."

"Am I a prisoner?" Chayin asked him, Carth's hand upon his arm.

"That is up to you. Prisoner or honored guest—your choice. When your time is upon you, we might aid you with the helsar. There is much you could learn here."

"But I may not leave?" Chayin's body was stiff and straight in the light of those tiny suns.

"Not at this time, no," Khys said, and waved his hand. The cahndor had been dismissed. For a moment, Chayin hesitated, as if he might speak. Then he turned and walked meekly beside Carth through wide double doors of black thala.

"Now," said Khys, as Carth closed the doors softly, "you may speak your questions, and I will answer them." And the dharen of Silistra sat himself down cross-legged before me. I knew not what to ask. I looked at that powerful frame, and could not believe my mind's assessment of his age. He hovered at that indeterminate point, like Sereth and Chayin, a mature male in his prime.

"You cannot be that Khys," I said.

He smiled, not unkindly, revealing perfect teeth.

"I walked the Parset Lands when deracou blew all the enths of the day, before the Parsets separated themselves from us. I have seen the dead sea there when its tide was up, before it was boiled away."

"I would not live so long," I said, chilled.

"It has its compensations. One hears the breathing of the changing climes."

"What will you do with me?" I could smell him, and it was a strange smell, from his flesh, but oddly familiar. My knees ached. I sought to move them from under me.

"Stay! Whatever I please, Shaper's daughter, I will do."

"And with Sereth?"

"I have given him a choice." The dharen shrugged. "I have his helsar. I have him. Eventually, he will serve me."

"And if he does not?"

"I can, if I must, instill in him such loyalty as I might choose. Eventually, he will serve me." His molten eyes narrowed, those long, thick lashes almost obscuring them.

"If you were to show him mercy," I whispered, "it could be a bridge over what lies between us."

"I need not bargain with you, little savage. You have not even the most meager understanding of your position. Stand up."

And I was quick to obey him, lest he stand me. My nails bit into my palms. I kept my clenched fists at my sides. My skin crawled at his touch. I stood very still, but my mind's despair and loathing I could not quell.

"Soon enough, you will not even recall such emotions," he said, encircling me with one arm. He guided me thusly to that curtained window and drew those dark hangings back.

Into the audience chamber poured the warm summer sun, glistening upon the clear green waters of the Lake of Horns. And upon those graceful, sinuous buildings that make up the dharener's city, all white and gleaming, did the sun shine. Wide walks threaded around the lake, and upon them I saw men and women strolling. And hulions. Hulions pad the streets of the dharener's city. They do the bidding of those who rule it. How greatly I had shortchanged those winged beasts, in my conception.

The city sits in a great forested valley, curled around the lake like a necklace of helsars. At the tip of the most easterly horn lies the dharen's keep, wherein I am kept. From my chamber, I see that same view, albeit from a slightly higher elevation.

Khys spoke long to me that day of what concerned him. He spoke of the fathers, and their history. Why he did so, I do not know. I will have lost it all, soon enough. I found, when I awoke this morning, that I did not know where I was. I shook upon my padded couch, sifting through what was left of my memories. My first two hundred years have slipped almost totally beyond my recall. I wonder if I will lose even the ability to read and write. I sorted through my pages, when I found them, as if they were the work of a stranger. And they reminded me. There is no one truth. Khys lies!

I had begged him, after he talked the sun to its rest that day, to let me write, in my confinement.

"Estrazi allowed that I might send him a message," I said softly to him, as we watched the sun set over the lush forests. "If I must sit so long in one place, it would give me something to do."

The thought amused him. He stroked his jaw reflectively.

"That would be the final touch!" he said at last. "But I doubt that you will have long enough to put down any extended missive. The damage you did yourself with all that uris is only beginning to affect you. Burned synapses, I am afraid, are beyond my powers. New paths will replace the old. It will not be painful," he added as I looked at him in horror, though I had glimpsed it when I spoke with Chayin. "What you have been will fade from you."

And I retreated from him until the window pressed against my back. Crying, I pleaded with him. He stopped me. When I at length regained control of my emotions, he gave back to me my body's command.

"Let me see Sereth," I asked him, over that elegant table upon which a most delectable meal had been set.

"You have hardly touched your food," the dharen said. Chayin, beside me, only played with the sauced, spiced denter before him. We had exchanged no word, the cahndor and I, since the meal began.

I turned myself to my plate, lest he force the food upon me. Never in my life had I feared anything as I feared his command of my limbs.

When I had cleaned it, he motioned Carth, who had stood the whole time behind him.

I went with him, docile, unspeaking, out those double doors and up two flights of some unfamiliar stone.

The chamber in which the dharen keeps me is soft and resilient. I cannot hurt myself. The couch is a barely raised dais, with no hard edges. A play of golden light is ever across these pale green walls, even at night. My couch has no covers, with which I could strangle myself. I have a window, which does not open, barred by golden light, beyond which my hand cannot pass, lest I find some way to shatter it.

The door, also, is thickly upholstered. Upon the inside of it is no handle or knob.

Carth has my care. He feeds me, and takes me out of the room twice daily to bathe and attend my needs. Those trips are my only exercise. I never see the dharen.

But I believe he sees me, he and his six brethren. In my dreams I have met them.

At first, I thought it could not come. I lay long

enths thinking of Sereth, of what had been between us. Surely, I thought, my memories of him will not pass from me. The scars, I thought, are too deep. What could have been ours, had we what others take so lightly—time and each other, and some shadow of a life together? Upon any scales of judgment, we deserved at least that.

Last night I lay, touching myself, as has become my habit, that I might imagine us once again together. And I got hardly a sense of him.

Carth told me yesterday that he would come for this account today, that I was to finish it. I read what I have written, and it recalled to me certain things: the way his hair falls over his eyes, the way he tosses his head like some defiant threx, one glimpse of his dark-tanned hand upon my breast. I will hold to those memories. I will not lose myself. I will not forget Sereth, whom I love.

Khys, in his arrogance, will surely pass this to you, my father. If, in your wisdom, you choose to withhold me your aid, then perhaps I will come to understand, in the fullness of time. Now I do not understand. I have seen brother turned against brother and the very fabric of time and space rent asunder. I have seen such carnage as I never dreamed could come to be. And if I have gainsaid your will, it was not by empty defiance, but out of need.

I have remembered that which you said to me, upon the red sea's floor. In it, I have found some small comfort.

Khys will fall afoul of his pretensions, as we all do.

And I? No matter what he tries to make me, I am still my father's daughter.

Postscript

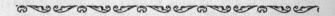

Today is Detarsa first first, 25,696. Last evening, I met the dharen, at a celebration in my honor, that of my birthday. Of course, it is an arbitrary date Carth set, for my true date of birth is unknown.

At Carth's bidding, I write this.

"Set down," he said to me yesterday mid-meal, "a short piece about yourself: who you are, what you are, what today will bring you." Carth is my teacher. He was, until last evening, the only man I had ever seen close at hand.

When I was found wandering the forests, I was chaldless, naked, bereft of memory. I could not speak a sentence in one language. My speech was a jumble of a hundred tongues, and quite unintelligible.

I do not remember, of course. Carth told me. My first memory is of him standing over me in this very room. And I was crouched in the corner, speaking as he described, terrified. We have come a long way, Carth and I.

We could not, alas, piece together the fragments of my past. Who and what I was remains a mystery. Carth has warned me of prying too deeply, lest whatever I will not remember rise up again and wipe out all I have learned.

And I have learned much, these last months: history, philosophy, politics, chaldra, languages. Carth says someday I will be very powerful. I will be trained as a forereader. I might even bear the arrar's chald.

Upon my neck I wear a band that keeps those powers in check, until I am skilled enough to use them. Without it, Carth has assured me, I would die.

It is not unattractive. In the mirror upon my chamber wall, it glows soft with light, setting off my copper skin with its gleaming. Last evening I wore a soft drape of gold metallic, to meet the dharen. It was an elegant garment, much different from the sleeveless thigh-length s'kim I usually wear.

I was excited, dressing. My fingers shook as I fastened the clips at my shoulders. I wondered what he would be like, if he would find me attractive. I have read extensively his writings. Much of what he has written is still beyond me. I sighed a trembling breath, arranging my copper-bronze hair in the mirror. I would meet the man who wrote *Ors Yris-tera!* I hoped he would find me pleasing.

I have read books, some true, some fictions, that Carth has chosen for me, books that made me anxious for the touch of a man. But Carth would not satisfy my curiosity.

I asked him several times, and he said only that I was not for him.

Then he brought me the gossamer cloth, and told me I would sup with the dharen.

I hoped he would find me pleasing, standing before the mirror. I had no way to adjudge myself. From a great distance, only, have I seen other women.

Carth came to fetch me, dark face smiling kindly, and we walked through the halls and down two flights of steps. I had never been farther than the end of my chamber's corridor. My stomach twisted and turned, my pulse thumped against my eardrums.

Imposing is the dharen's keep, I think. It is a high-ceilinged, thala-paneled place. I had read about thala. I ran my hand over the blue-black smoothness. Looking into its grain made me dizzy. It went down forever. I felt very small, and frightened, in the greatness of that room. All was blue-black and shades of silver. A silvery carpet covered the floor, thick and soft, with subtle, eye-catching designs. The lights seemed to hover in the air, dancing just below the muraled ceiling. All manner of animal life ranged there, in a lush jungle. I could not even guess at their names. Carth has barely started me upon flora and fauna. But it was very beautiful.

In the room were desks and tables, and numerous couches, arranged in groups, longer and thinner than my sleeping couch. Upon one table, tapers burned in silver holders, the flames flickering over covered dishes, surely silver. The table was round.

I perched myself upon the edge of the thick-napped, upholstered couch nearest the table, to await him. I played with the hair resting on my silk-draped thigh. I wondered how a wellwoman might await a client; how she would sit, how she would hold her breasts out, her tummy in, leaning forward, perhaps, with lips slightly parted. I laughed, pretending.

One of the double doors opened at that moment, and the dharen entered.

Golden-copper he is, lighter than I. And tall, with long legs and broad shoulders. He came toward me, his dark robe swirling around him, the great chald of Silistra glinting at his hips. A smile touched his lips. He reached out his hands to me. I gave him mine, and he clasped them warmly.

"What amuses you?" he asked me in a melodious voice.

"I am only pleased to be here," I said softly.

"You are very beautiful," he said, stepping back a pace. I wondered how many women those glowing eyes had scrutinized.

"Am I? As beautiful as a wellwoman, even? As Estri of Astria?"

He stared at me strangely, his eyes narrowed. They are so heavy-lashed, they seem oblong.

"Doubtless," he said at last. "You are, perhaps, more beautiful. You have read of her, of course."

I nodded, wetting my lips. "I have just finished it. Carth thought I should read it. She died from a similar affliction to mine. Could you not have saved her?"

"She was not sane. She lost more than memory. She had no will to live. It was a kinder thing we did. She craved death." He extended his hand to me, led me to table.

"You are far from the monster she painted you," I said to him as he seated me, then himself at my left hand. He smiled and brushed my cheek with his lips. I quaked within.

"Do you have any other observations upon her writings?" he asked as he served me cheesed tuns. His upper arms are very wide around, perhaps as wide as my thighs.

"Only that reading her made me anxious to know my womanhood." I stared brazenly into his eyes. "I had a dream about her lover, that I was with him," I whispered.

"Which one?" he said dryly.

"There was only one," I said, prodding my food with the two-pronged silver fork. "I would feel what she felt. I have been too long by myself." My eyes sought his, caught them.

He put down his fork and twisted in his chair. "Are you asking me?" he said levelly.

"Oh, no," I wailed, "I would not dare. It is only . . ." I hugged myself, flushed and miserable.

"It is only what?" he demanded, but softly.

"That I need some man's touch, that I may know maleness, and femaleness in that reflection. One can only get so much from books." I implored his understanding. "I was not being forward. Carth says you are my guardian. Forgive me."

He put his hand upon my arm. "Look at me," said Khys.

I looked at him. Never had I imagined such a man.

"Would you?" I whispered, leaning forward.

"I have had that intention," he said, "since I first saw you." And he got up from the table, food untouched. He walked to the dark-hung window and turned to face me.

"First," he said, "we must give you a name. Have you thought upon it?"

"No," I said, flustered. "I thought you would choose."

"Your first birthday, so to speak, cannot pass and leave you nameless. Pick a name, it does not matter what."

I whispered my choice to him, and he laughed, a gentle laugh. His fingers played in his chald.

"So be it. May you have better luck with it," he said.

And he called me to him by it, where he was at the plush-hung window. He was gentle with me, patient at my clumsiness. He seemed to take joy in my discoveries, though I knew nothing of how to please a man but what I had read. And it is very different from reading. His clear voice grew husky, his instructions terse. Afterward, kindly, he praised me, though I had trembled when I first saw him in his nakedness.

Hungry, he disdained the cold food upon the table and stepped out the door, fastening his robe around him. I lay where he had left me, too drowsy to move, content for the first time in passes. I had a birthday. I had a name. I had even had a man. I wriggled upon the silvery carpet.

By the time he returned, I had fastened the sheath once more at my right shoulder. I lay upon the midnight couch, half-reclining. I felt very proud, looking at him as he approached, that such a man had used me.

He sat beside me, fondled my breast lightly.

"You will bear me a son," he said.

"If it is within my power to do so," I breathed, bending my head to kiss his hand.

"It is already done." He laughed. I put my hands to my flat, hard belly wonderingly.

"I thought such could happen only after long and concerted effort," I disbelieved.

"I am the dharen," he reminded me. "Such a small feat is well within my capabilities. Are you displeased?" He narrowed his eyes, and for a moment I felt invaded.

"No," I said, "only disconcerted. It will be an honor."

"One you richly deserve." He chuckled, his hand running the length of my turned hip.

"You will not send me back to my chamber, will you?" I implored him.

"Only for a set's time, while your quarters are being prepared. We were not sure that you were ready. But I will visit you." He lifted my chin with his finger.

"And are you sure now?" I tried to hide my disappointment.

"Almost," he said, and his face went very stern. It was frightening to look upon.

"I have a new keeper for you. Carth has an emergency to tend. He awaits. Go and sleep well. I will visit you tomorrow." Reluctant, I got up and left him. I felt his eyes upon me until I closed the door and leaned back against it.

I stood there, shivering a moment. I smiled to myself, and turned to my new keeper. I marveled at how diverse men are. This morning I had seen only Carth. Now my eyes knew the dharen, and this man, also.

He was as tall as Khys, but not as broad. His skin did not shimmer. His hair and eyes were brown. He wore the arrar's chald, as did Carth, and plain leathers, almost black. He wore a weapons belt. Carth did not. His eyes were very deep under his brows, and I could not escape them. My back against the doors, my hands clenched behind, I looked at him, trapped.

"Let me take you back," he said at length. He hardly opened his mouth when he spoke. His words hissed upon a whisper like the wind against the tower. He was some sheathed weapon, cold as steel. He bore many scars, this man, and I had no doubt that he had earned them dealing death.

"Come with me," he said, with what could have been gentleness, and I let him take my shoulders and guide me up the stairs. His eyes never left me. The silence between us was deafening.

"I am Estri," I said to him, to break it.

"No," he said, shaking his head, "you are not." And there was a sadness in his voice that stopped me in the passage. He stopped too, and turned to face me. Muscles twitched in his jaw. He tossed his head.

"Just come with me," he said. "I am sorry. I knew it would be that name they gave you." And I looked at that man, trembling visibly in the corridor, and asked him his name. He spoke it. Tears filled my eyes for him, that he still carried such pain for his dead couch-mate.

"I did not realize," I said, touching his arm. "I did not mean to remind you."

"Let me take you back," he said, disengaging my hand, propelling me forward.

"Sereth," I said. He closed his eyes, opened them. "What?"

"You will find another."

And then it was he that halted. He left me and leaned on the corridor wall. I went and peered up into his face. I should not have. What was there was private grief. I put my hand upon his shoulder. He shivered. Not knowing anything else to do, I stood there with him.

"Sometimes I get dizzy," he said with a weak grin. "Too many blows to the head." He pushed himself away from the wall. I let my hand fall.

We walked the rest of the way in silence.

He opened my chamber and stood back.

"Go on," he said, his lean form tense, his eyes watchful.

"Carth comes in and sits with me. We talk. I am not sleepy."

"And I am not Carth. Have you no soul, woman? Leave me be. You will have your Carth back soon enough, from this timely emergency." And before his fury I ran into my chamber, and turned and put my hand upon the door, so that he could not close it.

"Why are you angry?" I asked him. "I have done nothing."

"I am not angry," he said, running his hand over his eyes, as if to clear them. "I have matters pressing. Remove your hand, and I will go find Carth."

"I had a dream about you once," I said softly.

His face changed. He took my hand from the doorjamb. Then dropped it.

His eyes searched mine. Whatever they sought there, they did not find.

"You had best content yourself with dreams. I value my life. I must choose well the moment to spend it," he said, and closed the door upon me. I heard the tumblers spin.

It amuses me to forward this to you, that you may be apprised of the fate of your envoy. Your daughter will bear my son, and when he is grown, I may choose to set him against you.

Be warned. Send no more manipulators into my domain.

Khys

Glossary

(P)   = Parset
(S)   = Silistran
(ST) = Stothric
(M)   = Mi'ysten
(MK) = M'ksakkan

Amarsa: (S) The eighth pass of the Silistran calendar; the pass of summer solstice.

aniet: (P) One of the seven interconnected underground life-support complexes that housed refugee Silistrans during the thousand-year period known as hide-days. The hide aniet lies under the dead sea in the Parset Desert; or the hide-name aniet, as Aknet aniet Beshost. Of all the hides of Silistra, the blood of aniet is the least common, being confined almost exclusively to the Parset Lands by an insular confederation of tribes who maintain there a strict autonomy. Almost one-half of aniet's survivors were of gristasha tribesmen, and this strong infusion makes "aniet's stamp" an easily recognizable Silistran type.

apprei: (P) The tapestried, pyramidal tents of the nomadic desert cities of the Parset tribes.

appreida: (P) The gathered appreis that constitute the

349

Parset tribal unit; any group of appreis containing representatives of the major facets of Parset life; the ground upon which rests the bulk of a given tribe.

apth: (P) These large and ferocious tusked beasts roam the barrens and foothills of the Yaicas, even venturing into the desert itself. The ill-tempered, pugnacious apth has a disproportionately small head, from which jut its savage tusks, set upon a thick and muscular neck. Where neck meets shoulder, the apth boasts an exaggerated crest, which in times of drought "humps" full with stored water. Apths, though formidable opponents even of men and dorkats, are increasingly rare and are under the protection of the cahndors and the god Tar-Kesa.

Arlet: (S) Well Arlet. Also, the lands controlled by her.

Arletian: (S) Of or pertaining to Well Arlet. In couching, any coupling attended by bondage or containing elements of submission; as criticism, excessive vehemence, or roughness.

arrar: (ST) The chald of the messenger, within which is woven every strand attainable on Silistra; the mark of the dharen's personal service; one who bears such a chald.

Astria: (S) Well Astria. The lands controlled by Well Astria, including Port Astrin, her dependent city. Sometimes, in colloquial speech, it may denote the Well Foundress: "By Astria!"

Astria Barina diet Hadrath: (S) The Foundress of Well Astria, great-grandam of Estri Hadrath diet Estrazi.

Baniese: (S) Of or pertaining to Baniev.

Baniev: (S) Silistra's most northeast coast port. Baniev's major exports are: the famed northern thala; danne, the yellow herb that grows high in the Sabembes; and the tri-sailed long ship whose fleetness has no equal even in the quays of Dritira.

bast: (S) The hide bast, which lies under Well Arlet and is said to extend under the Sabembe range. The hide name "bast."

binnirin: (S) A high-protein, high-fat grain that grows in numerous varieties all over Silistra. Anything tannish-brown may be called binnirin. From the grain comes flour and the fermented beverage brin, as well as oil and stalk fodder for denter and parr.

Bipedal Federate Standard Time: (MK) (BFST) Measured in hours, minutes, and seconds; an hour being equal to twenty-one twenty-seconds of an enth.

Bipedal Federation: (MK) (B.F.) The M'ksakkan confederacy of worlds as a whole, including both the Bipedal Federate Trade Union, (merchant arm) and the Bipedal Federate Group (the original fifty-five worlds, commonly referred to as the Inner Stars).

Bipedal Standard: (MK) (B.S.) Universal mean weights and measures.

bondrex: (S) A class of horned herbivores; any undomesticated grazer whose milk and meat are not coveted by man (except the steppe bondrex, prized and raised for its long, silky hair). There are nineteen species of bondrex cataloged on Silistra.

brin: (S) A mild intoxicant drink fermented from the binnirin grain.

brist: (S) A large and ferocious Silistran carnivore, hunted both for pelt and meat. Brist have a standing height of up to sixteen B.S. feet, a weight of up to twenty-five hundred pounds. Their appearance is generally manlike. The head is round, the jaw slung under and hinged below side-set ears. The whole body is covered with a thick hair coat, generally brown, much prized for its warmth and durability.

cahndor: (P) "Will of the sand"; the warlord of a Parset tribe; in usage, one who commands the speaker's allegiance and respect. The Silistran root word "chan" ("will of") has been adopted into Parset, with only its division into gender to differentiate it from its usage in the north. Whether suffix or prefix, "chan" is always female, while "cahn" denotes a male.

ca-nera: (S) Three-quarters of a nera.

Cathe: (P) The mythological winged slitsa, guardian of the Spirit Gate that opens upon the twin rivers of Ascension and Dissolution, and before whom every traveler freed of flesh must come in supplication, lest his journeys never end.

chald: (S) (Stothric: spirit-bond.) A belt of chains commonly soldered around the waist.

chalded: (S) Possessed of or wearing a chald.

chaldless: (S) Possessing no chald; one who has been either unwilling or unable to acquire chaldra; an outlaw; one who has been stripped of his chald for iniquitous behavior, and so disbarred from Silistran society.

chaldra: (S) Numerous volumes exist upon the subject of chaldra, first and foremost. *Ors Chaldra* (the dharen Khys, hide-year sixty-three); Khys's postulates of self-rule; the goal-seeking morality of Silistra in general, including both high-chaldra (tasks and responsibilities undertaken to strengthen the spirit form and increase survival potential of the eternal particle, the individual consciousness, or the flesh race as a whole) and low-chaldra (pertaining to the survival and betterment of the mundane individual, the acquiring of life skills of material import only); a trade or craft chain.

chaldric: (S) Demanded by chaldra; the "chaldric strands" that make up a chald; duties or labors determined by the Laws of Chaldra.

Clous: (S) The Silistran north star.

coin girl: (S) A girl who couches for pay outside the Well system.

Coseve: (P) The southeastern Parset Lands, holdings of the Cosever nation, whose color is green and whose device is a white sphere transfixed by lightning upon a beryl ground.

couch: (S) (n.) A sleeping platform, any surface used for coupling.

couch: (S) (v.t.) To copulate.

couchbond: (S) A companionship agreement between two consenting adults. (Low-chaldra.) The titrium couchbond strand is issued to the male at puberty after potency has been determined. No Day-Keeper need officiate at such an enchalding, nor is a chalder demanded by custom. The titrium chain may be inwoven or removed from a chald at the discretion of the two parties involved. There is no minimum or maximum time of couchbond.

couch-gift: (S) The tokens exchanged upon the assumption of couchbond, forever after the property of the individual in receipt. Also, any gift of sentiment.

couching: (S) (n.) Any single coupling; a style, as "an Astrian couching."

couch-mate: (S) Persons bound together by love and/or issue; in usage, those in extended couchbond, those who consider their relationship more binding than simple couchbond. Couch-mate denotes responsibility of a high moral order between two people. Gifting between couch-mates is traditionally regulated; one gives either the gift of life (progeny, animal or human) or the gift of death (knife or sword).

couch-met: (S) Met while performing well work; couching partners who have no previous acquaintance.

couch-price: (S) The fee a woman demands for her sexual services. Fees may range from as low as a titrium half-well for a coin girl to as high as fifty gold dippars for a *high-couch* girl.

couch-sisters: (S) Wellwomen; those of the same Well.

crell: (P) A subhuman status awarded humans in the Parset Lands. Crells are bred, bought, and caught: a foreign chald is reason enough for such immurement and exploitation of an unwary stranger.

crill: (S) The hide crill, under the city Nin Sihaen across the Karir-Thoss River, is the most westerly of all Silistran hides; the hide-name crill, as: Sereth crill Tyris.

crux: (S) One of the major Weathers of Life; time within which only that preordained may be done. Time so obscured that no foreknowledge may be gathered of what will occur therein. Colloquially, the abyss. Any time that spawns far-reaching changes whose effects and purposes are supernal in nature. Events that precipitate numinosity or nympholeptic response in the superconscious.

danne: (S) Psychotropic yellow herb that grows best at high altitudes in stony soil.

Day-Keepers: (S) The guardians of Silistran history, past, present, and future. The Day-Keeper hierarchy as a whole is referred to as the Dharendiil, a High Day-Keeper as dharener. Over these presides the dharen, the spiritual guide of Silistra.

Day-Keepers' Clock: (S) A mythical gnomon upon whose face all that ever was, is, and will be is inscribed. Usually an oath, as "By the Day-Keepers' Clock."

Day-Keepers' Roll: (S) The records of the dead, the archives into which name and history are entered upon an individual's death.

deep-reader: (S) One whose skills allow access to the deeper consciousness of another, exempting thoughts framed for communication. The value of deep-reading is considered by many to be greater than that of surface reading, for thoughts upon the surface, like the tip of an iceberg, give little and often faulty enlightenment as to what lurks beneath.   •

denter: (S) A large-humped, nub-horned animal, passive and tractable, raised for meat and dairy, and often used as a draft beast. This single-hoofed animal ranges from ten to fourteen hands and may reach a weight of thirteen hundred B.S. pounds.

deracou: (P) "The wind that devours"; most deadly of Parset sandstorms; the summer storms that yearly remake the desert's topography, which once blew all the year round upon the desert lands, and against which the Parset nictitating membranes and contractible nostrils were developed as survival modifications by hide aniet's Day-Keepers.

dharen: (ST) The spiritual ruler of Silistra; the supreme authority of the Day-Keeper hierarchy.

dharener: (ST) A high Day-keeper; one who holds the administrative rank of dharener; a hide council member. (In the Parset Lands, where the dhareners posture at autonomy, the hide council seeks no higher authority.)

dhrouma: (S) A drum made from the hollowed-out elbow of the onaric tree's branches. Once the curved tube has been aged, both ends are covered with gaen hide.

diet: (S) The hide diet, which extends under Well Astria, has her entrance on the banks of the Litess River, within the walls of the Day-Keepers' School; the hide name diet.

dippar: (S) Silistran coinage. One gold dippar is equalled by fifty copper dippars. Dippars are minted only in independent cities, as opposed to titrium and gold half-wells and wells, minted by the Well system. They are round with octagonal holes punched in mid-disk, and are intaglioed with a representation of the city in which they were struck.

Dordassa: (P) The land of the Dordassar tribesmen, which bisects the dead sea. Dordassa is bordered on the north by Nemar, on the east by the Embrodming Sea, on the south by Coseve, Menetph, and Itophe, and to the west by the tail of the Yaicas and the Opirian Sea. Her colors are cobalt and cinnabar, her device the cobalt dorkat upon a cinnabar ground.

Dorkat: (P) Wingless cousin of the hulion, the dorkat

has the same wedge-shaped head and pointed ears.
The hind musculature tends to be lighter, but the fore-
quarters are as heavily developed. Although the
cranial capacity is identical with the hulion's, dorkats
do not demonstrate more than half the intelligence of
their winged brethren. The nocturnal dorkat is preva-
lent in all the wilderness areas of Silistra, and its prey
is thusly varied, dependent upon what the area will
provide. They are exclusively carnivores, with pro-
truding incisors. Dorkats, unlike hulions, have been
known to turn man-eater, and are often troublesome
raiders to herders of domesticated beasts.

draw: (S) Draw time, one of the Weathers of Life, recognizable by the acceleration of the procession of
events, and to the individual by an increased sensitiv-
ity and awareness of proximity to crux. Draw time,
when properly exploited, is said to be the most fruitful of all the Weathers.

Dritira: (S) Fifth-largest Silistran city, largest southern
port. Dritira receives goods overland from Stra and
Galesh, and ships from every city with merchant
fleets. The Embrodming Inlet, which she shares with
the city of the written word, Yardum-Or, is the most
trafficked harbor upon Silistra. Dritira, as Yardum-
Or, is a dependent city to Well Oppiri, third most
prestigious of the Silistran Wells.

ebvrasea: (S) The largest of Silistra's omnivorous birds.
Ebvraseas have been known to achieve a wingspread
of sixteen feet or more. They are night hunters and
seldom venture out of their craggy realms. Ebvraseas
mate for life.

ei-jos: (P) The five-named human spirit as it is delineated by the religion of Tar-Kesa; folk representation
of the Tar-Kesian tenant that man is never complete
while enfleshed, and that human iniquity stems from
this inherent knowledge of the flawed nature of mor-
tality.

enth: (S) One twenty-eighth of the Silistran day; each
enth contains seventy-five iths.

Falls of Santha: (S) The great cascades at the source of
the Litess River, high on the Plateau of Santha in the
Sabembe range.

Feast of Conception: (S) The oldest performed ceremony
upon Silistra, dating back into prehistory. Before

Haroun-Vhass, the Fall of Man, Silistrans observed Feast of Conception.

fire gem: (P) A multihued precious stone mined exclusively in the Parset Lands, fire gems rival gol in hardness and durability and are much sought by gol-etchers.

firstcome: (P) Any individual whose actions seem to fulfill prophecy; a catalyst or agent of Tar-Kesa, sent periodically into the world to purge and prepare his children before He makes his presence felt.

forereaders: (S) Those females who have received training in the sorting of probability. Forereaders are the most powerful and prestigious women on Silistra, those whom the Day-Keepers have chosen to share their work, those whose innate foreseeing ability is .88999 or better.

forereader's disease: (S) An inability to discern the relative likelihood of manifestation of what is seen in the sort, followed by the appearance in the forereader of doubt and fear. Once this negative patterning has become firmly established in the viewer's conception, all incoming data are misread to accord with the interpretive viewpoint, a closed cycle of paranoia develops, wherein the forereader manufactures a false sort, reads it, reinforces the self-generated fear, brings into being that which is feared, is thusly upheld, and manufactures yet another false sort.

forereading: (S) Stochastic processing, the sorting of probability.

friysou: (P) A featherless, leather-winged scavenger common in the desert regions, the friysou's wingspread may approach that of the mountain ebvrasea. The friysou is not an aggressive predator, however, preferring to pick the bones of other beasts' kills.

gaen: (S) Most common of southern draft beasts, the gaen is a distant relative of the northern denter. This straight-horned herbivore is readily domesticated, placid of temper, and can haul up to ten times its own weight for considerable distances. Its heavy musculature, although a benefit to those who use gaen for draft, yields up a tough and stringy meat which is barely palatable; "gaen-eater" is an epithet applicable to any so lacking in life skills as to be reduced to depending for sustenance upon this slow-moving, dull-witted, untasty beast.

Gaes d'ar: (P) "You stand before me"; one of fifteen possible Parset greetings, the use of which is in a formal audience between two of markedly different stations.

gaesh: (S) The hide gaesh, beneath the jungle city of Galesh on the Karir-Thoss River. The hide name gaesh.

Galesh: (S) The city that feeds Silistra, Galesh lies in the most fertile Karir-Thoss Valley. The Galeshir swamps yield a number of medicinal herbs that cannot be found elsewhere, as well as the swamp kepher from whose scent glands come the base fixatives for the much-sought Galeshir perfumes. In this tropical climate the Silistran silkworm thrives; Galeshir carpets are second only to Parset rugs in their beauty and durability.

gol: (S) The excrescence of the golachit of Silistra. Gol comes naturally in five colors: blue, amber, white, silver, and red. Black or other adulterated colors are produced by feeding the golachit the proper melanis (harmless chemically treated fungi). Gol is considered superior as a building material because of its permanence; gol might last a man a lifetime, while iron, brick, and wood seem to wear away visibly under the Silistran eye.

golachit: (S) The great builder beetle of Silistra thrives both in a wild state in the gollands at the feet of the Sabembes, and in a mutually beneficial symbiosis with man. As with web-weaver and webber, so do golachit and golmaster blend minds and create together such beauty as would have remained unrealizable dream for either alone. The golachit is a scavenger by nature and finds both food and stimulation in this community with man.

golmaster: (S) One who enters into community of minds with a golachit; a golarchitect.

gristasha: (pre Hide Silistra) The dark-skinned primitives who formed one-half of the hide aniet, precursors to the Parsets, who still tattoo themselves as did their fierce progenitors. The Parset culture, in language and custom, bears heavily this gristasha influence.

Groistu: (ST) The constellation of the stones wielder,

which dominates the southwest quadrant of the Parset sky.

gul: (S) The ovoid, juicy fruit from which kifra is obtained; any of the three varieties of gul, the yellow, the orange, the purple-blue.

harinder: (S) A sepia-colored, thorned shrub ubiquitous upon Silistra. It is speculated that when the Polar Wastes are explored, some subspecies of harinder will be found there.

harth: (S) (n.) A common and tasty bird whose feathers are black and iridescent. The harth thrives in city and town, as well as plain and forest. He is a migrating bird, preferring warm weather. In the northern regions at harvest past, the sky is indeed "harth-black" with their numbers, screeching their distinctive "Hareee, haree" cry.

harth: (S) (adj.) Anything black and shining, especially black with blue or purple overtones.

helsar: (M) A bluish-white, crystalline life or prelife form said to be the reagent (in its shattered state) of life in a neighboring continuum. Helsars manifest upon a time-space world only contiguous to a disturbance such as is caused by flesh when first attempting the obviation of space.

hest: (S) To bend or twist natural law to serve the will; to command by mind; to cause a probability not inherent in the time to manifest. (The line between hesting and shaping is somewhat difficult to define when highly skilled individuals are concerned. The rule of thumb is held to be thus: if natural law must be remade or totally superseded, as in creating a permanent object such as a fruit or a star, one is shaping. If one is simply controlling an already existing object or event, as would be the case if one caused a fruit or star already in existence to alter its behavior but not its structure, one is hesting. The fruit or star one moves to the right or the left or higher in the sky by will would not have behaved in that fashion, but is still the same star or fruit as was a natural inhabitant of the time before the hest was applied. If one, on the other hand, creates fruit or star, one has brought into the time, by a suspension of natural law, that which heretofore did not exist. One shapes matter.

One hests time.) In usage, bringing in a hest, affecting probability.

hide: (S) The seven hides of Silistra: aniet, bast, crill, diet, gaesh, rendi, and stoen. Each hide supported a thousand survivors and their progeny through the long years of waiting until the planet's surface was again habitable. Under the aegis of the dharen's Day-Keepers and forereaders, the hides were built and operating sixty years before the projected disaster. But few believed, and thus only in hide aniet were there other than Day-Keepers and forereaders when the world exploded into war. It is said that the word "hide" derived from the scoffing and mocking of pre-hide Silistra at the project. "Khys's burrows" was another early name for the interconnected life-support complexes that saved what little of Silistra that was desirous of survival.

hide-days: (S) The thousand years of subterranean living, accounted hide-year one through one thousand. Our present calendar date of 25,693 is counted from the first year spent above the ground. All that occurred before hide-year one is termed pre-hide, or prehistoric.

hide-name: (S) Any of the seven hide-names: aniet, bast, crill, diet, gaesh, rendi, and stoen. Hide descent is always carried through the mother. The hide-name is second in the male, third in the female, and always takes lower-case honors.

high-couch: (S) Formally, the Well-Keepress, also any woman able to demand over thirty gold dippars per couching.

huija: (P) The metal-studded, braided lash favored by Parsets.

hulion: (S) The most intelligent animal on explored Silistra. The hulion—winged, furred carnivore of the Sabembe range—shuns civilization. They are known to have mind skills and a complex language, but are not symbolizers such as man. The hulion does as he wills upon Silistra, and none obstruct him. The high Sabembes and the unnamed western mountains are their domain of choice.

Inner Well: (S) The great central court within a Well's walls.

ith: (S) One-seventy-fifth of an enth.

Itophe: (P) The land of the Itophe, bordered on the north by Dordassa, on the east by Menetph, on the south by the Embrodming, and on the west by the southernmost Yaicas and the salt river Oppi. Itophic colors are gray and sepia, her device the triple triangle of sepia upon a field of gray.

jer: (P) A watering place in an otherwise arid region.

jeri: (MK) A costly and exotic M'ksakkan drink which mixes seven fruits with a char-filtered grain beverage; a sweet drink much favored by women.

jiask: (P) A Parset fighting man; one who has earned the jiask's chaldric strand.

jiaskcahn: (P) A jiask who rules over three hundred of his fellows.

kapura: (S) A drum similar to the dhrouma, but having a cylindrical, uncurved belly. The dhrouma produces a lower, drier sound than does the kapura.

kifra: (S) A Silistran drink made from crushed guls, a live fruit wine.

Liaison: (S) The contact officers installed as semipermanent officials on Bipedal Federate Trade Union worlds. The designation "First," "Second," etc., is Silistran, but indicative of the local M'ksakkan hierarchy.

Litess: The Litess River.

Menetph: (P) The southernmost of the Parset Lands, bordered on the north and east by Coseve, on the south by the Embrodming, and on the west and north by Itophe. The Menetpher device is the amber star upon a black ground.

Mi'ysten: (M) Name for both a planet and people. Experimental sphere of the Shapers.

M'ksakka: (MK) The administrative planet of the B.F. Group and Bipedal Federate Trade Union. M'ksakka is a highly industrialized world that exports all types of leisure and convenience machinery, a superior solar sail, and a synthetic shatterproof crystal.

M'ksakkan: (MK) Originating upon M'ksakka. All M'ksakkans, unless very high or very low in their society, bear the M' before their name; as M'lennin, or, conversely, Khaf-Re Dellin.

Morrlta: (S) The pelter town nestled in the foothills of the Sabembes.

narne: (S) A red, round fruit with crisp white pulp and a

distinctly salty aftertaste; the tree, which bears red leaves and fruits eight passes out of the year; the drink made from pulping the fruit.

Nemar: (P) The most northerly of the Parset Lands, bordering upon the Skirr valley in the north, the Sabembes in the east, Dordassa in the south, and the Yaicas in the west. At one time the border of Nemar included Mount Opir. The Nemarsi device is the slitsa wound around the Parset blade upon a field of crimson.

Nemarchan: (P) "Will of Nemar"; the woman, by tradition a forereader, who is leader over Nemar's tiasks.

nera: (S) 1.2 B.S. miles; Silistran measure of distance.

Oguast: A provisionally entered B.F. planet in Silistra's own sector. Oguast's surface is eighty-two percent water, her main exports are wistwa ivory and articles of superior ceramic process.

Ors Yris-tera: (ST) "Book of the Weathers of Life"; the divination system introduced by the dharen Khys during hide-days, along with the game itself, yristera.

owkahen: (ST) "The time coming to be"; those probabilities among all the available futures that will manifest as reality.

pandivver: (P) an insectivorous barrens bird whose favorite food is the hydrotaxic wirragaet.

parr: (S) The small, wiry-haired food beast of Silistra. The snub-nosed, flop-eared parr provides Silistra with meats, hide, fertilizer, and glue. It is said of a parr that only its hair does man no service.

parr-breeder: (S) One who raises parr; one who wears the low-chaldric brown strand.

parr-hide: (S) The sturdiest leather available on Silistra, parr-hide is thicker and less pliable than either tas or denter. Its main uses are in harnesses, footwear, armor, and weapon-related leathers.

Parset: (P) (adj.) Having origin in the Parset Lands.

Parset: (P) (n.) An individual of any one of the five Parset tribes.

Parset Lands: (P) The Parset Desert; the Parset barrens; the territories of the five tribes—Coseve, Dordassa, Itophe, Menetph (under which lies hide aniet), and Nemar. The Parset Lands lie at the bottom of Skirr Valley. They are bounded on the northeast by the tail of the Sabembes, on the east and south by the Embrodming Sea, and on the west by the southern Yaica range and the river Oppi.

pass: (S) One-fourteenth of the Silistran year; the Silistran lunation. Each pass is composed of four sets.

peg: (S) (v., to peg time.) To scale down one's time sense, to become concerned with the moment, to expand the moment. Pegging time is a prerequisite to all temporal skills. More formally referred to as "taking stance in the now," this process is the Silistran weapon against idleness and apathy, as well as the first step in sorting: discerning the probabilities available from the moment. The moment is infinitely fruitful; it is the mind's apprehension of it that is subject to famine and drought. If a man, at the end of the day, recollects only a blur of similitude, it is then incumbent upon him to redouble his efforts to "take stance," lest he come to the end of his life and find, in truth, that the days have all slipped away.

Port Astrin: (S) Well Astria's dependent city. Port Astrin, adjoining the Liaison's Port, caters more than any other Silistran city to off-worlders.

puiia: (P) A succulent with detergent and antibiotic qualities.

ragony: (S) Tan-and-black-striped hardwood from the deciduous ragony tree.

rana: (S) A hot, stimulating drink, rusty-brown in color, from the steppe-grown berried plant of the same name.

rana: (S) (adj.) Being of the color rana, rusty-brown.

rendi: (S) The hide rendi, under the city of Stra, which lies on the most western shores of the inland Opirian Sea; the hide-name rendi.

Sabembes: (S) The Sabembe range, sometimes called the Eastern Crags.

saiisa: (S) A term of disrespect usually applied to coin girls of questionable cleanliness.

sa-nera: (S) Full nera; one nera.

Santha: (S) The Plateau of Santha; the Falls of Santha.

sarla: (S) A summer-blossoming shrub often used in hedges, the sarla has variegated leaves and flowers, often producing blossoms of three or four colors simultaneously.

set: (S) Seven days; one quarter of the Silistran pass. Sets in a pass are reckoned first through fourth. "First third" would be the third day of the first set in a given Silistran pass.

Seven: (S) A man who has attained the rank of seventh in the council of seven Slayers that oversees the Slayers of a given hostel; in addressing one of that rank: "Seven"; in speaking of him, "the Seven" of a given hostel.

Shaper: (M) One who can control the constituents of matter and form them to his will.

Silistra: (S) The third planet of the star Veriti; in usage, the inhabited continent, exempting the Polar Wastes and those shores of which none are empowered to speak.

Silistran: (S) (adj.) Of Silistra.

Silistran: (S) (language.) Often called modern or New Silistran, the planetary tongue. Although some may not speak Darsti, the language of science, nor Stothric, the language of metaphysics, nor Parset, the tongue of the desert dwellers, all speak Silistran.

s'kim: (S) An unrestricting short garment worn by women, often white. A s'kim may be tied in numerous ways, and is differentiated from a short-length wrap by its strings at neck, waist, and hip.

Slayers: (S) The enforcement arm of the Day-Keepers, those who have tested for and been awarded the black-iron chain, chaldric strand of the Slayers. Slayers are an authority as accessible to one man as any other, and there is no man who is denied the strength of a Slayer's arm, be his need just and true, and his waist chalded. A Slayer is responsible to his Slayers' Seven and ultimately to the Day-Keepers for his actions, but in practice he is usually his own authority, responsible to the Law Within. The limit of fourteen Slayers upon any one commission, however, is strictly enforced. The Slayer's device is the crossed sword and stones in black, upon a silver ground. Their leather colors are slate and black. Subranks are indicated by belt colors and cords.

Slayers' Seven: (S) The top-ranking Slayers in a given hostel; the seven officials directly responsible to the Day-Keepers for the comportment of their hostel. Each is addressed by his rank number, "One" through "Seven."

slitsa: (S) Any legless reptile; of the class "slitsa." There are one hundred and five species of slitsa.

sort: (S) (n.) The probabilities inherent in a specific moment of time; those alternate futures available to one trained to seek them.

sort: (S) (v.) To "sort" probability; to determine in advance the resultant probabilities from postulated actions.

Stoth: (ST) The Stoth disciplines; the prehistoric philosophy and religion that were precursors to the Day-Keepers and the Weathers of Life.

Stothric: (ST) An archaic Silistran language; the language of metaphysics; the traditional garb of the Stoth priesthood.

Stra: (S) The city of Stra, upon the most westerly shore of the inland Opirian Sea. Stra is the mining capital of Silistra, the home of famed stra-metal, whose secret is considered Stra's greatest treasure. Stra also refines copper, bauxite, iron, and gold, all of which they mine in the rich Yaica range. Within Stra's gates are Well Frenya, and beneath her, the hide rendi.

stra: (S) That greenish metal refined in the city of Stra, whose resistance to corrosion and tensile strength are greater than that of Silistran steel.

ta-nera: (S) A quarter-nera.

Tar-Kesa: (P) The god Tar-Kesa, by whose laws the cahndors and dhareners rule the Parset Lands.

tas: (S) The woolly hill grazer whose flesh is most highly prized of all Silistran meats.

tas-skin: (S) Often referred to simply as tas, or tas-suede. The hide of the tas may be split very thin, and even in splits rivals the durability of leathers thrice as thick.

Tasa: (ST) (Stothric: be blessed.) The common Silistran farewell.

tasling: (S) A tas under six years of age.

thala: (S) The most costly hardwood upon Silistra. Northern thala, the preferred variety, is black with a blue cast. Southern thala, substantially less expensive, is black with brown overgrain. It lacks the sheen and depth of northern thala, but shares its near-imperviousness to weather.

Thrah: Iridescent long-haired pelts from the planet Torth; the animal from which the Thrah pelt comes is about the same size as a brist and might be mistaken for one, but for the long, multicolored coat and the fact that the thrah walks on all fours and is mute.

threx: (S) The preferred riding beast of Silistra. The threx may range from fifteen to twenty hands in height, from one to two thousand B.S. pounds. It prefers meat but can subsist upon almost anything. It is readily domesticated up to a point, but remains a moderately dangerous animal at all times. Threx can reach a speed of up to forty neras an enth for short periods, and in endurance races have been known to make as much as six hundred neras in four days. Threx are readily trained and often war-trained. Threxmen are fond of saying that there is no weapon but man more dangerous than threx. The threx of the north and the Parset threx, who has two vertebrae fewer than his northern cousin, are in some other ways dissimilar: the Parset threx has a more efficient metabolism, nictitating membranes, nostrils that can be closed at will, and greater strength and stamina than the common Silistran threx.

tiask: (P) A Parset warwoman; one who has claimed the tiask's strand.

tiaschan: (P) A tiask in command of three hundred of her sisters.

titrium: (S) A pinkish metal similar to gold but less costly. Titrium is the metal of the couchbond strand, and the half-well titrium coin. Titrium is a product of the city Torwin.

Torth: The planet Torth, from which Silistra buys more goods than from all the other star-worlds combined. Torth sculpture, whether out of metal or stone, or in the form of "Torth sculptured hangings" is much sought upon Silistra. A Torth sculptured hanging is basically a thick-piled tapestry worked upon a very fine grid with threads woven from the Thrah-hair, and then carved to various depths, revealing at each level different tones of color.

Torwin: (S) The city Torwin, from which comes titrium. Torwin is sometimes called the musicians' city. Both players and makers of instruments throng Torwin from elsewhere on Silistra, to study the aural arts. Torwin, upon the Karir river delta, has both a sea and river port, and from its ships tropical fruits and certain crustaceous delicacies north.

tun: A starchy, black-skinned tuber with yellow pulp that grows in stony, sandy, or even poor soil.

uris: (P) A species of succulent that grows wild in the Parset Lands; the stimulant drug made from the uris plant.

uritheria: (P) A beast from Tar-Kesian mythology, said to have ignited the sun in the sky; the cahndor's device.

veil: (P) A colloquialism for forereader's disease.

webber: (S) The arachnid artisans who produce, in cooperation with web-weavers, web-cloth and web-work.

web-cloth: (S) A nearly indestructible material made in collaboration by web-weavers and webbers, Silistra's largest arachnids.

web-fiber: (S) The web-strands used for ropemaking when optimum strength is required and the fact that web-fiber rope cannot be cut is no deterrent. Web-fiber is produced only by training webber-weaver pairs, and is much less common than hemp rope.

web-weaver: (S) One who enters into community creation with a webber.

web-work: (S) Open-weave, diaphanous body dressing, usually geometric in pattern; more than lace and less than cloth, very similar to the unguided work of webber alone.

Well Arlet: (S) The second most prestigious Well on Silistra lies in the elbow of the Sabembe range, above the hide bast.

Well Astria: (S) The most venerated Well on Silistra, Astria bears the name of the Well Foundress Astria Barina diet Hadrath, author of the Well Woman's Ors (Stothric: book). Astria was the premier Well, and although different in trappings and style, in substance every Well upon Silistra is patterned after the Astrian form. Well Astria lies upon the plain of Astria, fifty-eight neras from hide diet and the Day-Keepers' School.

well tokens: (S) (gold and silver.) Must be purchased with regular coinage or won in the pass and set games. Well tokens from one well may not be used in another, nor are they considered coinage per se.

wind from the abyss: (S) In the *Ors Yris-tera* (Book of the Weathers of Life), written by the dharen Khys, is the first known reference to the wind from the abyss, and it is from this book of divination that the term came into general usage. Who of Silistra has not at one time or another thrown the bone yris-tera pieces onto the three level board and found himself delineated as the "ebvrasea upon the square of overriding purpose"? Says the ors: "His wings beat upon the wind from the abyss." And: "Stalking is assiduous; Stalking culls the weak from the strong; In both the hunters and the hunted does it perform this function." (Khys, from the divination "Stalking.") In common usage, the chill of premonition, the physical forewarning of danger that may not be avoided. "Before Stalking, who can stand but those who also stalk?"

wirragaet: (P) An insect that lies dormant just under the desert sands when insufficient water is present for its survival, to rise up in clouds containing tens of thousands when roused by the presence of moisture in the air. The wirragaet is the preferred food of the pandivver, whose long beak enables it to hunt them beneath the sands.

Wirur: (ST) Constellation of the winged hulion, containing "at the tip of his westward ear" the north star Clous.

wistwa: The great sea beast of Oguast. It is maintained by Oguasti that two tall men, one upon the other's shoulders, could stand within the rib cage of the wistwa, and that the top man might then stretch his arms upward in vain to touch the backbone of the great sea beast of Oguast; the ivory of such a beast.

Yaicas: (S) The Yaica Range, the longest chain of mountains upon known Silistra.

yellow crier: (S) A bright yellow bird that might lie in the palm of a hand. In flight the yellow crier's wings are invisible. It darts at great speed and low altitude after the insects that are its prey. Its beak is as long again as its head, and from its mouth comes a sound most like a screaming child's.

yit: (S) A small, furred burrowing animal, the yit is often found in proximity to man. The yit is a cozener and thief by nature, stealing even the homes of other yits.

yra: (P) The Parset military unit of twenty-one; also, twenty-one.

yris-tera: (ST) "The weathers of life"; the name given to
the divinatory game that is the accompaniment to the
Ors_ Yris-tera. Yris-tera consists of three slotted
boards, each of which is divided into forty-nine
squares, nine of which are holes, or "slots." When assembled, the placement of boards is as follows: on
the top, the board of catalysts; in the middle, the
board of movement and manifestation; on the bottom, the board of outcome. The sixty pieces, traditionally carved of bone, are shaken in a cylinder, one
end of which has seven holes through which the
pieces may fall onto the boards. The yris-tera piece
breakdown is as follows: one Well, one child, one
star, two flames, two dayglasses, two scrolls, two
sheaves of binnirin, two waves, two parr, four
women, four men, five ebvrasea, eight threx, eight
spears, eight shields, eight swords. When one piece is
joined within a square by another, the piece value is
thereby altered, yielding up such additional specifics
as: Day-Keeper = dayglass/man, forereader = day-
glass/woman, slayer = sword/man. Yris-tera, in all
its complexity, has been well delineated by the
dharen Khys, its creator, and interested parties might
refer to his abridged manual *Yris-tera* and to the *Ors*
itself.

Silistran Calendar

pass of winter solstice Orsai
Tisera
Cai
Macara
Detarsa
Jicar
Finara

pass of summer solstice Amarsa
Cetet
Enar
Brinar
Decra
Sisaen
Laoral

ABOUT THE AUTHOR

JANET E. MORRIS lives in Hyannis, Massachusetts. She is thirty years old, and is a professional musician who sings and plays the bass guitar. Until her first smashing success as the author of *The High Couch of Silistra*, she had written one other very short story which had never been published. *The Golden Sword* is the second book in the *Silistra* trilogy.

OUT OF THIS WORLD!

That's the only way to describe Bantam's great series of science-fiction classics. These space-age thrillers are filled with terror, fancy and adventure and written by America's most renowned writers of science fiction. Welcome to outer space and have a good trip!

☐	THE MARTIAN CHRONICLES by Ray Bradbury	2440	$1.75
☐	STAR TREK: THE NEW VOYAGES by Culbreath & Marshak	2719	$1.75
☐	THE MYSTERIOUS ISLAND by Jules Verne	2872	$1.25
☐	A CANTICLE FOR LEBOWITZ by Walter Miller, Jr.	2973	$1.75
☐	HELLSTROM'S HIVE by Frank Herbert	8276	$1.50
☐	THE DAY OF THE DRONES by A. M. Lightner	10057	$1.25
☐	THE FARTHEST SHORE by Ursula LeGuin	11599	$1.95
☐	THE TOMBS OF ATUAN by Ursula LeGuin	11600	$1.95
☐	A WIZARD OF EARTHSEA by Ursula LeGuin	11609	$1.95
☐	20,000 LEAGUES UNDER THE SEA by Jules Verne	10325	$1.25
☐	STAR TREK XI by James Blish	11417	$1.50
☐	ALAS, BABYLON by Pat Frank	11502	$1.95
☐	FANTASTIC VOYAGE by Isaac Asimov	11527	$1.75

Buy them at your local bookstore or use this handy coupon for ordering:

Bantam Books, Inc., Dept. SF, 414 East Golf Road, Des Plaines, Ill. 60016

Please send me the books I have checked above. I am enclosing $_____ (please add 50¢ to cover postage and handling). Send check or money order —no cash or C.O.D.'s please.

Mr/Mrs/Miss_____

Address_____

City_____State/Zip_____

SF—11/77

Please allow four weeks for delivery. This offer expires 5/78.

RAY BRADBURY

*America's most daring explorer
of the imagination*

☐ S IS FOR SPACE	(11017—$1.50)
☐ SOMETHING WICKED THIS WAY COMES	(10750—$1.75)
☐ THE HALLOWEEN TREE	(10610—$1.50)
☐ THE ILLUSTRATED MAN	(10557—$1.75)
☐ DANDELION WINE	(10430—$1.50)
☐ R IS FOR ROCKET	(10367—$1.50)
☐ TIMELESS STORIES FOR TODAY AND TOMORROW	(10249—$1.50)
☐ I SING THE BODY ELECTRIC	(2882—$1.75)
☐ MACHINERIES OF JOY	(2834—$1.50)
☐ THE WONDERFUL ICE CREAM SUIT & OTHER PLAYS	(11582—$1.50)
☐ THE MARTIAN CHRONICLES	(2440—$1.75)
☐ GOLDEN APPLES OF THE SUN	(2247—$1.25)

Buy them at your local bookstore or use this handy coupon for ordering:

Bantam Book Catalog

Here's your up-to-the-minute listing of every book currently available from Bantam.

This easy-to-use catalog is divided into categories and contains over 1400 titles by your favorite authors.

So don't delay—take advantage of this special opportunity to increase your reading pleasure.

Just send us your name and address and 25¢ (to help defray postage and handling costs).